√   1/07

DOUBLE DEAD

DOUBLE DEAD

TERRY HOOVER

FIVE STAR

An imprint of Thomson Gale, a part of The Thomson Corporation

THOMSON

™

GALE

Detroit • New York • San Francisco • New Haven, Conn. • Waterville, Maine • London

Hoo

LIBRARY OF CONGRESS CATALOGING-IN-PUBLICATION DATA

Hoover, Terry.
    Double dead / by Terry Hoover. — 1st ed.
      p. cm.
    ISBN-13: 978-1-59414-587-2
    ISBN-10: 1-59414-587-3 (alk. paper)
    1. Private investigators—North Carolina—Charlotte—Fiction. 2. Mistresses—Crimes against—Fiction. 3. Bankers—Fiction. 4. Charlotte (N.C.)—Fiction. I. Title.
PS3608.O6255D68 2007
813'.6—dc22   2006029410

First Edition. First Printing: January 2007.

Published in 2007 in conjunction with Tekno Books and Ed Gorman.

Printed in the United States of America on permanent paper
10 9 8 7 6 5 4 3 2 1

This book is dedicated to the brightest, most talented and generous group of women it has been my privilege to know: Cathy Pickens, Dr. Ellores Brailey, Dr. Paula Connolly, Dawn Cotter, Dr. Susan Luck, Nancy Northcott, and Ann Wicker.

But most of all, to Harry, who could have done it much better, but gave me the courage—and the freedom—to try.

CHAPTER 1

July 4, 1961

The telephone jerked him from a heavy, dreamless sleep without registering on his consciousness. He sat up and stared into the darkness, wondering why he was awake. The phone rang again and his body reacted instinctively to its strident summons, propelling him across the room and into the hall without conscious thought.

" 'Lo." He slumped against the wall, shivering in thin cotton jockey shorts.

"Greg? Are you awake?"

A flare of irritation as he recognized John's voice helped dispel some of his stupor. "Yeah," he lied.

"I'm afraid I have some bad news, Greg. Your mother's dead. I'm sorry, but she's dead."

"But I . . . How did . . . ?" His vision contracted into a pinpoint as shock sucked the air from his lungs. He doubled over, struggling for breath. John's voice continued as a buzz from the receiver, but he'd ceased to comprehend. Instead, he concentrated on taking slow, deep breaths until, gradually, the pounding in his head subsided.

"What happened?" he interrupted.

"Wha . . . ?" Confused, John sputtered to a stop. "I just told you."

"Tell me again."

John's sigh carried clearly over the wire. "She wanted to go out to the cabin, but when we got there, I couldn't do anything with her. She kept hollering for me to leave her alone. So I came home and went to bed, but I got to worrying what she'd get up to out there by herself, so I went back out to see about her and she was dead."

"You left her out there like that, by herself?"

"We'll talk about it when I get there." As always when cornered, John retreated into his customary tone of command. "Now listen, son. I'm gonna bring her home. Watch for me, but don't turn on the porch light, hear?"

He didn't answer.

"Greg?"

"I'm here."

"Wait for me. I'll be right there."

He hung up and turned toward his mother's room. It was a bad dream. Her light would be on and she'd be propped up on her elbow, demanding to know who was calling at such an hour.

Her room remained dark and silent.

He crammed his fist against his mouth and fled to his own room. His jeans and t-shirt lay across the end of his bed where he'd dropped them a few hours earlier. He pulled them on, then dragged the chenille spread off his bed and wrapped it around his shoulders. The fabric brushed the stack of baseball cards on his desk as he passed, sending them cascading to the floor, but he didn't notice. The spread trailed behind him as he stumbled through the house, turning on lights in every room.

Until he came to his mother's room. He hesitated in his mother's doorway for a long time but, in the end, could not force himself to enter. He went back out to the living room and sank down on the edge of the sofa, hugging the spread to his shoulders as he rocked back and forth and waited for John to bring his mother home.

★　★　★　★　★

It seemed years had passed when he finally heard the tires of John's Cadillac crunch over the gravel, but the mantel clock showed it had been less than an hour since the phone had awakened him.

He rose and went to peer out through the backdoor screen. He could just make out the gleam of John's white shirt in the darkness as he stepped out of the car.

John crossed the yard, yanked open the screen, and squeezed past him into the kitchen. His white shirt was streaked with dirt. His face, too, was deathly white, and sweat trickled down his sideburns. A sour smell of whiskey and fear hovered in the air around him.

"What the hell are you doing with all these lights on?" John demanded. "We might as well be on the damn stage." He strode through the house, snapping switches, and returned to loom over Greg. "C'mon, let's get her inside."

He trailed John out to the car. John wrenched open the door, and Greg saw his mother in the weak yellow glow of the dome light. She lay sprawled in the floorboard, head and shoulders draped over the hump, her face mercifully shrouded in the shadows on the far side. She was barefoot.

John straightened up briefly to survey the neighboring houses. Their occupants slumbered peacefully, oblivious to the wordless shrieks of alarm from the crickets and cicadas. Satisfied, he wedged his shoulders into the narrow opening and grasped her under the arms. Grunting with the effort, he dragged her from the car and laid her down on the grass.

"You take her under her knees," he ordered. "I'll take her shoulders."

Greg was racked by a spasm of shame as he realized he was afraid to touch her.

"It's all right," John urged.

Slowly, Greg bent and slid his hands under her knees. Her skin was cool, but not cold or waxy the way he thought dead people were supposed to feel. He lifted and felt her body resist. Then her chest collapsed like a broken board, emitting a weird sound halfway between a gasp and a groan. He looked up at John, but tears blurred his vision. "Are you sure she's dead?"

"Of course, I'm sure," John snapped. "C'mon." He shoved his hands under the shoulders and heaved. Her head lolled back between his arms. "Let's go."

He began to back toward the house. But the oversized basket on Greg's bicycle, leaning against the stoop, snagged his sleeve. "Goddamn it!" He shook free. He jerked his head left, then right, checking for signs of life from the surrounding houses.

They managed to wind through the darkened kitchen without bumping into the table or chairs, but as they negotiated the narrow hallway, one of her arms slipped free and banged against the doorjamb. Greg bit his lip hard to stop the scream that bubbled up from his chest.

They laid her down on the bed. John leaned against the wall, one hand splayed against his chest as he bent over, struggling to catch his breath.

Greg's eyes were riveted on his mother's face. "What happened?"

Enough light from the streetlight penetrated the blinds for him to see that her hair was stringy and disheveled. Her eyes were closed. Even in the darkness, the bruises stood out lividly against the pale flesh of her arms and legs.

"I don't know," John panted, shaking his head. "Heart attack, maybe, or she poisoned herself with that stuff she was drinking." He raised his eyes to look directly at Greg for the first time. "We both know it could have happened anytime, anywhere, the way she was going. As far as anybody else has to know, she died right here in her bed, in her sleep, of a heart attack. That's all anybody has to know and there won't be any ugly talk."

When he didn't answer, John straightened up and crossed the room to drop a heavy hand on his shoulder. "We don't want a scandal, do we?"

Greg gazed down at his mother, but still he didn't speak. John grasped him by his other shoulder and turned him slightly so he could look into his face. "You stand by me on this, son, hear? I'll look out for you, see you're taken care of. You don't have to worry about that."

He raised his eyes to John's. John flinched, but didn't loosen his grip. Slowly, Greg nodded.

"Good." John's relief was as palpable as a third presence in the room. He turned toward the bureau, his movements brisk and sure again. He yanked open the drawers and pawed through the slips and panties. "Where are her pajamas?" he asked over his shoulder.

"Why?" But he knew the answer even as he asked, and his heart gave a painful lurch.

"She wouldn't sleep in her clothes." John straightened up and looked hard at him. "We have to put her pajamas on her." He held up a pair of pink cotton pajamas. "These'll do."

Greg stood in the shadows and watched as John rolled his mother over to struggle with the zipper on her dress. His big hands were clumsy. As he fumbled with it, the fabric ripped and the dress fell free from her shoulders. She was naked under the red-and-white-striped sundress. Greg turned his head.

"Hand me those." John held out his hands for the pajamas.

He picked them up from the foot of the bed. Her scent, comprised of her perfume, the hair spray and soap she used, rose from the fabric.

"Pick up her legs," John ordered.

He did as he was told. John forced her feet through the legs and wrestled the bottoms up over her hips. Sweat rolled down his face. "You'll have to help me with the top," he panted.

He held the sleeve while John forced her arm through. He looked away while John propped her up to thread her other arm through the opposite sleeve. When he looked again, John had laid her down and was struggling with the buttons. Then he drew the sheet and spread up over her chest and laid one arm across the sheet, the other against her pillow.

"That's all we can do for her now," John gazed down at her. It was impossible to see his expression in the darkness. He wheeled abruptly and left the room.

Greg stood by the bed feeling helpless. He should *do* something, but he couldn't think. He lifted her hand and pressed it to his cheek. Tears squeezed from under his tightly shut lids onto the cold flesh.

After a minute, he scrubbed his face on his sleeve and went out to the living room. John sat by the picture window, the tip of his cigarette glowing in the darkness. "Sit down, son."

He perched on the edge of the sofa and concentrated on the tip of the cigarette as it jerked up and down with John's words. It flared briefly as he took a deep drag.

"I'm sorry about your mother, son." John ground out his cigarette in the ashtray on his knee and leaned forward, a silhouette in the darkness. "But there's nothing we can do for her now, except protect her."

Greg stared at him, giving nothing away.

"We don't want a scandal, Greg. That's something we can do for her. Do you understand?"

He nodded.

"Good. Now listen to me very carefully. I want you to call the police and tell them you got up in the night and found her like this, hear? Tell them . . . I don't know, tell them something didn't look right to you so you went in to check on her and she wasn't breathing, so you called for help. Can you do that?"

He nodded again, not trusting himself to speak.

"I'll help you make the call, then I have to go. I can't be here when the police arrive. But it'll only be a little while and you'll be all right. Do you understand?"

"Yes."

"All right." John rose. He hesitated in the doorway, as if to speak.

Greg felt himself shrink. If John touched him now, he might scream. But John thought better of whatever he'd thought to say, and passed on into the hall. Greg stared into the darkness and listened as he dialed.

"Greg? It's ringing."

He took the receiver and listened to the rings until someone answered. "This is—" his breath caught in his throat. "This is Greg Green," he managed. "I need help. My mother is . . . I can't wake her up."

He gave the officer his address and even remembered to thank him. He replaced the receiver.

"You did fine." John patted his shoulder. Greg couldn't suppress a shudder. John dropped his hand. "It won't be long now and remember, I'll take care of everything. You just stick to our story, all right?"

"I've got it."

He watched through the screen as John pulled away. Long after the taillights had disappeared around the corner, he continued to gaze into the darkness after him. Finally he turned and went to the linen closet in the hall. He groped behind the folded sheets and towels until his fingers found the bulky package where she had hidden it, wrapped in white tissue. He carried it out to the living room and sat down in the chair John had vacated, the package cradled in his lap. Tears slid down his face and were quickly soaked up by the flimsy paper. It was the

last birthday gift his mother would ever give him.
Tomorrow—today—he turned thirteen.

CHAPTER 2

I was feeling pretty good as I tossed my overnight bag in the back seat and climbed behind the wheel. I turned on the radio. ". . . in reaction to growing concern over the latest salvo from the John Birch Society, President Kennedy today—" I twirled the dial. Michael was still rowing that damned boat ashore. I turned it off.

While everybody else had been enjoying watermelon and fireworks yesterday, I'd spent my holiday looking for a church bookkeeper who'd been forging checks. He got away with it for quite a while, because the treasurer was eighty and suffered from cataracts. But when the treasurer dropped dead of a heart attack, the board of deacons heaved a sigh of regretful relief and quickly appointed a sharp young vice-president from one of the banks to replace him. The bookkeeper knew his Call Had Come From Up Yonder, and he disappeared along with two hundred dollars from petty cash.

The church didn't want to go to the police because of the scandal, so Susie's principal, who's on the board, suggested they hire me to look for him.

I figured the guy would head for a big city where he could get lost and that he'd stay in the state where his North Carolina I.D. wouldn't leave a trail, at least until the heat was off. Raleigh's the nearest town of any size, so I hit the highway, stopping at every cheesy motel along the way.

My hunch paid off at a motor court on Raleigh's outskirts.

The bookkeeper had registered under a phony name, but the desk clerk recognized his picture in the church directory.

I took a room across the courtyard where I could keep an eye on him and called the treasurer. Then there was nothing to do but wait.

He arrived a little after nine with the minister in tow, and the three of us strolled over to pay a call. The look on the bookkeeper's face when he found us on his doorstep made up for the wait.

After a couple hours' argument, the church agreed not to prosecute if the bookkeeper would make good on what he'd stolen. I wondered how he was going to do that without a job, but it wasn't my problem and I'd done what I'd been paid for, so I left them hashing out the details and went to bed.

I was bushed, and despite the heat, the lumpy motel mattress, and the scratchy sheets, I slept later than I'd planned. The others had all gone when I packed up and checked out.

Okay, so I'm not exactly Sam Spade. But it pays the bills, and I knew when I gave up being a reporter for a private investigator's license two years ago, it would take time to land the big cases. The church had paid me a three-day retainer in advance. Since I'd struck it lucky and found my quarry on the first day, even after deducting my modest expenses—a few gallons of gas, the cheeseburger I had for dinner, and the cost of a cheap motel room—I'd still come out ahead.

My conscience nudged me to suggest I should refund the balance of the retainer. But if they ended up having to prosecute, which I fully expected they would, I could wind up spending at least a day in court. I could use the money as well as they could in the meantime.

The drive home was as dull as a Sunday afternoon. Nothing on the radio but housewives discussing their love life or their laundry problems, and preachers exhorting me to repent, and nothing to do but steer and count tobacco fields. I soon fell into a sort of waking trance, daydreaming of a beach vacation with Susie and the kids. Except for a very cheap weekend at Myrtle Beach last summer, when we'd lived on peanut butter and jelly, we hadn't been able to afford a vacation since I quit the *Times.* In my heart, I knew Susie'd probably insist on using the money for something sensible like groceries or shoes, but for a few hours, I could dream.

By a freakish coincidence, Susie quit her job at the paper the same day I did. Given everything that happened, though, maybe it wasn't coincidence. Maybe somebody was looking out for us. She was lucky enough to find a job teaching high school English and surprised to find she enjoyed it. It's not exactly how she'd planned to use her journalism degree, but there are worse jobs and she's home by the time the kids get out of school. She was even lucky enough to pick up a six-week session of summer school. I didn't want her to take it, but the money had come in handy.

Even with her salary, we barely make ends meet. Between us, we cover the house payment and the groceries and I manage to make my office rent and the phone bill every month, but cases are still sporadic and I can never be sure when the checks will show up. Every month we live on the edge. If the Falcon dies on us or one of the kids gets really sick, it could be enough to push us over.

The first thing you notice as you approach Charlotte is the steeples, the white ones that soar heavenward to proclaim the glory of God and those of concrete and glass that proclaim the glory of commerce. A mixed message, maybe, but it seems to work. Go to work, go to church, and you'll be rewarded. And most of us are. The rich live in big white houses in Myers Park; the rest of us make do with a two- or three-bedroom ranch in the self-contained villages we call suburbs. Even our poor are working class. And nobody seems to have a problem with worshiping two gods.

But for every one of those soaring steeples is a cinder-block palace where the lights are dim for reasons other than economy and people go to do what they don't talk about at the neighborhood cookout. Whatever they get up to in those places on Saturday night, most of them are cleaned up and in their appointed places in the pew on Sunday morning, so I guess it balances out.

And, as I rolled in, I had to admit it's a pretty town. We're known as the City of Trees, and on that hot July afternoon, I was grateful for every one of them. I hit town just late enough to run into rush-hour gridlock, so it was nearly dinnertime when I pulled into the driveway.

"Sonuvabitch!"

I threw up a protective arm and whirled, expecting a fist or a club coming for my head, but there was nobody there. I slumped against the car door and waited for the roar in my ears to subside. As it did, I became aware of banging and more curses from the yard next door. I peered through the curtain of wilted honeysuckle to see my neighbor, Ron, waltzing with a piece of corrugated sheet metal twice his size.

Ron's a great guy. You couldn't ask for a better neighbor, but he's one of those guys who can turn the simplest chore into a project. He ordered a bomb shelter from some mail-order outfit back in April after the Bay of Pigs. The massive carton, containing a Japanese Army surplus Quonset hut, arrived marked "Made in Japan." Unfortunately, so were the instructions. He would've sent it back, but he couldn't fit the pieces back into the carton.

"How's it coming?" I called.

"Damn thing's defective," he panted. "How 'bout giving me

18

a hand?" He made the mistake of loosening his grip. The sheet landed on his head with a noise like a cartoon sound effect.

"Uh, maybe after supper," I replied, backing away. "I think Susie needs some help in the kitchen."

I found her gazing into the refrigerator as if it contained the secrets of the universe. She'd traded in her high heels and stockings for a pair of Bermudas and bare feet. I paused for a moment to admire the view before I kissed the back of her neck.

"Whatcha looking for?"

"Frostbite," she sighed.

The box fan droned in the window, struggling to exhaust some of the day's heat, but it would be hours before the sun sank low enough to give us any relief.

"You had a call." She backed out of the refrigerator with a handful of celery, shut the door with her hip, and gestured toward the phone with her elbow.

"Yeah?" I filched a stick of celery from the pile on the counter and ran it under the faucet.

"Mm. George Warren." Her tone was a little too nonchalant, and she didn't look at me. "He must've been trying the office all day and figured he'd catch you at home. His number's on the counter."

Warren's a legend, one of the most famous attorneys in the state, hell, in the *country*. The kind who has his picture taken with governors and senators and whose name is always being tossed around when they're looking for a candidate for something.

I'd never actually met him, but I'd seen him in action. Not that he spends much time in court these days. When you're that good, your cases don't make it to court. Which, I guess, is one of the reasons people pay top dollar to hire him. The stories told about him in the newsroom, though, have become legends.

Now the legendary George Warren was looking for me. Either

my reputation had grown overnight or I'd stepped in something on a case that was a lot bigger than I'd realized.

Susie made the kids turn down the TV while I dialed.

"Mr. Warren? Steve Harlan. I understand you've been trying to reach me?"

"Yes, Mr. Harlan." His voice matched the image, rich and smooth as blended bourbon. "Thank you for returning my call. Your wife tells me you've been out of town."

"Had to go to Raleigh. Just got in."

"I see. Then you probably haven't had an opportunity to see the papers yet."

"Just the Raleigh paper this morning."

"Are you familiar with John Lattimore?"

"The president of State Mutual Bank?" Who also owns half the prime commercial real estate in town. Was he suing me?

"The same, I'm afraid. Mr. Lattimore has been charged with murder."

I took a minute to digest that one. Lattimore was a big deal in town, the son of a wealthy, respected family and a member of the country club set. I'd never interviewed him, but I'd covered enough Chamber luncheons to recognize him by sight. He had a reputation in the newsroom as an arrogant bastard. I admit to a pang of nostalgia and, if I were being honest, some envy, as I imagined the excitement in the newsroom about now. Newspapering is like malaria. Once it gets in your blood, it's there to stay.

"Mr. Harlan?"

"Sorry. I'm here."

"I've been retained to represent Mr. Lattimore and was hoping you might have some time available over the next few weeks. I realize this is short notice, however. Perhaps you're too busy?"

He probably knew otherwise, but I played along. "I think I can manage."

"Splendid. Why don't we meet in the morning? Would nine be convenient?"

"I think so."

"Good. I'll look forward to meeting you then." He gave me the address and bade me a courtly goodnight.

I realized, as I stood there with the receiver in my hand, I hadn't asked for any details. Some detective.

I glanced at Susie, who was pretending to be deaf. She looked back at me from the corner of her eye. I snatched her up, spatula and all, whirled her around the room and planted a big smack on her cheek. I put her down, but I didn't let go.

"He wants you on the Lattimore case?" she asked. Her green-gold eyes were bright.

"You read about it?"

"Are you kidding? Ben gave it two pages and a couple side-bars and so did the *Courier* this morning. Jackie didn't get that kind of coverage in Paris. This is the break you've been waiting for."

"You've waited a long time, too."

Susie's the first and only woman I ever loved for more than a few hours. We were both journalism majors at Carolina so our paths crossed fairly often and after our first meeting, I made sure they crossed as often as possible. She swears I fell in love with her because she's smarter than I am. She's probably right.

The kids descended on us, flinging themselves at my legs and clamoring to be let in on the excitement. Christine is nine, a beauty who mercifully doesn't know it yet, with her mother's infectious grin and blue-green eyes fringed by thick, dark lashes. But Susie is dark and Christine's hair is the color of expensive champagne. Adam, at seven, is like looking into a mirror. His big, brown eyes can reduce his mom to mush and she's a tough cookie.

"We're going to be rich," I shouted, scooping them up, one

under each arm. I rubbed my beard across their cheeks until they squealed.

"Out," Susie ordered. "I can't cook with everybody underfoot. Adam, get Daddy the newspaper."

Susie hadn't exaggerated. In sixty-point type, the headlines screamed: "Millionaire Charged in Secretary's Death."

The dead woman was Delores Green, forty years old, secretary for an insurance company uptown, divorced, with a teenage son. Her neighbors and co-workers were quoted saying the usual things: "nice, quiet, a good worker, a devoted mother." I noticed "respectable" was missing and wondered whether it was significant by its absence.

The kicker came at the bottom of the first column.

"According to the dead woman's son, 13-year-old Greg Green, Lattimore called him in the early morning hours to say his mother had died. The boy told police that he helped Lattimore carry his mother's badly bruised body into the house, dress her in pajamas and place her in bed hoping to 'avoid a scandal.' "

I read the graph again but it didn't get any better. I scanned the rest of the story, looking for cause of death, but there was nothing other than the cryptic reference to her "badly bruised body." A sidebar on Lattimore recapped his career and listed his civic activities and club memberships. A wife was mentioned halfway down in the story, which also carefully pointed out the couple had been "estranged" for some time.

I read between the lines, as I was intended to, that Lattimore had apparently had something going with the dead woman. I studied her picture. It was a studio portrait, probably the most flattering the family had been able to dig up, but even with special lighting and retouching, she could never have been called a siren. Dark-haired with big, soulful eyes, she'd been carefully posed, but it was obvious she was carrying a few extra pounds. I was willing to bet Lattimore's wife was a knockout. It's the guys married to dowdy frumps who go for the flashy babes. The ones married to beauties tend to go for the soft, comfortable type.

I'd call Ben after supper for the inside scoop.

Ben came to work at the paper about a year behind me and we hit it off right away. Nobody in the newsroom knew what to expect when word got out that they'd hired a Jewish kid from New York. The old timers treated him like an exotic animal they weren't sure was housebroken.

The only thing we had in common at first was a cockeyed sense of humor, but it was enough. We make an odd couple, I guess, kind of Sheriff Andy meets the rabbi, but he's a hell of a newspaperman and one of the brightest guys I've ever met. Few people take enough time to see past his intellect and cynical New York veneer to his heart, which is as big as Montana.

Susie and I don't see as much of him since he made city editor last year, but I usually talk to him every couple weeks and he drops in for dinner whenever he can make it. "As one of three Jews in North Carolina, it's not like my dance card is filled," is the way he explains it.

If anybody knew the inside story, it would be Ben, and I wanted all the background I could get before I met with Warren.

Over supper, we chatted about the day. Adam, who has a confused idea of what I do—something between Superman and Marshall Dillon, I think—wanted to know if I'd caught the bad guy.

"He's not a real bad guy," I explained. "He just did something wrong and he had to face up to it. It's important to face up to your mistake . . ."

But he'd lost interest. "Dad?"

"What?"

"Why do they call 'em colored fountains when they're white?"

"Huh?"

"Granny took us to Clark's today and I hadda go to the bathroom and they had a sign over the fountain that said it was colored, but it was white and she wouldn't let me drink." He managed to get it all out without stopping for breath.

Susie and I exchanged glances across the table. I should have been better prepared, but coward that I am, I'd hoped this day wouldn't come for a while. The phone rang and I grabbed for it like a life preserver. It was the mother of one of Christine's friends offering to load up a crowd of kids for a trip to the drive-in.

"Please, please, pleeease? It's Elvis." Christine clasped her hands under her chin and danced an anxious jig.

"Yuck," Adam announced.

"Well, you don't have to go, sport," I said.

"Yeah." Christine stuck her tongue out at him. I pretended not to see.

"Oh, I might as well," he backpedaled. "There's nothing else to do."

Christine paused just long enough to throw her arms around my neck before racing off to gather up stuffed animals and pillows.

We got the kids off, then Susie washed and I dried. As soon as I'd put away the last dish, I dialed the newsroom.

"*Times*, newsroom," barked a voice I didn't recognize. I asked for Ben.

"Uh, he's pretty busy right now, can he call you back?"

"Tell him it's Steve Harlan."

"Harmon?"

"Harlan. H-a-r-l-a-n."

"Hang on."

Obviously, my legend did not live on.

"L'chaim, y'all." Ben came on the line sounding half strangled, which told me he was in his usual position—feet propped on the desk, rear end precariously balanced on the edge of his chair, which would be pushed back into the aisle to accommodate his long, skinny legs. After a day like today, his wiry red curls would be standing up like cheap carpet. Ben's hair is his barometer. As long as he has enough to pull, tug, or otherwise abuse, he'll never have an ulcer.

"You still breaking your mother's heart?"

His wealthy parents are always after him to come "home" to New York and settle down, but he sticks around. It could be making city editor, but I suspect it has more to do with that blonde in Classifieds, an old-fashioned, foot-washing Southern Baptist.

"Find me a Jewish girl who can make cornbread and black-eye peas like Susie, I'll marry her in a minute," he retorted.

"Since when are black-eye peas kosher? You have any idea what's in those?"

"On second thought, I'll just take Susie. You don't deserve her anyway."

"Tell me what you've got on Lattimore and she's yours," I promised.

"Ready to come back to work?" He lowered his voice. "Name your price, buddy. There's nobody left in the newsroom who could handle this one like you."

"I believe it was another gifted writer from North Carolina who said you can't go home again. That was somebody else in another lifetime."

"I hear you." A silence fell between us.

I broke it, finally, by filling him in on my call from Warren. There was another silence when I finished that brought me down to earth with a thud. Maybe I'd put my former life behind me more than I realized if I could be that stupid. I'd been so

25

excited I hadn't stopped to consider this wasn't just another story we could laugh about over a beer. It was a major murder investigation, and if I became part of the investigation, and thus the story, I was putting Ben squarely in the middle of a professional and ethical dilemma.

"Oh, hell, I'm sorry, Ben," I said. "I don't know where my brain was."

"It's not a problem," he said quietly. "We don't have anything at this point you couldn't worm out of your police buddies anyway. If you take the case, *then* we'll worry about what's on and off the record."

"Are you sure?"

"Hey, it's all academic at this point. You haven't been formally retained, right? Until tomorrow, you're just curious like everybody else in town."

"Thanks."

"Don't worry about it. But it's going to cost you a beer and some of Susie's cooking."

"You got it."

"Wadda you want to know?"

I thought about it for a minute. "What tipped the police off that things weren't what they seemed?"

"Your boy panicked. He tried to rig it to make it look like she died in her sleep, but when they saw the bruises, even those morons Bennett and Lang could figure out nobody's that hard a sleeper and they hollered for Owens."

"Bennett and Lang?"

"What can I say? It was a holiday."

Bennett and Lang are detectives. At least, they work in the Detective Division, but their toughest assignment is usually picking up the Chief's dry cleaning. They would never have caught the call if the division hadn't been seriously shorthanded for the holiday. Owens, the lieutenant in charge of the division, is another story. He's a solid cop, a rarity in a department where a guy's voting record carries more weight than his ability. Like all cops, Owens has a love-hate relationship with the press, but he always played straight with me and I tried to return the favor.

"What about cause of death?"

"Nothing definite so far. We haven't heard anything on the autopsy report and the police aren't talking," Ben replied. "The only thing everybody seems to agree on is that she was pretty banged up."

"No stab wounds, no gun shot?"

He hesitated. "No, but there are some wild stories going around."

"Like?"

"Weird stuff—bite marks, mutilation, that kind of thing."

Terrific. I finally get my big break and my client turns out to be a pervert. "Well, Fitzgerald said rich people are different from you and me."

"I'd take my chances," he replied.

"You're in the wrong business for that."

"Tell me about it."

"What about the boy?" I asked.

"He stuck to the story Lattimore gave him for a while, may even have believed it. He's just a kid. But when the cops told him it wasn't natural causes, he told 'em what really happened and they had Lattimore inside so fast, Fireball Roberts would've been green."

"Anything on the wife?"

"A ringer for Liz Taylor, I hear. Comes from one of your fine old families up in Virginia somewhere. Word is, a lot of people thought she married down when she married Lattimore, despite his money, but they were married for more than twenty years before they split up."

"Recently?"

"Couple years."

"What've you got on the Green woman?"

"Just the usual, so far, but we're working on it. Listen, they're calling me, I gotta go. Call me . . ." he trailed off. By tomorrow, everything could be different between us.

"You'll hear from me," I promised.

"Ciao." He hung up.

I wandered out into the backyard and plopped down in one of the lawn chairs. It protested and I made a mental note to get around to re-webbing it sometime this century. Dusk had come and gone, but the sky retained that incredible blue tinge it gets just between daylight and dark. *L'heure bleu,* the French call it. It was quiet on the other side of the fence; Ron must have given up for the night. The bugs were making their own midsummer night's madness, but the mosquitoes weren't out in force yet, so I sat, watching the stars and thinking.

After a while, Susie came out to take the laundry off the line before the dew fell. I gave her a hand and then we sat, companionable and quiet in the twilight.

She stirred. "The boy bothers you." It wasn't a question.

I nodded. I lost my father when I was ten, not much younger than Greg Green, and it hit me hard. I hadn't cried much, but I spent a lot of that summer alone behind the azalea bushes.

"You having second thoughts?"

I gazed up at the rising moon as though it held the answer. "If Lattimore killed her, he deserves everything that's coming to him. But he's supposed to be innocent until proven guilty, and I guess I won't know until I hear his story."

She reached for my hand. "Do what your gut tells you, Steve. There'll be other cases, other breaks. If you don't like it, walk away. We'll be okay."

I couldn't think of anything to say, so I just squeezed her

hand and we sat, enjoying the night, until the mosquitoes drove us inside.

CHAPTER 3

I told myself I wasn't nervous, but I checked for yellow stains under the arms of my white oxford-cloth shirt and tied three knots before I was satisfied with my tie. Susie pretended not to notice. I dropped her at school and nosed the Falcon in front of a parking meter by five of nine.

Warren's office, like that of nearly every other attorney in town, is in one of three identical red brick boxes that squat across from the courthouse cannon. Lawyers are crammed in there like sausage in a skin, but they put up with the inconvenience to be close to the action. Information flies across the street so fast, we used to swear they have the courthouse pigeons on retainer.

I was so caught up in my own thoughts, I forgot about reporters. As I rounded the corner, I spotted a *Courier* photographer I knew and two reporters I didn't, loitering on the courthouse sidewalk keeping an eye on Warren's front door. I ducked back before they spotted me and made my way across the parking lots to the back door of Warren's building.

Maybe I still look like a reporter; fledgling private investigators don't make enough to dress well either. The porter tried to stiff-arm me, but I showed him my license and convinced him I had an appointment upstairs.

I didn't fare much better with Warren's henna-haired watchdog in the front office. It was probably the beard.

Thanks to my years as a reporter, I have plenty of practice

disarming suspicious secretaries, so I gave her my "aw shucks" grin, the one that always earned me an extra slice of pound cake from Pickle Bryson's mom.

But Warren's watchdog had been "aw shucked" by the best in her time. I finally persuaded her I wasn't Fidel disguised in a cheap suit, and the calendar on her desk insisted someone with my name had a legitimate appointment.

"Go on in," she said, giving me that same look my fourth-grade teacher used to. The one that says "cute doesn't buy any bananas, buster."

My grin doesn't work on Susie either. I'm gonna have to work on it or start hanging around dumber women.

I knocked once on Warren's door and obeyed a summons from within, but stopped short in the doorway. I guess subconsciously I was expecting a Southern version of Judge Hardy, somebody with a stiff back and manners to match. Warren looked the part, all right, right down to the gold watch chain draped across the vest of his black suit and patrician features topped by a head of snowy white hair that would set my mother swooning.

But the man the newspapers had tagged "a legend in jurisprudence" sat at his desk, in the middle of a room that resembled my grandfather's general store more than a law office, expertly spinning a yo-yo.

He gave me a sheepish smile. "I can walk the dog, but this rock-the-cradle thing is giving me fits. I'm determined to get it before my grandson comes to lunch Sunday."

"Afraid I can't help you with that," I replied with a smile. Struggling to extricate his fingers from the yo-yo string, Warren got up and moved a pile of papers off a chair so I could sit down.

The phone buzzed for his attention. I tried not to listen as I gazed around his office. There was plenty to look at. The usual

31

diplomas and certificates were all but buried under pictures, mementos, and more pictures. I spotted a stuffed fish, a battered putter mounted over a photo of Warren with Arnold Palmer, and an honest-to-God horse collar that looked as though it had seen some use. His law diploma from Carolina occupied pride of place, mounted in a gold frame with one of those little lights over it. A fellow Tarheel. One point in my favor.

Law books filled the floor-to-ceiling bookshelves along one wall. The shelves on the opposite wall were stuffed with everything from leather-bound first editions to tattered paperbacks. I could have sworn I saw a whole row of Erle Stanley Gardner.

"Now then, Mr. Harlan." I turned my attention back to Warren. He'd managed to free his fingers during his conversation. "You've read the papers?"

"Yes sir, I have."

"Then you have some idea what we're up against."

The "we" was a good sign.

"My client has gotten himself into a world of trouble and it's going to take a big shovel to dig him out." But he didn't look worried as he leaned back in his chair and rocked gently. "To make matters worse, he has spoken quite freely to police without benefit of counsel. Unfortunately, that's done and can't be undone. My biggest concern at this point is the boy."

"Precisely," he said, responding, apparently, to the feelings that must have shown on my face. "Public sentiment will run very strong against him for involving the boy."

He rose and went to the window, speaking over his shoulder. "The press is going to eat us alive," he said. "We got off easy yesterday because of the holiday, but they're out there now," he gestured out the window, "digging and burrowing for dirt. It's the story of a lifetime, of a career, for a newsman. There's money, scandal, prominent people. They'll be all over it like a duck on a June bug."

I kept quiet, reminding myself I was on the other side, now, but something in my stillness must have communicated itself to him.

He turned back from the window with a smile. "Forgive me, I realize I'm speaking of your former colleagues. I didn't mean to imply any disrespect. I don't fault them for it. In spite of what I just said, I'm a strong advocate of a free press. I don't know any good attorney who isn't. As a matter of fact, I became a fan of your work after your series on integration."

"Thank you." I tried to hide my surprise.

"There is no denying, however," he went on, "that your background could be a plus for us." He watched my reaction from under bushy, white eyebrows.

"Let us be clear, Mr. Warren. Are you looking to hire an investigator or a press agent? Because if it's the latter, I'm afraid I'm not your man. I could suggest several names if you like."

Warren held up a hand. "I'm sorry, Mr. Harlan. I put that badly. I assure you I have no interest in hiring a 'mouthpiece' and if I had, I wouldn't insult you by asking. I have too much respect for you to suggest anything of the kind."

I put my hat back on my knee.

"I simply meant that your background is an added advantage in dealing with your colleagues. You may be able to offer suggestions on how we might best handle the situation, minimize the damage, so to speak. There's also the undeniable advantage that the reporters will consider information we decide to share with them with far more credibility if it's the result of your work or its validity is confirmed, even implicitly, by you."

"You are aware of the circumstances around my . . . leaving the *Times?*"

"Of course. But after what happened, certainly no one could

fault you," he replied. "And while many of your colleagues are still employed by the paper, it is under new ownership and new management."

For once I kept quiet while I chewed it over. He still hadn't answered the sixty-four-thousand-dollar question. But did it really matter why he called me? This was probably the biggest case to come along in the last fifty years and it could make my new career. I owed it to Susie and the kids not to pass up the opportunity. On the other hand, if I fell flat on my face, I'd fall hard and I couldn't expect any mercy from the guys on the street, not even my former colleagues at the *Times*. If I'd had another hand, I'd have added, did I really want to help get this guy off if he was guilty? Susie's voice saying, "Walk away, Steve. We'll be fine," was overlaid by the image of her tired face as she folded clothes at midnight.

"Well, Mr. Harlan?"

"Did someone refer you to me?"

"No. As I said, I followed your work at the *Times* so I was aware when you left the paper to become an investigator. And our little circle," he made an encompassing gesture I took to indicate the legal fraternity that surrounded us, "is a small, rather incestuous one, if you will. I've kept abreast of your career."

"Well, I'm flattered, of course. But there are other, more experienced investigators available. Why me?"

He studied me a moment before responding. "I have been an attorney almost as long as you've been alive. I flatter myself that after all these years I'm a good judge of people. You strike me as intelligent. And you know this town. The police and the reporters know you, you know the D.A. and his staff."

I waited.

Warren leaned forward and clasped his hands together on the blotter. "There are many good investigators with years of experience available and undoubtedly, I have messages waiting out there from many of them, offering their services. So let's just leave it that this will almost certainly be a long, tiresome, and essentially unpleasant case and I'm indulging myself the luxury of choosing an investigator with whom I feel comfortable."

There seemed no adequate response to that.

"Are we agreed then?" he asked, rising.

I stopped him with a gesture. "There is one more thing. Your client has never made any secret of the fact he considers reporters a necessary evil. And he can afford any investigator he wants, including those you mentioned. How is he going to feel about it?"

"My client," he replied in a tone as dry as his law books, "has placed himself in very great jeopardy by his own actions. If he is indicted, he stands a very real chance of going on trial for his life." He took his hat down from the rack and plopped it on his head. "In other words, Mr. Harlan, for the first time in his life, my client may have to lump it. Shall we go?"

"Where are we going?"

"To the jail. Time is precious and I want you to hear John's story firsthand. Then we can discuss where to start."

He held the door open for me. "Miz Turner, we're going to the jail now. Would you be so kind?"

She rose and crossed to the window. I tried not to stare. Underneath that battered old desk and plain brown dress was a pair of legs a chorus girl would kill for. And she had to be sixty if she was a day. At Warren's nod, she ostentatiously parted the Venetian blinds and peered out. She nodded to us and we slipped out into the hallway.

"What was all that about?"

"Thanks to Miz Turner, the reporters who are no doubt lurking out front will assume I'm about to slip out the back," he replied as he pulled a small key from his pocket. "While they're racing around there, where Fred will keep them busy, we'll stroll over to the jail."

He led me past the elevator to the stairs and down to the coffee shop on the ground floor. He nodded to the Greek proprietor, who made a big show of winking back. Warren slipped behind the counter and through the curtain into a dark, odorous storeroom.

"I am relying on your discretion as a gentleman," he said with mock solemnity as he nudged aside a carton of ketchup to reveal a door. He unlocked it and led me down a long, empty corridor that seemed to run forever. We eventually emerged on the sidewalk a block below his office. There wasn't a reporter in sight. He strolled through the crosswalk like an emperor as I trailed behind, feeling as insignificant as the guy with the broom at the end of the parade.

CHAPTER 4

Warren parked me in an interview room while he went in search of his client. To take my mind off the overpowering odor of sweat and pine-scented disinfectant, I made some notes and scribbled out a few questions.

It didn't take long to jot down the few facts I had, and Warren still hadn't returned. As the minutes crawled by, I amused myself by studying the colorful, if misspelled, obscenities etched into the bile-green walls. I'd been reduced to doodling by the time Warren finally appeared with Lattimore in tow. There was no deputy with them. Whether that was a testament to Warren's importance or Lattimore's, I wasn't sure.

Warren performed the introductions. I stood up to shake Lattimore's hand across the scarred table. I noticed a fresh bandage on the back of his left hand. Lattimore nodded but didn't speak. I nodded back, studying him and trying not to be too obvious about it.

He wore dark slacks and a white dress shirt, open at the neck. They didn't look as though they'd been slept in, so someone must have brought him fresh things this morning. He'd made an unsuccessful attempt at shaving, probably the best he could do with an electric razor and no mirror. Up close, I was struck by his size, well over six feet tall and two hundred pounds. His hands matched the rest of him, big, meaty, and plenty strong, as I'd discovered when we shook hands. If he hit you, you'd stay hit. I disliked him on sight, but told myself it was an instinctive thing, the resentment of the haves by the have-nots.

We settled ourselves around the table. Lattimore lit a cigarette.

"John, I'd like you to tell Mr. Harlan about the events of this weekend," Warren said.

"There's no point. The whole thing is stupid," Lattimore protested, exhaling smoke through his nostrils. His already florid complexion grew darker and, being a crackerjack detective, I deduced he was probably a heavy drinker with a temper to match. "They can't hold me. They've got nothing. They think they've got a big case, gonna make a name for themselves off me."

He spoke to Warren and ignored me like a bug on the wall. Spending the night in jail didn't seem to have made much of an impression on him. I decided to see for myself.

"You're in jail, Mr. Lattimore."

He stiffened and turned to glare at me. The reflection off his glasses made it impossible to read his eyes, but I didn't need to see them to know that he was having a hard time with the idea he wasn't calling the shots.

"Owens doesn't need you to make his reputation," I continued. "You wouldn't be here if he and the D.A. didn't think they have a case. I need to know what that case is if I'm going to poke holes in it."

He studied me for a minute, then turned to look at Warren, who met his gaze squarely but didn't change expression. Lattimore shrugged and ground out his cigarette. He planted his elbows on the table and leaned toward me. "What do you want to know?" His tone was challenging.

"Tell me about Delores Green."

"Delores. Lord, where to begin." He sighed and leaned back in his chair, running a hand through hair that was beginning to retreat. "I've known Delores for ten or twelve years. Greg was just a baby; she hadn't been separated long when we met."

"How did you meet her?"

"Somebody introduced us, I don't remember who."

"What was your relationship with her?"

Warren interrupted. "We should bear in mind, Mr. Harlan, that what Mr. Lattimore tells you may not be covered by client confidentiality and you could be called to testify."

I got the message. "Where was her husband?"

"Down in the eastern part of the state somewhere." Lattimore waved a dismissive hand. "He remarried not long after the divorce, but he died about two years later. Heart attack, I think."

No jealous husband in the picture, then. "What's the actual charge?" I asked Warren.

He replied in a voice bland as grits. "They're asking for Murder One."

I struggled to conceal my dismay. Murder in the first degree means premeditation. In this state, it also means the death penalty. I studied the initials gouged into the tabletop. If Lattimore had gotten Warren's message, and I felt sure he had, he'd tell me only what I needed to hear. The rest I'd have to find out for myself.

"Why don't you just tell me what happened?" I invited.

"Where do you want me to start?"

"At the beginning will be fine."

"Let's see." He leaned forward again. This time, it was his turn to study the initials. "I called Delores late in the afternoon, about six, to see if she wanted to have some supper, but there was no answer. I kept trying until about seven-thirty and still didn't get an answer, so I just fixed something at the house and didn't think anything more about it."

"That was Sunday?"

"Yeah." He lit another cigarette. "A little before nine, I went to the store. I rode by Delores's while I was out. Greg was out in the yard with some of the neighbor boys. He told me Delores had gone to the office about three and he hadn't heard from her since.

"I rode by her office, but it was dark and I didn't see her car in the parking lot. I thought she might have stopped by Peggy's—that's Peggy Summerfield, one of her girlfriends—but her car wasn't there and neither was Peggy's. So I went back by the house but she still wasn't home."

"Why were you so anxious to find her?" I asked, still trying to get a feel for their relationship.

Lattimore glanced at me, but his eyes slid away. "Not many people know—*knew*—about it, but Delores had a drinking problem. A bad one. She managed to cover it pretty well, but it's been worse lately. She could be falling down drunk at dinnertime, but she'd get up next morning and go to work and nobody would ever guess a thing."

"Did her son know about it?"

"It wasn't something we talked about, but he knew and he looked after her when she was 'sick,' we called it. If it was real bad, he'd call me."

I nodded without comment.

"So I was worried something might've happened, she'd had an accident or something," he continued. "No matter how bad she was drinking, she tried to be a good mother. She wouldn't have stayed gone that long without making some arrangements for Greg or at least letting him know where she was, unless she was hurt or . . ."

"Passed out?"

"Or dead."

No one spoke for a minute.

"So what did you do?"

"Greg and I started calling around looking for her. We called a couple of her friends, but nobody had seen her. I sent Greg back outside and called the hospitals, but they didn't have anybody who matched her description. By then it was pretty late, so I went out and told Greg to spend the night with his friends and I got in my car and rode around for a while, checking places she liked to go."

"Such as?" I asked.

He named a couple supper clubs and restaurants and I made a note of them.

"No luck?"

"No. Greg was taken care of, so I went home and went to bed. I didn't know where else to look."

His concern for the boy didn't jibe with his actions later, but I decided to work up to that gradually.

"Did she . . ." I hesitated. "Is there anyone she sees?"

"A boyfriend?" Lattimore shot me a sharp look. "Nobody special." His shrug said it didn't matter, but I wondered. "If she had a date, she would've told Greg."

"I see. So when did you see her next?"

"I called Greg at the neighbors as soon as I got up Monday morning, but he hadn't seen or heard from her."

"You didn't go in to the bank?"

"Nah, we both took Monday and Tuesday off to make a long weekend."

"What time was that?"

"About nine."

"Who are these neighbors?"

"The Rosinskis. They have two boys; the younger one is Greg's age. The older one is off at school somewhere. A little before lunchtime, about eleven, I guess, I called the house again. Greg said some man had just dropped Delores off and driven away in her car. Greg said she was in pretty bad shape. I didn't like the sound of that, so I got over there as quick as I could."

"Bad shape, how?"

He considered a minute. "Greg didn't say and I just assumed he meant she was drunk. And she was. But she looked like hell. Her hair was a mess, her clothes were all dirty, and she had some scrapes on her face, here," he indicated his nose, "and here, by her eye. She had bruises up and down her arms and a big one on her knee that was starting to swell up."

"Where'd she been?"

"I couldn't get much out of her. She was still pretty drunk. Greg and the little Rosinski boy were standing there, taking it all in, so I sent them outside and tried to get some sense out of her."

My glance strayed to the bandage on his hand.

"I didn't beat it out of her," he said, noticing my glance.

"I didn't say you did." I kept my tone level.

"It wouldn't have done any good anyway. She wasn't making any sense. She just kept mumbling about watching the water. I thought maybe she'd gone out to the cabin, but she said not."

"What cabin?"

"It's just a little weekend place I have down on the river. We used it a lot when my kids were small, but hardly anybody goes there now. Delores and I used to, sometimes."

I got the picture. Having a twelve-year-old around would certainly cramp your style.

"What about the guy? Did she tell you who he was?"

"What guy?"

"The guy who brought her home."

"Oh, him. It was just the guy from the gas station. She'd been having trouble getting the car to start in the mornings, so she took it in on Friday but they couldn't find anything wrong with it. It did the same thing when she tried to start it Sunday morning, so she took it back by the station and got the guy to drive her home. He drove it back to the station to check it.

"I cleaned her up a little and put her to bed, then I went home," he continued. "I hadn't had any breakfast and I was hungry."

He held up his bandaged hand. "That's how I did this. Burned it taking a ham out of the oven. Then I laid down and took a nap like I usually do on Sunday afternoon. Delores called about dinnertime and said she was going to the ABC store. I reminded her it was closed and told her I'd bring a bottle over."

I raised my eyebrows but didn't look up from my notes.

"If I hadn't, she'd have gone out looking for a drink," he said, his tone defensive. "She was in no shape to drive, and in her condition, anything could have happened."

"I thought her car was in the shop."

"It was in the driveway when I got there." He shrugged. "I guess the guy brought it back. Anyway," he continued, "when I got to her house, this guy and his wife from the next street over were there, making themselves at home."

"The Rosinskis?"

"Nah, they're okay. These people, the Hemingways, they're real white trash. The wife's been working temporary at Delores's office for a couple weeks and they live over on the next street, so Delores started giving her a ride to work and they've been freeloading ever since. Delores even loaned 'em her car once or twice before I put a stop to it."

"Why did they borrow her car?"

"I don't think they have one," he replied. "Anyway, Hemingway spotted the bottle and hung around. I figured what the hell, and poured everybody a drink. Delores had one, then she went back to her room and laid down. The wife, Elvira's her name, she went back there and sat with her for a while. Hemingway and I sat in the kitchen. About ten-thirty, eleven o'clock, Elvira came out and helped herself to another drink. Delores got up too and said she was hungry. I told her to put some clothes on

and comb her hair and we'd go get something. The Hemingways took the hint and left. Delores and I left right behind
them. But when we got in the car, she wouldn't tell me where
she wanted to go. We rode around for a while, arguing, and I
started in on her about where she'd spent the night."

"Wait a second." I held up a restraining hand. "Where was
the boy all this time?"

"He'd gone over to some kid's house to work on a jalopy.
The kid's car crazy. He spends all his time working on one or
reading about 'em or pestering his mother to let him drive hers.
I put my foot down about that, too."

"Did you get any more out of her about Sunday night?"

"Some. She remembered leaving the house and told me she
gave Hemingway a lift uptown to catch the bus, then she went
shopping for Greg's birthday. Maybe that's why she told him
she was going to the office. She stopped by a drive-in on Wilkinson and got some chasers and had a few drinks, but after that,
nothing. She went blank. Swore the only thing she could
remember was looking at the water. I asked her again if she
went to the cabin, but she said no. Maybe she dreamed about
water."

"What about the bruises? How'd she explain those?"

"She didn't. Said she didn't know how she got them. We rode
around for at least an hour arguing, but she swore she couldn't
remember anything after leaving the drive-in until she woke up
in her car the next morning."

"Go on."

"Well, after a while, she decided she wanted to go out to the
cabin. She wanted to know if I had anything to drink out there.
I told her she didn't need anything else to drink. But she just
kept on and on at me, so I agreed. We weren't that far from the
cabin anyway."

"Where is it?"

"Off Highway 49, almost to the South Carolina line. It's not even paved, just a dirt road. You'd miss it completely unless you know where to look."

"Uh huh."

"Well, we got to the cabin and she flopped down on the sofa while I looked for something to drink. I found a bottle with enough in it for a couple of short ones and poured us both one. She downed hers pretty quick and started to stagger around. I don't understand it. Two small drinks and she was as sloppy drunk as anybody I've ever seen.

"We argued some more, mostly about her drinking. She'd promised a few weeks ago she was gonna quit, pull herself together, but she's been worse than ever. When I mentioned Greg, she got ugly. I guess she felt guilty. Anyway, she just got worse and worse. After a while, she sprawled out there on the sofa and told me to leave her the hell alone. I was pretty fed up by then, so I decided to do just that and let her sleep it off."

For all his pretense of disgust and disapproval at Delores's drinking, he seemed awful quick to pour it down her, but maybe it was his way of trying to control her intake.

"Was she awake when you left?"

"I don't know. She didn't say anything when I turned off the lights."

"You weren't worried about leaving her alone out there?"

"Not really. There's nobody around to bother her. There was no more booze and I locked her in when I left so if she woke up, she couldn't go out and fall in the river. There's some stuff in the cabinets—coffee and cereal and stuff—so I knew she'd be all right until morning. I figured by the time she woke up, she'd be feeling so lousy, she might be more inclined to listen to reason."

"What time was it when you left?"

"Midnight, maybe."

"You went home?"

"Yeah," he replied. "I'd had enough, so I went home and went to bed."

"Wait a second," I held up a hand. "Let's back up for a minute. When you first arrived at the cabin, did you see anything to suggest she'd been there the night before? Car tracks? Things moved around, out of place?"

"Nothing."

"Okay, sorry, go ahead. What made you go back out?"

He fiddled with the cigarette pack and didn't meet my eyes. It was the first time he'd shown any real sign of nervousness.

"I woke up about two." He still wasn't looking at me. "I laid there a while and got to thinking about her out there by herself. I knew she couldn't get out, but she could've broken a glass and cut herself or set the house on fire trying to light the stove. So I got up and dressed and drove back out."

He shut his eyes briefly and drew a deep breath. "She was on the floor. I thought she'd rolled off the couch. I went over to pick her up and as soon as I touched her, I knew she was dead."

"Why?"

"I'm not sure. She was just so still—dead weight. I just about died myself. I thought I was gonna have a heart attack right there. I tried to find a pulse or a heartbeat, but I couldn't get anything. I was scared to death."

"You're sure she was dead?" I persisted.

"Yeah."

"But how did you know? It's very important that you remember." I didn't even want to think about what the prosecution would do with this if they got him on the stand.

"I don't know. I just knew. She wasn't breathing, nothing."

"Was she cold? Stiff?"

He reflected a moment. "No."

"What did you do?"

"Well, I sat there and tried to think. All I could think about was the scandal." He glanced at me, but I didn't react. "Then I remembered how, when some politician conks out in the wrong bed, the cops just move him to a room down the hall, you know? And I thought, why not? I could take her home, put her in bed, and nobody would know the difference."

"Except Greg."

"I couldn't sneak her in without his knowing it," he said. He looked everywhere but at me. "I was trying to do him a favor."

I let the silence hang until it grew heavy.

"Look, she was dead," he burst out. "There was nothing that was gonna change that. I was trying to protect him. How would you feel having your mother's picture all over the papers, having everybody in town find out she drank herself to death in some guy's cabin out in the woods?"

Not to mention how his wife, his friends at the country club, and the bank's board of directors might feel about it.

"So what did you do?"

"I carried her out to the car and laid her on the back seat. Then I went back in and gathered up all her stuff—her pocketbook and her shoes and stuff—and put them in the car. Then I called Greg and told him what had happened."

For somebody in the throes of panic, he was awfully cool about covering his tracks.

"How did he react?"

"He didn't say anything much. I think I told him she'd had a heart attack, but he didn't seem to take it in. I locked up the cabin and drove the back way to Delores's house. Somewhere along the way, she . . . she fell off the back seat." He swallowed hard. "I didn't stop. When I got to her house, Greg was waiting for me. He helped me carry her in and we changed her into her pajamas and put her into her bed." He heaved a gusty sigh. "Then I left."

That brought my head up with a jerk. "What?"

"I left."

"You left?"

"Yeah."

I gazed at him for a moment without speaking. "What about the police?"

"Oh. Well, Greg called them. I told him what to say, that he'd gotten up in the night and found her—like that. I explained to him that was the best way—so there'd be no talk later . . ." His voice trailed off.

"Did you go straight home?" I kept my voice even and noncommittal, but it was an effort.

"I parked around the corner until I saw the police car arrive. They were there in about ten minutes. Then I drove home."

I couldn't think of anything to say.

"I . . ." Lattimore hesitated. "I had her clothes, the dress and stuff she'd had on. I didn't know what else to do with them, so I balled them up and put them in my car. When I got home, I burned them."

"Burned them?"

"In my trash can. I didn't know what else to do with them." He looked to Warren for support. "I couldn't just throw them away. What would the garbage man think if he found a woman's clothes stuffed in my trash can?"

I didn't dare look at Warren. I didn't know what Lattimore's garbage man might have thought, but I could just imagine the transports of joy the D.A. would have if he found out about it.

"Did the boy . . . did he accept your explanation for what happened?"

"It was the truth. He didn't say much. I figured he was in shock, but he understood and he went along with it once I explained why it was for the best." Lattimore looked from me to Warren again as if hoping for absolution.

I, too, looked at Warren and received an imperceptible nod.

"How's your relationship with Greg?" I asked.

"You know how kids are." Lattimore leaned back in his chair, relaxed now that the hard part was over. "Greg's an only child. Delores spoiled him and it's come back to haunt her when he got older."

"Haunt her how? Has he been in trouble?"

"The usual stuff. Talking back, thinking he was too big to have to listen to her anymore. I tried to ride herd on him some and he resented it. But, hell, I'm the closest thing to a father he's ever known."

"How much of this did you tell the police?"

"All of it." He shrugged. "Once Greg told them what really happened, there was no reason to lie." He dropped his fist on the table with a thump and leaned toward me. "The only thing I'm guilty of is trying to avoid a scandal. There was no murder. She had a heart attack and died in the wrong place at the wrong time and I tried to put the best face on it." He gestured toward the window. "Any minute now, they're gonna figure that out and they'll be over here with their tails between their legs to apologize. But it's too late. The damage is done. I've seen the papers and when I get out of here, I'm gonna make those bastards sorry they were ever born." He shoved his chair back and rose, ready to do battle.

Warren was on his feet. "I don't want to hear any more talk like that outside this room, John." He put a placatory hand on Lattimore's shoulder. "Right now, we have to concentrate on getting you out of here. I have a meeting with the district attorney in"—he consulted his watch—"less than an hour. Do you have everything you need, Mr. Harlan?"

"For the time being."

But I was sorely puzzled. Lattimore was no expert. If he hadn't panicked, if he'd taken her to a hospital, Delores Green might be alive. But at worst, he should have been looking at a manslaughter or negligent homicide charge. That was a long way from Murder One—and way too close to the gas chamber. Either he wasn't telling the truth or there was something else going on. But what?

Even if Lattimore knew the answer, he couldn't—or wouldn't—tell me. But I knew someone who could.

CHAPTER 5

I waited in the corridor, grateful for the fresh air, while Warren took Lattimore back to his cell. His bearing when he returned was as dignified as ever, but he looked as though he'd aged ten years. He opened the door to the interview room. "Let's step in here for a minute."

As soon as the door closed behind us, he sank heavily onto the nearest chair and rubbed a hand over his handsome face.

"Give you a hard time?"

"No, but this is hard for both of us," he said. There was real pain in his eyes. "John and I've never been what you'd call friends, but I've known his family for years. We know the same people, we've attended the same weddings and graduations and funerals for twenty years. Hard as it is for me to see him like this, it's even harder for him to have me see him like this."

"You could've called the deputy to take him back to his cell," I said.

"No," he sighed. "It's the least I can do for him. He'll suffer enough humiliation before this is over. In some ways, it's a blessing he's in here where he's protected from the worst of it."

I couldn't argue with that. We sat for a while, lost in our own thoughts, until I finally broke the silence. "How do *you* feel about his story?"

"It has the value of simplicity," Warren replied, staring thoughtfully into space. "In my experience, the guilty usually err by being too elaborate. They have an explanation for everything. If he'd killed her, I think he'd have come up with a more plausible story, certainly better than this one. But he seems genuinely surprised they even suspect him of killing her."

"You don't think he was just counting on his name and reputation to protect him?"

"No," he replied. "I think he honestly believed he'd get away with it." He focused suddenly on me, a direct and penetrating gaze. "You don't like him much, do you?"

I hedged. "Let's say he doesn't fit my image of a banker."

"It's all right." He waved a hand. "There's no rule that says we have to like our clients. And John's not easy to like. I can't say I've ever cared much for him myself. He's brash, arrogant, overbearing, and sometimes downright crude. The difference is, I understand him, you see. I knew his people. His daddy came to town with nothing and became one of the wealthiest, most powerful, and respected men in this town. And that wasn't easy during the Depression. Despite what you might think, it's not easy being a rich man's son.

"John's mama was a wonderful woman. She and my mother were in the DAR together. John was their only son. From the time he was a little boy, his father groomed him to take over. But for some reason, John was never able to measure up to his daddy's expectations. I don't know whether the fault was truly with John or with his father's expectations. But naturally, when John finally slipped the leash and went away to college, he raised more than his fair share of hell and his daddy never let him forget it.

"John's a smart man. He's not a natural-born banker like his daddy, but he understands money. His real talent is property—real estate. Over the years, he managed to convince his father to invest in some prime properties and they've done very well. He had some good ideas, but his daddy never could see it. Even after John was grown and married, had a family of his own, his daddy still told him how to dress, where to live, what kind of car to buy. I get the impression that when his father died a few years ago, John went off the rails. I don't know whether he was just used to having his father to keep him on the straight and narrow or he was making up for lost time."

He rose and began to pace around the little room. "Fortunately, he married a woman just like his mother. Deborah Lattimore comes from a good family. The term doesn't mean much any more, but Deborah is a lady. A lot of people said she married beneath her when she married John, and he knew it. That's not an easy way to start a marriage, but they did all right. Not perfect, but they bumped along. They've raised three fine children together. No doubt, knowing John, he has had his little adventures, but he must have been reasonably discreet if he had a relationship with this woman for ten years and I didn't hear a whisper of it."

He sighed again and placed his palms down on the table, leaning his weight against them. "I've known John Lattimore all his life. Like most of us, he's a lot of things, not all of them good, but I honestly do not believe he's a murderer. And I owe it to his mama and daddy to do everything I can for him. I need your help, Mr. Harlan. Nobody says you have to like him or even approve of him. Just help me save his life."

His ice-blue eyes held mine and I had the eerie feeling that he saw clear through to a little boy behind a hedge of azaleas. I was beginning to understand why he was a legend. Even if he was playing me like a violin, he did it with a master's touch so that, to my surprise, I found I didn't mind. Something passed between us without words. Warren gave a slight nod of satisfaction. I flipped open my notebook.

"The bruises. Our client seems to think she died of a heart attack. But what if she was in worse shape than he realized? What if she had an internal injury or a concussion and nobody realized it?" The more I thought about it, the better I liked it. Warren paid me the compliment of looking interested.

"She'd have put the headache down to the hangover," I continued. "Or maybe what everybody thought was a hangover to end all hangovers was a concussion. And if she was drinking on top of it . . ."

"He did say she seemed unusually inebriated for the number of drinks she'd had," he agreed.

"But even if that's the case, he'd still look good for it," I said. "Cops like to keep it simple and they're usually right." I ticked off the points on my fingers. "He was the last one to see her alive. He admits bringing her home dead and tries to cover it up. If he told the police they'd been arguing the night she died, that'd be the icing on the cake. But what I don't understand is why they moved so fast. Lattimore's not just some guy who slugged his old lady too hard after a few drinks. I'd think they'd want to be very sure of their ground. Especially King. He and Lattimore probably belong to the same country club," I said.

"We all do," Warren replied absently.

Floyd King's the district attorney, a political animal so slick he borders on the slimy. But maybe I'm prejudiced. I've never trusted men with big, horsy grins, and whenever King slaps me on the back, something he doesn't bother to do since I left the newspaper, I'm reminded of Mr. Ed.

"The other thing that bothers me is the premeditation angle," I said. "Even if Lattimore did kill her, maybe knocked her around so she hit her head or something, I don't see how they can argue premeditation. It just doesn't fit."

"But she had the bruises when she came home on Sunday," Warren pointed out. "At least two people saw her, the boy and the service station mechanic, so they should be able to back up his story. Unless the boy lied to police, and I can't think why he should."

I could, but I kept my thoughts to myself.

"Let's look at it the other way," Warren said. "John insists she drank herself to death. Is that possible? If she was able to function, get up and go to work every day, it doesn't sound as though she was suffering from cirrhosis of the liver or something of that sort. Suppose John's right, and she had a heart attack. Wouldn't that show up in the autopsy?"

"I don't know," I said. "If there's any way to tell, Doc would find it."

"Only if he was looking for it," Warren pointed out.

Doc Winston, the county coroner, is a character, but sharp as they come. He takes orders from nobody but God, so if the police were convinced it was murder, it had to be on his say-so.

"I've never known Doc to get through an autopsy so fast," I said. "He's thorough and he's careful. I've seen him keep the body-bag boys standing around for hours if he's not satisfied about something. They must have rushed the autopsy through."

"And maybe if they did, they made some mistakes," Warren said. "Even Doc's not infallible, although you'll never convince him of that."

"The way I see it, we're left with three options." I counted them off on my fingers. "One, she died as a result of injuries inflicted by a person or persons unknown on Saturday night. Two, she died of natural causes and Doc missed it in the autopsy. Or . . . our client's lying and he killed her."

"We're assuming, you know, that *someone* caused those injuries," Warren pointed out. "What if it wasn't someone but something? According to what John tells me, she'd already had one accident while intoxicated. What if she inflicted those injuries herself?"

"An accident?"

He nodded.

"If her car had been damaged, the guy from the service station should have noticed," I said. "Lattimore says the car was at the house when he arrived Sunday night. He would have noticed if it was banged up."

"True," Warren admitted. "But I was thinking more of the night she died. Maybe she fell and hit her head at the cabin."

"It's possible," I agreed.

He drummed his fingertips on the table and frowned. "I'd give a lot to know why they're so confident. King is dragging his feet on bail and that looks bad, like John's some sort of mad dog killer who's a menace to society. I can't imagine Floyd would take a step like opposing bail unless he was very sure of himself."

"Or blinded by ambition," I said. "King's never made any secret that he aspires to greater things. Maybe he sees this case as the springboard he needs to get his name known statewide."

Warren gave a slight but unmistakable shudder of distaste and looked at his watch. "I'd better go. Where will you start?"

"I have a source in the Detective's Division who may be some help, and I want to get hold of the guy at the service station as quickly as possible."

He nodded. "Let me know what you find. If I'm tied up, leave word with Miz Turner."

He started out, but turned back when he reached the doorway. He gestured toward one of the more colorful suggestions etched into the paint. "Is that possible, do you think?"

"Only in South Carolina."

We left the jail by the front door this time and were immediately surrounded by reporters, heat, and humidity that wrapped around us like cellophane. I could feel my shirt and tie wilting. The reporters crowded close, lobbing questions like pop flies. I spotted a cameraman from the local television station and discreetly straightened my tie.

"Are you working on the case, Steve?" someone called from the back of the crowd. I recognized Kent Rose, who replaced me on the police beat, and blessed Ben's little Jewish heart.

"I've been retained on Mr. Lattimore's behalf," I replied.

"What will you be working on?" He fed me my cues as we slowly pushed our way through the crowd.

"Proving Mr. Lattimore's innocence," I replied, softening it with a smile.

"What's Mr. Lattimore's frame of mind?" one of the *Courier* reporters asked Warren.

"As good as can be expected," he replied. "He had a comfortable night and he remains optimistic that we can, with Mr. Harlan's help, clear up this terrible misunderstanding soon."

I tried to hide a smile, but my jubilation was short-lived.

"How long have you been an investigator?" called a weedy little guy I didn't recognize.

"Two years."

"Is this your first murder case?"

"Yes." I began moving faster.

"Has Mrs. Lattimore been to see her husband?" asked Kent.

I could have kissed him, but I'm sure Warren would have preferred strangulation. "I'm not certain who has visited," he replied.

We'd reached the street by this time. "I'm sorry, gentlemen, but I'll have to ask you to excuse me," he said. "I have a meeting in a very few minutes."

They trailed him for a few yards, calling out more questions, but he threw up a genial hand and disappeared across the street and into his building with practiced speed. I took the opportunity to slip away to my car.

Kent was waiting for me, leaning on the fender.

"Oldest trick in the book."

"Learned from the best," he replied. "What've you got for me?"

"C'mon. I just talked to Lattimore for the first time. I haven't even had a chance to look at my notes."

"You'll have to do better than that."

We'd known each other a long time, and despite our competition at the paper, we'd become friends of a sort. He had a job to do and I knew it.

"I swear, I don't have anything yet, not even an idea. I'm just getting started."

"You're definitely on the case, though?"

"Yeah."

"Ben wants to do a profile on you. We'll need a new picture."

So it was tit for tat already. Somehow, I didn't think that was quite the way Ben had worded it, but I knew how the game was played. If Warren expected to get double value from me, it seemed only fair I get some benefit out of it. And he'd made no secret of my involvement; he'd even tossed out my name gratis.

"Tell you what," I suggested, "bring the photographer by the office this afternoon. Maybe I'll have something by then. About three."

At least it wouldn't make today's deadline.

"Hunh uh. How about one?"

"That won't give me much time," I protested.

"I have faith in you." He flipped his notebook shut and pushed himself upright. "Hell, by then, you may have the whole thing wrapped up."

"I won't make much money that way."

"One o'clock," he repeated, pointing his pen at me.

"One o'clock," I sighed. I slid behind the wheel and turned the key, but as soon as Kent was safely out of sight, I killed the engine and clambered out again. I kept a wary eye out for reporters and cops who might recognize me as I circled behind the building and made my way to a diner on the corner of Graham and Alexander.

The diner was cool and dim and smelled of bacon grease and coffee. They hadn't cranked up the grill and deep-fat fryers for the lunch crowd yet, and the place was deserted except for the cook and the waitress. I chose a booth in the corner, where I couldn't be seen from the door but had a clear view of the street. The cracked vinyl of the booth made my thighs break out in a sweat and I gave silent thanks for the seersucker pants that would disguise the wrinkles being pressed into the backs of my thighs.

I ordered a Coke, extra ice, from the waitress, who heaved a long-suffering sigh like she'd been counting on my tip to put her on Easy Street, and trudged off. I picked up a menu to hide behind.

For thirty minutes, I sipped my drink and watched the sidewalk, but there was no sign of Hilda.

Hilda has worked in the Detective Division—hell, be honest, she's run the Detective Division—so long, she's like a piece of the furniture. She and Owens have a good arrangement. He calls her ma'am; she graciously allows him to run the investigations. They get along fine.

I was beginning to wonder which would go first, my bladder or my supply of dimes, when she rounded the corner.

I tensed, ready to toss my change on the table and take off if it looked like she was heading for the coffee shop across the street, but she passed it without a glance.

She proceeded regally down the sidewalk, looking neither right nor left, her long, pigeon-toed feet slapping the sidewalk, white plastic pocketbook clutched in the crook of her elbow. Her gauzy, flowered-print dress did little to soften her angular body and only emphasized the ugly little spaniel haunches of her collarbones. The bright sun was merciless to her frizzed, permed hair, dyed an unlikely shade of auburn. Hilda's face could stop a clock, but at that moment, I could have kissed her.

She had always treated me with the same disdain she heaped on all men, until the day I accidentally stumbled on her guilty secret.

I'd been going through the previous night's arrest reports at the desk. As I turned to leave, I bumped into her, knocking the folder she was carrying to the floor. It fell at my feet like a gift from the gods. As I stooped to gather up the scattered requisition forms, I spotted pages of typed manuscript.

"You write?"

She snatched the pages from my hand. "Mind your own business."

I picked up another page at random and scanned it. It was a *True Confessions* piece. The style was lurid, but it showed some talent.

"Did you write this?"

"If you breathe a word, I'll have you banned from the station," she threatened in a fierce whisper. Ugly red color crept up her neck.

"My lips are sealed," I promised, rising. "But why the secrecy? This is pretty good."

"Well, nobody else seems to think so," she said stiffly, but I saw a small blaze of hope in her bulging blue eyes.

I recognized that look, torn between a desperate desire for encouragement and shame at being caught with literary pretensions. I'd seen the same look in veteran reporters' eyes as they shamefacedly tossed a manuscript on the table after a few late-night beers.

"Who doesn't think so?" I asked.

"Editors." She began stuffing the pages helter-skelter into the folder.

"Take it from me, there are plenty of editors out there who don't know good when it hits them between the eyes. May I read it?"

My motives were selfish. I admit it. I was only interested in making points with she who knew everything that went on in the cop shop and controlled it with an iron fist in a white nylon glove. If wading through a few pages of purple prose was all it took to get on her good side, I was game.

"What for?" She clutched the folder protectively to her flat chest.

"I think it shows real talent." I gave her my most earnest and sincere face. "Perhaps I could make some suggestions. I do know a few people . . ."

"Oh, what the hell." Blindly, she thrust the folder at me and blundered off down the hall.

I took it home that night and waded through it with Susie. For what it was, it wasn't bad, and I told Hilda so the next day. She asked some intelligent questions and paid attention to the answers.

A week later, she stopped me in the hall and slipped me another folder containing a revised version. I couldn't find anything to fault with it and told her so. I helped her write a cover letter and promptly forgot about it.

Two weeks later, I was again flipping through the arrest reports when she sidled up beside me and thrust a check for twenty-five dollars under my nose.

"They bought it?" I found, to my surprise, I was genuinely pleased.

"And asked to see more," she replied with the first thing like a smile I'd ever seen on her sharp face.

She churns them out by the dozen now, not under her own name, of course, and often uses some of the actual cases that come through the Detective Division for ideas. She taps away on her old portable typewriter in the attic most evenings. Her "invalid" mother thinks she's doing overtime for the department and frets that she's working too hard, but since the extra money pays for the mother's weekly trips to the beauty parlor, she does her fretting quietly in the downstairs parlor where it won't disturb Hilda.

I kept my word and Hilda's secret. In return, she became one of my best sources. I call on her only when absolutely necessary or I need ironclad confirmation. The Chief is livid about departmental leaks, but it never occurs to anybody to suspect Hilda.

I waited until she'd ordered before I climbed up on the stool next to her.

"Move down," she muttered without turning her head.

I obeyed, putting an empty stool between us. "Relax, nobody from the station ever comes here," I said.

"They've clamped the lid down tight on this one." She spoke out of the side of her mouth. She was really enjoying this.

"How do you know which one?"

She favored me with a withering look.

"Sorry, Mata Hari, I forgot who I'm talking to."

I thought I saw the ghost of a grin as she sipped her iced tea.

"Well?" she asked finally.

"Well, what?"

"You've never joined me for lunch before, so I assume you want something."

"Hilda, I'm wounded."

She shot me a look that could have melted bullets. I know when I'm licked, so I pulled out my notebook. "What can you tell me about cause of death? How'd they get from a couple of bruises to Murder One?"

"A couple bruises?" Her penciled eyebrows rose to meet the sausage curl on her forehead. "She was black and blue from head to toe. I heard Doc counted more than a hundred. Somebody beat that woman to death is how they got Murder One."

"Are you sure?"

"I saw the pictures."

"Can you get me one?"

"Not a chance. The Lieutenant has 'em locked up. It's more than my life is worth to try."

I figured I might as well know the worst. "Hilda . . ." I hesitated, wondering how to phrase my next question to a woman old enough to be my mother. "Was there any talk about . . . ?" I raised my eyebrows and hoped she'd get the idea.

"You mean was she interfered with?" Hilda pursed her mouth. "No, nothing like that."

That was a relief. "I hear there are some wild stories going around."

She snorted. "I've heard 'em, but not from anybody with any sense."

"What about blood tests?"

"Blood tests! Nobody's ordered any blood tests, far as I know." She was clearly intrigued. "They'd have to send 'em clear to the FBI in Washington."

"Check on it for me, will you? It could be important."

"I guess I can do that," she consented.

Delores's mechanic was looking more and more important, and I wanted to get to him before the police got there first and shut him up.

"Thanks, Hilda, you're a wonder." I fished out my wallet, but she impaled me with a steely glare and I put it away.

"Hold your horses, Sherlock. There's more."

"Yeah?" I sank back down on my stool. She glanced around, but we still had the place to ourselves.

"I heard the Lieutenant and the Chief with King this morning. He wants to oppose bail and the Lieutenant was trying to talk him out of it."

"How come?"

"I think the Lieutenant's worried King may have jumped the gun. If Doc hadn't been so certain, I don't think he'd have gone for the warrant a'tall. But you know how much the Lieutenant respects Doc. If Doc says it was murder, that's good enough for him."

"Just this once, I hope he's wrong. Thanks, Hilda." I risked death by planting a kiss on her cheek and escaped before she recovered.

CHAPTER 6

The sidewalk was hot enough to blister the soles of my feet through my shoes. I paused to let my eyes adjust to the glare and checked my watch. Nearly noon. There wasn't much time before I had to meet Kent.

As I trudged back to the car, it occurred to me I'd been in such a hurry to catch Hilda, I'd forgotten to put another penny in the parking meter. Sure enough, there was a pink ticket fluttering under the wipers. I snagged it and stuck it in my pocket instead of the glove compartment, where Susie would run across it. There went my lunch money for the week.

Fortunately, the service station Delores used was nearby. If it hadn't been so hot, I'd have walked. Instead, I rolled down the windows and let the breeze cool me for a few blocks.

The station looked deserted, but the big bay doors were open and I heard a radio somewhere inside. I carefully avoided the bell cord. No sense getting off on the wrong foot by dragging the guy out in the hot sun if I wasn't going to buy anything.

I followed Patsy Cline's voice to a tiny office behind the pyramid of oil cans and posters encouraging me to "Go Esso" for Happy Motoring.

The gas jockey, or maybe he was the manager, was polishing off a meatloaf sandwich and poring over a parts catalog. The sight of the sandwich reminded my stomach I'd had nothing but a couple gallons of coffee and Coke since breakfast. I rapped

65

on the door with my knuckles and nearly gave the poor guy a
heart attack.

"Oh, hey, sorry. I didn't hear you come in." He stumbled to
his feet, still chewing, and wiped his hands on a rag dangling
from his pocket. The little embroidered oval on his coverall told
me his name was Terry.

"It's okay. Don't let me interrupt your lunch. I'm just looking for some information."

He shrugged, unfazed. Not the manager, apparently. "You
lost?"

"Not exactly. I was hoping to talk to whoever was here
Sunday morning. Would that be you?" I gave him my best good
ol' boy grin.

"Could be." He wadded up the waxed paper from his
sandwich and tossed it over his shoulder without looking. It
banked off the wall and into the wastebasket without even graz-
ing the sides. "Me and Jack were both here Monday morning.
What can I do for you?"

"A lady came in that morning with a"—I consulted my
notebook—"a black '58 Chevy. Did you help her?"

"Nah, that was Jack," he said with obvious relief. "I was working on a transmission in the back when he came in and said he
was gonna drive the lady home and check out the car. He
shouldn'ta, we was fixing to get busy, but he took off before I
could say anything."

"Is he here?" I looked around hopefully. In my experience
most people are just naturally inclined to be helpful.

"Nah." Terry sounded aggrieved for the first time in our short
acquaintance. "He hasn't shown up since Monday. Ain't called
or nothing either. I had to work the holiday all by myself
yesterday. And lemme tell you, I was busier'n a cat covering shit
on hot bricks."

"You know where he lives?"

"Rooming house over on West Boulevard, I think. Something the matter with the car?"

"No, nothing like that." I decided I'd get more by confiding than withholding. "I'm a private investigator." I gave him a quick peek at my license. "You read in the papers about the big murder case?"

His eyes grew round. "The one they arrested that Lattimore fella for? You think Jack's mixed up in that?"

I sent up a silent prayer of thanks to Perry Mason for making detectives out of everybody. "No. But the woman with the Chevy is the one who got . . . who died," I explained. "Did you see her when she came in?"

"Nope." He shook his head regretfully. "Like I said, I had my head in that transmission the whole time. I heard the bell and hollered to Jack and he went out to see about it. A minute or so later, he stuck his head in and said he was leaving and pfft, he was gone, like that." He snapped his fingers.

"What's Jack's last name?"

"Cotter. Jack Cotter."

"Do you have a phone number or address for him?" I had hopes of the battered filing cabinet in the corner.

"Huh uh. All the pay records and such are at the main office."

My chances of getting anything there were slim and none, but I'd give it a try. In the meantime, I left Terry one of my cards and asked him to call me if he heard from Jack or he showed up. But somehow I had a feeling it wasn't going to be that easy. I thanked him and headed for the car.

"Hey!"

I turned back.

"Which side you working for?" he called.

"The right one, I hope," I replied and loped back to the car.

★　★　★　★　★

I debated my next move as I sat at the light. Hilda's information explained a lot, but it sure didn't jibe with Lattimore's description of Delores's injuries. I was suddenly less certain we wanted to find the elusive Jack. If Delores had looked as bad on Monday morning as Hilda described, Jack would surely have mentioned it to Terry when he got back to the station. If not, when and where did she come by more than a hundred bruises? The police were putting their money on Lattimore. I was still on the fence.

There could be any number of explanations for Jack's disappearance. Maybe he'd found a better job. Maybe he'd been on a bender and hadn't seen the papers. Maybe he had and didn't want to get involved. Maybe he was holding out for the highest bidder. Any of those explanations was preferable to the alternative—that Lieutenant Owens had already gotten to him and convinced him to make himself scarce until the hearing.

When the light changed, I hung a left and circled the block until I found a pay phone. The midday sun turned the glass and steel booth into a greenhouse. By the time I'd found the number for the station owner's office, I was soaked with sweat. But the frigid reception I got from the secretary cooled me off in a hurry. It looked like I'd have to hit all the rooming houses on West Boulevard until I found Cotter.

Back in the car, I drummed my fingers on the wheel in frustration. Lattimore claimed he had no idea where Delores could have gone Sunday night. So who might?

I dug through my notebook until I found the address for Delores's friend, Peggy. She wasn't far away and there was no point making the round of Delores's favorite watering holes yet. They'd either be closed till evening or in the middle of the lunch rush. Maybe Peggy could narrow it down for me.

Her address was a red brick apartment house on Morningside overlooking the new park and just around the corner from my office. The front door stood open to catch any stray breezes and I recognized the heavy organ from the theme of "As the World Turns." I knocked and the volume went down. A white-haired woman who looked old enough to be Delores's mother appeared but didn't unlatch the screen.

"Help you?"

"Sorry to bother you." I gave her my 'aw shucks' for good measure. "I'm looking for a Mrs. Summerfield."

"I'm Miz Summerfield."

"Mrs. Peggy Summerfield?"

"That's right. Are you a reporter?"

"No ma'am. I'm an investigator. I understand you were a good friend of Delores Green."

"An investigator, you say? Are you with the police?"

"No ma'am. I'm a private investigator, but I am working on the case."

"What do you want with me?" Nothing good, her tone implied.

I stifled a sigh and launched into my spiel about how everybody was entitled to a fair trial. I dropped Warren's name, hoping it would carry some weight.

"You're working for John's lawyer? Law, why didn't you say so?" She unhooked the screen and shooed me inside, talking a mile a minute. "Come in the house. This whole thing is just terrible. Why, if Delores had any idea they had John down there in that jail, she'd just die!"

Her hand flew to her mouth as she realized what she'd said. Her pale blue eyes filled with tears. She removed her glasses to mop them with a tissue that looked as though it had already seen a lot of use.

"I'm sorry. Law, how awful of me." She groped blindly for

the edge of the sofa and sat down. "I had to go down there, you know."

"To the jail?"

"No, the funeral parlor," she explained. "They called. They needed something to cover her arms—the bruises, you know. I took a white sweater of mine down there. They'd done a nice job. She looked so natural—just like she'd laid down there for a nap." Her kindly blue eyes filled again and threatened to spill over.

I crouched at her feet and offered her my handkerchief. Something about her made me feel protective. She reminded me of my mother's friends—simple, good-hearted women growing tentative with age.

"That was very kind of you," I said gently. I suddenly realized she was the first person I'd heard express any grief or sorrow over Delores's death. Years of interviewing the families of the victims and the accused should make conversations like this easier, but it doesn't. "Had you been friends a long time?"

"Oh Lord, yes." She stopped to calculate. "Ten years or more. We used to work together down at the dairy. I was in bookkeeping; she was secretary to Mr. Hollings." She pronounced it sec-a-tary.

She wiped her eyes and replaced her glasses. They immediately fogged up again.

"Did you know Mr. Lattimore, too?"

"Oh, yes. My husband and I thought the world of both of them."

"Yes ma'am. So you knew he and Miz Green were . . . friends?" My calf muscles were screaming by this time, but I didn't want to interrupt the flow. I tried to shift my position without being obvious about it, but she noticed and jumped to her feet.

"I'm so sorry. I haven't even offered you a chair. Sit right down here." She directed me toward a big, black Naugahyde monster in the corner, the only piece of furniture that wasn't flowered, covered with a tatted doily, or shrouded under protective plastic.

"That's my husband Don's chair. He says it's the only chair in the house that's fit for a man's you-know-what."

I sat and immediately sank into the Black Hole. Don must have a heck of a you-know-what. I struggled upright and perched precariously on the edge.

"Would you like some iced tea?" she asked. The last thing I wanted was something else to drink but I smiled and allowed as how that'd be nice.

As the swinging door whooshed behind her, I caught a whiff of fresh biscuits and fried chicken from the kitchen. She returned a minute later bearing a sweating aluminum tumbler on a plastic tray.

"I'm afraid I interrupted your lunch," I apologized as she fussed around with napkins and coasters.

"Oh, I had a sandwich a while ago. I was getting my supper started early. Then I can just heat everything up when Don gets home. I don't think a man ought to have to come home to a hot house after working all day, do you?"

"I guess not."

She finally had everything arranged to her satisfaction and plopped down on the plastic-covered sofa. The backs of my thighs began to sweat in sympathy. She picked up a magazine from the coffee table and fanned herself with it. I caught a whiff of Tussy bath powder.

"You say you've known Delores a long time?"

"Oh, yes. She was just a young girl, really, when she came to work at the dairy. I felt sorry for her, having to raise that little boy all by herself. I kind of took her under my wing and she used to say I was just like a second mama to her." She lowered her voice confidingly. "Course, from what I understand, her real mama wasn't much account."

"No? Why was that?"

"She drank." She leaned back and waited for my reaction. I shook my head sadly so as not to disappoint her.

"Killed herself a few years back. She was cooking supper one night and just walked in the bedroom and laid down and turned on the gas. Left a whole chicken burning up in the pan. But the terrible thing was, it was Delores found her. That's why I was so shocked what she said Thursday night."

"Thursday night?" I was so distracted trying to figure out why the combination of hot chicken grease and gas hadn't blown up the whole neighborhood, I thought I'd missed a connection somewhere.

"When Greg called me over there."

"I see." But I didn't.

"Delores takes these pills to calm her down. I guess she forgot how many she'd taken and got confused and took some more. Greg got scared and he called me to come."

I bent my head to my notebook to conceal my heightened interest. I looked up with my reporter's face—an expression of mild interest with just a small frown to betray polite skepticism. It's an old trick, but it almost never fails. Even the most reluctant interviewee will start to squeal like a pig to convince you how important their information is. "Really? What kind of pills?"

"Some kind of tranquilizers the doctor gave her. I couldn't blame her. It was so sad, you know." But she looked excited as she leaned forward to lay a hand on my arm. "There she was, raising that boy by herself, holding down a job, and in love with a man who could never marry her."

"So you knew Mr. Lattimore was married."

"Of course. But there was never any *love* in it. Both the

families had money, you know." There was awe in her voice. That's the kind of thing rich people do, it implied. They merged rather than married, like banks. It was obvious she found the whole thing terribly romantic. I felt a pang of pity. She was a nice woman, trapped in an ordinary existence and making the best of it, finding her excitement where she could. I suddenly wondered if Susie ever felt that way.

"You were telling me about Thursday night?" I prompted.

"Well, Greg called about suppertime and I could tell he was upset. He told me what had happened and asked me could I come over there. So I did. I was real surprised when I got there 'cause Delores was up walking around. She had on her pajamas, though, and she was real groggy. I got her to go lay down and called the doctor. He didn't seem very worried, just said to give her lots of black coffee. So I made some and took it in to her. She didn't want it, but I got a little bit of it down her and it seemed to help. I stayed with her for a while, just sat with her, you know. But that's when she said it." She sat back, satisfied, as though everything should now be clear as day.

"Said what?" I asked as gently as I could.

"Well, I told her she ought to take a vacation, get away from things for a while. And do you know what she said?"

"No." I made a conscious effort not to grit my teeth.

"She said, 'The only place I want to be is with my mama.' And to think, now she is with her mama." She fumbled for the tissue again.

"Do you think she meant it?"

"Oh, no, never." She was shocked by the suggestion.

"Did you see or talk to her on Sunday?" I asked.

"No, she called me from work on Friday. I think she was unhappy with me for calling the doctor. But I didn't know what to do." She looked at me, begging for understanding.

"I'm sure you did the right thing. She was probably just

embarrassed. Who is her doctor?" I pretended to look for it in my notes.

"Dr. Morgan, over in the Doctors' Building."

"That's right. So you didn't talk to Delores on Sunday at all?"

"No."

"I see. Well, thank—"

"It was Monday."

"Monday?"

"Yes, I called her."

"Did you see her?"

"No, John answered the phone and said she'd taken a pill and was lying down. I don't think it could have been good for her to take all that many pills, do you?"

"No ma'am. Tell me, Mrs. Summerfield, just between you and me, did Delores drink much?"

"Drink? Why, no. Whatever gave you that idea?" Her surprise seemed genuine.

"She didn't drink?"

"Well, I mean, she might have one at a party or something like that. Who told you that Delores drank?"

I backpedaled as gracefully as I could. "Well, I just wondered, you know. Sometimes these things are inherited."

"Not Delores. Not after what she went through with her mama. It got so bad, after the girls were up some size, her daddy finally divorced her."

"Divorced Delores's mama."

"Well, that's what I said."

"Yes ma'am, you did. Mrs. Summerfield, do you have any idea where Delores was on Sunday night?"

"Sunday? No, where?"

"She didn't come home Sunday night. When you talked to her on Friday, did you mention if she had plans?"

"No, but we didn't talk but a minute. Did you ask John or Greg?"

"They spent most of Sunday night looking for her. In fact, Mr. Lattimore mentioned he rode by here that evening thinking she might be with you, but no one was home."

"I can't think where . . ." she said, vaguely. "Oh, I know. We ran over to the Woolworth for a minute. I needed some stockings. But I can't imagine Delores didn't come home. She wouldn't stay out all night like that and not let him know where she was. Even if she was just over here, playing cards or something, you know, she always called and checked on him a couple times."

"Lattimore?"

"No, Greg. She was a very good mother."

"I see. Well, thank you, Mrs. Summerfield, you've been a big help." I struggled up from the depths of the monster. "If you happen to think of any place Delores might have gone or if you remember anything that might help, I'd appreciate it if you'd give me a call." I handed her one of my cards.

"Well, of course I will, but I can't imagine what it could be that would be any help. But I know Delores would want me to do anything I can." She looked distressed. "Do you think I should go see John down at the jail?"

"I don't think that's necessary. I'm not even sure they'd let you see him. And with any luck, we'll have him out of there soon. The preliminary hearing should be in the next few days."

"Well, all right, if you think so." She looked unconvinced.

"It's not really the place for a lady." I patted her on the shoulder and struggled out of the chair.

"You might ask Mimi, I guess."

"I'm sorry?"

"Where Delores was Sunday night. Delores might have said something to her," she explained, not very helpfully.

"Who's Mimi?"

"Mimi Brown. She's a friend of ours, plays cards with us and so on. She used to work at the dairy, too." She gave me Mimi's address. I thanked her and headed for the door.

"Oh, Miz Summerfield, one more thing." I turned back.

"Of course."

"Could I please use your bathroom?"

CHAPTER 7

I took the office stairs two at a time, almost bowling over Mrs. Bruno, who has run the insurance office downstairs since Lincoln's first term.

My office is in a two-story building on the corner of Commonwealth and the Plaza, where the nice brick bungalows give way to the bank, the grocery store, and the library. Something closer to the police station and the courthouse records would be nice, but my clients, who seem to expect to dodge bullets to reach my door, are reassured by the respectable neighborhood. I can't afford uptown rents anyway.

I tripped over the pile of mail that had accumulated during my absence, but I ignored it as I lunged for the phone. I caught Kent just as he was going out the door and put him off until the next day. He wasn't happy about it. I rashly promised to call him back with something usable before deadline but it wasn't enough. He extorted a promise of breakfast the next morning as well before he let me off the hook.

As I headed back out to the car, I caught a whiff of the special from the Diamond Grill two blocks up. Tuesday meant it was country-style steak and gravy over rice. I tried to ignore it, but I had to turn up the radio to cover the rumbles of protest from my stomach.

Peggy had told me Mimi worked, but her address on Kenwood was only a few blocks away, so I decided to swing by and at least stick a card in the door. To my surprise, I found her at home, catching up on her ironing.

"The plant shuts down for the whole week of the Fourth," she explained as she unplugged the iron and led me into the living room.

Mimi looked to be about Delores's age, maybe a few years farther into her forties. With her dark hair and eyes, she looked a little like Delores. But Delores's extra padding had given her a feminine softness. Mimi's was poured into some kind of latex armor that didn't bear thinking about in July.

"Peggy called to say you might be coming by." She offered me a cigarette from the cut-glass bowl on the table. I declined. She lit one for herself and fanned the smoke away from her face.

"I was hoping you might have some idea where Delores was Sunday night," I explained. "Miz Summerfield didn't know and suggested Delores might have mentioned it to you if she had plans."

She snorted, sending streams of smoke from her nostrils. "No, I don't imagine Delores discussed her plans with Peggy."

"Why's that?"

"Delores was my friend and I'm sorry she's dead, Mr. Harlan, but just because she's dead doesn't make her a saint. Don't get me wrong. Delores wasn't a tramp, but she liked to have a good time. It's just that her idea of a good time was a little different from Peggy's."

"So you do know where she was Sunday night?"

"Nope, sorry." She shrugged her broad shoulders; her bosom went along for the ride. I tried not to stare. "I just figured if Peggy didn't know it was because Delores didn't want her to."

"When was the last time you saw Delores?"

"Let's see, today's Wednesday." She squinted up at the ceiling as she thought. "It was Wednesday of last week. We had supper at her house. Or rather, I had supper."

"How's that?"

"Well, Greg and I had barbecued chicken. Delores had Jim Beam."

For the second time, I had to struggle to keep my face impassive. One of the first things you learn as a reporter is that no two people see things or remember them the same way. They'll differ in a hundred small details, and it has no significance. But when two people have completely contradictory takes on a situation, you know you're on to something.

"Did she drink much?"

"Not for a fish," she replied cheerfully. "Look, I liked Delores. A lot. But I figure the only way you're going to get at the truth is if we all level with you."

"I appreciate that. How long did you know Delores?"

"Lord, since Moses was a pup. We met when she came to work at the dairy right after she split up with her husband."

"Was she drinking then?"

"Not really. She was never what you'd call real stable, but she didn't start drinking hard until a couple years ago."

"After her mother died?"

"Oh, you know about that, do you?" She raised one eyebrow and something clicked. Jane Russell with a little Bette Davis thrown in. "Now that you mention it, it was after her mother died. But it wasn't really a problem. She'd show up for work once in a while with a hangover, but she always showed up. Delores was smart. She'd come in on the weekends when we had reports to get out and sometimes she took things home to work on." She leaned over to stub out her cigarette in a big ceramic ashtray that resembled a pancreas.

"When did it become a problem?"

"It's hard to say. It might have been about the time she figured out John was a dead-end street."

"You know Mr. Lattimore?"

"Sure. I worked for him for a couple months when I was between jobs—collecting rents, carrying papers back and forth, that kind of thing."

"What was their relationship like?"

"I think she was in love with him at first. At least she said she was. But I don't know how much of it was love and how much she was impressed by his money and his reputation." She folded her arms over her formidable bosom and shook her head. "But it didn't take long for her to figure out there was no future in it. John wasn't going to leave his wife for Delores."

"But he did, didn't he?"

"Not until a year or two ago. By then, they'd gotten to be like an old married couple anyway. They fussed and fought, but they stayed together. Lord knows why. John was never what you'd call romantic. Delores got real excited about something one time and flung her arms around his neck. John pushed her away, told her to stop acting like a teenager. You could tell he was embarrassed. Delores dated other guys and I don't think she made any secret of it, but John never seemed to mind much."

I'll admit I don't have a lot of experience in this area, but Mimi's description didn't sound like my idea of a torrid affair between a man and his mistress. It sounded more like most of the marriages I know.

"Did their fights ever get physical?" I asked.

She shook her head. "Not that I knew of and I think Delores would have told me. I never understood the two of them, but the arrangement seemed to suit them and it wasn't any of my business."

She stared past my shoulder, lost in thought. I waited.

"I guess one reason I'm not all broke up about the whole thing is cause deep down I knew it was coming," she said finally.

"What makes you say that?"

"I don't mean I thought he was gonna kill her. I don't know

what happened out there the other night, but I have a hard time believing John killed her. It's just that after seeing her the way she was the other night, I was sort of expecting it. Running her car into a tree or something, maybe. Walking out in front of a car. But not this."

"Tell me about the other night."

"She seemed fine when I got there. She had supper started and she didn't act like she'd been drinking. But she offered me one and I said yeah, so she poured us both one. She knocked hers back while she was standing there at the stove. But she must've been hitting it before I got there, 'cause it wasn't five minutes later, I heard a noise and when I turned around, she was slumped over the stove like she was gonna pass out. I grabbed her before she went into the frying pan face first and sat her down. She was pretty bad. Greg came in and got upset, but I told him the heat had gotten to her while she was cooking."

"Did he believe you?"

"I doubt it, but he pretended to. Anyway, I finished cooking supper and put it on the table, but Delores was in no shape to eat it. She couldn't even get the fork to her mouth. I had to put a dish towel in her lap because the food was falling out of her mouth." She shook her head. "Poor kid. I felt sorry for him. He didn't say a word during dinner, just shoveled the food in and took off as fast as he could. I put Delores to bed and cleaned up the supper dishes."

I tightened my lips and concentrated on keeping my gaze steady, but I could feel a stinging behind my eyeballs and a corresponding tingle in my nose. "Did you see her take any pills while you were there?"

"Pills?" She seemed genuinely surprised. "What kind of pills?"

"Her tranquilizers."

"Delores didn't take any tranquilizers I know of."

"Are you sure?"

"Listen, the only way Delores could have been any more tranquil than she was the other night, was if she was already dead."

My little chat with Mimi had been enlightening, but it put me way behind. I ran yellow lights all the way across town keeping a wary eye in the rearview mirror for cops.

My luck held until I got to West Boulevard, where I found a half-dozen rooming houses to every block. The neighborhood had been one of the nicest in town back in the twenties, but as the children grew up and moved away, the neighborhood declined as neighborhoods will. Normally, they would have languished for twenty years or so, becoming a little more faded, a little more dated, then young families would start to buy them, fix them up, and voila, you have revitalization. But the city's decision to convert the old air terminal three miles away into a genuine airport was the death knell. The last of the original residents fled. The smaller houses were turned into rental property, mostly for colored families. The large, gracious ones that fronted on West were chopped up into rooming houses. The regal, sheltering oaks and magnolias had fallen to the bulldozers during the last road widening, leaving the houses exposed, faded matriarchs with their slips showing. The once-green lawns were now dirt parking lots for cars that had seen better days. Even from the street, I thought I could smell mothballs, but maybe I read too much Thomas Wolfe.

I'd resigned myself to pounding the pavement when I spotted a dingy little drugstore on the corner. I shoehorned into a parking space and went in. The scent of camphor was even stronger inside. It fought with stale cigarette smoke, cheap hair tonic, and onions from the grill. I considered ordering something to eat, but the hot dogs rolling around inside the glass case looked as old and tired as I felt.

Stifling a sigh, I ordered a Coke from the old guy behind the counter. He obliged but instead of moving away, he lingered, wiping circles on the six inches of counter not covered with placards of stomach powders and hairnets.

"Worked here long?" I asked.

"Long enough," he replied. "Thirty-two years."

"Thirty-two. Imagine that. I guess you probably know everybody in the neighborhood."

"Most," he agreed.

"I was hoping to run down a buddy of mine lives around here, but I don't have an address for him."

"Close friend, is he?"

"Army buddy, actually. Last I heard, he was living in a rooming house on West Boulevard, but I lost the letter and I can't remember which one."

"Uh huh. What's your buddy's name?"

"Jack. Jack Cotter."

He pretended to think it over. "Jack. Jack. Let's see, there's a big fella by the name of Jack, blonde hair, 'bout five-foot-eleven or so, used to room with Miz Liza. That be him?"

"Well, it's been a while since I've seen him," I hedged.

"Then there's that fella, little runty guy with curly black hair, named Jack, lives on the corner of West and South Tryon with Miz Vanizer. Buys Wildroot."

I'd been made. He was enjoying himself now.

"Gee, if I could just remember where he said he worked," I said. "Seems like he was working as a mechanic somewhere."

"Uh huh. That'd be the one at Miz Vanizer's then, I 'spect."

"D'you think so?"

"Reckon so. You can tell by the hands. That grease gets worked in around the fingernails, you can't never get it out."

"That sounds like him, then. Thanks." I got up, leaving my

Coke untasted and poured all my change out on the counter. "Uh huh." He was still wiping the counter and smiling to himself as I let myself out into the sunshine.

CHAPTER 8

Vanizer's had nothing about it to distinguish it from any of the others except the smell of age and mildew lurking beneath several decades of boiled potatoes. I hesitated in the foyer while my eyes adjusted to the gloom.

"Got one room, upstairs in the back, rent's twenty dollars a week. No smoking or cooking in the rooms."

"I'm not looking for a room." I peered into the dimness behind the stairs.

"Oh, I beg your pardon." A wizened little gnome in a print dress materialized from the shadows. Even without the hump on her back that forced her to gaze down at her ugly black orthopedic oxfords, she wouldn't have come much higher than my elbow. A coronet of braid atop her head gave her an extra half inch.

"Can I help you?" she asked politely. She peered up at me sideways through thick, rimless glasses that gave her frog eyes.

"Yes ma'am, please." Despite her odd appearance, she had a certain dignity that demanded good manners. "I'm looking for one of your boarders, Mr. Cotter."

"I'm afraid you're too late," she said. "He paid his rent and moved out a few days ago."

My heart sank. "Can you recall exactly which day?"

"Monday evening."

"Did he leave a forwarding address or mention where he was heading?" I asked without hope.

"Sorry, no," she replied. "They seldom do."

"Was anyone with him?"

"He had a car waiting outside and there was a man in the passenger side, but I'm afraid I didn't pay much attention."

"Do you remember what kind of car it was?"

"I'm afraid I don't know one from the other," she said. "Is there some kind of trouble?"

"No ma'am. I was just hoping to ask him some questions."

"Police?" She cocked her head at me like a bird.

"Private investigator."

"Ah," she nodded. "I had a feeling something was going on."

"Why's that?"

"Well, he was wearing new clothes and he got behind the wheel when he left. He's never had a car while he was living here. Never paid his rent on time, either, so I wondered if he'd come into money from somewhere."

I'd been prepared to find Cotter had flown the coop, but his sudden affluence was unexpected. I fought down the thought that Lattimore had money and wasn't behind bars until late Tuesday afternoon.

"Do you happen to remember what color the car was?"

"Tan," she said decisively. "That much I'm sure of. It was tan."

"You've been very helpful. If you happen to hear from him, would you let me know?"

She agreed and I left her one of my cards, making four in one day I'd given away, a new record.

Back at the office, I used up several precious minutes filling Warren in on my afternoon and convincing him to let me release the details of Delores's disappearance on Sunday night.

"There's an old saying in my profession," he said. "Never ask a question unless you're sure you already know the answer."

"That's what people like me are for—to find the answers," I replied. "Somebody may come forward and even if they don't, why not give everybody something else to chew on, muddy the waters a little to take some of the attention off Lattimore? Cotter's sudden wealth worries me even more than his disappearance. What if somebody doesn't want him available? With enough money, you can disappear for a long time—maybe forever if you're lucky and you're careful. And we don't have forever. If we can turn up someone else who knows where Delores was on Sunday night or saw her with the bruises before she got home Sunday morning, King might think twice."

He was quiet. I wondered whether the same question was in his mind that had been in mine ever since I heard Cotter had taken off. Had John Lattimore paid Cotter for his silence and financed his flight so he couldn't contradict his story?

"What if they take their information to the police?" Warren asked.

"If they do, I'll know about it and from what my sources tell me, I think it would be enough for Owens to pressure King to take another look at the case," I replied.

"All right," he capitulated. "As you say, we don't have much time. It looks as though King is going to oppose bail and I'd like to head him off at the pass if we can."

It would cut my billings considerably if we wrapped it up that easily, but the publicity would make up for it.

"How much time do we have before the preliminary?" I asked.

"With luck, a week or more. Without it, maybe forty-eight hours. I'll probably know tomorrow," he replied.

"What about this tranquilizer angle?"

"It bears looking into, particularly if there was no blood test for barbiturates. But that will be a matter for the trial and I hope it won't come to that."

"You have any objection if I ask a few rhetorical questions of an expert I know?"

"Can he be trusted to be discreet?"

"As the grave."

"Not, perhaps, the happiest choice of words," he replied and hung up.

I decided to take that as a yes.

I depressed the button and dialed the *Times*. Whoever answered laid the phone down while they went in search of Kent. I listened nostalgically to the din of deadline: ringing phones, people yelling over the clacking of typewriter keys, and the clamor of the Teletype bell. I love it; I guess I always will, but I realized I didn't miss it anymore. It was a good feeling.

"Rose," Kent barked.

"It's me. You better get Ben on."

"Ben! Pick up two!"

"Nice of you to drop in," Ben greeted me.

"Anything to oblige. Ready?"

"Go."

I ran it down for them, making sure to work in that Lattimore and the boy cooperated in the search on Sunday night and that Lattimore had taken responsibility for seeing Greg was taken care of by friends when his mother couldn't be found. Ben asked the questions while Kent concentrated on getting it all down. I didn't mention the restless Mr. Cotter. I preferred to find him myself if possible, but I emphasized we were interested in talking with anyone who had seen Delores Sunday night or Monday morning.

"Got it," Kent said, and he was gone.

"So, you're official?" Ben lingered long enough to ask.

"Looks that way."

"We'll talk." Then he was gone too.

I dallied long enough to comb my hair and wash my hands

before I headed for the hospital. Something about hospitals always makes me feel like I should have clean hands when I go in.

When I asked for Gary at the front desk, the nurse on duty checked her watch and suggested the cafeteria. As I made my way down the halls, I pondered how anyone could eat in a hospital. I was so hungry my stomach thought my throat had been cut, but one whiff of that hospital smell—that combination of floor wax, alcohol, disinfectant, and something more sinister, and my appetite disappeared.

I spotted Gary studying a display of congealed salads. As I joined him, it occurred to me how much the gelatinous masses resembled gall bladders and livers. I turned to get Gary's opinion on the matter and realized he wasn't staring, he was asleep.

"Gair?" I tugged gently on his sleeve.

"Coming!" he shouted, looking around wildly. "Start a hypo of nitro and three cc's of—"

"Gary! Relax. It's me, Steve."

"Steve." He peered at me through bloodshot eyes. "Damn, I didn't know you'd been sick."

"C'mon Gary, let's sit down."

I relieved him of his tray and led him over to a table. He folded into a seat and propped an elbow on the table to hold up his head, limp as the stethoscope that dangled from his pocket.

Gary and I go way back, all the way to Carolina. He was pre-med; I was poor. He studied round the clock; I was night manager at a gas station. He spent a lot of nights studying with me after the library closed. I once heard Susie describe him to a potential blind date as "dark and broodingly handsome in a Heathcliffish sort of way."

I studied him now and decided bloodhound would be more like it. Brown hair, big, drooping brown eyes set in a long, brown face. Of course, I've never seen him after a full night's sleep. Who knows. Maybe with a shave and eight hours under his belt, he'd look like Laurence Olivier.

"Listen, Gair, can you drink yourself to death?" I reached over and helped myself to a French fry.

"Not unless I get a night off," he replied, his eyes already at half mast.

"How long you been on?"

"What day is it?"

"Wednesday."

"What year?"

"Never mind. You gonna eat that?" Surrounded by the sight and smells of food, hunger was overcoming my squeamishness.

"Eat what?"

"Here." I shoved some French fries onto a napkin and helped myself to the tossed salad, leaving him the burger and a piece of pie.

"Eat," I ordered.

I waited until he'd finished most of the burger and looked marginally more alert.

"Gary, I need some help. Is it possible to drink yourself to death?"

"Sure. People do it all the time. We get three or four stiffs in here a month. Derelicts, mostly."

"Yeah, but can you do it all at one time?"

"God knows, I've tried."

"I'm serious. Can you drink so much at one time you have a heart attack or something?"

"The alcohol alone won't cause a heart attack, but if you were scheduled for one, being drunk could certainly complicate things."

"How?" I asked around a mouthful of salad.

"Because you'd be too drunk to holler for help."

I opened my mouth to ask another question, but he was off and running.

"There's alcohol poisoning, but that's tough."

"Why?"

"Well, most people just pass out before they consume that much alcohol."

"What if they drank a lot?"

"Well, there's cirrhosis of the liver, but I assume this was an unexpected death?" He pondered. "It's hard to say without knowing more."

So I told him everything I knew about Delores's drinking and the tranquilizers.

"The tranquilizers, of course, could change everything. But they'd show up right away in an autopsy."

"But only if you test for them, right?"

"True."

"Would that be a given?"

"Depends. If you were looking for cause of death, you'd almost certainly test for barbiturates or poison. But if the cause of death was fairly obvious, probably not. The city doesn't have facilities for running the tests and they'd have to spring to send them to Raleigh or Washington, I'd think."

"How long after can you run those tests?"

"Depends," he said again. "Not more than a day or two for blood or tissue samples and they'd have to be stored properly." He sighed. "That's about all I can tell you without knowing more specifics."

"Like what?"

"Age, general physical condition, that sort of thing. How old was she?"

"Forty."

"Height? Weight?"

"Height, I don't know. Weight, maybe one thirty, one thirty-five."

"Her mother drank?"

"Yeah."

"And she, the dead woman, I mean, hid her drinking?"

"From most people, yeah."

"Well, she fits the pattern."

"What pattern?"

"Children of alcoholics are way more likely to become alcoholics and because they're so used to covering for their parents, they're good at hiding their own problem. Tell me more about the episodes where she passed out after a drink or two."

I gave him all the details I could remember.

"Now that could be helpful. Sounds like reverse tolerance."

"What's that?" I had my notebook out now.

"Well, I'm not an expert, but after a certain point, a heavy drinker's liver simply can't process the alcohol anymore and their tolerance goes way down. They can get falling down drunk on one or two drinks. It happens toward the later stages and it happens in women faster than in men."

I had a brainstorm. "Alcohol dilates the blood vessels, right?"

"Right."

"So, would it make you more susceptible to bruising?"

"In a manner of speaking, I guess."

"How's that?"

"Drunks tend to fall down a lot."

"Can you die from this reverse tolerance thing?"

He hesitated. "Not necessarily, but it indicates the late stages of alcoholism. If your victim was that far along, alcohol poisoning becomes more of a possibility. Alcohol is a depressant. If you drink enough, it suppresses the signals from your brain to your heart and lungs. You go into a coma and just stop breathing."

"Thanks, Gair, you've been a big help."

"Anytime." He waved a weary hand. "We're open twenty-four hours a day, no waiting, free Green Stamps."

I was halfway down the hall before I remembered and turned back. Gary was sitting where I'd left him, sound asleep. I hated like hell to wake him, but it was important.

"Gair?" I touched his shoulder.

"Wha . . . ?" He stared up at me blearily.

"We never had this conversation, okay?"

"What conversation?"

"Sweet dreams, Gair."

I hadn't realized how late it had gotten. The sun had slipped behind the trees, softening the hard yellow glare of afternoon to the gray of evening. In the west, the sky was the color of a bruise and a fitful breeze promised a thundershower before midnight. I hoped Susie hadn't held dinner for me. A lot had happened since I'd kissed her goodbye—I checked my watch—ten hours ago.

My mother-in-law's station wagon was parked in front of the house. I was surprised to see my mother's Buick behind it. As always, my first heart-stopping fear was that something had happened to Susie or the kids. But there was no smoke or blood, no ambulances or police cars. Everything seemed quiet.

But appearances can be deceiving. I let myself in the back door and all hell broke loose.

"Well, hello, Mr. TV Star!" Mother fluttered up from her seat at the kitchen table to peck my cheek.

"Daddy!" Adam barreled through the doorway and flung himself at my legs. Christine appeared from nowhere and squirmed under my arm to twine her arms around my waist.

Susie looked up from the dishes in the sink. "He saw you on TV coming out of the courthouse and nothing I could say would persuade him you hadn't been arrested."

She gave me a tight smile, but I could read the tension in every line of her body. She loves both our mothers dearly, but it drives her crazy to have people underfoot in our small kitchen.

"I told him," Christine announced from the lofty heights of nine-year-old wisdom. But she didn't loosen her grasp on my waist and I dropped a kiss on her forehead before I bent to unwrap Adam from my leg.

"Everything's okay, sport. See, I'm here, safe and sound." I hefted him up in my arms. He burrowed his face into my neck.

Still holding them both, I leaned over precariously to plant a kiss on Susie's cheek.

"Sorry, I'm late," I said. I gave her a look that apologized for much more.

"No problem. Have you eaten?"

"I had a bite with Gary at the hospital. He sends his love." I knew he would have if he'd been conscious.

"How is he?"

"Tired."

"Yep, that's Gary." She placed the last dish in the drain and wiped her hands on the towel.

"How's the case going?" My mother hovered behind me, avid for news. "We watched you on the television with that Mr. Warren. Such a *distinguished* man. You looked very handsome too, dear. If you'd just shave off that beard, everyone could see how handsome you are." She patted my arm. Susie and I traded amused glances over her head and the tension in the air evaporated.

My mother-in-law appeared in the doorway. "Steve. You must be worn out. Here, sit down. How 'bout some tea, or would you rather have Coke?"

I shuddered. "No, thanks, Helen. I've had enough liquids today to last me a lifetime."

She looked puzzled but mercifully asked no questions. "C'mon sweetie, let Daddy get his tie off." She gently unwound Adam's arms from my neck. "Let's take this boy to the car wash and scrub those bumpers. C'mon, Christine, I'll put your hair up in curlers for you." She led them down the hall to the bathroom. I sank into a chair, suddenly weary beyond belief.

"What's he like?" my mother persisted.

"Who?"

"Warren."

I obliged with all the details I thought would interest her.

"Did he do it?"

"Who, Warren?"

"Oh, you! Of course not. Did he kill that poor woman?" She lowered her voice. "Were they . . . you know . . . carrying on?"

I put her off. "I don't think Mr. Warren wants me to discuss the details of the case before the trial, Mom. If there is one."

That got a raised eyebrow from Susie but seemed to satisfy Mother.

"Oh, well, I'm sure he knows what's best." She rose and gathered up her purse. "I'd better be going if I'm going to make it home before dark. Thank you for dinner, dear." She kissed Susie's cheek. "I'll just go back and say good-night to the children before I go."

Susie saw her out and returned to the kitchen. There were splashes and riotous laughter from down the hall, but it was quiet in the kitchen. Susie stood behind my chair and worked magic on my shoulder muscles with cool fingers.

I rolled my head forward to give her more room to work. "Oh. That's wonderful. How did you know?"

"You think you're the only detective in the family?" she replied. "Besides, you look like you've been dragged through a bush."

"I guess it has been a long day. I didn't realize how long until

I slowed down and it caught up with me."

"Is it going well, or are you too tired to talk about it?"

I was so tired my brain ached, but thinking out loud to Susie always helps me pull things together. Maybe she'd see something I didn't. I poured it all out, not bothering to put it into any coherent order. She knows me well enough to follow my mental shorthand without much trouble. I'd just about run down when the phone rang.

"I'll get it," Susie said. "Unless there's been another murder, you're unavailable." As she stretched across the counter to snag it, I admired the strip of flesh exposed when her blouse rode up. Maybe I wasn't as tired as I thought.

"Hello? Yes, this is the Harlan residence." Silence. I turned to see her big, dark eyes narrow. "Oh, yeah? Well, why, don't you . . ." She made a few suggestions that put the graffiti writers at the jail in the shade. "Hello? Hello?" She slammed down the receiver. "Ha! They can dish it out, but they can't take it," she announced with satisfaction.

"Who was it?"

"Crank call about the case. It's been one after another since dinner."

"Susie? Is something wrong?" Helen appeared in the doorway, her face worried.

Susie made a visible effort to calm herself and forced a smile. "Prank call. Teenagers should be sent to boot camp for the summer."

Helen's no fool, but after a glance at me, she wisely decided to let it go. "The children are ready to be tucked in."

"I'll come," Susie said and brushed past her.

"I'll be there in a minute," I called after her.

It was very quiet in the kitchen for a beat. Helen looked at me gravely. "It'll get worse, won't it?"

"I'll do my best, Helen."

She knew what I meant.

Her face softened. "I know you will. But it'll be ugly, won't it?"

"Probably."

She patted my shoulder. "You're a good man, Steve."

That's high praise from a mother-in-law. "Thanks, Helen."

I watched her out to her car from the front porch. The dampness in the air was rising. As I watched, a fork of lightning streaked to the ground in the west. It was probably already raining out at the river. That made me think of Lattimore's cabin. I stood, enjoying the cool breeze, and thought about a dead woman with a musty-smelling cabin for a tomb. Who was Delores Green? A drunk, a party girl, or a devoted, hard-working mother who turned to tranquilizers and booze to soften the hard edges of her life? Despite all I'd learned today, I had more questions than answers.

I went back in and met Susie coming down the hall.

"Suse?" I put my arms around her. "Tell me about the calls?"

"Most seem to feel public hanging is too good for him and don't appreciate your efforts to get him off," she said, keeping her voice low. "Judging from their limited vocabularies, I'm assuming they're not Lattimore's country club pals. This one was along the lines of, 'Tell your hotshot private-eye husband to give it up if he knows what's good for him. That rich bastard deserves to get what's coming to him.' "

I tightened my arms around her. "I'm sorry."

She shrugged. "Goes with the territory."

It certainly wasn't the first time. I'd had the number changed to an unlisted one when I went on the police beat to make it harder for disgruntled defendants or unhappy cops to find me, but it isn't hard to find if you want it badly enough. A few bucks to a clerk at the newspaper or access to a cross-reference directory would be enough.

Susie gave me a forgiving smile. I bent to kiss her. She felt good and I lingered until Adam's voice floated plaintively down the hall.

"Daddy? Are you gonna tuck me in?"

"Coming, bud."

"You know where to find me," Susie whispered and slipped out of my grasp.

I said goodnight to Adam and spent a few minutes with Christine. I was heading toward the bedroom when the phone rang again. I snatched it up.

"You got something to say, say it to me!"

"And good evening to you!" Hilda sniffed.

"Sorry, Hilda. We've had some crank calls. I thought you were another one."

"You were right about the blood tests," she plunged in without further preamble. "Nobody's ordered any."

"Thanks, Hilda. I appreciate it."

"There's more."

"Yeah?"

"Your lady friend's not dead."

"What?"

"When the packet came over from the mortuary, there was no death certificate. I called to ask about it and the girl said Doc told her to hold up on it."

"So legally, she's not dead."

"Got it."

"Anything else?"

"Isn't that enough?"

"It's wonderful, Hilda. Thanks a million."

I hung up and stood mulling over what she'd said. Maybe Doc wasn't as certain about the cause of death as he thought. Things were looking up.

I went through the house turning off lights and locking up. I slipped into the bedroom and shucked out of my clothes in the dark, leaving them in a pile on the floor. I slid under the sheet and stretched out a hand. "Suse?"

Her only response was a ladylike snore.

CHAPTER 9

I woke to find myself staring into the face of a gargoyle that smelled of Corn Flakes. I shut my eyes. Dreaming of gargoyles with Corn Flakes on their breath had to indicate something seriously screwy in my psyche. I opened my eyes again and blinked. The gargoyle blinked and drew back. It was Adam, his face scant inches from mine.

"Are you up?"

I mumbled something incoherent, but it seemed to satisfy him. Mission accomplished, he zoomed off to spread more sunshine. I stumbled to my feet and shuffled down the hall toward the bathroom.

As I drew even with Christine's room, her door flew open and she bounced into my chest so hard, it knocked both of us back a step.

"Daddy!" She made a big deal out of covering her eyes. Pink foam rubber curlers bobbled madly about her face.

"What?"

"Don't you have a robe or something?"

"A robe?" Actually, I have three hanging in the back of my closet, the accumulation of several Father's Days and Christmases, but I always figured they were in case I had to go to the hospital."

"Yes, a robe." She rolled her eyes. "It's not couth to go around in your boxer shorts."

Couth? Before I could form a reply, she flounced into the

bathroom and shut the door. I considered beating on it and standing on my parental privilege for first dibs, but I suddenly felt too old and melancholy. Instead, I trudged back to the bedroom and dug a robe out of the closet. I headed toward the kitchen where I could hear Susie and Adam doing a duet on "Itsy Bitsy Spider."

"When did your daughter become Emily Post?" I collapsed into a chair. I'm not a morning person. I'm barely a person at all before coffee.

"Who's Emily Post?" Adam demanded.

Susie raised an eyebrow at my robe and laughed. "It's a stage. Nine-year-old girls are older than dirt. Don't worry, she'll regress when she turns into a teenager."

"Please. Not before breakfast."

She slid a mug of coffee in front of me and kissed the top of my head. "Sorry about last night."

"S'okay." I started to wave my hand but decided it was too much trouble and propped my head on it instead.

"Same time, same place tonight?"

"You're on. Can you get your mother to drop you at school this morning? I'm supposed to meet Kent at seven-thirty."

"I don't see why not." She went off to hustle the kids into some clothes for the ride.

I studied the pattern in the Formica and sipped my coffee while I waited for the day to come into focus. Unfortunately, it bore a whole lot of resemblance to yesterday.

By the time I finished my coffee, things didn't look quite as overwhelming. By the time I'd showered and shaved, I felt damn near invincible.

Kent was waiting for me at the Diamond with a fresh copy of the *Times*. I skimmed the story while he ordered for both of us. They'd done a good job with it and I told him so.

"Thanks," he said, to me and the waitress as she set two plates in front of us. She rewarded him with her best smile.

Susie describes Kent as drop-dead handsome and dead boring. He's all right, if you like the matinee-idol type: blue eyes, wavy black hair, a Kirk Douglas chin, and lots of white teeth. A face like that is wasted in newspapers, so he does a lot of community theater. He's played Lancelot almost as many times as Goulet.

"I see the boy's staying with an aunt somewhere. You had any luck talking to 'em yet?" I asked.

"They've taken a powder," he replied out of the side of his mouth. He started talking like that after he took over the police beat. "I've got one of the neighbors watching the house, but they've gone under cover somewhere."

"They'll probably shoot me on sight if I show up, but let me know if you hear anything, would you?"

"Sure thing," he promised. "Same goes for you."

I changed the subject. "What's the *Courier* got?"

"Not much." Satisfaction oozed from him like the butter melting on his grits. "The usual sources at the cop shop are shut down tight and probably will be for a while. Their lead story was what Lattimore ate for lunch in his cell followed by a rehash of the arrest."

"You got anything good for today?"

"Other than an interview with a real live private eye?"

"Watch it unless you wanna find that photo of you in tights on the newsroom bulletin board."

"Soon as we get through with you, we're heading out to the cabin, get some shots of the crime scene." I gave him a look and a raised eyebrow at that. He ignored both. "Looks like the funeral will probably be tomorrow or the next day depending on when they release the body," he added.

"Here?"

"South Carolina."

"You covering it?"

"Unless there's something else going on I should know about." He wiggled his eyebrows at me.

We chewed in silence for a few minutes, then Kent raised his head suddenly to ask, "Do you miss it?"

"Sometimes," I replied. Like now, when it should have been me on the other side of the table asking questions about the biggest murder case this town had ever seen. I recognized the avid curiosity Kent was struggling to conceal, remembered the controlled tension in every line of his body as he tried to act nonchalant.

But this time I had more answers than he did. I was closer to the story than I could have ever dreamed when I was a reporter. In many ways, it's still the same job: asking questions, ferreting out information a crumb at a time.

"I always thought you got a raw deal," he offered, slurping his coffee.

One that had left him sitting pretty behind my desk, I thought, but aloud, I said, "Nobody made me leave. I guess I dealt myself out."

The truth was, leaving the paper was the hardest thing I'd ever done. Being a reporter was the only thing I'd ever wanted to do. But it was done almost before I knew it. Afterward, I was forced to realize how much of my identity was wrapped up in what I did for a living. I didn't just have to find a new career, I had to find a new "me." It has taken a long time, and there are days I'm not sure I'm there yet. But in the process, I've learned something about how everybody in this life tries to find the role, the mask, that fits most comfortably and then spends the rest of their life struggling like hell not to let it slip. Most succeed, but at the cost of never finding out who's really under the mask. Somehow that understanding lets me be a little more forgiving, a little more tolerant, so maybe some good has come of the experience.

I changed the subject and we swapped gossip until the check came. Kent pointedly ignored it. I paid. We strolled the few blocks down to my building, where we found the photographer waiting for us.

As I unlocked the office door, I saw it for a moment through Kent's eyes—not quite seedy, but definitely shabby. The furniture's secondhand, the walls bare except for a copy of my license and my diploma from Carolina. It's clean, but that's about all you can say for it.

Kent gave it a thorough once-over, but covered it by turning to the photographer. "What do you think, Bobby? Can we get something at the desk or will you get too much glare from that window?"

Bobby grunted in response and began to set up his lights and tripod. That seemed to settle the question, so I sat down behind the desk. Kent's interview style had improved with practice, but it was still an uncomfortable exercise being on the other side of the notebook.

Kent gestured at the photo of Susie and the kids on my desk. "You wanna work in the family?"

I hesitated.

"C'mon," he coaxed. "It's a new angle for a private eye. Makes you look like a Boy Scout."

"Yeah, I know. But no names or mention of the neighborhood, okay?"

He raised his eyebrows.

"I'm probably overreacting, but we had some crank calls at the house last night. I think it made Susie a little nervous." I'd have a reason to be nervous if Susie heard me say that. If she's ever been afraid of anybody or anything, it'd be news to me.

"Gotcha." He turned to Bobby. "You through here?"

But Bobby had apparently used up his allotment of words for the day. He looked up from packing his gear to give Kent a withering glare.

I stood up and rolled my head around to relieve the kinks. "This must be my punishment for subjecting other people to this all those years. I feel like an idiot."

"Don't sweat it, buddy. We'll make you look good." Kent clapped me on the back then ruined it by adding, "Anything for a friend of the big guys upstairs."

"Their best friend is whoever brings in the hottest story," I replied, clapping him on the back. My way of not-so-subtly reminding him where yesterday's scoop came from. He had the grace to turn red. He and Bobby cleared out of my office in record time.

I checked my watch. It was still early. I had things to do, but it was too early for most of them and I wanted to stick by the phone in case the story brought some calls.

I dragged out the typewriter, rolled in paper and carbons, and started typing up my notes. My two-fingered typing style may not be elegant, but it's fast. Even so, it took several hours to transform my scribbles into coherent prose. The phone remained stubbornly silent. By the time I finished, the kinks in my neck and shoulders had turned into knots.

I separated the copies and stuck them in a folder. Then, feeling like a second-rate spy, I stowed them in the massive black Mosler safe I bought from my Uncle Boyd when he sold his furniture store. I'd had visions of clients asking me to deliver ransom payments or blackmail payoffs. But so far, the most important things in it are copies of my tax returns from '59 and '60.

I felt silly, but it was beginning to sink in just how big a case this was going to be. I didn't want some overzealous reporter or cop helping themselves to my notes. I didn't think Owens would condone anything like that, but there are a couple guys in the Detective Division who've pulled worse to make points.

My grandmother used to say, "Be careful what you ask for, you just might get it." I'd been hungry for a big case, something I could sink my teeth into and make a name for myself. I'd gotten it all right—in spades. Thinking of spades made me think of graves and that reminded me of Peggy trotting off to the funeral home to perform one last favor for her friend.

Some fresh air and a change of scenery were definitely called for. I decided to drop off my report at Warren's office in person.

I'd learned my lesson and kept my charm buttoned up as I crept into Miz Turner's domain. She swiveled away from her typewriter and eyed me up and down, presumably to make sure I wasn't packing a gat or concealing a bomb, before she deigned to announce me.

"Your investigator's here." She spoke into the phone without taking her eyes off me. I stood up very straight and tried to look like Paul Drake, but in my heart I knew I didn't have the shoulders or the dimples for it.

"Go on in." She waved in the direction of Warren's door and dismissed me from her attention.

"Ah, Steve. Good morning." Warren rose and came around the desk to shake hands. "Do you mind if I call you Steve?" He ushered me to a chair as though I was royalty instead of a hired hand.

"Not at all."

"Coffee?"

"Thank you, no. I've had plenty," I replied. "I just came by to drop off my report."

"Excellent." He took the folder from me and began to leaf through it. "Did you learn anything helpful from your medical source?"

"You'll find the details in my report, but based on what he . . . what I was told, together with what we know of Delores's history and some things I picked up from her girlfriends, cause of death is looking more promising." I gave him a quick summary of what I'd learned from Gary about reverse tolerance.

"We now have an independent witness, Delores's friend, Mimi, who saw her get falling down drunk on one drink only a few days before she died. Then there's Delores's remark to the other friend, Peggy Summerfield, the night she took too many tranquilizers, about wanting to join her dead mother. That was what, seventy-two hours before she died? To me, that adds up to a woman in trouble—suicidal or at least seriously depressed."

"Mmm." Warren was deep into the pages, but he waved for me to continue.

"This woman was in deeper trouble than anybody realized. I find it interesting that one friend knew about her drinking but not the tranquilizers and the other knew about the tranquilizers, but Delores was able to keep her from finding out about the drinking."

"What's this about the death certificate?" He marked the place with his finger and looked up.

I shrugged. "The information's reliable. Practically from the horse's mouth."

"Your contact considers it significant?"

"Apparently so. The word to hold up the certificate came straight from Doc."

"That is interesting."

"Could they be having second thoughts?" I could see my retainer flying out the window.

"That's probably too much to hope for," Warren replied. "But it's valuable information all the same. It would be risky, but *if* it looks like the grand jury is going to hand down an indictment, we could use it to force King's hand on bail. Or persuade the grand jury to hand down an indictment on a lesser charge. Otherwise, we holler habeas corpus and point out they're proposing to try a man for murder when the coroner hasn't even ruled it murder."

"You're the expert, but you're right. It sounds risky to me. Wouldn't we be better off leaving them a hole to back out of?"

"Certainly," he replied. "I hope we won't have to use it. But if it looks as though they'll get an indictment anyway, it will at least force them to commit on a cause of death."

"So you think it will come down to a question of cause of death after all?"

"It's much too soon to say until we see what evidence they present at the preliminary hearing," he said. "But those bruises are going to haunt us. A jury is going to take one look at John and those hands of his like canned hams and they won't have any trouble believing he beat that woman to death. Even if we get him off with cause of death, everybody in this town will go to their graves convinced he beat her up, unless we can demonstrate where she got those bruises."

He leaned back in his chair and regarded me over his glasses. "Murder never dies. It affects everyone whose life it touches, for the rest of their lives. If John is to have any kind of life at all when this is through, he has to walk out of that courtroom not just acquitted, but vindicated."

That seemed a lot to hope for given the general reaction to his involving a thirteen-year-old boy, but I kept my thoughts to myself. "Any idea how soon the preliminary might be?"

"I should know something by the end of the day," he replied. "But I expect King will push for as soon as possible. My wife tells me several people cut him dead in the Club dining room last night. He's going to be anxious to get his licks in."

I gathered up my briefcase and hat. "Any instructions? I thought I'd keep working on where Delores spent Sunday night and see if I can turn up anything on our missing mechanic."

"No, that's fine. Keep working on that. I'd also like to know more about the tranquilizers she was taking." He rose and came around to usher me out.

"We need to find out what pharmacy she used," I said.

"I'm going over to the jail later. I'll see if John knows anything about it," he promised. "Check back with me after lunch. If he knows anything, I'll have it for you by then. I'll also need her doctor's full name and address in case we decide to subpoena her records."

"How about I try and talk to her doctor first?" I asked.

"Do you really think you can get anything out of him?"

"Nothing to lose by trying." I shrugged. "He might be willing to part with a little information if it will mean keeping his name out of court. That kind of notoriety is bad for business. Especially his business."

"I suppose it's worth a try," he agreed. He opened the door and gestured me out ahead of him. "Let's check with Miz Turner and see if this morning's story has generated any calls."

"Seven," she reported. She consulted her notebook. "Four who didn't match the description, one report she was pinching the tomatoes at the Park-N-Shop on Wilkinson Boulevard, another that someone who looked like her hogged the dryer at a Laundromat on South Boulevard all night, and one man who insists she was his long-lost cousin—"

"Did you get his name?"

"—from Argentina." She glared at me over the top of her reading glasses.

"Right. Thank you. Well, it was worth a try." I was halfway out the door when something else occurred to me. "If the preliminary's this week and they get an indictment, how long have we got before trial?"

"It depends on when the superior court judge sits next," Warren replied. "It could be as little as a month. Ordinarily, I'd delay as long as possible and let some of the hoopla die down, but if they refuse bail, I'll push for the earliest date we can get."

I winced. "That's not very long."

"I doubt John would agree."

I headed back to the office and put in a half hour on the phone calling in favors at the credit bureau, the driver's license office, and the police records office. If people had any idea how much personal information about them is lying around in file folders just waiting for someone to ask, there'd be a riot.

At the moment I was only interested in whatever I could find on Cotter—former addresses, traffic tickets, previous employers—anything that would give me a line on where to start looking.

The most it cost me was a pair of wrestling tickets and I have an arrangement with a lady in the ticket office at the Coliseum who owes me a favor. I'd beaten the cops to a call at a frat party that turned ugly one night and hauled her son home in my back seat, saving him from a night in the drunk tank and her from public disgrace.

I cajoled Mrs. Bruno into listening for my phone for the usual price of a dozen Krispy Kreme doughnuts, although privately, I thought she was beginning to resemble a big, round doughnut.

I hadn't lied to Warren about my agenda for the day, but there was one stop I hadn't mentioned.

"Well, hey there, if it ain't Sam Spade." Terry greeted me like a long-lost friend. "Say, listen, I haven't seen hide nor hair 'a Jack since you were here yestiddy or I'da called you."

"S'okay." I stuck out a hand for him to shake. After a minute's hesitation, he wiped his hand on the rag in his back pocket and worked my hand like a pump handle. I guess not many people offer to shake hands with a mechanic.

"In fact, I think you'd better start looking for a new partner." I hoisted myself up on the drink box. It was blessedly cool on my backside.

"That a fact?"

"Yeah. Cotter's landlady says he packed his bags and moved out Monday evening."

"Well, how 'bout that."

"I was wondering if you've ever seen this guy around here." I pulled out the picture of Lattimore I'd clipped from yesterday's newspaper.

Terry studied it. "Why, sure, I know Mr. Lattimore. He's been bringing his car in here for years."

"He's a customer?" My heart sank, but it made sense. If Delores was having car trouble, she'd naturally ask Lattimore about it and he'd send her wherever he took his car. I should have thought of that.

Terry looked over his shoulder before he answered. "Not a real good one, if you know what I mean."

"How's that?"

"These rich guys, they're all the same," he confided. "Like to throw it around, put on a big show, but in real life, they squeeze a nickel till it—"

"Hey Terry, you seen the three-quarter socket wrench?" A red-faced guy with sandy hair stuck his head through the door. "Oh, sorry, I didn't know you was talking to somebody."

"This here's the private investigator I told you about that's working on the big murder case," Terry told him.

"How ya doing?" I nodded.

"This is George. He's helping out for a few days till we can get somebody to take Jack's place."

I could have sworn George deliberately averted his face, but he muttered, "Pleased to meetcha," before disappearing back into the gloom of the garage. He seemed to have lost interest in his missing socket wrench. Probably behind on his car payments or his alimony. A lot of people suddenly develop a guilty conscience and a burning need to be someplace else when they find out what I do.

I turned back to Terry. "You were telling me how Lattimore squeezes a nickel?"

"Yeah. He drives a big, fancy Cadillac, but he don't take care of it. Jack was always trying to tell him he'd save money in the long run if he'd just bring it in regular for maintenance, but no, he'd drive it till something went wrong, then bring it in and want reconditioned parts to boot. Took his own sweet time paying his bill, too. Sometimes I'd have to remind him a coupla times, you know?"

"Wait a minute. You're saying that Cotter knew Lattimore too?"

"Why, sure. Unless it was something big, Jack usually took care of him."

I felt like the bottom had just dropped out of my elevator. I hated to ask, but I had to know. "Terry, what color is Lattimore's Cadillac?"

"Black."

Well, hallelujah for small favors.

"Has he been in recently?"

"I don't recall so, but lemme check." He flipped through the tin box on the counter until he found what he was looking for. "Nah, he's overdue for an oil change and lube job. Hasn't been in for months."

"How come you didn't mention this when I was here yesterday?"

He looked hurt. "Well, gee, buddy, you didn' ask."

★ ★ ★ ★ ★

I found Dr. Morgan listed on the eighth floor of the Doctor's Tower, a highfalutin' name for a plain old ten-story office building. The "o" in his name on the door was missing and the "n" wasn't long for this world. I was surprised to find the waiting room empty. Maybe Wednesday was his golf day.

The green vinyl sofa was rump-sprung, the linoleum had been scuffed bare in spots by nervous feet, and there was an air of neglect about the dog-eared magazines and wilting plants. A curtain of dust hung lazily in the sunshine that pierced the dusty Venetian blinds.

But the nurse who appeared in answer to the tinkle of the bell was crisp and efficient. Her eyebrows looked starched into place and her uniform was so white, I needed sunglasses. She gave me a professional smile as she walked briskly to the desk, picked up a white card, and poised her pen over it expectantly.

"Yes sir, how can we help you?"

"My name's Harlan." I gave her one of my cards. She read it and made a face like she'd smelled something bad. "I'd like to talk to Dr. Morgan. It won't take a minute."

"I'm sorry. Dr. Morgan doesn't see anyone without an appointment." She handed back my card.

I looked around at the empty waiting room. "I'm sure he's very busy." I lowered my voice. "It's about one of his patients." Just in case she thought I was there for some nasty divorce thing.

"We don't release information on our patients." She slammed her desk drawer shut as though it would close the question once and for all.

"As an occasional patient myself, I appreciate his discretion." I gave her my best sincere smile. "It's really just a question of getting a few facts straight."

"I'm sorry, it's out of the question." She rose and waited for me to take the hint.

"If we could clear up these few minor points, it would save us having to subpoena the doctor later."

That got her attention. She frowned and drummed her nails on the desktop. "Wait here," she said finally. "I'll see if he has time to see you." She marched to the frosted door and closed it smartly behind her. I heard a murmur of voices behind it. I moved away from the door when they stopped.

"Dr. Morgan will see you now."

She held the door open for me. I glanced down at her and smiled my thanks as I passed and was startled to see what looked like fear in her eyes.

Morgan's office was like a cave after the bright sunshine outside. The only illumination came from a lamp on the desk that cast a pool of light on the blotter. When he leaned forward, it reflected off his thick, silver hair. His face was ruddy, probably from hours on the golf course. I bet he was a killer with the old ladies.

"You're looking for information on one of my patients?" he demanded. As I suspected, his eyes were blue, but one of them was what my grandmother used to call a "wall eye" that wandered off to the left. In spite of myself, I found my own gaze wandering after it.

I dragged it back and gave him a reassuring smile. "Just trying to verify a few facts."

"I don't make a habit of discussing my patients," he snapped.

"No sir, I understand. But in this case, I don't think your patient will mind. May I sit down?"

I sat before he could refuse. This close, I could see a layer of ash down the front of his white coat. A mist of brandy fumes wafted across the desk to engulf me. That explained the ruddy complexion. He lifted his hands from his lap and clasped them together on his desk blotter, but not before I noticed how they shook.

I knew now why his waiting room was empty. It also answered the question of why he had prescribed tranquilizers for a woman he had to know was an alcoholic.

"Delores Green *was* one of your patients?"

He wiped his mouth with a shaking hand and didn't answer.

"You know Mrs. Green died Tuesday?" I prodded.

"Of course I know. I read the papers."

"There seems to be some question about the tranquilizers she was taking." If he chose to infer it was the police asking the questions, that was his problem.

He didn't answer. He seemed to have slipped into another world.

"Did Mrs. Green have a drinking problem?" I persisted.

That snapped him out of his brandy-induced haze. "Even if I could answer that, I wouldn't. Who the hell do you think you are, coming in here asking about people's private lives?"

His face grew redder and little bubbles of spit appeared at the corners of his mouth. He staggered to his feet suddenly, pushing his chair back so hard it bounced off the shelves behind his desk and rolled back to hit him behind the knees. He collapsed into it with a whoof that unleashed a new waves of fumes in my direction.

"Look, Dr. Morgan, all I want to know is what kind of tranquilizers you prescribed for Delores Green. Now you can either tell me and I'll go away, or we can subpoena her records and drag you into court to testify. Somehow, I don't think you'd like being up there in that witness stand. And I suspect the few patients you have left wouldn't like it very much either."

"Are you threatening me, young man?" He struggled up out of his chair again, his recalcitrant eye rolling wildly.

Braving the fumes, I leaned across the desk, stared him

straight in his good eye and drew a deep breath, but before I could let him have it, the nurse burst into the room.

"Doctor? Is everything all right?"

"No, it's not all right," he shouted. She rushed over to put a hand on his shoulder. "Comes in here and wants to know all about people's private lives." He collapsed into his chair and subsided into mumbles. She murmured quietly to him.

I gathered up my hat from the chair. "See you in court, doctor."

I found a pay phone in the lobby pharmacy. I'd just begun to dial when there was a knock on the glass. It was Morgan's nurse.

"I'll be done in a—"

"Please, Mr. Harlan, could I talk to you?" She wrestled open the door and plucked at my coat sleeve.

"What is it?"

"Not in here." She looked over her shoulder. "In the lobby. Please?"

She dragged me to a corner behind a plastic potted plant. "Please, Mr. Harlan, you can't subpoena Dr. Morgan."

"Oh, but we can." Although I wasn't nearly as sure as I sounded.

"No, you don't understand." She wasn't so crisp now. "He isn't really like that."

"Like what?"

"Like . . . that. Like you saw him upstairs."

"A rum-soaked old quack who should've been struck from the Medical Register years ago? You coulda fooled me."

"Dr. Morgan is . . . was, a good doctor," she said. "He's a good man. He hasn't always been like this." She looked around to make sure no one was listening. "It's his wife," she whispered.

"What about her?"

"She's . . . she's dying. Cancer. There's nothing more they

can do for her. She's his whole life, Mr. Harlan. They don't have any children. He's watching her die and there's nothing he can do for her. It's killing him too."

She bit her lip. "I . . . I wrote those prescriptions for Mrs. Green. There aren't many patients left. Most of them are old and they just call when they need their prescriptions refilled. I know I shouldn't have, but Mrs. Green was so insistent and I was trying to save Dr. Morgan all the worry I can. Please, Mr. Harlan, you can't call him to testify. It'll destroy him. All he has left is his good name. Don't take that away from him."

I thought for an instant about what it would be like to have to watch Susie die, but it was too horrible. My mind veered away.

"All right," I sighed. "I'll do my best to keep his name out of it. But I need to know what she was taking, how much, and when it was renewed last."

"I wrote it down for you." She fished a folded prescription slip from her uniform pocket. "It's all there." When she handed it to me, there were tears in her eyes. "Thank you."

"What will you do when it's over?" I asked.

"Oh, I'll be fine," she said with an attempt at a smile. "The hospitals are always looking for nurses to work the night shift."

I handed her one of my cards. "I have a friend who'll be setting up his practice in a few months. He could use somebody like you. Gimme a call if you're interested."

"Thank you."

"The preliminary's set for day after tomorrow." Warren sounded tired after his session with Lattimore.

"Do you need me there?"

"I think you should be there to hear what the prosecution has to say," he replied. "It'll be our first opportunity to see what they have. They'll have to put Doc on the stand, and I'm sure they'll have the boy testify."

"Poor kid."

"Yes." He fell silent for a moment. "I did get one piece of information for you. John wasn't sure what kind of tranquilizer Delores was taking, but he told me that he was with her on Friday afternoon when she had the prescription refilled."

"You mean the Friday afternoon after the Thursday night when she took too many and Peggy Summerfield had to come over and pour coffee down her?"

"The same."

"Well, whadda you know." I digested that nugget for a minute. "I got the name of the tranquilizer and the dosage from her doctor, so it looks like we're in business."

"Why do I have the feeling it's better if I don't inquire how you came by that information?"

"Oh, ye of little faith."

"Not at all. You've done quite well."

"Should I meet you at your office before the hearing?"

"I'll probably be with John," he replied. "And I think it would be best if you keep a low profile and sit in the gallery with the rest of the spectators."

I thought fleetingly of telling him about the story on me that would appear in tomorrow morning's paper, but he'd find out soon enough.

"But come early," he continued. "There's bound to be a crowd."

"I'll be there."

I grabbed a grilled cheese sandwich and a milkshake at the pharmacy counter before making the rounds of Delores's favorite watering holes. I started with the drive-in on Wilkinson since that was the last place she told Lattimore she'd been.

The west side used to be the primary residential area of town, but when the postwar families began moving to new neighbor-hoods on the east side, it became strictly blue-collar territory with Negroes manning the line between the bungalows of working-class white families and Wilkinson Boulevard. And the buffer was growing thinner all the time. Once a respectable, if not very attractive, commercial main drag, Wilkinson had deteriorated into an ugly string of fried-chicken joints, used-car lots, machine shops, and empty storefronts. Most of those were fast becoming cinderblock palaces with neon beer signs and cracked parking lots. The Big Chief drive-in was one of the few remaining landmarks from the neighborhood's palmier days. I'd cruised its parking lot many a night in my youth.

"Sorry." The carhop shifted her gum and her weight from right to left. The badge strategically pinned over her left breast said her name was Patti. "They're all a blur after a while, but I'm pretty sure I'd remember a lady by herself in the middle of the afternoon. Besides, women are lousy tippers."

"All of 'em?"

She preened and fluffed her short skirt. "Sure. They're jeal-ous."

"How about the car?" I described it for her again. "That ring a bell?"

"Nah."

"You're sure."

"Sure, I'm sure."

I wasn't convinced she was sure of her own name. I looked around. "How 'bout one of the other girls? Maybe they'd remember."

"I was the only one working. Judy and Sandra don't come on Sundays."

Just my luck. Where's Nancy Drew when you need her?

Patti shifted her weight and the gum back to the right. It was fascinating to watch.

"Well, listen, Patti, if you think of anything, anything at all, give me a call, will you?" I handed her one of my cards.

"Sure." She glanced at it without interest, stuck it in her waistband, and skated away. I watched her and stopped myself just in time from wondering what the younger generation was coming to.

I spent the rest of the afternoon showing Delores's picture to shifty supper-club managers and bored waitresses. If there's anything more depressing than a beer joint or a club in daylight, I'd hate to see it. It's not just the customers who look better in dim lights.

A couple of them thought they recognized her, which wasn't surprising, but no one remembered seeing her that night. I finally gave up and called it a day. There was always tomorrow. Besides, I had a date.

Chapter 10

Thursday was a washout. None of my sources turned up anything on Cotter. It was as if he'd never existed before he arrived in Charlotte. Which made me pretty sure Cotter wasn't his real name, but a lot of good it did me. Without something like a social security number to go on, I was stuck.

Warren spent most of the day in "consultation" so we spoke only briefly when I called to report my lack of progress. We agreed to meet back at his office after the hearing.

I was still racking my brain for some other avenue to explore as I battled traffic on my way to the courthouse Friday morning. I expected a crowd, but the courthouse lawn looked like a Cecil B. DeMille movie. A caravan of cars snaked around the courthouse at a crawl searching for a parking space. I finally extricated myself from the parade and found a space in an hourly lot six blocks away.

The dusty azaleas on the courthouse lawn were taking an awful beating as the crowd, mostly women, swarmed across the grass like lemmings, jostling and jockeying to beat each other to the door. Nourished by a daily diet of juicy tidbits courtesy of Ben and his cohorts, their appetite for the story had become voracious. Most of the people fighting for a glimpse of the hearing had never heard of Lattimore before his arrest. Now he was discussed and dissected over every coffee pot, bridge table, and break room in town.

I spotted one of the courthouse regulars, evicted from his

usual spot by the door, lounging against a column giving passersby the evil eye.

"How ya doing, Doy?"

"Been to two World's Fairs and a goat fucking and I ain't never seen nothing to beat this," he replied sourly and spat for emphasis. It succeeded in thinning out the crowd around him considerably.

I grinned at him and raised my hat, but there was no time to reply as the crowd swept me through the doors. We hit a bottleneck in the corridor, where scaffolds, buckets, and drop cloths crowded the hallway. The reek of fresh paint hit my sinuses like a sledgehammer. Some poor guy in overalls stood pinned against the wall balancing an open bucket of paint over his head. "S'cuse me, ma'am, coming through. S'cuse me. Ma'am?"

No one paid any attention. I wondered how long he'd be able to hold that bucket before he dumped it on someone's head.

I knew how he felt. I was packed in, bobbing in a sea of women, engulfed in a cloud of Tussy roll-on, mothballs, and Evening in Paris. It was like being smothered to death in a giant cupcake.

Drastic measures were called for. I began to squirm and twist, inching my way forward. I bumped into a firmly packed haunch and got glared at by its owner, but kept on squirming till I'd worked my way up to a little blue-haired lady near the front of the crowd. I tapped her on the shoulder. "S'cuse me. I'm so sorry, but could we just scoot through here? My little girl has to get to the bathroom."

"Why, a'course you can." She tried to twist around, but we were packed in too tightly for her to look down. "Do you need me to take you, baby?"

"Thank you, we'll manage. C'mon honey, this way," I spoke over my shoulder as I squeezed through the tiny opening.

"But, I don't see . . ." Her voice floated after me as I pushed on through the crowd.

The crush thinned out by the elevators. I paused to pull myself together and knock the dents out of my hat.

"Magazine, mister?" There was a tug at my sleeve. I looked down at a little colored boy of about nine or ten.

"Not right now, son." I turned away.

"But they're real special magazines," he insisted. He rolled his eyes toward the stack in his hand. *True Confessions.* With a piece of paper peeking out from between the pages of the top copy.

"Sure, okay, how much?" I glanced around, but no one was paying any attention to us.

"Two bits."

"Here you go." I handed him a couple quarters. He pocketed them and slipped into the crowd slick as a garter snake. I tucked the magazine under my jacket and made for the men's room. Once inside, I slid the bolt home before I took the magazine out. Inside was a photocopy of Greg's statement to the police. I blessed every hennaed hair on Hilda's head and sat down to read it.

But by the bottom of the first page, I wasn't smiling anymore. In his arrogance, Lattimore had underestimated just how much Greg resented him. The police had given him his chance to crucify Lattimore. I had no doubt they'd egged him on, but it was obvious the kid had it in for Lattimore in a big way. I had to get to Warren and fast.

I barreled out of the stall like Elliott Ness, straight into the arms of Jeff Phillips, my former counterpart for the *Courier.*

"Well, well, if it isn't Sam Spade," he said, grabbing my elbows to steady me. "Glad to see you've improved your taste in literature since you left the *Times.*"

I looked down and realized I was still clutching the magazine.

"My Son Forced Me Into a Life of Sin" was blazoned across the cover in big red letters.

"Oh, this? I found it in the stall." I tried to crumple it up, but it was too stiff.

"Uh huh." He tapped my chest with his pad. "Well, let me know when you're ready to move up. My kid's got some Superman comics you might like. But now you're a big-shot private eye, got your picture in the paper, you've probably got your very own x-ray glasses. Seen in any good motel rooms lately?"

"Matter of fact, I thought I recognized your wife the other day." I paused before the mirror to straighten my tie before I let him have the punch line. "And thanks for the offer, but when I'm in the mood for fantasy, I'll read the *Courier.*"

I stuffed the magazine in the trash can, hoping like hell it didn't have a mailing label on it, and beat it out of there. Greg's statement was burning a hole in my pocket.

I plunged back into the crowd and fought my way to the courtroom doors just as the bailiff pulled them shut. "I need to get in there."

"Yeah, you and everybody else." He turned his head and sent a stream of tobacco juice into the brass spittoon.

"But I'm with the defense."

"I don't care if you're with the FBI. I got my orders. No standees. Once them seats is filled, that's it."

He tugged his shirt down over his bulging belly and planted his feet like he was putting down a tap root.

I started to argue, but he wasn't listening. His attention had been caught by something over my shoulder.

"Did you say the dee-fense?" He straightened suddenly. "Why, that's different. Hold your horses a minute." He squeezed through the double doors and pulled them shut behind him.

I turned to see what had prompted his sudden change of heart. Lieutenant Owens stood at the back of the crowd. His big Irish potato of a face was expressionless, but his right eyelid slid slowly shut. I gave him a nod as I slipped through the doors the bailiff held open for me.

With his belly leading the way, he bulldozed through the crowd to a bench three rows back from the railing. He pointed out a space about six inches wide next to a hefty lady wielding a crocheting hook. Madame DeFarge with a blue rinse and more rolls than a bakery. She glared at me as I squeezed in. I pretended not to notice, but kept a close eye on that hook.

I craned my neck for a glimpse of the defense table, but there was no sign of Warren or Lattimore. The courtroom, even with its high ceilings and rotating fans, was already heating up from the crush of warm bodies and the morning sun streaming through the enormous, two-story windows. The remodeling was supposed to include air-conditioning, but with typical bureaucratic common sense, some pencil pusher had decided it would be the last thing to be installed.

The crowd parted momentarily. Two rows up to my left, I spotted a young boy in a Madras sport coat in the first row behind the prosecutor's table. He was seated next to a gray-haired woman in a flowered hat; the aunt, I assumed. She gazed straight ahead. Greg sat with his head bowed, cracking his knuckles. His dark crewcut looked like he'd just come from the barber shop. Without the coat and tie, he could have been any thirteen-year-old kid.

Unwelcome memories rushed over me as I studied him, a boy with a child's face and the carefully cultivated mannerisms of a man. For a few agonizing moments, I felt what he was feeling, the pain and bewilderment, the agony of being the center of attention when all he wanted was to crawl in a hole with his grief. I even knew his secret shame—that his first thought and constant worry was what would happen to him now that his mother was dead. I ached to tell him all orphaned children feel that way, but I knew that even if I could reach out to him, he wouldn't allow it. Too much time had passed. He had already begun building the walls that would contain his grief and keep out the rest of the world.

Mike Higgins from the D.A.'s office sat scribbling notes at the prosecution table while his boss hovered over him. King stood in front of the table with his hands in his pockets, trying to look important and nonchalant at the same time. His suit, an unfortunate shade of tan, only heightened his resemblance to Mr. Ed. As the minutes ticked by with no sign of Lattimore or Warren, I expected him to start pawing the ground.

At the last minute, they slipped in through a door behind the witness stand, unnoticed by most of the crowd. Warren was relaxed, smiling and nodding to acquaintances as though his presence was nothing more than a routine formality, a minor inconvenience. The wily old fox had not only saved Lattimore from running the gauntlet outside, he'd succeeded in making King look like an eager rookie.

By contrast, Lattimore's face could have been carved from marble. He took his seat quickly, turning his back on the spectators, most of whom hadn't registered his presence yet.

I shielded my notebook with my hand and scrawled a hasty note. I didn't dare try to pass Warren the statement in open court, but I could at least warn him. I grabbed a passing bailiff and asked him to hand the note to Warren. He read it and turned to look for me in the crowd. He nodded his thanks and bent to speak to Lattimore, but before he could say more than a few words, the clerk bawled, "All rise!"

We clambered to our feet. While the judge arranged his robes, Warren whispered to Lattimore and shoved a pad in front of him.

The judge banged his gavel. "Bailiffs, get these people into seats or out of the courtroom." People began to clamber over each other for the few remaining seats. The unlucky ones grumbled as they were escorted out. As soon as the doors thudded shut behind them, the judge banged the gavel again to make sure he had everybody's attention.

"This court will come to order. And I do mean order," he added sternly. "I see some crackers and Co'Cola bottles. There'll be none of that in my courtroom. And there'll be no noise or outcry. Any disturbance from anybody but these lawyers and I'll throw you in jail for contempt of court. Any questions? Fine. Mr. King?"

There was a hasty whispered conference at the prosecution's table. With some difficulty, Higgins unfolded his six-foot-four frame. His height was a big asset when he played guard at State, but in the ordinary world, he's like Gulliver in Lilliput. "If it please the court, we'll take up the State versus John Lattimore, case number 7984."

Still smarting from Warren's one-upmanship, King had apparently decided to exhibit a little sangfroid of his own and let Higgins carry the ball.

"All right, let's proceed," said the judge.

"Your Honor," Warren rose. "For the record, we would like to notify the court that I, George Lee Warren, will be representing Mr. Lattimore in this matter."

"So noted. Mr. Higgins, call your first witness."

"The State calls Detective Horace Bennett."

Bennett lumbered up to the stand. His fat, pale face glistened with sweat. He ran a finger under his collar as he took the oath.

Higgins led him through his identification, the call from the prowl car officers who responded to the scene, and, finally, his arrival at the house.

"And what did you find when you arrived?" he asked.

"We found a young boy who told us he was the son of the deceased." Bennett stopped and waited for his next cue.

"What did he tell you?"

"He told us he woke up in the night to . . . to . . ." He licked his lips and looked to King, but there was no help from that direction. "To relieve himself. Said he looked in on his mother in her room and something about her didn't look right, so he went in and tried to wake her. But he couldn't get her to wake up, so he called us."

"Did you examine the deceased?"

"Well, we didn't disturb the body," Bennett said. "We felt for a pulse, but we couldn't find one. We called her name a few times, but she didn't respond. So my partner went out to the car to radio for an ambulance."

"What did you observe about the condition of the deceased?" Higgins asked.

"Objection," Warren rose. "The witness is not competent."

"The witness has been a city detective for ten years," Higgins retorted. "He is certainly competent to describe what he observes at a crime scene."

"Overruled," said the judge. "The witness will confine himself to describing what he observed without drawing any conclusions."

"Thank you, Your Honor," Higgins said. "Mr. Bennett, will you please tell us, in layman's terms, what you observed about the condition of the deceased?"

Bennett looked confused. "Well," he began hesitantly, "the first thing we noticed was the bruises she had on her."

"Can you describe them?"

"Well, there was bruises all up and down the insides of her arms. And she had like a shiner by one eye, a couple bumps and scrapes on her cheek, and her nose looked like it was swole up some."

There was a murmur from the spectators. The judge banged his gavel a few times and glared at them until they subsided.

"What did you do next, Mr. Bennett?" Higgins asked.

"Well, we went out to where the boy was sitting in the living room and told him we thought his mother might be dead. He said he thought so too. My partner sat down and talked with him and tried to find out was there a relative or somebody we could call to come get him, and I looked around while we waited for the ambulance."

"Did you observe anything pertinent at the scene?"

"Well, I found a spot of what looked like dried blood on the floor in the bathroom. And we found a picture on the coffee table."

"A picture?" Higgins turned from his pacing.

"Yes sir. It was a picture of a man."

"Did you recognize the man in the picture?"

"Well, yes sir, I thought I did, but I asked the boy to be sure."

"And what did he say?"

"He said, 'That's my mama's boyfriend. That's John Lattimore.'"

The crowd went into an uproar. The judge had to beat on the gavel for quite a while to get them quieted down again. "Another outburst like that and I'll clear this court," he warned.

"Mr. Bennett," asked Higgins. "When did you first begin to suspect Mrs. Green had not died a natural death?"

I expected Warren to object again, but he merely looked interested.

"Well, sir, when Doc . . . Dr. Winston, the coroner, told us it was murder."

This time the spectators contained themselves, but only just.

"Objection," Warren called calmly as if it were understood.

"Sustained. The purpose of this hearing is to determine whether it was, in fact, murder, Mr. Bennett," the judge told him.

Bennett turned scarlet and glared at Higgins as though he

suspected him of deliberately setting him up.

"I beg your pardon," Higgins said. "I'll redraw the question. Mr. Bennett, at what point did your suspicions begin to focus on Mr. Lattimore?"

"Well, we called him at his office, but his secretary told us he was taking the day off. So we went to his house and asked him did he know Miz Green . . . the deceased. He said he did, he was a 'friend of the fambly.' " He rolled his eyes so the crowd wouldn't miss the irony. "So we asked him would he come down to the station and help us with our inquiries. He said he would come down in a little while and we left."

At the murmur that followed that remark, Higgins quickly moved on.

"What did Mr. Lattimore tell you when you took his statement? Excuse me, his first statement?"

"We asked him when he had last seen the deceased. He said he saw her on Monday and again on Monday night. Said he'd been at her house Monday night and left about eleven and went home to bed. Said he didn't know anything else until the boy—"

"That would be the deceased's son?" Higgins prompted.

"Uh, yeah. Said the boy called him that morning and told him he'd found his mama dead in bed."

"Your Honor, so as to cut down on the confusion, let the record identify the boy referred to, the son of the deceased, as Greg Green," Higgins said.

"Noted."

"Now then, Mr. Bennett, did Greg Green call Mr. Lattimore in your presence?"

"No, sir. I didn't see him make any phone calls while I was there."

"Was he at the house the whole time you were there?"

"No, sir. He give us a name and phone number of his aunt. She arrived 'bout a half hour after we called her and packed him some clothes and got him outta there before they drug . . . before they removed the body."

"Now, I believe Mr. Lattimore later made a second statement, is that correct?" Higgins asked.

"Yes sir."

"And was that statement different from his first statement?"

"You might could say that." Bennett reared back in his seat and grinned at the crowd. Most grinned back at him.

"Could you please give us the gist of Mr. Lattimore's second statement?" Higgins asked.

"The wha . . . ?"

"Could you tell us, briefly, what he said in his second statement?"

"Oh. Yeah. Well, we didn't have any cause to hold him after we talked to him the first time, so we thanked him and let him go. A couple hours later, Doc . . . Dr. Winston, notified us that the deceased had died from foul play. So we called the boy's aunt and asked her to bring him back down to the station so we could ask him some more questions.

"She did and we told him what the coroner had said. That she didn't die from natural causes, but somebody killed her. So that's when he told us what really happened and we went and got Mr. Lattimore and brought him back down to the station to answer some more questions."

He paused to catch his breath. I realized the rest of us were holding ours so as not to miss a word.

"As soon as he came in, he saw the Green boy and he turned real white. I thought he was gonna pass out."

"Mr. Lattimore turned pale?"

"That's right."

"Did Greg say anything to him?"

"No. He just looked at him as he went by."

"I see. What did Mr. Lattimore have to say then?"

"Well, the only thing he changed was he told us that he'd been at Miz Green's house on Monday night like he told us the first time, but he didn't leave and go home at eleven. Said the both of them—"

"He and Mrs. Green?"

"Yes sir. He and Miz Green left the house together around eleven and went out to a cabin he has down on the river. He admitted to us they argued on the way. He said they stayed at the cabin for a while, then Miz Green decided she wanted to spend the night at the cabin. But he didn't want to stay, so he left her there and went home and went to bed."

He paused again to wipe his face with a handkerchief. Beside me, Madame DeFarge whipped out a cardboard fan bearing a picture of Jesus and began working up a sweat with it. I leaned forward and tried to discreetly peel my damp shirt from my back.

"He said he woke up in the night and got to worrying about her out there by herself," Bennett continued. "So he dressed and drove back out and found her dead on the floor."

"I'll just bet," my seatmate whispered in a voice you could've heard clear out at the river. The judge glared in our direction.

"What did he tell you he did next?"

"He said he called her house and talked to the boy. He told him his mama had died and he was gonna bring her home. Then he drug her out to his car and put her in the back seat."

"What did he do when he had the body in his car?"

"He said he drove to her house, Miz Green's, and drove up to the back door and carried her in the house."

"Did he say if anybody helped him carry the body into the house?"

"No sir."

"Did he say which room in the house he carried the body to?"

"No sir."

"Did he say whether he just laid her in bed or he undressed her and put her to bed?" A note of desperation was creeping into Higgins's voice. He dared a glance at King but got no help there.

"He didn't say, just said he put her to bed."

"Did he state what he did then?"

"He said he told the boy, Greg, to call the police and then he left and went home."

"Lord have mercy," whispered Madame DeFarge in spite of herself.

Higgins let the silence hang for a minute. "Did you ask him why he did not take Mrs. Green to a hospital for medical treatment or contact the police himself?"

"Yes sir."

"What did he say?"

"He said that on account of he was a prominent person, he didn't want to get mixed up in it."

There was no way Higgins could top that shining moment. "The State has no further questions for this witness," he said.

"Mr. Warren?"

"Thank you, Your Honor." Warren rose and approached the bench. I craned my neck. Lattimore had his head down, still writing.

"Mr. Bennett." Warren gave the fat detective a respectful nod. Bennett looked startled. "Mr. Higgins tells us you have been a detective for ten years. Is that correct?"

"It sure is," Bennett replied defensively. "Ten years this October."

"Thank you. And in those ten years, how many homicide scenes would you estimate you have seen?"

Bennett cut his eyes toward King's table.

"Mr. Bennett?"

133

"Well, that'd be hard to say."

"Well, just an estimate. Ten? Twelve? A hundred?"

"Not that many." His voice was low.

"I'm sorry?"

"I said, not that many."

"Not how many? Ten? Or a hundred?"

"Three." Bennett shifted in his chair again.

"Thank you. And during those ten years have you had any special training in pathology?"

"Huh?"

"Pathology." Warren rephrased the question. "Have you had any training in observing or assessing bodies?"

"Oh. Well, they taught us how to check to see if they're dead." Bennett cut his eyes at King again.

"I see. So you couldn't really say how recent or severe the bruises you observed might be?"

"Uh, no. I guess not."

"Thank you. Now you say that Mr. Lattimore told you he saw Mrs. Green on Sunday and again on Monday night. Is that correct?" He turned to await Bennett's answer.

"That's right."

"Did he mention whether he saw Mrs. Green at any time on Sunday?"

Bennett wasn't sure how to field that one. He opted for caution. "No."

"No, he didn't mention it, or no, he didn't see her?" Warren prompted.

"He . . . he mentioned that he didn't see her," Bennett replied.

"Did he explain why he didn't see her?"

"He said he went to her house early Sunday evening but she wasn't home."

"Was anyone at home?"

"He told us that he spoke to the deceased's son at the house."

"Did he tell you the content of that conversation?"

"He did. He said he asked the boy where his mother was, but he didn't know."

"Did Mr. Lattimore tell you what he did then?"

"Yes sir. He went looking for her. Said he went to her office and some friends' houses and some other places she liked to go, but he couldn't find her anywhere."

"Did he explain why he was so anxious to determine her whereabouts?"

"He said he was concerned about her." Bennett smirked in spite of himself.

Warren had been standing with his hand on the railing of the witness box. At Bennett's words, he moved away. It was a simple, but eloquent gesture. Even Bennett caught the intent and flushed.

"Did Mr. Lattimore say why he was so concerned about her?" Warren asked. I realized that by moving away, he'd also forced Bennett to raise his voice so that his answer came loud and clear all the way to the back rows and the Negroes up in the balcony.

"He said the deceased had a drinking problem and he was afraid she'd had a accident."

Warren paused for a fraction of a second to let that sink in. The crowd didn't let him down. They kept quiet under the judge's stern eye, but there was plenty of shifting and shuffling and raised eyebrows. I spotted Kent in a corner scribbling furiously in his notebook while trying to blend into the woodwork.

"What did Mr. Lattimore tell you he did then?"

"He said he went into the house and called the hospitals to see if they had anybody who sounded like her."

"Someone who matched the description of the deceased?"

"That's what he said."

"And did they?"

"No." As Bennett's replies became shorter and more truculent, Warren grew more polite. He leaned forward attentively to catch Bennett's answers as if hanging on every word and gave a gratified nod after each response. The result was to make Bennett very nervous.

"Did Mr. Lattimore mention whether the deceased's son was present during this time?"

"No. He said he sent him outside while he called."

"Thank you. And what did Mr. Lattimore tell you he did next?"

"On Sunday or Monday?" Bennett asked.

"After he called the hospitals on Sunday night."

"He left and went home."

"He went straight home?"

"Well, we didn't ask him if he stopped anywhere."

"I beg your pardon. What I meant to ascertain was whether he went home and left the boy alone in the house."

"Objection." At a nudge from King, Higgins was on his feet. "Mr. Warren is wandering down the trail with questions that have nothing to do with the matter at hand."

"Are you going somewhere with this, Mr. Warren?" the judge asked.

"I most certainly hope so, Your Honor," Warren replied. It earned him a few snickers.

"Then let's get there, shall we? Answer the question, please, Mr. Bennett."

"He said he arranged for the boy to spend the night with some friends," Bennett said. Then he added just loud enough to be heard on front rows, "Least that's what it said in the newspapers."

I expected Warren to call him on it or have the judge do it, but he seemed content to let it hang in the air. As the silence grew longer, Bennett realized he'd gone too far. He slowly turned the color of one of my grandmother's prize tomatoes.

Having scored enough points for the moment, Warren strolled over to the defense table, picked up his legal pad and spent the next ten minutes leading Bennett through Delores's return home on Monday.

"Did Mr. Lattimore indicate whether Mrs. Green offered any explanation for her injuries?"

"No sir."

"He didn't indicate whether she was able to explain the injuries?"

"He said"—Bennett consulted his notebook again—"she was in no fit shape to explain anything."

"Thank you for clearing that up," Warren inclined his head. "I have just a few more questions. In your capacity as an investigating officer on this case, did you have any occasion to visit Mr. Lattimore's cabin?"

"I did."

"How would you characterize the cabin, Mr. Bennett?"

"Characterize it?"

"Would you describe it as luxurious, for example?"

"No, I wouldn't say that."

"Comfortable?"

Bennett squirmed. He dug around in his ear and rubbed his face till I thought his nose would fall off. Warren waited.

"Rustic!" Bennett finally said proudly. He even forgot himself so far as to beam at Warren. "I'd have to say it was kinda rustic."

"Excellent. That gives us a very clear picture," Warren congratulated him. "Can you recall, Mr. Bennett, how do you reach this cabin from the highway?"

"Well, there's a dirt road runs about a quarter of a mile from the road to the cabin."

"And is there a path from the dirt road to the door of the cabin?"

"It looks like there might've been at one time, but it's mostly overgrown now."

"So it could be somewhat hazardous to navigate in the dark?" Warren asked.

Bennett looked wary. "I s'pose it could be."

"One last question, Mr. Bennett. Do you recall whether there are steps leading to the door of the cabin?"

"Yes."

"What type of steps are they?"

"Well, uh, to the best of my recollection, there are three, or maybe four, steps at the bottom, of concrete block, the flat kind, and then maybe another three made of boards."

"Thank you, Mr. Bennett. You've been most helpful."

Bennett scowled.

"The State calls Dr. Henry Winston," Higgins extricated himself from under the desk again.

The crowd sat up and prepared to enjoy themselves. Madame DeFarge dug an elbow in her neighbor's ribs.

Doc prides himself on being a "character." He claims to speak several languages and he's always rhapsodizing about Mozart and Haydn. "There's nothing like some Courvoisier, a good Havana, and a little Mozart to get the stink out of your nostrils after digging around in somebody's insides" is one of his favorite sayings.

His audience usually consists of cops who are doing good not to run out of grocery money before they run out of month, but they don't seem to resent it. In fact, one of the favorite pastimes down at the station is swapping Doc stories. They're proud of having a real doctor for coroner. It's an elected position and there aren't usually many volunteers. Most towns make do with the local undertaker. There's even one small town up in the mountains where the coroner is the fry cook at the local diner.

But Doc is unique in that he's not only a real doctor but a certified pathologist, as he had just finished telling Higgins.

"How long have you been the county coroner, Dr. Winston?"

"Going on for twenty years now," he replied.

"Do I hear a stipulation that Dr. Winston is an expert pathologist?" beseeched the judge.

"We so stipulate," Warren replied.

"Let the record so indicate," the judge said and waved at Higgins to get on with the matter at hand.

"Dr. Winston, in your capacity as coroner of this county and as a physician, on the fourth of July, 1961, did you make an examination and autopsy of one Delores Green?"

"I did."

"Where did you view the body?"

"At Jergen's Funeral Home."

"Would you tell the court what you found on arriving at Jergens' Funeral Home in reference to Delores Green?"

Doc settled back a little in his seat and prepared to perform. "I found the body of a normally developed white female who appeared to be between thirty-five and forty-five years of age. I found multiple bruises on her body."

"What do you mean by multiple, Doctor?"

"I estimate there were well over one hundred bruises on her body at the time I examined it." Madame DeFarge and her companion exchanged a satisfied glance.

"And on what portion of the body were these wounds?"

"They extended from the scalp to her feet."

There was another murmur from the crowd, but the judge was too interested to caution them.

"Could you describe the wounds to the court, please?"

"The majority of the wounds were small," Doc replied. "There were several fairly large wounds. The largest was on the left knee."

"What color were the wounds, Doctor?"

"They were mottled; some were light and some were dark."

"Did you find any other wounds on the lower portion of the body?"

"I did."

"Describe them, if you will."

"The upper and lower thighs, the upper and lower legs, and the anterior surface of her feet."

"What about the area of the vagina?" Higgins did his best to sound matter-of-fact, but a dull red crept up the back of his neck. I almost felt sorry for him.

"There were a number of bruises around the vagina."

That brought whispers from the women in the crowd.

"What about her buttocks?"

"There were bruises on the buttocks."

"You mentioned earlier finding bruises on the head. Could you describe the wounds you found on the head, please?"

"The deceased was a dark-headed woman and the wounds did not show up at first on external examination, but when I reflected the scalp—"

"Excuse me, Doctor, when you say 'reflected the scalp' . . . ?"

Doc bestowed a smile, that just missed patronizing, on the crowd. "When I was performing the autopsy to remove the brain, I peeled the scalp and laid it forward over the face, and found some fifteen to twenty bruises in the tissue beneath the scalp," he explained.

There was an expectant pause. I leaned forward to see King whispering to Higgins.

"Mr. Higgins?" the judge prompted.

He straightened up hastily. "I beg your pardon, Your Honor. Dr. Winston, do you have an opinion, satisfactory to yourself, as to whether or not the deceased had a concussion of the brain?"

I couldn't believe it. Were they throwing in the towel? Why

hadn't Hilda told me?

"That is a definite possibility," Doc replied easily. Too easily.

"Did you examine the tissues from the neck area of the body?" Higgins asked.

"I did."

"What did your examination reveal?"

"There were hemorrhages in the subcutaneous tissue, that is, the tissue underlying the skin." He threw that out, graciously. "At the base of the brain, I found what is commonly called a whiplash injury of minor type."

Had he changed his tune about the cause of death or was he just covering himself in case of an appeal? Higgins didn't look concerned, which meant the answer didn't surprise him. I sneaked a glance at Warren, but he was too experienced a hand to look anything but interested.

"Could you describe what you mean by whiplash injury, Doctor?"

"By whiplash, I mean that one of the vertebrae in the neck had crossed over the other one to produce some trauma or injury to the spinal cord."

"Did you observe any fracture of the vertebra?"

"I did not."

Higgins led him through a few more technical details, more to establish credibility than anything else. I let my eyes and my attention drift for a minute or two. My attention was jerked back when Higgins produced his finale.

"Dr. Winston, based on your examination, your observations, your professional experience"—he spun it out, building the suspense—"your autopsy and your findings from your examination, do you have an opinion, satisfactory to yourself, as to the cause of death of Delores Green?"

"I do."

"What is your opinion, Doctor?"

"I find that the deceased died as a result of injuries multiple and extreme." The syllables rolled off his tongue.

"Do you have an opinion, satisfactory to yourself, as to whether or not the injuries that you observed were caused by external violence?"

"Objection," Warren called.

"Sustained. Rephrase the question, Mr. Higgins."

"Yes sir. Dr. Winston, based upon your examination and autopsy, do you have an opinion, satisfactory to yourself, as to whether or not the injuries you observed were of sufficient severity to have caused shock resulting in the death of Delores Green?"

"Object to leading," Warren said.

"Sustained."

Higgins gave up and went for the question that would get him the answer he wanted. "What is that opinion, Doctor?"

"The injuries I observed from external examination of the body were sufficient to have caused her death by shock."

"Thank you, Doctor." Higgins sank down into his seat.

Warren timed it nicely, giving us just enough time to catch our breath before he rose. He gave an almost imperceptible bow in Doc's direction, the ritual acknowledgment of one opponent to another. Doc stroked his silver mustache and returned the salute with a slight nod.

Warren made the first feint. "Dr. Winston, when did you say you first saw the body of the deceased?"

"Approximately nine a.m. on the morning of July the fourth."

"Do you have an opinion, satisfactory to yourself, how long that body had been dead?"

"I do not."

"I believe you stated the deceased was a normally developed white female?"

"That is correct."

"And that you observed multiple bruises on her body?"

"That is correct."

"Now Dr. Winston, from your examination of the deceased, did you arrive at an opinion as to whether some of those bruises were old and some of them were new?"

"I could not."

"At the time you conducted your examination of the body, had it been embalmed?"

"It had."

"That is to say, the blood had been removed from the body?"

"That is correct."

"Now, Doctor, when you examine a body for postmortem purposes, what is the effect of an examination conducted after the blood has been removed?"

Beside me, Madame DeFarge gave a delighted shudder that shook the bench.

"Very little if one is trained in that type of investigation."

"I'm sorry?"

"There is little change."

"When you refer to wounds that you found on the body, do you include in that term, the word 'bruises'?"

"Yes, bruises."

"Do you also include breaks in the skin, abrasions?"

"Yes."

"Did you find any wounds, that is, bruises, on the body of the deceased that also included abrasions?"

"There were a few such areas on the upper and lower extremities."

"Were these piercing-type wounds, or abrasions?"

"They were abrasions."

"That is to say, a friction-type break in the skin?"

"I could not say, really, whether they were caused by friction, only by some external force."

"How deep were these wounds or abrasions that you observed?"

"They were all superficial."

"So none of these wounds or bruises that you saw was sufficient to have caused death?"

"No."

"Dr. Winston, did you explore any of these bruises by opening them up?"

"I made a few small incisions."

"How many of the bruises did you explore?"

"Approximately fifteen or twenty."

"Now the bruises that you found, Doctor . . . are bruises caused by leaking of blood out of the tissue surrounding the circulatory system?"

I saw how Warren had spent his time yesterday.

"That is correct."

"When you opened up these bruises with your instruments, did you take any tissue from them?"

"I did not."

"So you opened several of the bruised areas with your instruments but you did not take any tissue from them?"

"That is correct."

"Did you know where the body had been, Doctor? Did you know anything about the route it had traveled before you saw it on the examining table in the mortuary?"

"I did not."

"You are aware, now, however, are you not, Doctor, that the body was taken from the place where she died, to her home, then from her home to the hospital where it was pronounced dead, and from the hospital to the mortuary?"

"Object to his understanding." I'd begun to think Higgins and King had nodded off. "The only way he could know any of that information would be from hearsay," Higgins complained.

"Sustained."

"I'll withdraw the question." Warren began to pace in front of the stand, his eyes cast down as though in deep thought. Doc watched him with a sardonic smile.

"With reference to the neck injuries that you described as a whiplash injury, that injury could have occurred in transporting the body after death, could it not?"

"Object!"

"Overruled."

"That is true," Doc conceded.

"In other words, in moving the body of Mrs. Green from place to place, with the head uncontrolled, you could sustain a whiplash injury?"

"Of the type I found, which was minor."

Warren conceded the point with a small nod before getting down to serious business. "Dr. Winston, will a dead body bruise after death?"

"It will."

"And isn't it true that, alive or dead, some people are more susceptible to bruising than others?"

"Yes, that's true."

"Had you ever had occasion to examine the deceased before you performed the autopsy?"

"I had not."

"So you are not familiar with the ease with which she would have bruised?"

"I am not."

"You are, however, familiar with the term lividity, are you not?"

"I believe I've heard of it once or twice." The spectators rewarded him with a few titters.

"What is lividity, Doctor?"

"It is a settling of the blood to the dependent portion of the body after death that causes a fresh pigment discoloration, which later turns to a light purple, and finally, almost a black discoloration."

"In plain English, then, the blood runs downhill to whatever part of the body is lowest and pools there?"

"Something like that."

"And causes the skin to turn dark, either purple or black, I believe you said, so that it resembles a bruise?"

"That's more or less correct."

"And you stated that at the time you examined this body, the blood had been removed from it?"

Doc retreated into pedantry. "It is impossible to remove all blood during the embalming process. Enough is removed to allow the mortician to introduce the embalming fluid, but it's impossible to remove every drop of blood from a dead body."

"Could any of the wounds or bruises you saw be attributed to lividity?"

Doc relaxed. "No," he stated positively.

"Dr. Winston, what did you do with the blood that you removed from Delores Green's body?" Warren asked, as if suddenly struck by the thought.

Touché. Doc stiffened ever so slightly.

"The blood was actually removed by the mortician whom I had trained to do so," he answered. "He handed it to me and I sealed it. I personally carried it, under seal, to my laboratory, where it remained until I released it to a city detective."

"Was it your intention to have an examination made of the blood?"

There was a block of ice in my gut. What if Hilda was wrong?

Doc hesitated for a fraction of a second, just long enough to reassure me. "It was."

146

"Do you know whether this examination has been conducted?"

"I have not received a report." Doc carefully kept his eyes forward, away from the prosecutor's table.

"Dr. Winston, have you signed a death certificate in relation to the death of Mrs. Green?" Warren asked suddenly.

"I have not." Doc responded easily, but again, he held himself very still.

"Why have you not, Doctor?" Warren asked mildly.

"I am waiting for the final blood report."

"When you receive the final blood report, it will assist you in reaching a conclusion as to the cause of death for Mrs. Green, is that correct?"

Doc hesitated. "That is correct."

"But when asked by the assistant district attorney just a few moments ago, you seemed very certain about the cause of death. Are we to understand, then, Dr. Winston, that your investigation into the cause of death for Mrs. Green and your opinion as to the cause of death are inconclusive at this time? Or have you revised your opinion in the last quarter hour?"

There was a heavy silence. "If the blood had not been obtained for analysis, the death certificate would have been signed by now. I am awaiting the result of the blood test," Doc replied. He shifted in his chair and fingered his mustache again.

"Why are you awaiting the result of the blood test, Doctor?" Warren pressed.

"It may be helpful in determining the degree of shock and contributory factors."

"It might also change your opinion, too, mightn't it, Doctor?" Warren insisted.

"It could."

"Doctor, during the autopsy, did you take tissue from any other portions of the body?"

"I did."

"What portion?"

"The brain, the spinal cord, the lungs, the liver, the kidneys, and other organs in the body."

Warren suddenly shifted tack. "At this time, at this very moment, then, your investigation into the cause of death is inconclusive, is it?"

"I have not signed the death certificate."

"Answer the question please, Doctor," the judge instructed.

"I have found enough—"

"Just answer the question, please Doctor," the judge interrupted again.

"Yes. The investigation is inconclusive in that I have not received the blood report." Doc maintained his urbanity with an effort. "But I have found enough to be satisfied that these injuries could well be the cause of her death. The reason I'm waiting on the blood report is to be a little more elaborate in writing my report and signing the death certificate." Butter wouldn't have melted in his mouth.

"The real reason you're waiting for the blood test is to rule out other causes, isn't that correct, Doctor?" Warren asked.

"Not other causes, corroborating causes."

"I beg your pardon?"

"In other words, if this woman had a high blood alcohol or high barbiturate situation, that would be an aggravating factor."

The spectators exchanged glances. They'd been left behind in this verbal swordplay but they scented blood.

"Could a high blood alcohol or barbiturate level be sufficient in itself to have caused death?" Warren asked.

"It could be."

"And would that be shown by blood test?"

"I don't know. I have no report."

"But if that condition existed, it could be demonstrated by a blood test?" Warren persisted.

"Certainly."

Warren's voice was quiet, but it carried clearly to the back of the courtroom. "And if the blood contained a sufficient quantity of blood alcohol or barbiturate to be lethal, you would change your opinion as to the cause of death, would you not?"

"She's dead, okay? She's dead, dammit. Just stop it!" Greg's voice rang through the courtroom. He was on his feet. He pounded his fists on the railing, his face red and contorted. His aunt sprang up and put her arms around his shoulders and tried to ease him back into his seat. He shook her off and sat down, his face in hands.

Warren turned. His face was inscrutable, but I was close enough to see his eyes. They were the saddest eyes I've ever seen. King was on his feet but Warren beat him to the punch.

"Your Honor, may we request a recess?"

CHAPTER 11

King and Higgins hustled Greg out of the courtroom. The aunt trailed behind clucking like a chicken. Warren and Lattimore disappeared through the same door they'd come in. The rest of us stayed put. Nobody wanted to risk losing their seat.

The minutes ticked by—ten minutes, twenty, a half hour—still nobody moved. Beside me, Madame DeFarge's fan struggled to keep pace with her jaw. ". . . lived in that big house on Magnolia," she nattered to her companion.

"Which one?"

"The big white one with the green shutters."

"The one with the nasturtiums?"

"No, the other one."

"Isn't that where old Miz Barrett lived?"

Madame DeFarge snorted. "You're getting senile, Lillian. Miz Barrett lived at the other end of Magnolia. Her house backed up to the Latham's."

"It did not. The Lathams lived on the corner."

"They most certainly did not. I went to school with Betty Latham all the way through eighth grade and I know for a fact . . ."

Much more of that and I'd have been on trial for murder, but mercifully, the clerk came in and called us back to order. Madame DeFarge dropped her crochet hook as she struggled to her feet. Resisting the urge to poke her with it to see if she'd deflate, I handed it to her politely. She glared at me. So much for lost opportunities.

The prosecution team came back in first. They clustered protectively around Greg, who was pale and red-eyed but composed. Warren and Lattimore followed a minute later.

"Now then, where were we?" the judge asked as he took his seat. The clerk murmured in his ear. "That's right, I believe Dr. Winston was in the middle of his testimony." He looked to the court reporter for confirmation, but Warren rose.

"I have no further questions for Dr. Winston."

"So be it. Mr. Higgins?" The judge raised his shaggy eyebrows and peered over his glasses at the prosecution's table. "You may call your next witness."

"The State calls Greg Green, Your Honor."

The courtroom was hushed as Greg took the stand. He repeated the oath in a voice that cracked.

Higgins led him gently through the preliminaries—name, age, address.

"How long have you known John Lattimore?"

"Since I was a baby, I don't know. I don't remember. He's just always been around." Greg's voice was barely audible. He stared at the railing in front of him.

"So Mr. Lattimore is really the only father you've ever known?"

"No."

"I beg your pardon?"

"My father's dead." Greg raised his head and looked out at the crowd for the first time as if defying anyone to disagree with him.

"But he's been around all your life, you say?"

"Yeah."

"What was your relationship like?"

Greg shifted in his chair. "Well, he'd come around all the time."

"What do you mean by 'all the time'?"

"Well, whenever he felt like it. Any time of the day or night, he just came and went like he pleased."

"Did your mother object?"

"I don't know. I don't guess so."

"But you did?"

Greg shrugged and didn't answer.

"I'm sorry, Greg, the court reporter must have an answer for the record."

"I don't know. I was just a kid."

"Would you say your relationship with Mr. Lattimore was cordial?"

"I don't know what you mean."

"Well, was it friendly?"

"We got along okay sometimes."

"Did you argue?"

Greg hunched his shoulders and shifted in his seat. "Sometimes."

"What did you argue about?"

"Just different stuff. He'd boss me around, tell me what to do. Sometimes he'd make fun of my friends or stuff like that."

"Did he tell your mother what to do?"

Greg hesitated. "Yeah. Kinda. Well, not really. She wouldn't let him. But if he didn't like something, he'd just say real snotty things."

"What kind of things?"

"Well, like if Mom was talking about somebody at work or about going somewhere with one of her friends he didn't like, he'd say sarcastic things about them or he'd make fun of the restaurant or the movie. Like, if he didn't like it, nobody should think it was any good. He'd make fun of it. Like, 'Everybody knows that place is no good.' Like that."

"Did they argue?"

"Sometimes."

"Did the arguments ever get violent?"

"What?"

"Did they shout at each other? Throw things?"

"Objection!" Warren called. "Mr. Higgins is leading the witness."

Higgins appealed to the judge. "Under the circumstances, Your Honor, I don't think it could be called leading."

"I'll allow a certain latitude under the circumstances," the judge ruled.

"I never saw them throw things."

"Did you hear them shout at each other, Greg?" Higgins asked.

"Sort of. Sometimes they would raise their voices. But if they were mad, they'd just get real sarcastic—you know, just saying it real mean."

"Did Mr. Lattimore ever strike you, Greg?"

"Yeah. Yes." Every eye in the place bored into the back of Lattimore's head.

"More than once?"

"Yes."

"Did he strike you with his hand?"

"No. With a switch."

"How old were you at the time?"

"The last time?"

"Yes."

"Last summer."

Warren was on his feet again. "Objection. Mr. Lattimore is not accused of harming this young man. This is nothing more than a fishing expedition to discredit Mr. Lattimore."

So, why, I wondered, had he allowed the question at all?

"He has a point, Mr. Higgins. Do you?"

"I'm merely trying to determine the relationship between this boy and Mr. Lattimore and the tenor of the household."

"I think we have the picture. Let's move on."

"Yes, sir." Higgins turned back to Greg. "Greg, did Mr. Lattimore ever bring liquor to the house?"

Greg shrugged. "Sure, all the time."

"Did he offer liquor to your mother?"

"Sometimes."

"Did you see Mr. Lattimore drink this liquor?"

"Yes."

"Did your mother drink with him?"

Greg hesitated again and finally opted for noncommittal. "Sometimes."

"Did he, did Mr. Lattimore encourage your mother to drink with him?"

"He . . ." Greg struggled to make his meaning clear. "He would ask her if she wanted one, but—"

"Thank you, Greg." Higgins cut him off and changed course. "Now, Greg." He paused to assemble his features into his most sincere expression. "I'm going to ask you about the night your mother died. I'm sorry to have to ask you these questions, but you understand that it's important we establish what happened that night?"

"Yes." Greg stared at his feet.

"Now, on the night your mother died, July the fourth, when did you see her last?"

"About five-thirty."

"Five-thirty in the afternoon?"

"Where were you after that time?"

"I went to a friend's house. I—"

But Higgins cut him off again. "Now, let me ask you to back up to Monday, the day before your mother died, for a minute. When you saw your mother that morning—"

"Monday?"

"That's right. On Monday morning. Now you told police she had some bumps and bruises?"

"Yeah, she looked—"

"And I believe you stated to the police that shortly after she arrived home that Monday morning, Mr. Lattimore called?"

"Yeah. He asked if she was home. I told him she was and he came over."

"And you were there when he arrived?"

"Yeah."

"How did he seem?"

"I don't understand."

"Was he angry? Concerned?"

"He was . . . um, he was aggravated."

"Aggravated?"

"Yeah."

"What did he do?"

"He said something like, 'You've really outdone yourself this time, Delores.' And he started asking her where she'd been. But she didn't tell him and he started getting mad. But then he turned around and saw me and Em—"

"Em?"

"My friend, Em Rosinski. He lives across the street."

"Go on."

"Well, he turned around and saw us and he told us to go outside. I didn't want to go, but he yelled at us and told us to go outside, so we went."

"Did you hear any more of his conversation with your mother?"

"I heard the door to her room slam and I could hear him yelling." His voice quivered. He looked like he was going to cry again.

Higgins gave him a minute to pull himself together. Greg took a deep breath and visibly brought himself back under control. I swallowed a lump in my own throat the size of a cantaloupe.

"Did you see your mother again that day?"

"Umm, just a little bit. She stayed in bed most of the day. I went over to my friend's house and when I got home, she was sitting in the living room watching TV. She said goodnight and I went to bed."

"How did she look then?"

"I couldn't really see all that good. She had the lights off except for the TV."

"Did you see her the next morning?"

"Yeah. She was in the kitchen when I got up."

"How did she look then?"

"I don't understand what you mean."

"Did her bruises . . . did she look better or worse than she did when she came home Monday morning?"

"Uh . . ." Greg rubbed his face hard. "She looked worse. Her nose—"

"Thank you, Greg. Now I'd like to return to the events of the third, excuse me, actually the morning of the fourth, when Mr. Lattimore brought your mother home. What time was it when you were awakened?"

"About two-thirty, I think."

"Would you tell us, please, what happened?"

Greg took another deep breath. I realized I was holding mine.

"I was asleep. And the phone rang. It was him."

"Mr. Lattimore?"

"Yes. He told me . . . he said my mother was dead."

"Go on, Greg," Higgins said gently.

As Greg related the grisly events of that night, I purposefully detached myself and scanned the courtroom, gauging the effect of his words. Across the aisle, a woman wept quietly, gloved fingers pressed to her lips to forestall a sob, but for the most part, the room was utterly silent. The crowd was frozen, hardly daring to breathe. If Jesus Christ and all his disciples had suddenly materialized behind the judge's bench, no one would have taken any notice. I forced myself to tune in again, listening carefully for any discrepancies between Greg's version and Lattimore's. The facts were essentially the same, but there was something about hearing the vivid details from this young boy that invested them with macabre horror. In spite of that, Greg's version didn't differ substantially until he came to the end.

". . . I asked him why we had to do that, put her in pajamas and all, and he said so there wouldn't be any talk."

"Is that all he said, Greg?"

"He said, 'Stick by me on this, Greg, or I'll take care of you.' "

My stomach did a slow roll and came to rest somewhere around my Adam's apple. I caught Madame DeFarge watching me from the corner of her eye and realized I was gulping great, slow draughts of air in an effort to ease the tightness in my chest. My fists were clenched, my whole body ached with tension. God only knows what my face looked like. To reassure her, I gave her a wide and totally inappropriate smile, which probably only made me look that much more like a lunatic. She edged closer to her companion. The spectators could no longer contain themselves. But the crowd subsided quickly under the judge's gavel, rather than miss a word.

"And so you helped him?"

"Yes."

"And after you helped him undress your mother," Higgins paused ever so slightly to let that sink in, "what did Mr. Lattimore do?"

"He told me to call the police and tell them that I woke up in the night and found her dead, asleep."

"And you did that?"

"Yes."

"And then what did Mr. Lattimore do, Greg?"

"He left."

"He left you alone in the house?"

"Well . . . except for my mom."

Higgins surveyed the crowd, then, deliberately, turned his gaze on Lattimore. "I have no further questions, Your Honor."

It was after noon. I thought Warren or the judge might call for a lunch recess, but Warren dived straight in.

"I, too, am sorry to have to ask you to relive these painful memories, Greg, but I'm sure you're old enough to understand that a man's life is at stake here, so it's important that we have all the information."

Greg didn't answer, but Warren didn't seem to expect one. He proceeded, gently but inexorably, to repair the damage Higgins had done.

"Do you have a job this summer, Greg?"

"I have a paper route and sometimes I work at a drugstore."

"How do you deliver your papers?"

"On my bike."

"And how do you get to your job at the drugstore?"

"Sometimes my friend's mom takes us."

"And the other times?"

"Sometimes he would take us."

"He being Mr. Lattimore?"

"Yes."

"Did you work at the drugstore on the Friday afternoon before your mother died?"

"Uh, no."

"What did you do that afternoon, Greg?"

"Friday afternoon?"

"That's right."

"Um, I don't . . . I'm not sure."

"Were you up early?"

"I don't remember."

"Were you awake when your mother left for work?"

"No."

"Were you up by, say, ten o'clock?"

"I think so."

"Did Mr. Lattimore come by the house that afternoon, Greg?"

"Um . . . yes. He brought my mother home."

"Did he stay at the house for a while?"

"Yes."

"Did the two of you work in the garden that afternoon, Greg?"

Greg was puzzled and visibly wary. "Yes."

"How long would you say the two of you worked in the garden, Greg?"

"About two hours, maybe."

"And did you argue during that time?"

"About what?"

"Anything. Did you argue or disagree about anything during the two hours you worked together in the garden?"

"No."

"I see. So there were times when you got along quite well with Mr. Lattimore?"

"Sometimes."

"Now, Greg, you stated that Mr. Lattimore struck you with a switch as recently as last summer, is that correct?"

"Yes."

"Why did he do that, Greg?"

"I . . . I don't remember."

"Did your mother ask him to do that, Greg?"

"I don't know."

"I'm sure you can if you try, Greg. It wasn't that long ago."

"I don't remember."

Warren walked back to the table and consulted his yellow pad. "Did your mother ask Mr. Lattimore to switch you because she discovered you had snuck out of the house one evening to go riding around with one of your friends in a car he 'borrowed' from his parents without their knowledge?"

"I don't remember," Greg insisted stubbornly.

By leaning forward, I could just see King's profile. It looked as though it had been carved from petrified wood.

"But that wasn't, in fact, the last time Mr. Lattimore struck you, was it, Greg?"

A murmur rippled around the edges of the courtroom.

"What do you mean?"

"He whipped you, again, at your mother's request, as recently as this spring, didn't he, Greg?"

"Yes." His voice was barely audible.

"And can you remember why Mr. Lattimore struck you at that time, Greg?"

The aunt leaned forward and tugged on King's sleeve. He shook his head ever so slightly. She settled back in her seat.

"Yes."

"Was it because your mother discovered you had been helping yourself to money from her purse?"

"It was a mistake . . . she forgot she told me to."

The outrage of the unjustly accused rang in his tone. And the sad thing was, she probably had during one of her binges. For a moment, I hated Warren but it was only a fraction of what I felt for Lattimore at that moment. He, of all people, should have been ready to give Greg the benefit of the doubt where Delores's memory was concerned.

"I see." Warren walked back to the table and braced himself on his elbows, his back to the crowd. "You said that your mother and Mr. Lattimore occasionally argued. Did you ever hear them argue about liquor or drinking?"

Greg looked at the prosecution table for help, but none was forthcoming. "Yes."

"What did they argue about?"

"He—"

"Mr. Lattimore?"

"Yes sir. He would yell at her sometimes because he said there was too much gone from the bottle."

"The bottle of liquor?"

"Yes." Greg shifted in his seat. He laced his fingers and braced his elbows on the chair arms.

"Did Mr. Lattimore object because he thought your mother had drunk the liquor from the bottle?"

"Well, it wasn't me!" He sat up straighter in his chair.

Warren looked at him for a moment. His voice was gentle. "No, Greg, I have no doubt of that." He picked up his tablet and consulted it.

"Greg, I'm going to ask you to tax your memory once more. Do you recall the Thursday night before your mother died?"

"Thursday?"

"Yes, that would have been the evening of the twenty-ninth. Do you recall your mother taking some pills that evening?"

"I didn't see her take any."

"Perhaps not. Do you recall, however, that she became ill and you called one of your mother's friends and asked her to come over to your house because you were concerned about your mother's condition?"

Greg shifted in his seat. "She was sick. She didn't feel good."

"And did you call someone to come over because you were alarmed?"

Greg looked at the floor. "Yes."

"And do you recall that your mother's friend came to the house and gave your mother black coffee for several hours?"

"I don't know about any coffee."

"Did you hear your mother make the statement to her friend that evening that she, quote, 'Just wanted to be with her mother'?"

"I didn't hear her say that."

"Is your grandmother living, Greg?"

"No."

Madame DeFarge and her companion exchanged looks.

"Let's move forward now, if we may, Greg, to the evening of Sunday. When did you last see your mother on Sunday, Greg?"

"She left at about three because she said she had some paperwork to do at the office."

"Did she tell you what time she would be home?"

"No."

"And did your mother return home that evening, Greg?"

Greg looked at his feet again. "No."

"Did you see Mr. Lattimore on Sunday evening, Greg?"

"He came over after dinnertime looking for her. I told him where she went."

"And was that the last time you saw him that evening?"

"No. He came back about a hour later."

"Did he tell you where he had been during that hour?"

"He said he'd been looking for my mother."

"What did he do then, Greg?"

"Objection, Your Honor." Higgins half rose from his seat. "We've covered this ground with Detective Bennett."

"Sustained."

"Did Mr. Lattimore leave you alone in the house that night, Greg?" Warren asked.

"Your Honor," Higgins complained.

"Move on, Mr. Warren."

"Yes sir." Warren inclined his head. He locked his hands behind his back and began to stroll gently up and down. "Greg, you stated that Mr. Lattimore said to you, 'Stick by me on this or I'll take care of you?" He laid extra emphasis on the last few words.

"Yes."

"Is it possible you could be mistaken, Greg? Are you sure he didn't say, 'Stick by me on this, I'll take care of you'?"

For the first time, Greg looked directly at Lattimore. There was no sign of the frightened boy anymore.

"No," he said softly "I'm sure. He said if I didn't stick by him, he'd take care of me."

Warren regarded him silently, but Greg's eyes remained fixed on Lattimore.

Lattimore's shoulders slumped. He shook his head and looked down at the table.

"I have no more questions," Warren said.

The judge stirred. "Then we are adjourned for two hours. We will reconvene here at three-thirty. And I want to see counsel in my chambers." He banged the gavel and disappeared in a swirl of robes.

I rose stiffly and joined the throng shuffling toward the doors. I looked up to see Owens standing stolidly by the doors surveying the crowd without expression. Our gaze locked. His face didn't change, but I read a message in his eyes. I just wished like hell I knew what it was.

CHAPTER 12

The sunlight streaming through the blinds made silver wraiths of the steam rising from my coffee. Beside it, the headlines screamed up at me. "Lattimore Bound Over On Murder Charge." I'd already read it twice.

It had been a long night. Every time I closed my eyes, I saw Greg's face. My professional detachment, carefully acquired and nurtured during my years as a reporter, was crumbling. In a dingy interview room at the jail, I had been able to listen to Lattimore's bald recital with nothing stronger than contempt. But hearing Greg relive that night in a packed courtroom had rocked me in ways I hadn't anticipated.

By the small hours of dawn, I'd more or less come to terms with the personal humiliation and professional embarrassment my resignation would cause. As I showered, shaved, and drove to the office, I rehearsed my speech. But somehow I couldn't bring myself to pick up the phone. I sat with my feet on the desk and twisted the cord of the Venetian blinds into a little noose over and over again. The sigh of the pneumatic door at the foot of the stairs floated up to me, followed by footsteps on the stairs, but I still didn't get up.

A peremptory knock. The door opened before I could respond. Warren stood in the doorway. "May I come in?"

"Of course." I stumbled to my feet and indicated the visitor's chair. Warren removed his hat and tossed it on the rack as though he'd done it every day of his life. He carried his own cardboard cup of coffee.

"May I sit down?" he asked. I nodded. He settled himself in the chair and took a sip with a sigh of contentment. "Your coffee's getting cold," he observed mildly.

"Yep."

"Quite a day yesterday." He indicated the newspaper with a nod of his head and took another sip. I didn't answer. "Still, we didn't come out too badly. Thanks to you."

"No." It came out sounding more curt than I intended. "I suppose not."

Silence descended again. The minutes ticked by, but Warren seemed content to sit and sip his coffee in companionable silence. Finally he drained his cup, set it down, pulled an immaculate white handkerchief from his pocket and dabbed at his mustache. "Let's go for a ride."

"A ride?" I was startled enough to drop my feet to the floor. "Where to?"

"There's someone I want you to meet." He took his hat from the rack and held mine out in mute invitation. I settled it on my head and followed him down the stairs.

The maid who answered our ring was the tallest Negro woman I'd ever seen. Indian ancestry was unmistakably stamped on her high cheekbones and hawk-like nose.

"Miz Lattimore's lying down," she informed us. "She ast me to get her up when y'all came. You just make yourselves at home and I tell her y'all are here." She ushered us into a small room at the back of the house.

The foyer was pretty much what I'd expected, thick red carpet and a chandelier straight out of *The Phantom of the Opera*. But the room the maid ushered us into had been furnished by someone with taste. It was warm and comfortable, a woman's room but without frills or fuss. Large windows overlooked the backyard and let in warm sunshine that picked out the colors in the flowered chintz slipcovers and highlighted the gleam of old, polished wood. A table under the window was covered with photos. A wedding portrait from the Gay Nineties stood shoulder to shoulder with a recent shot of a toothless infant of uncertain sex.

"My grandson," said a voice from the doorway.

"Deborah. How are you?" Warren held out his hands to her. She gave him both of hers as they touched cheeks.

"I'm fine, George. It's good to see you."

She turned to me. "You must be Mr. Harlan. I'm Deborah Lattimore." She extended a cool hand. "George speaks very highly of you. I understand we have a great deal to thank you for."

"I'm happy to do whatever I can."

I had to concentrate on not stuttering. I'd been told she was a looker, but looker didn't begin to cover it. Dark hair swept back softly from a perfect brow punctuated by delicate, naturally arched eyebrows. Her pale apricot lipstick perfectly matched her sleeveless linen dress.

She had to be in her late forties; she'd just admitted to being a grandmother, but her skin was smooth and unlined except for the laugh lines around her eyes. God, her eyes. Deep pools of green surrounded by a ring of gold. A snatch of poetry floated through my head—something about forest pools and golden autumn leaves. They were eyes to make a poet of a man.

"Please sit down," she invited.

I realized I was still clutching her hand. Her gentle smile was forgiving. She was probably used to it.

"Birdie?" She turned to the maid hovering protectively in the doorway. "Would you bring us some coffee, please?"

"Yes ma'am. Bring you some of that pound cake I made too."

"Thank you, Birdie. That would be nice."

" 'Bout time I got you to eat sumpin," Birdie's mutter floated back to us as she stumped down the hall. "Ain't eating enough to keep a bird alive."

Mrs. Lattimore turned back to us with a smile. "You're in for a treat, Mr. Harlan. Birdie's pound cake is famous."

I smiled back. I'd gladly have eaten nails if it would make her happy.

She turned back to Warren and asked about his wife. I took the opportunity to study her. Despite her poise, there was tension in the line of her back and faint shadows under those magnificent eyes. Her skin was almost translucent in the sunlit room.

She and Warren chatted until Birdie returned with the tray. There was a polite tug of war between the two women over the cake. Birdie stood, mute and stubborn, while Mrs. Lattimore cut herself a sliver. She picked at it until Birdie, satisfied, went away. As soon as the door closed behind her, Mrs. Lattimore put the plate down and turned to Warren.

"Now, George, I want you to tell me everything. Everyone's trying so hard to protect me, I could scream."

He paid her the compliment of giving her a direct answer. "I would've liked for John to walk out of that courtroom a free man, Deborah. You know that. But he'll be released on bail this afternoon. And I believe we have a good case. I don't want to encourage you with any false hope, and obviously I can't go into details at this point, but I think I can say honestly our chances for an acquittal are good."

"Thank you, George," she said quietly. "It helps to know where things stand. How is the boy?"

If Warren was surprised by the question, he covered it well. "He's as good as can be expected, I think. He's staying with family out of state until the trial."

"That poor child has had to grow up so fast." She spoke

matter-of-factly. "He's been the only grown-up in that family since he was just a little bitty thing."

She smiled faintly at our faces. "I've shocked you. Did you think I didn't know?"

For the first time since I'd known him, Warren seemed at a loss. He glanced at me, but I had no help to offer. "I'm sorry, Deborah," he said. "I know this must be difficult for you."

"It's humiliating," she said simply. "But people will feel sorry for me. Not enough to keep 'em from talking, but they'll be sympathetic all the same. It's the children I worry about."

She caught my glance at the table of photos and smiled ruefully. "You're right, of course. They're hardly children anymore. Do you have children, Mr. Harlan?"

"Two."

"Then you'll forgive my being a protective mother. They're not children any more. But that makes it worse. The boys are just getting established in their careers. My youngest, Dennis, just graduated and went to work for an architect last year. My oldest son, Robert, will have it the hardest. He works at the bank with his father. And my daughter . . . well, you know how fathers and daughters are. It was very hard for her when her daddy and I separated."

A short silence fell.

"Deborah," Warren began. He stared at his hat, turning it over and over in his hands.

"Yes, George?" I think she knew what was coming.

Warren sighed and met her eyes. "We may need you to testify, Deborah."

"Of course, if you think it will help." She rose and went to stand at the window with her back to us. With one perfect finger she traced the carving on a picture frame. Warren remained fascinated by his hat. The room was very quiet. So quiet I could hear the drowsy hum of a lawn mower somewhere outside and

Birdie rattling dishes in the kitchen.

"There are some questions I have to ask you, Deborah," Warren said to her back. "Personal questions—about John, about your life together. They're none of my damn business, but I . . ."

"I understand, George." She turned back to face us and braced herself against the table. "There'll be no secrets left by the time this is over. I know that. Anything you don't ask, Floyd King will. And there are some things you *should* know if you're going to help John. I'd rather they came from me. But there's one thing I have to tell you and I want your promise it won't leave this room, George. You mustn't even let on to John that you know."

Warren held up a warning palm. "I'm not sure that's a promise I can keep, Deborah. I'll use anything I have to keep John from going to . . . prison."

She studied us for a moment and sighed. "I suppose you're right. And it's not as though it will make any difference to the verdict. But I think it will help you understand. I almost wish I *could* get up on the stand and tell it. Maybe it would help people understand. Not that what he did wasn't wrong. It was. It was hurtful and foolish, but I don't believe John killed her, George."

"Neither do I, Deborah."

She came back and settled into her chair, folding her arms protectively across her chest. Warren fished a yellow tablet from his black satchel.

"You have to know that Delores Green wasn't the only woman in John's life," she began. Warren's dismay was almost comical. "He's been running around with other women for years. He didn't bother to hide it. The whole point was for people to know."

"Why?" Warren asked.

"Because he had a problem. He couldn't . . ." She looked

away. "He couldn't function." She seemed relieved when the words were finally out.

"You mean he couldn't function as a man? He was impotent?" Warren asked.

"Is that the word for it? Then, yes, I guess that's what he was."

"But . . ." Warren searched for a delicate phrase. "Your children."

"Oh, he wasn't always that way. It was just after our last, Dennis, was born."

"I see."

"It wasn't just me. He couldn't . . . I don't think he could . . . perform . . . with anyone. It was some medical thing. After a few years, he broke down and had surgery, but it didn't do any good. That was the worst, I think. When he had to accept it wasn't going to go away. And you know him, George. You know what he's like. If he couldn't perform, he had to make everybody think he was the biggest Casanova in town."

"So the whole time he was seeing Delores Green . . . ?"

"I can't be certain, of course. But I can't see any way they could have . . . been intimate."

"But they had a relationship for what? More than ten years!"

There was amused pity in her smile. "People stay together for a lot of reasons that have nothing to do with love, George. Personally, I suspect very few of them have anything to do with love, but maybe I'm just being cynical in my old age."

She got up and began to wander around the room, picking up knickknacks and putting them down again without seeing them. "It's ironic in a way. If it hadn't been for Delores Green, I think John would have left me years ago. It was just too humiliating for him. But as long as he had a 'mistress,' he could fool everybody. Maybe he thought he was fooling me. And as long as he had me, he had an excuse not to marry her." She stopped by the window to stare out at the flower beds. "But Delores Green had one advantage I could never compete with. She needed him. She was a mirror that reflected the image he needed to see—the image of a big, important man."

She turned back to us with a smile. "That's not entirely true. John wouldn't have left while Big John was alive. How about that? I have my father-in-law and my husband's mistress to thank for keeping my marriage together."

"Did John ever strike you or the children, Deborah?"

"No, of course not. He might've swatted the boys when they were little, but mostly he left that sort of thing to me."

"Until John developed his problem, was your marriage a happy one?"

She shrugged. "As happy as most, I expect. He loved the children when they were small, but after they got up some size, he didn't quite know what to do with them. He expected too much. Especially from the boys. With Big John for a father, he didn't know any other way.

"And yet," she added thoughtfully, "the worst of John's troubles didn't start until Big John died. John was always full of plans of what he was going to do when he was finally in charge. I don't mean to make it sound like he was waiting for Big John to die, but when he did, John just fell apart. He was like a weather vane in a hurricane."

She stopped talking, lost in her thoughts. Warren continued to scratch away at his pad, but he shot me a meaningful glance from under his eyebrows.

"Mrs. Lattimore . . ."

"Yes, Mr. Harlan?"

She came out of her reverie and turned to me with a gracious smile. I knew very well why Warren had brought me here, but even with all my disillusionment, it was hard to bring the words out under her gaze.

"In view of everything he's put you through, why are you still willing to testify for him?"

She straightened her back, lifted her chin, and gave me a look I'll never forget. There were generations of Southern steel in her eyes, but the rebuke was as gentle as her Virginia drawl.

"He is still my husband, Mr. Harlan, and the father of my children. And whatever else he may be, he is not a murderer."

It was a quiet ride back to the office. I had lost none of my ambivalence; if anything, meeting Deborah Lattimore had only magnified my confusion. But she had succeeded in reducing her husband from a monster to a human being again, a flawed man with his own demons and desires—and while I didn't dislike him any less, I could—almost—feel sympathy for him. Nothing could ever make up for what he'd put Greg through, but I was beginning to understand his panic. John Lattimore was a man to whom appearances meant everything and secrets were a way of life.

Warren pulled up to the curb and sat with the engine idling. Waves of heat rose from the sidewalk, making everything waver and shimmer as if underwater. The maples lining the sidewalk had already given up. Their leaves drooped, listless and still, providing no relief.

"What do you think?" Warren asked.

I got out of the car and leaned my head back in the window. "I think, Mr. Warren, that you could sell road kill at a church picnic."

"I'm not sure you intended that as a compliment, but I can't say that in your shoes I'd feel any differently. Does this mean you'll stay on for the trial?"

"I'm not a quitter, Mr. Warren. And as a very wise man once said to me, we don't have to like our clients, just protect them."

He held out his hand. "Thank you," he said quietly. "If you'll stop by the office later, I'll have Miz Turner type a list of the witnesses we expect King to call for the trial."

"I'll stop by later this afternoon."

"Good hunting, Mr. Harlan."

I stood on the sidewalk with my hat in my hand and watched him nose the big, black car into traffic.

Back in the office, I slanted the blinds against the broiling sun and switched on the rotating fan. It did little more than stir the hot air around and flutter the papers on my desk, but it was better than nothing. Maybe when this was all over, I'd be able to afford one of those new window air conditioners. Nothing like a little comfort to help you forget your scruples.

I dialed the Detective Division and doodled dollar signs on my desk blotter while I waited.

"Detective's Division," Hilda snarled.

"It's me."

"You have some nerve calling here . . ."

"I know. I'm sorry, but it's important . . ."

"Where are those supplies I ordered last week?"

"You can't talk?"

"That's right! Last week."

"I got it. Just listen, okay? Can you get me a copy of Bennett's report?"

"No, that will *not* do!"

"Can you get a look at it?"

"Well . . ."

"I need to know about a barbiturate bottle—probably in her bedroom or bathroom." I spelled out the name for her.

"You haven't heard the last from me," she warned.

"Thanks, Hilda."

There wasn't much else I could do until I had the list of witnesses, so I walked up to the Diamond for some lunch, torn between hurrying to avoid sunstroke and moving slowly so I

Terry Hoover

wouldn't ruin my shirt.

The breeze from the overhead fans was soothing on my damp skin as I wrestled open the door, which always stuck in hot weather. Two guys at the counter glanced at me in the mirror and turned to whisper to each other. By the time I made my way to a booth in the back, the whole place was silent.

"Hello, darlin', what you want to drink?" The waitress was vaguely familiar, but I had to get her name, Katrina, from her nametag. Probably one of Nick's far-flung relatives from Greece who are always coming and going. For some reason I've never been able to fathom, nearly every restaurant in town is owned and operated by Greeks. I guess one settled here, did well, and sent for his relatives, and pretty soon the word was out. Katrina placed her bulk between me and the rubberneckers and fished a pencil from the depths of her raven beehive.

"Is my fly open or did I grow another nose?"

"You famous now, darlin', " she said in a stage whisper. "You got your picture in the papers, been on TV. Maybe we put your picture up there." She winked and waved her pencil at the fly-specked photographs of hockey players and wrestlers that lined the walls, all with suspiciously similar autographs.

"I'll have the meatloaf and iced tea."

"Comin' up!" She bustled away to harangue the cook. I ignored the stares and pretended to be engrossed by the pictures of pecan pie and ice cream behind the counter.

CHAPTER 13

As it turned out, the list wasn't ready until the next morning. When I picked it up, there was a note attached asking for a complete background check on Delores. I'd have done it anyway for my own benefit, but now I could bill for it. It would mean running down everything from her credit rating to her boy-friends, on top of tracking down all the potential prosecution witnesses and coaxing them to talk. I started estimating billable hours as I headed for the car.

Elvira Hemingway, Delores's neighbor and sometime co-worker, was at the top of the list, so I decided to start with her.

I knew the neighborhood, forty or so small homes built after the war, occupied by white-collar families, clinging tenaciously to the coattails of the well-to-do neighborhood behind it—Latti-more's neighborhood. A section of new homes and a half-dozen duplexes went up a few years ago to house the families of return-ing Korean vets. From the letter appended to the Hemingways' house number, I assumed they were in one of those. But out of curiosity, I made a slight detour past Delores's house first.

It stood between its neighbors, a neat, unremarkable brick bungalow with fake Tudor timbering. Somebody, probably one of the neighbors, had cut the grass recently. There was no hint of the drama that had taken place behind its blind windows. Whatever secrets lay behind them remained hidden.

A flash of white caught my eye. I turned my head in time to

see a curtain drop across a neighbor's front window. I moved on.

The Hemingways had the front half of a duplex on Lennox. A bedsheet sporting faded teddy bears covered the picture window. The reek of fresh paint hit my nostrils. Someone had just moved in or out. As I pressed the bell, I hoped for my sake it was in.

The only response to my ring was an ominous echo. I waited a few minutes and pressed it again. People seemed to be developing a bad habit of vanishing whenever I turned up. Ten o'clock in the morning, maybe they were at work. But the house had an empty, untenanted feel that made me uneasy. I debated sticking a card in the door, but thought better of it. I had turned to leave when I saw the sheet twitch.

"Mrs. Hemingway?" I raised my voice. "Mrs. Hemingway, I'd like to talk to you about Delores." Maybe she'd think I was a relative from out of town. If I could get her to open the door, I had a good shot at getting inside. Cops have authority on their side, but I'd spent years learning to get people to talk.

The door opened a crack. "I'm sorry. I was vacuuming and didn't hear the bell."

Yeah, and my last name's Rockefeller. "You *are* Mrs. Hemingway?"

"Yes, I'm Miz Hemingway."

She stepped closer to the screen. Her fingers scrabbled at the V of her blouse. I fished out a card and held it up just far enough away so that she had to open the screen to read it.

"I'm sorry to bother you, but there are a few questions I need to clear up."

"I don't know . . ." She glanced over her shoulder as if seeking approval from someone inside. "I'm not sure I should be talking to you."

"Oh, it's nothing major." I pulled open the screen and edged over the sill, gently forcing her back a step. "I just need to check some of the details of your statement."

"Well . . ."

I took off my hat and let the screen shut behind me. Up close, I caught the stink of a fresh permanent from her blonde curls. Between the paint fumes and the ammonia wafting from her head, the house would be unbearable by afternoon.

"May I sit down? This won't take long."

"Well, all right." She scooped up an armful of clothing from the sofa. "The place is kind of a mess. We just moved in and I've been working, so we aren't real organized yet."

A family of lipstick-stained coffee cups and glasses scattered about called her a liar. Movie magazines were splayed on the floor; a grimy brassiere lay draped over the arm of the Morris chair in the corner. A family of migrant workers couldn't have made that big a mess in a month.

But I gave her a sympathetic smile. "Moving's a chore, isn't it? Where'd you move from?"

"Oh, not far. Just a mile or two. We needed another bedroom for my little girl."

That explained the Barbie doll whose plastic stiletto heel was firmly rooted in my backside. Mrs. Hemingway ignored the brassiere and perched on the arm of the chair. Her faded pedal pushers exposed an ankle liberally peppered with stubble. Her thin, sleeveless blouse needed a wash and a couple of buttons.

"I have a little girl. How old is yours?"

"Uh, seven. She just turned seven." She dragged her attention back to me with an effort.

"Mine's nine."

She sprang up from the chair. "Would you like something to drink? A Co'Cola? Beer?"

"Not for me, thanks. But you go right ahead."

"I believe I will, if you don't mind. It's so *hot,* isn't it?"

She escaped to the kitchen, wrestling the accordion door shut behind her. I listened but didn't hear any ice trays or cabinet doors banging. I leaned over to sniff a sticky glass on the coffee table. Cheap gin. With the point of my pen, I rifled through the pile of unopened mail on the table looking for a previous address, but everything was addressed to Occupant.

"There, that's better." She breezed back in. There was no glass in her hand but she seemed relaxed and even gave me a crooked smile. Or maybe it was the lipstick she'd applied that listed to the left.

I pretended to consult my notes. "I understand you worked with Delores?"

"I did. I work for a secretarial agency. I worked in Delores's office for a few weeks while one of the girls was out having a baby."

"And you and Delores got to be friends."

"Well, friendly. Since we live . . . lived, so close, we rode back and forth to work together."

"You took turns driving?"

"Well, no. We don't have a car right now. My husband is looking around . . . somebody made him such a good offer for ours he sold it, but we haven't decided on a new one yet."

"Then I guess it worked out nice that you and Delores met and could ride together. Did she ever talk to you about John Lattimore?"

"Well, we met him at the house several times. He's real nice—not at all snooty like you'd expect from a bank president. My husband and him had a lot of things in common. They liked to talk about business things—the stock market, interest rates, and so on."

"So you got to be good friends too."

"Well, not what you might call good friends . . ." She backtracked, torn between hobnobbing with the swells and getting too cozy with a murder suspect.

"Mrs. Hemingway, did Delores ever say or do anything to give you the impression she was afraid of Mr. Lattimore?"

"Why, no." She paused for the briefest fraction. "They were always a happy couple."

"Did they seem happy to you Monday night?"

"Well . . . they weren't really together all that much that evening."

"How do you mean?"

"Well, Delores wasn't feeling well and a lot of the time we were there, she was lying down in her room and Mr. Lattimore was in the kitchen talking business with my husband."

"What does your husband do?"

"Well, he, uh, he was a supervisor for a moving company."

"Really? Which one?"

Her fingers worked at the collar of her blouse again. "Well, he's not there anymore . . . he hurt his back and had to give it up."

"Oh, that's too bad. What's he doing now?"

"He's, uh . . . listen, I really think you ought to talk to him." She sprang up from the chair. "Why don't I go call him?"

"I can come back and talk to him later when he gets home from work. I just have a couple more questions. Did Delores say anything to you Monday night about the bruises on her face and body?"

"I really think my husband should be here before I talk anymore. I need to call him anyway." She looked at her bare wrist. "I was supposed to call him at his break to see if he needs me to pick him up."

"But you don't have a car."

"Well, I can borrow my mother's car when I pick up my little girl. They don't live far."

"Well, if you'd feel more comfortable, go ahead and call him."

She edged toward the door. "We don't have our phone hooked up yet. I'll have to go around to the other side and use my landlady's phone. I won't be but a minute."

I stood up. "Would you rather I wait outside on the porch?"

"No! No, that's fine." She flapped a hand to indicate I should sit back down. "I'll just be right back."

I watched from behind the sheet until she disappeared around the hydrangea bush. As soon as she was out of sight, I made a quick tour of the other rooms, starting with the master bedroom. Clothing was draped over every available surface. The furniture hadn't been much when it was new and that was a long time ago. I couldn't bring myself to lift the mattress and look, but I'd have bet my next check there was a girlie magazine under the bedsprings. It would take longer than I had to make any kind of a thorough search in there.

The smaller bedroom was the little girl's. It was neater, simply because it was almost empty. A stuffed bunny propped in a miniature chair leered across the teacups at a naked, raddle-haired doll. A carelessly made-up mattress took up most of the floor in the opposite corner.

I'd just started on the medicine cabinet when I heard the door slam on the other side of the duplex. I nipped back to my seat on the sofa and was flipping through a movie magazine when she returned. "Any luck?"

She was flushed and out of breath. "He'll be here in just a few minutes."

"Well, that's fine. Now to get back to—"

"It's so *hot* in here," she interrupted. "And this paint is just awful. Why don't we sit out on the porch where there's a breeze."

"That's fine."

"Are you sure you wouldn't like something to drink?" She edged toward the kitchen.

I took pity on her. "Well, if you're sure it's no trouble."

I sat back down and waited. The minutes passed, but she didn't reappear. Nor was there any sound from the kitchen. I put my ear to the accordion door. "Mrs. Hemingway? Can I give you a hand?"

"Be right out," she caroled. She emerged, bearing a tray and two plastic glasses. "Oh, I forgot the crackers."

She turned back, but I inserted my frame between her and the kitchen.

"That's all right. I'm not very hungry. Shall we?" I held the door open so she had no choice but to go. But as soon as we stepped onto the porch, she began fussing over the chairs.

"Oh, these are just filthy. You'll ruin your suit. Let me get something to wipe that out with."

I caught her gently but firmly by the elbow. She was stalling. And she was scared. She was obviously a weak sister anyway, but there was something else going on. If I was going to find out what, I had to do it before her husband showed up.

"What are you afraid of, Mrs. Hemingway? Has somebody threatened you? Told you not to talk to anybody?"

" 'Course not." But she wouldn't meet my eye. "I'm not afraid of anything. Or anybody."

"Look, let's sit down here and . . ." But she wasn't looking at me. I let go of her elbow and turned in time to see the black Ford slide to a stop behind my car. Behind me, the front door slammed shut. I heard the thunk of the lock.

Lang unfolded his lanky legs from the Ford's passenger seat. By the time Bennett wrestled his belly from under the steering wheel, they'd been joined by a patrol car. It pulled up in front of my car, neatly boxing it in. Two uniforms emerged and took up positions on the sidewalk. They didn't speak. There was nothing threatening in their attitude or expression, but they didn't take their eyes off me.

I watched Lang lope up the walk, Bennett waddling in his

wake, and wondered for the hundredth time what joker had paired them as partners. It's impossible to see them together without thinking of Mutt and Jeff.

I took a stance in the center of the top step and waited. For once, I kept my mouth shut and let them make the first move.

"You got no business here, dick," Bennett rasped. He paused to wipe his red face with a grubby handkerchief. "And don't think just 'cause'a your face, you can get away with playing stupid. You know better than to go harassing prosecution witnesses."

I stuck my hands in my pockets and made a conscious effort to relax my shoulders. "Harassing? Who's harassing? The lady offered me a beer. No trouble here till you showed up. Why don't you go on back to the pound and find another ankle bone to gnaw on."

I was just hoping to keep him off-balance until I could find a graceful way out. I knew King had sent them to roust me and I was fairly sure their orders didn't include arresting me and having it wind up on tomorrow's front page. But I couldn't be certain. I took a casual step down and waited to see how they'd react. They didn't budge, but they didn't brace me either.

"One a these days, that smart mouth's gonna get you in trouble you can't get out of, buddy-ro." Bennett thrust his face in mine, breathing cigar breath in my face. "And I wanna be sure to be around to see it."

"Don't count on it, Bennett." I poked a finger into his gut and used it to push him aside. I squeezed past him and eased down another step. "I'll be dancing at your funeral if you don't lay off the biscuits and milk gravy. Don't you know that stuff gives you hardening of the arteries?" I was safely on the bottom step now.

"Harlan!" Something in his tone made me turn around. His little piggy eyes narrowed until they almost disappeared into the folds of fat. "Consider this a friendly warning. Leave the prosecution witnesses alone. I trip over you again, I'll stomp you like a bug."

"Better bring a chair." I glanced back at Lang, who hadn't uttered a word. "Nice talking to you."

There was an itch between my shoulder blades where their eyes bored into my back. The uniforms fell into step behind me as I passed. I pulled out and the patrol car made a U-turn to fall in behind me. It hung behind me like a bad smell all the way to the office.

I called Warren as soon as I got back to the office. He was less upset than I expected.

"Can they do that?" I asked. "Keep me from questioning witnesses?"

He heaved a sigh strong enough to ruffle my hair through the wire. "Technically, no. But the fact that the Hemingway woman called King . . . you're pretty sure that's what happened?"

"Oh yeah. I blame myself for that. I shouldn't have let her out of my sight, but short of tackling and hog-tying her, I couldn't think of any way to stop her."

"Not your fault. But it's your word against hers. 'Course, it also tells us she's uncomfortable about something."

"You want me to back off on the witnesses for a while?"

"Hell, no. But we're gonna have to pick our battles and with John just out on bail, this is one I'm not ready to fight yet. Just step carefully. Are the police still outside your office?"

"Nah. They dropped me and disappeared."

"Good. Call me if you have any idea you're being followed or they try to interfere with you."

I promised to get my notes over to him first thing in the morning and hung up.

I spent an hour reviewing the meager information Warren

had been able to provide on Delores. It wasn't much, but it was a start.

I grabbed a sandwich and spent the rest of the afternoon at the courthouse and the Motor Vehicle Bureau. By the end of the day, I was several bucks and more than a few favors in the hole, but I had copies of Delores's and Greg's birth certificates, her divorce decree, driving record, and credit report. Hey, when it comes to excitement, those guys on *77 Sunset Strip* got nothing on me. But then they don't have to call home and explain to their wives why they won't be home for dinner—again.

I was back on Delores's street by dusk, when I figured most of the neighbors would be inside, digesting their supper in front of the television. I parked under some trees at the far end of the block and fished out the sample case I keep under the seat for just such an occasion. To a casual observer, I looked like an insurance salesman, a sight to send even the nosiest neighbor scurrying for cover.

In some backyard children chanted, "Ain't no bears out tonight, Papa shot 'em all last night." Shrieks followed as the "bear" charged out from her hiding place to pursue her tormentors. A brother and sister on bicycles pedaled past, too intent on their argument over a jar of lightning bugs to pay any attention to me.

I ditched the case behind some bushes before I rang the Rosinski's bell.

"Comink, comink," intoned a deep voice from inside. The front room was dark. A burly figure appeared from a lighted doorway down the hall and lumbered toward the door, pulling up suspenders as he came. "Yah?"

"Mr. Rosinski?" I could make out no more than a substantial silhouette outlined against the greenish light spilling into the hall.

"Yah."

"I'm Steve Harlan. I'm an investigator. I'd like to talk to you about Delores Green."

The porch light went on over my head, luring a thousand bugs to their deaths. Apparently satisfied with what he saw, Rosinski unhooked the latch and opened the screen wide. "Come in. You want a beer?" Without waiting for an answer, he turned and headed down the hall. I followed, trying not to bump into the furniture in the dark.

The glare in the kitchen made me blink. Exotic smells hung in the air, but the table, counters, even the sink, gleamed spotless and sterile under the fluorescent overhead. A damp dishtowel draped over the oven door handle was the only sign the kitchen had ever been used.

Rosinski hooked a chair with his foot and gestured me into it. "Sit." I sat.

He bent double and fished inside the refrigerator with a massive arm for a beer, which he plunked down in front of me. He lowered himself into his chair with a grunt and took a healthy pull from his own can.

"You police?" he asked.

"No. Private investigator."

"Ah. So, what you want to know?" He swiveled around to rest his meaty forearms on the table. His hair, though still thick, was white so I put him in his late fifties, maybe even his sixties, but vigorous and strong as a bull. His neck and shoulder muscles strained the seams of his cotton undershirt.

"I understand Greg and your son, Em, are friends. Did you know Greg's mother very well?"

He gave the question serious consideration. "Pretty good. She seem like a nice woman. It's a bad ting for a boy to lose his mother that way. Who look after him now, huh?" he demanded. He shook his head and contemplated his knuckles. "A bad ting."

"Mr. Rosinski, I understand people don't like to speak ill of people after they're dead, but . . ."

He reared back in his chair. "What, you tink I lie?"

"No sir. It's just that some of my questions might seem . . . indelicate. You know what I mean? People tell you things that might not be true but the only way to find out is to ask."

"Okay, okay." He returned to studying his hands.

"Did you ever see any evidence that Delores drank or had a drinking problem?"

"No. She seem like nice lady. She work hard, she take care of the boy. He was always clean, you know? He's a good boy." He shook a finger like a sausage at me for emphasis. "He behave himself. He help my Em sometimes with his . . . what do you call it?"

"Paper route?"

"Yah. Paper route."

"I'd like to talk to Em. Is he here?"

"His mother's gone to pick him up." He glanced at the wall clock over his head. "They be home fifteen, maybe twenty minute."

"Did you ever meet Mr. Lattimore?"

"I see him couple times, maybe, in the yard. But talk, no. I see the car there sometimes."

"Did Greg ever talk about him?"

"Not much. I tink . . ." He fished for the right word. "It embarrass him his mother has a boyfriend." He leaned toward me, man to man. "At first, he tell us he is his uncle."

"Mr. Lattimore?"

"Yah. I tink because he is there"—he waved his hand—"early, late."

"Did Mrs. Green have a good reputation with the neighbors?"

"Yah. Everybody here know each other. Is nice neighborhood. Everybody friends."

"Nobody gossiped about her? Sometimes, an attractive woman on her own like that . . ."

He made an eloquent sound in the back of his throat. "You work hard, you don' have time to gossip."

"Do you know a woman by the name of Elvira Hemingway?"

"Who?"

"Elvira Hemingway. She was a friend of Delores's, rode to work with her sometimes. She and her husband live in one of the duplexes over on Lennox. A blonde woman, about this tall?"

"That one!" He made another sound, ruder.

"You know who I'm talking about?"

"Yah. I know. She and dat husband of hers." I raised my eyebrows in question. "What do you call it?" He muttered to himself in Polish. "White trash!" he said finally, triumphantly.

"How do you mean?"

But he couldn't find the words he wanted. "She was here . . . dat morning. In he . . . her, what do you call it?"

"Bathrobe?" I hazarded. "Nightgown?"

"No. Trousers, you know . . ." He gestured at his ankles.

"Pajamas?"

"Yah! And the tings in her hair?"

"Curlers?"

"Yah."

"What morning was that?"

"The morning she die. The police were at the house and dat woman, she was over here: 'Oh, he kill her, he kill her.' " His voice rose to a falsetto as he clapped his hands to his cheeks and wagged his head in imitation. " 'I know it. I know he kill her some day.' "

"She said that? 'He killed her. I knew he would kill her some day'?"

"Yah. Dat's what she say. She sit right dere," he pointed to my chair. "And she said dat." He tchted again.

I opened my mouth to ask a question but I was interrupted by the slam of the screen door. A woman's voice called out. Rosinski responded with something that sounded like Polish for "in here."

Mrs. Rosinski, a dark, handsome woman, stopped short in the doorway at the sight of me and my notebook. She glared at me and snapped out a question in Polish. His answer didn't please her. She shot something sharp back at him. He barked back, but he hunched his shoulders and didn't meet her eye. She began to berate him in Polish.

I decided it was time to intervene. "Mrs. Rosinski? I'm Steve Harlan. I'm looking into Delores Green's death."

She gave me a hard stare in reply. It might have turned into a standoff if Em hadn't appeared at her elbow. The boy had his mother's dark good looks and height, but there were signs that once past the gawky stage, he would also have his father's strength.

"Mama?"

She snapped an order at him without taking her eyes off me. He began to argue, but she cut him off. I moved quickly before she banished him to his room.

"Em? I'm Steve Harlan." I maneuvered around Mama's elbow and stuck out a hand for him to shake. He looked surprised and more than a little pleased. "I'd like to ask you a few questions if you don't mind."

He opened his mouth to reply, but Mama beat him to it. "He have nothing to say. He has done nothing."

"Nobody has accused him of anything. I just have a few questions about the information he's already given the police. I'll ask them right here in front of you and Mr. Rosinski."

"He has nothing to say," she repeated.

"Mama!" Em protested.

"Mrs. Rosinski, I understand. I have a son of my own. And a

daughter. Believe me, I wish neither of these boys had to get mixed up in this. But it's an important matter. A man's life is at stake. A man with children and grandchildren of his own. In this country, a man is innocent until he's proven guilty in a fair trial." From their age and heavy accents, I was gambling they'd immigrated to the States after the war. "I need Em's help."

She opened her mouth to retort, but Papa Rosinski snapped sharply at her. She turned without another word and disappeared.

Em took the whole scene in stride. My little speech had inflated his pride. The hard part now would be separating the cold facts from his eagerness to play up his part in the story.

We settled ourselves around the table. I took out my notebook. Father and son followed my every move as if they expected me to pull a rabbit out of my shirt pocket.

My first question was a bluff. "Now, Em, you've signed the statement you made to the police, haven't you?"

"Oh, yes."

"Good. And have they been in touch with you about testifying at the trial?"

He looked to his father for guidance. "They say maybe, maybe not," Mr. Rosinski said.

"That's fine. Now, Em, I'd like for you to just run over what you told the police for me. As carefully as you can. Would you do that?"

"Which part?"

"Start with Monday morning when Mrs. Green came home. No, the night before. Sunday night. Greg spent the night with you, is that right?"

"Yes."

"Was that something you had planned? That he would spend the night with you?"

"No."

"Why did Greg spend the night with you that night, Em?"

He studied the pattern in the table. "It got late and his mother wasn't home yet, so he brought him over here."

"Mr. Lattimore?"

"Yes."

"Did Greg's mother come home that night that you know of, Em?"

He shrugged. "She wasn't home the next morning. Greg had breakfast over here, and then he went home. I think he wanted to look for her."

"Did you see Mrs. Green when she came home?"

He shook his head. "After."

"After she came home?"

He nodded. "Greg called me to come over. At first, I said no, because I saw his car there."

"Mr. Lattimore's car?"

"Uh huh."

"Why didn't you want to go over when he was there?"

He risked a sidelong peek at his father. Rosinski looked up from his beer and gave him an infinitesimal nod.

"I didn't like him. And I didn't like being over there when he was. It was . . ."

"Tense? Uncomfortable?"

"Yeah. Him and Greg didn't get along. There was a lot of yelling."

"Greg and Lattimore?"

"Yeah, them, too. But him and Greg's mom argued sometimes. Sometimes they were just kidding around, but I couldn't tell. And sometimes they'd be kidding around but you could tell they really meant it."

"I understand. But you did go over to Greg's house that Monday morning?"

He nodded again.

"Did you see Mrs. Green?"

"Yes."

"Now this is important, Em. Did you notice any marks or bruises on her face?"

"I couldn't really see her that well. When I went in, they were back in her room. The door was open and I could see her moving around in there, but Mr. Lattimore was standing in the doorway talking to her. Mostly I just heard her answer him."

"So you couldn't really see her face clearly?"

"No. After a while, they started to argue. We turned up the TV and tried not to listen, but they got louder."

"What did they say?"

"I can't remember the exact words. He was mad at her. I think 'cause she stayed out all night." He looked at his father again out of the corner of his eye. "He kept asking her where she was."

"Uh huh."

"Greg got up and went and stood in that little hall between the living room and the bedrooms. After a minute, he turned around and saw him there and told him to get out."

"Lattimore told Greg to get out?"

"Yeah. And he said, 'Take that boy with you.' Greg didn't want to, but he yelled at him, so I said, 'Come on, we'll go over to my house.' And that's what we did."

I made my next question sound deliberately casual. "Did Greg ever mention that Lattimore hit his mother or did anything, you know, to hurt her?"

He shook his head. "No. He hated him. But I never heard him say anything like that."

I probed a little to see if he knew more about what went on in the Green household than he was telling. But he said he didn't and I believed him. Out of embarrassment or shame, Greg had kept things to himself.

"Thank you, Em. I appreciate your help. I'd like to talk to your father again, okay?"

Mrs. Rosinski must have been hovering nearby. She materialized out of the gloom. "No more," she decreed. "We don't need trouble. We have nothing to do with that over there."

She jerked her chin in the direction of the Green house. She began to rattle away in Polish at her husband. He responded in kind. I'd obviously overstayed my welcome. I wouldn't get anything else tonight, so I decided to make a graceful exit.

"Thank you, Mr. and Mrs. Rosinski. You, too, Em. You've been a real help."

Em grinned, but the older Rosinskis were having too much fun to pay any attention to me.

CHAPTER 14

I joined the stream of umbrellas flowing down the sidewalk toward the Liberty Building, where they eddied briefly in the revolving door before being sucked into the lobby. The weather gods had decided to remedy the summer drought all at once. The city was awakened before daylight by thunder and torrential downpours. The promised dawn never materialized. At eight-thirty in the morning, all the cars headed into downtown had headlights on. I had water in my shoes and my pants legs flapped wetly against my shins.

I handed my card to the receptionist. She consulted the bank of blinking lights on her switchboard and informed me Mr. Chambers was on the phone but promised to let him know I was waiting just the minute he was free. I deposited my umbrella in the stand along with the others and settled down to wait.

Rows of identical offices—identical size, identical shape, with identical curtains and chairs—formed a "U" along the outside walls. The front wall of each office was half glass, giving me a clear view of men in shirts and ties doing whatever it is insurance men do—like calculating how many years guys like me have left. It also gave them a clear view of the scenery in the secretarial pool, which was set up in a big, open bullpen like a newsroom. I entertained myself by trying to guess which of the junior-executive types Delores had worked for.

Within minutes, it was obvious the office telegraph had done its usual efficient job. There were a lot of furtive looks in my direction and a sudden blizzard of urgent papers to be delivered from office to office.

The receptionist held a low-voiced conversation on her headset. I caught the words "detective" and "Delores." A minute later, an older man in a coat and tie appeared and held out a manicured hand. "Mr. Harlan? I'm Bob Chambers." He gave me a firm handshake and the professionally sincere smile they flash when they throw out terms like "permanent disability" and "death benefits."

Chambers ushered me to a corner office and shut the door. His office had a window to indicate his senior status, but the decor was basically the same. "How can I be of help to you, Mr. Harlan?" he asked with an easy smile. He shifted sideways in his chair, however, as he spoke, and crossed his arms and his legs.

"I'm looking into Delores Green's death. I'd be interested in anything you can tell me about her."

"I'm not sure I can help you much," he replied. "I haven't been here in the Charlotte branch long. I knew Delores of course, but I can't say I knew her well."

I couldn't place his accent. Neither northern nor southern, it was remarkably unremarkable, the voice of someone who has lived in a lot of places and learned to blend in quickly. This job, this corner office, was probably just one of a half-dozen stops on his way up the corporate ladder.

"Was she a good worker?" I asked.

"I can't recall we ever had reason to complain of her work," he replied.

"Was she out much?"

"Not that I recall. I do remember that she seemed to have a lot of stomach problems. She kept a bottle of Bromo-Seltzer on her desk, but lots of people have nervous stomachs, especially in this business." He laughed, but the directness of his gaze said he understood the significance of what he was telling me.

"Did you ever see anything in her appearance or behavior to indicate she'd been drinking or had a hangover?"

He considered that briefly. "No, I can't say I did. I'm afraid I really don't know much that could help you, Mr. Harlan. And the company is anxious to keep our name out of the matter as much as possible."

"I can appreciate that. I'm not looking to cause any problems, but I'm sure you understand, I have a job to do just like your own investigators." He inclined his head fractionally in acknowledgment of my point. "Perhaps I could talk to some of the people she worked with. You sit beside the same person for seven or eight hours a day, you make conversation. After a couple years, even a couple months, it's amazing how much you know about them when you really think about it."

He studied me for a minute without speaking and seemed to come to a decision. "Look, Mr. Harlan, I'll tell you what. I have to leave town this afternoon; I'll be gone a few days. But there are a couple women here in the office who were friendly with Delores. If you'll promise to keep our name out of it, I'll talk to them for you. If they know anything that might help, I'll try to get them to call you—privately—away from the office. How's that?"

"Fair enough." A promise doesn't cost anything and I was fishing anyway, hoping to come up with the names of other people to talk to—maybe a previous boyfriend or two. "There is one other thing. I'm interested in another woman, a friend of Delores's who worked here briefly, named Elvira Hemingway. Like the writer. Do you remember her?"

"Sorry. The name doesn't ring a bell."

"When you talk to the women, could you ask about her as well?"

"Certainly."

He ushered me out to the lobby, where we shook hands. "Sorry I couldn't be more help," he said for the benefit of the bullpen. But he winked as he held the door for me.

"S'okay. Thanks for your time."

As long as I was downtown, I stopped back by the Credit Bureau. For two bucks, a stale doughnut, and some vending machine coffee, I came away with a copy of the Hemingways' credit report. I stuck it under my jacket to protect it from the rain as I sloshed back to the car, but the sheer weight of the envelope promised some interesting reading.

Back at the office, I propped my wet shoes in front of the fan to dry and put on a pot of coffee. While it perked, I tried Hilda again.

"Can you talk?"

"Just a minute." The receiver hit her desk with a clunk. I caught a murmured conversation before somebody hung it up.

"Hilda? Are you there?"

"Shhh!" Her voice was just above a whisper.

"Sorry. I thought you'd hung up."

"I'm in the Chief's office. Too many big ears around my desk these days."

"Do you have anything for me on the barbiturate bottle?"

"Lord, yes. Your little barb-bi-tiate bottle is stirring up a hornet's nest."

"How come?" I parked the receiver under my ear and stretched for my pad.

"King and Doc and the Lieutenant spent two hours behind closed doors in King's office. You could hear 'em yelling clear down the block. And they were hollering about bar-bi-tiates." I didn't ask how she knew what happened behind closed doors in King's office two blocks away, but I didn't doubt a word. "Doc came out looking like he'd seen a ghost and the Lieutenant came straight back here and called Bennett and Lang on the carpet. He tore a strip off both of 'em, but they swore up and down they never saw anything like that anywhere in the house and there's no mention of it anywhere in the reports."

"How about the autopsy report?"

"Don't know and can't find out. It's locked up in the Lieutenant's files."

"Okay, Hilda, thanks—"

"Hold your horses! The Lieutenant sent 'em back out to the house this morning and told 'em to turn it upside down until they find that bottle."

"No sign of 'em back yet?"

"No." Her voice became muffled and I knew she was consulting her gold pendant watch. "They've been gone more'n two hours now."

"Will you let me know?"

"No promises."

"That's good enough. Thanks, Hilda. I owe you one."

"One!" Her sniff carried clearly over the wire as I laid down the receiver.

Warren's number was busy, so I drove over and walked into a tumult that made the Israelites' exodus look like a Sunday drive. An army of baby-faced clerks, laden with books and papers, scurried back and forth under the stern eye of Miz Turner, who stood calmly in the center of the chaos snapping out orders and generally enjoying herself.

She barely spared me a glance. "Go on in." She jerked a thumb at Warren's door, whipped the pencil from behind her ear, and turned back to the young man who cowered at her side. "Where did you learn to cite a precedent, young man? Don't they teach you anything these days?"

"No ma'am. I mean, yes ma'am," he stammered. I left her to her fun.

"Come in." Warren's reply was muffled. The reason became obvious when I tried to open the door. Yellow legal pads and stacks of papers littered the floor. Warren sat hidden behind piles of legal tomes stacked in precarious piles on his desk. Dozens more, bristling with little slips of yellow paper, lay open on every surface. He raised up to peer cautiously around one of the stacks.

"Steve!" He jumped up and grasped my hand like a drowning man. "Come in, come in and sit"—he gazed helplessly about the room—"down."

I couldn't help laughing. After a second's hesitation, he joined in, before putting an admonitory finger to his lips. "Shhh. Miz Turner will make us stay after class."

"Where did all the kids come from?" I asked.

"Stole 'em," he replied. "Called up a friend of mine who's on the faculty at the law school, who pulled some strings." He lifted a stack from the nearest chair and placed it on the floor, where it promptly slid into a heap. He ignored it.

He cleared a hole between the stacks on his desk and sat down, peering expectantly at me through the opening. "What's the latest?"

As succinctly as possible, I brought him up to speed.

"I knew it," he crowed. He slapped the desk with his palm, setting off yet another avalanche. "I knew Doc was bluffing about those blood tests. I guarantee you those samples are on their way to Washington right this minute and I'll bet they left here so fast they were smoking!"

"You knew he hadn't tested?"

"Once I had him on the stand, I was certain of it. I filed a motion yesterday for them to release samples so we can have our own tests done."

"You did?"

"I did. And I'm gonna file another one right now to force King to turn loose of those statements and the crime scene report. By the end of the day, he'll be chewing up nails and spitting out battleships. Miz Turner!" He barreled out the door, scattering papers like leaves in his wake. His voice dwindled away down the hall. "Miz Turner!"

For lack of a better idea, I sat and waited. Within a minute, he blew back in as precipitously as he'd blown out. He snatched his hat down from the rack. "Let's go."

"Where are we going?" This was becoming a bad habit.

"To talk to John."

"Don't you have to file something?"

"Oh, Miz Turner will take care of that. C'mon, let's get out of here before she comes up with something else for me to do." Awed clerks flattened themselves against the wall as we fled down the corridor.

"What if he's not home?" I panted after him.

"He'd better be," he tossed over his shoulder. "I told him in no uncertain terms to stick close to the house."

I was in for another surprise when we pulled up in front of Lattimore's house.

"Isn't this . . . ?"

"Yep," Warren confirmed. "Deborah's backyard is on the other side of that fence."

"It's none of my business, but isn't that kind of odd?"

"John has never spent a penny he didn't have to." He slammed the car door. "This was his mother's house. After she died, he kept it as rental property. When he and Deborah separated, I expect he just gave his tenants notice and moved in."

He hadn't exaggerated about Lattimore's father keeping him

on a short leash. I could have thrown a rock and hit the house Lattimore shared with his wife and children for more than two decades. I wondered if Mrs. Lattimore had ever felt like doing just that.

Lattimore didn't seem surprised to see us. "Come on in," he said as he stepped aside to let us enter. He'd lost some color from spending so much time indoors and I thought his clothes hung a little more loosely on him, but he seemed as vigorous as ever. His nervous energy was overwhelming. It seemed to dim the light in the room.

He'd made little effort with the house. The furnishings were good, but arranged for convenience rather than effect. There were no pictures or knickknacks, and only Venetian blinds to shade the windows. The whole place had a temporary feel.

"How are you, John?" Warren asked as he seated himself on the sofa.

"I'd be a hell of a lot better if those damn reporters would stop pestering me," Lattimore replied. He'd remained standing. "Y'all want a drink?"

Warren refrained from pointing out it was only an hour since lunch. "Nothing for me, thanks."

"You?" Lattimore turned to me. I wasn't sure whether he'd forgotten my name or couldn't bring himself to say it.

"No thanks."

He concealed his disappointment. "Have a seat." He pointed to an upholstered chair and settled himself in a worn wingback chair that already bore the clear imprint of his body. "What's up?"

I waited for Warren to speak, but he nodded to me. "It's the tranquilizers Delores was taking," I explained. "You were with her on Friday afternoon when she had the prescription refilled, is that right?"

"Yeah. Right after supper we rode up to Stanley Drugs and picked it up."

"Did you actually see the bottle? I mean, close enough to see the label?"

"No."

"But you're certain that's what it was."

"I didn't pay much attention. She was always taking some damn pill or another to lose weight or calm her down or something. She had more aches and pains than a pin cushion. What is all this anyway?" He looked from one to the other of us.

"We're reasonably certain Doc *didn't* test Delores's blood for alcohol and barbiturates," Warren said. "We think they're on their way to Washington to be tested right now. But there's no sign anywhere in the crime scene report of the bottle of tranquilizers and Mr. Harlan has determined that the police detectives didn't find it the first time they were at the house. They're back there now looking for it."

"Why is it such a big deal?" Lattimore asked.

"It may not be," Warren answered. "They may simply have overlooked it. It's only important if they don't find it because there's a very good chance that the tests will be inconclusive. If I understand correctly what Mr. Harlan has explained to me, it could be too late. The blood samples may be spoiled if they weren't handled properly. If that happens, that little bottle may become very important."

He gave me more credit than I deserved. I'd completely forgotten that. His genial, grandfatherly facade was so good, even I had been lulled into forgetting he was one of the most feared and respected defense lawyers in the country.

"Can't you just put out one of those, what do you call it—those subpoenas and get the druggist or the doctor to say she had'em?" Lattimore asked.

201

Warren and I exchanged glances. "We can," Warren admitted. "If the blood tests are inconclusive and *if* the police don't find the bottle, we can use that to our advantage. But what if they do find the bottle and there's just the right number of pills missing? Or they turn out to be cold pills?"

"I'm sure they were tranquilizers," Lattimore insisted.

"Did you see the bottle again after Friday night?" Warren pressed.

"Hell, I don't know." Lattimore hitched forward in his chair and plowed his fingers through his hair.

"Think, John," Warren urged. "Can you remember the last time you saw it?"

"I am thinking," he replied. "But like I said, there were always pill bottles lying all over the house."

"What did she do with it when you came in from the drugstore?" Warren asked.

Lattimore closed his eyes in thought. "We came in the back door into the kitchen. She opened it right then and took one with some water from the sink."

"Did she put it down on the counter?" I asked. "On the kitchen windowsill?"

"It's no use. If I noticed, I can't remember now," Lattimore said.

"Where did she usually keep them?" Warren asked. "In the kitchen? On her nightstand? How about the medicine cabinet in the bathroom?"

"Her purse!" Lattimore said suddenly. "She carried them around with her in her purse."

"Her purse." Warren looked at me. "You gathered up her things at the cabin and put them in the car. What did you do with her purse?"

Lattimore closed his eyes again. "I carried it in. I put it . . . I think I laid it down either on the coffee table or her dresser.

That's where she usually left it."

"John." Warren leaned forward and looked intently at Lattimore. "Will they find your fingerprints on the purse?"

"I don't think so," he said slowly, not looking at either of us. "I wiped it off with my handkerchief."

"Did you tell the police you brought it back with you?"

"I . . . I can't remember."

"Think, man!" Warren urged. "It's important."

Lattimore opened his mouth to reply, but he was interrupted by a heavy knock at the door. He left us to answer it. We heard a murmur of voices, then Lattimore's rose above the rest, loud and agitated. My first thought was a persistent reporter.

Warren, however, was quicker on the uptake. He rose to face the door as Lattimore returned, trailed by Lieutenant Owens and several uniformed officers.

"Lieutenant," Warren said, his tone polite and noncommittal.

Owens nodded. "I have a search warrant here, Mr. Warren, authorizing me to search these premises."

"May I see it?" While Warren read, Owens surveyed the room, missing nothing. We exchanged nods. The only sounds in the room were Lattimore's breathing and the rustle of pages as Warren perused the warrant. He handed it back to Owens. "You don't really expect to find anything, do you?" His tone was mild.

"Not my job to expect," Owens grunted. "The district attorney has ordered me to execute this search warrant and that's what I aim to do. I also have another warrant, here—" He held out his hand. One of the patrolmen placed a paper in it. "—authorizing me to search the cabin belonging to Mr. Lattimore located at"—he squinted at the paper—"Route 5, Box 21, Highway 49." He handed it, too, to Warren.

"I presume it says much the same thing?" Warren didn't bother to unfold it.

"It does."

"Do I have to put up with this?" Lattimore demanded.

"I'm afraid so, John."

"God damn it," Lattimore swore. "If there is one thing out of place—" he began.

"That's enough, John," Warren said sharply. "Lieutenant Owens is doing his job. He has a legal right to search these premises. I suggest we move outside and let the officers get on with it."

"But, I—" Lattimore began to protest. Warren shot him a steely look and took his arm. Lattimore let himself be led outside without any further complaint. I followed them around the corner of the house to the patio. We settled ourselves on the rock wall that surrounded it, as far as possible from the house. I glanced up at the second-story windows, where I could see the officers moving about.

"They must not have found the bottle," Warren said in a low voice. "The search warrant specifies any and all personal possessions belonging to the deceased. Including clothing." He looked at Lattimore.

Sweat trickled down Lattimore's sideburns, but he said nothing and didn't meet Warren's eyes.

"John? Where did you burn her clothes?"

"In the trash can."

"Where is it?"

"I got rid of it."

"John!" We turned to see Deborah Lattimore at the back fence, looking worried.

"Oh, Lord," Lattimore muttered. He crossed the yard to speak to her. Two uniforms appeared around the side of the house and began to probe in the leaves of the rhododendron.

"Come on," Warren said. He led the way around the far side of the house to the carport. He leaned against the bank of cans and folded his arms. "Sit on that one," he ordered. Mystified, I perched one hip on the can lid. "Look natural," he said with a wry smile.

Lattimore found us there a few minutes later. "What the hell are you—"

"Hush!" Warren ordered just as Owens appeared. "Are we in the way here, Lieutenant?" Warren asked.

Owens eyed him suspiciously. "We need to look in that storage room there." He pointed to the door to my right. "Is it locked?"

"No. There's nothing in it but the lawn mower and a bunch of yard stuff," Lattimore said.

Owens nodded to one of the uniforms. We waited in uncomfortable silence broken only by the patrolman's sneezes as he rooted among the grass clippings and cobwebs.

Warren removed his hat to mop his face with a handkerchief.

"What you sweating for, Mr. Warren?" Owens asked. "Not nervous, are you?"

"I'm sweating, Lieutenant, because it's ninety-seven in the shade," Warren replied. He fanned himself with his hat. Although the rain had long since stopped, the humidity was thick enough to cut with a knife.

"Ahchoo!" came another vigorous sneeze from the storage room.

"Bless you," Warren said absently.

The patrolman emerged with a red face and grass clippings all over his black uniform. He shook his head at Owens. Owens wheeled and shouted for the other officers. He stared suspiciously at the three of us. "I'll take the keys to that cabin, Mr. Lattimore," he said. His eyes were on Warren. "Or you can accompany us in your car and be present during the search."

"You're damn right I'll—" Lattimore began.

"I don't think that will be necessary, Lieutenant," Warren

interrupted. "You'll see the keys are returned?"

"Of course." They stared at one another for a long moment. The Lieutenant broke first. He took the key from Lattimore's outstretched hand and weighed it in his palm. "We'll be back." He turned and left without another word.

No one spoke until the sound of the police cars died away.

"Just what the hell did I miss here?" Lattimore asked.

"Did you ever read *The Purloined Letter*, John?" Warren asked "The what?"

"*The Purloined Letter*. It's a story by Edgar Allen Poe about a missing paper. Everyone in the story is looking for it, but they can't find it because it's hidden in plain sight." He stood up and turned around. In silence, the three of us gazed at the shiny, new galvanized trash can on which he'd been leaning.

CHAPTER 15

"I'm beginning to feel like the Maytag man."

"Making yourself unpopular are you?" Warren put down his pen and leaned back in his chair. "A former reporter should be used to that." He smiled to take the sting from his remark.

After the breakneck pace of the first week, the investigation seemed to have bogged down. I'd spent the past six weeks digging out details and talking to more people than I could count. I was racking up billable hours and reams of reports, but I didn't seem to be making much progress. I'd tried telling myself every investigation has its low points. The only thing to do is keep slogging and keep a sharp eye out for the one detail, the loose thread that will unravel the whole knotty thing, but I was still discouraged.

I wasn't the only one unhappy about my progress. Kent Rose was breathing down my neck for something juicy. I'd been able to feed him a few things here and there, but as the trial drew nearer, both papers were struggling to maintain the fever pitch they'd stirred up.

"We are apparently the only two married men in town this summer," I told Warren, trying to match his light tone. "An amazing number of them have taken their families on extended vacations, and their secretaries have no idea when they'll be back."

Chambers had been as good as his word. I'd heard from two of Delores's cohorts in the secretarial pool who supplied me with a list of men who had squired Delores at one time or another. The results of my efforts to learn anything from them lay forlornly on Warren's desk.

"Well, you apparently haven't come completely empty-handed." He perched his glasses on his nose and reached for my report. His eyebrows rose at the first name on the list, a very married attorney whose office was only two floors below us. Also on the list were two insurance salesmen in Delores's office, a local grocery store manager, a guy whose profession I hadn't been able to learn even after a visit to his office, and a used-car lot owner in Gastonia who does his own commercials and is universally despised by everybody who owns a television set. But, fortunately for me, his third wife had already filed for divorce, so he had nothing to lose by being frank. And frank he had been.

"Good Lord, I eat there!" Warren looked up from the car dealer's account of his last "date" with Delores, in the back of his Cadillac behind the Lotus Blossom only a few weeks before her death.

"Me too."

"Anything else here?"

"Nothing much. Just some background I picked up on the Hemingways."

"Mmm. Anything useful?" He dropped the pages on the desk, removed his glasses, and rubbed his eyes.

"Not really. You wouldn't be thrilled if they moved in next door, but it wouldn't matter because they'd probably be gone in six months. They have a list of outstanding collections and previous addresses as long as Higgins's arm. And the husband's driving record is about as bad. Not that it matters. That 'real good offer' Mrs. Hemingway said they got for their car? It came from the finance company when it repossessed the last one."

"Ah, I recognize the type. Well, perhaps this will make you

feel better." Warren withdrew an envelope from his desk drawer.

"What's this?"

"A check for your first month's retainer plus overtime and expenses."

"Oh. Thanks."

I tried to force some enthusiasm into my voice, but I couldn't meet his eyes. After weeks of interviews and hours poring over statements until we were both cross-eyed, we should have some better answers by now. But we were no closer to coming up with anybody, other than our client, who looked good for Delores's murder. Or to discovering how and where she'd spent Sunday night. Jury selection was scheduled to start in a few days and I still hadn't found the answers to the big questions. Fortunately, no other clients had called with work that needed doing urgently and, from time to time, I worried about that and about what would happen when the case was over. But I didn't have time to worry long.

"Steve." Warren leaned across his desk. "You've earned every penny. You've worked like a Trojan these past weeks. Your wife has probably forgotten what you look like. Take her out to dinner somewhere nice and forget about this case for a few hours."

Physician, heal thyself. I wasn't the only one showing the strain. Warren's usually ruddy face was pale and he'd lost weight.

"It's not that I don't appreciate it—"

"But you're not satisfied." He leaned forward in his seat and laced his hands together on the blotter. "That's what made you a good reporter; it's what makes you a good investigator. I know how you feel, believe me. But as much as I'd like to solve this case, we have to face facts. We may never know for sure who or what killed Delores Green. The best we may be able to hope for is to create a reasonable doubt that John did it. And that's my job."

★ ★ ★ ★ ★

Susie said pretty much the same thing, but I missed it. We were seated at a window table at Manicotti's with the lights of the city spread out below us. Susie looked like a million bucks in a little black number and pearls, and I was in blue—a blue funk.

"I'm sorry, what did you say, hon?" I straightened in my chair and made an effort to look interested.

"I said," she repeated in the slow, measured tone she uses when she means business, "Warren is right. You've done your job. Which is *not* to solve the case or to get Lattimore acquitted. And he's obviously satisfied with your work." She gestured at the elegant surroundings.

"You're right. I just feel like I'm spinning my wheels."

She heaved a wife sigh, long-suffering and patient. "You went through this on every story."

"I did?" Stung, I looked up from my soup.

"You do. When things slow down and it looks like nothing's going to break, it drives you nuts. But something always does and then everything is wonderful again." She broke her roll in half and spread butter on it.

"I've covered every angle I can think of and every angle War-ren can think of, but nothing's shaking."

That was the gospel truth. Everything seemed to be at a standstill. I'd turned up nothing on the missing pill bottle or our missing mechanic. The one bright spot was that the police hadn't had any luck finding them either. We'd struck out on the blood tests, too. Warren dragged King and Doc back into court, but they swore there wasn't enough blood left to share and there was no word yet from the FBI.

"I think you've accomplished plenty," Susie retorted. "Didn't you say Warren was pleased about the tranquilizer angle? And you dug that out." She paused while the waiter deposited steam-ing, fragrant plates of spaghetti Bolognese before us. We breathed in the rich aroma of herbs and garlic and closed our eyes in silent homage before attacking it with our forks.

"That's our best hope so far," I admitted around a mouthful. "As long as that bottle doesn't turn up full of pills before the trial, we can plant some serious doubt in the jury's mind. But it all depends on the results of the blood tests." Warren had already talked with a high-priced pathologist in Baltimore who'd agreed to fly down to testify if we needed him. "I just have this nagging feeling I've missed something."

"Well, go back to the basics," Susie said. She ticked them off on buttery fingers. "Who, what, when, where, why, and how."

"Those are the basics of writing a story."

"Which *you* said are the same questions to be answered in an investigation," she shot back.

"We know the what, the where, and the when," I said. "The why we may never know and the how is still in question. And I'm afraid the jury will have no trouble deciding the who for themselves."

"Yeah, who last saw the victim alive," she agreed. She twirled another forkful of noodles.

"Thanks to our brethren in journalism, I don't think there's anybody within four states who doesn't know who was with Delores last."

But Susie wasn't listening. She stared at me, her fork halfway to her mouth.

"Suse? What's the matter?"

Her spaghetti slithered unnoticed from her fork. "Wait a minute," she said. She stared at the tablecloth for a minute before raising her eyes to me. "Look at it from the other way. We know, or we think we know, who was with Delores last before she died. But what about the other thing?"

"What other thing?"

"Where she was Sunday night." She laid down her fork and

leaned across the table. "Who was the last to see her before she disappeared on Sunday?"

"Greg."

"Unh-unh."

"Sure, he was. She told him she was going to the office."

"But she had company for part of the ride," she prompted.

Company? "Hemingway!" Every eye in the restaurant swiveled in my direction. But I didn't care. "She gave that Hemingway guy a lift to work."

"Right. Maybe she said something to him about where she was going."

"And the police didn't talk to him. They took a statement from the wife about what happened at the house Monday night and let it go at that. What's his name?" I reached for my notebook, but for the first time in weeks, I'd left it at the office. "Susie, you are a pearl among women. Brilliant *and* beautiful." She gave me a cool, complacent smile. "Eat up. I'm going to buy you the biggest, gooiest dessert they've got then I'm taking you dancing at the Pecan Grove."

"All that for a suggestion? What if he doesn't know anything? Or he won't talk to you, either?"

"I'll make him talk. Something's going to break. I can feel it now. I just need to swing by the office on the way and check my notes . . ."

Susie sighed and signaled the waiter for the dessert tray.

According to Greg's statement, Delores had left the house that Sunday afternoon around three. Just to be safe, I was parked down the street from the Hemingways' house by noon. It was a long, hot vigil. I passed the time debating whether it was worse to pull surveillance in the heat of summer or the dead of winter. Definitely summer, I decided as sweat trickled down my back and threatened to puddle in my shoes. At least the heat kept everybody inside with the shades pulled.

About ten to three, a Plymouth coupe pulled up in front of the Hemingways' house. The driver honked a tattoo on the horn. I slid down in the seat and turned the key. Hemingway emerged from the house and turned back with his hand on the knob to speak to someone inside. The sun in my eyes made it hard to tell much about him. I caught a glimpse of profile and light hair as he ducked into the passenger seat.

Neither man glanced my way as the Plymouth pulled away from the curb. The Saturday afternoon traffic was light, so I had no trouble keeping them in sight as we wound through shady side streets. I rolled the windows all the way down to take advantage of the breeze.

The Plymouth signaled for a left into a filling station at the corner of Providence and Queens Road. I sailed past and pulled into the lot of the Colonial store in the next block. Hemingway hopped out, waved, and went inside. When he didn't come out after ten minutes, I was sure he was an employee, not a customer. Across the street from the station was an ice cream parlor with a big front window. I decided to take it as a sign from God. Thirty minutes and a double cone of lime sherbet later, I made my move.

Hemingway was alone in the pit, his back to me as he rummaged in a toolbox.

"Mr. Hemingway?"

He whirled to face me, the wrench in his hand suddenly a menacing weapon.

"Sorry, didn't mean to startle you." I threw up placating hands.

"Something I can help you with?" He lowered the wrench and forced a smile, but his eyes remained wary.

"My name's Harlan. I'm looking into Delores Green's death."

"You a reporter?"

"No, I'm an investigator. Actually, I met your wife the other week, but I'm afraid I may have upset her. Hope there are no hard feelings."

Hemingway became downright jovial. "Oh, that." He waved the wrench. "Don't worry about it. You know how women are. Get all het up over things. She was all stirred up 'cause the police told her she'd have to testify at the trial. She didn't even know when it was going to be, but nothing would do but she take a day off work to get one of them stinking permanents so she'd look nice in court. Women."

"I guess Delores's death was a real shock to her."

"Yeah. It was a real bad thing. A real shame." He looked appropriately sorrowful.

"I was hoping you could help me with something."

"I don't know much that'd be any help. It's my wife the police talked to."

"Well, to tell you the truth, it was Sunday I was wondering about."

"Sunday?" He licked his lips and looked confused.

"That's right. I understand you caught a ride with Delores to work that afternoon."

"Oh, sure, sure. That's right. She gave me a lift to the Square so's I could catch the bus. But what's that got to do with her dying?"

"Oh, I don't know that it has anything to do with it. I was just wondering if she mentioned where she was headed."

"Oh. Well, now let me think on it." He furrowed his brow in thought. Something about him looked vaguely familiar, but nothing I could put my finger on. His face was ordinary, the kind you could pass on the street a dozen times without noticing. "She was heading to work . . ." He snapped his fingers. "I got it. It was almost the boy's birthday and she said he had his heart set on one of those, what do you call'em?" He mimed a swing with the wrench. "A tennis racquet. She was gonna go see about a tennis racquet."

"Did she say which store?"

"Sorry, but I don't recall."

"Did she say anything else?"

"Not really. We just talked about this and that, making polite, you know. I didn't really know her all that good."

"I thought I understood from your wife that y'all spent some time at her house and she'd loaned you her car a couple times."

"Oh, once or twice when we were over there, she'd ask us to stay for a cold drink. And I run up to the store for mixers or cigarettes in her car a time or two. We wasn't really on borrying terms."

"Oh, I see. Are you sure Delores didn't say anything else that might help?"

"Nah. I'd sure like to help you if I could, but it was mostly just chitchat about the weather and such."

"Well, thanks anyway. And tell your wife I'm real sorry if I upset her the other day."

"Oh, don't pay no attention to her. You know . . ."

"Yeah. Women."

Back in the car, I rolled down the windows and pondered what I'd learned. Not much, I decided. Hemingway had been surprisingly helpful, considering his wife had called the cops on me, but most professional deadbeats are the nicest guys you'd ever want to meet. His ingratiating manner had been perfected by years of practice. I stared unseeing at the dashboard, shifting the facts this way and that, willing them to fall into some sort of coherent pattern. Suddenly I bolted upright. Filling stations. Mechanics. A clue, in tiny, white numerals stared me in the face.

It was time to go see my ol' buddy, Terry.

He seemed genuinely glad to see me. "Cracked the case yet?" he asked with a knowing grin that crinkled the sun-reddened skin around his blue eyes. For just an instant, I could imagine him as a young man, cherub-cheeked with a snub nose and blonde hair that had long since fled.

"Not yet, but I think you could help."

"Well, I'd shore be happy to try."

"Do you keep mileage records on your regular customers?"

"Usually, so we can keep up with how long it's been since their last oil change or how many miles is on the belts and things."

And I'd thought the four years I'd spent in the grease pit had been wasted. "How about Delores Green?"

"I 'spect so. We can check." He gave his hands a lick and a promise with a rag and led the way into the office. While he rifled through the battered tin box that served as his filing cabinet, I helped myself to a Coke from the icebox. I dipped my handkerchief into the frigid water and wiped my face with it.

"Here we go." Terry pulled a dog-eared card from the box. "What do you want to know?"

"Did anybody write down the mileage when she brought it on Friday?"

"Well, let's see." He ran a blackened finger down the column as I craned over his shoulder. "The last one is June 30—29,456 miles."

"Nothing for the third?" But I could see for myself the rest of the card was blank.

"Looks like either Jack didn't check it when she come in Monday morning or didn't bother to write it down."

"I sure would give a lot to find that boy," I muttered.

"Nothing, huh?" he asked sympathetically.

"Not a trace. I can't even find anybody who knew him. He's the original Mystery Man."

"Well, now, I might be able to help you out there. There's a coupla guys work at the other stations, get together sometimes and play poker on Saturday night. Some of 'em might have known Jack better'n I did. Maybe you could talk to them."

"Are you playing tonight?"

"We sure are. We was gonna play over at the one on Central, but you want me to, I can call 'em and see if they'll move it over here."

"That'd be great. What time?"

"We don't start till after we close up at nine. Give everybody time to count the money and lock up, call it nine-thirty or ten?"

"I'll be here. Thanks, Terry, you're a pal."

"You might want to bring some beer," he called after me.

I put in a few hours at the typewriter until shadows appeared on the sidewalk below my window. Late afternoon on a summer Saturday is my favorite time. The light softens to a golden mellow glow, the whole, long lazy evening stretches before you. Time seems to stand still.

The case was far from solved, but at least I was moving again. I felt so good, I called Susie and told her to fire up the grill. Ron and Donna from next door came over with their kids. We enjoyed a smoky feast of hot dogs and hamburgers, baked beans, and Susie's killer coleslaw, followed by Donna's wonderful brownies. With nuts. The kids shrieked and romped through the sprinkler until it was too dark to see. We toweled them off and stuck them into bed too tired and sated to make more than token protests. A perfect evening. I kissed Susie, told her to expect me when she saw me, and headed uptown.

The station was dark except for a hundred-watt bulb over the front door. My rap on the glass summoned Terry from the back.

"I brought the beer." I held up two sweating six-packs.

"Great." He relieved me of one of them. "Now, these fellas'll talk the hind leg off a donkey, but I wouldn't start out asking questions right off," he suggested in a low voice. "Just let me work it in kind of gradual."

"Whatever you think."

"What's your game?"

"Poker?"

"Well, we ain't here to play tiddlywinks."

"I, uh, I don't really play."

He stopped dead and gave me a look of equal amazement and disgust. "You never played poker?"

"Just never learned."

"Now that might be a problem." He rubbed his face, the calluses on his palm rasping on his chin stubble, as he eyed my Madras shirt and khaki pants. "Then again, if you can afford to lose a little, taking a few bucks off a Joe College like you just might soften 'em up."

"So in other words, I just sit back, keep my mouth shut, and look stupid?"

"That's about it," he agreed.

It looked like a long night.

He led the way to the party. "This here's the fella I was telling you about," he announced, waving the six-pack like a talisman. "Name's Harlan." Three heads swiveled in my direction.

"This here's Bob." Terry motioned to the skinny one with wavy brown hair and a sunburned face. Bob raised rheumy blue eyes behind dime-store glasses and nodded. "This is Herman," Terry continued, pointing to the oldest member of the trio, who had a snowy crew cut and jowls, "and this is Larry." Larry sported an Elvis pompadour ten years too young for him and a face pitted with acne scars.

"Harlan here is a virgin," Terry announced. He plunked a cold beer in front of each man to sweeten the news, but Larry looked sour. "He's been too busy chasing bad guys to learn, so I told him we'd teach him a thing or two about the game." He winked.

"S'matter, didn't they play poker at your frat house?" Larry's Adam's apple bobbed as he took a thirsty swig from his bottle. When he lowered the bottle, it was half empty.

"Didn't have time," I replied, straddling the kitchen chair Terry offered. "I worked my way through school. As night manager of a filling station, matter of fact."

Larry grunted. Behind his back, Terry gave me a thumbs up.

"We gonna play cards or we gonna gab all night?" Herman asked. From his tone, he didn't really expect an answer. They'd memorized this script a long time ago.

"Okay, deuces and jacks wild. A dollar a hand's the limit," Terry instructed.

For the next half hour, I stumbled through hand after hand and had no trouble losing every one. Larry made no effort to hide his disgust, but since his was the highest pile of quarters, he didn't complain aloud. Bob and Herman kept their eyes on their cards and said little.

"How come George didn't play tonight?" Terry asked, eventually.

"Who knows?" Bob replied.

"Who cares?" Larry asked.

Terry shot me a look.

"Who's George?"

"You met George the other day when you was by here," Terry replied.

"I did?"

"Yeah, he helped out over here for a while after Jack took off."

"Guy with blonde hair?"

"That's him."

"Whatever happened to Jack anyway?" Herman spoke for the first time in several minutes. "I'm in. Raise you a quarter."

"I wisht to hell I knew," Bob replied. "Hit me, Terry. Sumbitch owes me five bucks."

"You seen the last of that five bucks," Larry said. "King high. Read 'em and weep." He slapped his hand down on the table and fanned the cards.

"Shit." Bob threw down his hand in disgust.

"Anybody ever ask George?" Herman asked.

"Ask him what?" Larry asked.

"Where Cotter got off to."

"Who cares?" Larry repeated impatiently.

"Were they buddies?" I asked.

"Thick as thieves," Bob said.

"You know, I thought George reminded me of somebody the other day. There used to be a guy in my outfit with sandy hair and eyebrows like that," I said. "I wonder if they're related."

"Anybody know George's last name?" Terry asked helpfully.

"Same as that guy killed himself a few months back," Bob offered.

"What the hell are you talking about?" Larry asked. He cut the deck and began to deal a new hand. Nobody protested.

"That big fella with the beard. You remember. He blew his head off with a shotgun."

"Oh yeah, that writer fella," Herman agreed.

"You mean," I asked, faintly, "Ernest Hemingway?"

"Yeah, that's him," Bob said.

"Let me get this straight. The guy I saw over here that day is George Hemingway and he and Jack Cotter are friends?"

"That's right," Bob said.

If I could have kicked myself in the pants, I'd have stood in line to do it. No wonder George had looked familiar. I'd seen him right here in the very service station where Delores Green brought her car. As I stared at the Esso posters lining the walls, I was struck by a thought.

"But George works at a Sunoco station."

"Same fella owns it," Terry said. "He's got a coupla Esso stations, but he owns two or three others under his wife's name."

"And George worked here?"

"Nah, he just helped out here once or twice when I was short-handed," Terry replied.

"Terry, why didn't you tell me George Hemingway and Jack Cotter were friends?"

"Well, geez, buddy . . ."

I held up my hand. "I know, I didn't ask you."

"That's right."

"Are we gonna play or we gonna talk about those South Carolina hicks?" Larry demanded.

"They're from South Carolina?" I asked.

"Yeah, George is from down around Gaffney, wadn't it?" Herman asked Bob.

"Yeah and Cotter's from Kershaw."

"Kershaw? You mean Cheraw?" I asked.

"No, Kershaw. It's a little bitty wide place in the road."

"He wadn't no such thing," Larry interrupted. "He was from McBee."

"No, it was Kershaw," Bob replied.

"You a damn liar," Larry replied, his face turning red. I counted five empties by his elbow. "I know damn well he was from McBee. We talked about fishing on the Wateree."

"He might've fished Wateree, but he was from Kershaw," Bob replied without looking up.

Larry opened his mouth, but I got there first. "Is Cotter married?"

"Not anymore," Herman offered. "I think he was hiding from his ex-wife."

"What's he look like?" If he was using a different name, I'd need a physical description to trace him in his hometown.

"Nice-looking fella," Terry said. "A little shorter than me, 'bout five eight, what, a hundred sixty pounds?" he asked Herman.

"A hundred seventy," Herman replied.

"Yeah, maybe. Curly black hair, real blue eyes. 'Bout thirty-five, I guess."

That matched the description the druggist had given me.

"Did he ever drive a beige or tan car?"

"Nah, don't think he even had a car," Herman replied.

"Can we play some damn cards here?" Larry interrupted.

"Getting too rich for my blood," I excused myself, rising. "You guys have cleaned me out of everything but pocket money. I'd better be on my way."

"Guess you college boys don't know everything after all," Larry grunted.

I decided to let him have that one. "Guess not," I said.

"I'll let you out," Terry said. I said goodnight to Bob and Herman. Larry ignored me and stumbled off in the direction of the bathroom.

I shook Terry's hand at the door and thanked him. "I feel bad I didn't think to suggest this before," he apologized. "I never knew George and Jack were buddies. Jack never talked much and George is kind of a floater."

"It's okay. I've gotten a lot of good information here tonight."

"Yeah?" He brightened.

"Oh yeah," I assured him. I clapped him on the shoulder and turned to go. The air was split by a deafening crack. I felt a sharp sting on my cheek. The next thing I knew, I was on the ground with Terry on top of me. My head swam from lack of oxygen and the combined fumes of gasoline and beer. Before I could get my breath, the air was split again. Chips of concrete rained down on us. Somewhere, an engine raced. By the time Terry scrambled up and helped me to my feet, the street was silent and deserted again.

Bob and Herman spilled out the door, wide-eyed. Larry followed, struggling with his fly. "What the hell was that?" Bob panted.

"Sumbitch shot at us." Terry pointed out the bullet holes in the wall inches from where we'd been standing.

I limped over and sat down on a bumper to take stock. The knee of my pants was torn, likewise the skin under it, and the heels of both hands. I put a careful handkerchief to my cheek. It came away bloody.

"You okay, buddy?" Terry asked.

"The fall did more damage than the bullet, I think." I stood up and discovered my knees were shaky. "Did you see the car?"

"Naw. I saw the flash and hit the dirt, but I think it was a truck," he replied. "Whyn't you come on inside and get cleaned up? I got a first aid kit in the back."

"No, really, I'm okay."

"You go home looking like that, you're gonna scare your wife into fits," he insisted firmly. "At least put some Mercurochrome on those scrapes and stick a band-aid on'em."

The fellas moved aside as Terry helped me into the office.

"You've sure pissed somebody off." Larry lounged in the doorway, rolling a toothpick from one corner of his mouth to the other. There was a new respect in his glassy stare. Getting shot at, it seemed, was even more manly than playing poker.

"Seems that way," I agreed.

"We oughta call the police." Herman appeared behind Larry in the doorway.

"No!" They turned startled faces to me. "I'm not exactly in

the cop's good graces right now. I'd just as soon keep this quiet. If there's any damage, I'll take care of it," I told Terry.

"Nah. It missed the glass. Just a couple dents in the wall. I'll slap a little paint on'em, nobody will notice." He stood back and surveyed his handiwork on my face. "You sure you don't wanna call the cops?"

"I'm sure."

"You want somebody to follow you home, case they're out there waiting for you?" Larry offered eagerly.

That was a chilling thought, but I didn't want any company for what I had to do next.

"I appreciate it, but they probably just meant to scare me. I've got a couple stops before I go home, anyway."

I thanked Terry again and shook hands all around. I looked back in my rearview mirror as I left, to see them clustered around the door, staring at the bullet holes.

Reaction set in once I was alone. My hands shook so hard it was difficult to grip the wheel, and I checked my rearview mirror every few seconds. Reaction was followed closely by confusion. I'd been plodding along for weeks, getting nowhere but ruffling no feathers. Now all of a sudden, people were shooting at me. But for what? What had changed? If I'd kicked over the wrong rocks digging into Delores's life I'd have expected a reaction before now. After some reflection, I decided the difference was that today I'd refocused my attention on Delores's whereabouts on Sunday night and within hours, I was dodging bullets. I scoured my memory until it was raw, but I couldn't recall anything I'd learned that would have been worth someone taking a shot at me. I didn't know what else to do but press on.

It took about ten minutes to reach Delores's neighborhood. I cruised her block twice, checking for dog walkers or insomniacs, but every house was dark. Her Chevy was a dark shadow under the trees at the end of the driveway.

I parked three blocks away under the shadow of an elderly elm and waited a few minutes for the rest of the adrenaline to fade and my heart to resume its normal beat. I eased out of the car as quietly as possible. To my overwrought nerves, the snick of the car door sounded as loud as a gunshot. I waited for the neighborhood dogs to set up an alarm, but they remained quiet.

I pocketed my flashlight. I didn't want to use it until I had to. I kept to the grass to muffle my footsteps and gave the gravel drive a wide berth as I approached the car. I reached for the door handle. At that moment, a car turned the corner. Its lights swept the yard. I hit the grass face first and prayed.

The car slowed. My heart came to a complete stop. But the car kept going and a minute later, the slam of its door carried clearly to me over the night air. Probably a neighbor coming home from the late show. I sat up and checked to be sure I wasn't wearing any garden slugs while I waited for my breathing to return to normal. Several minutes passed before my blood pressure retreated from petrified to somewhere around just plain scared.

I got up, took a careful look around, and tried the driver's side door. Locked. All the doors were locked. Damn. I cast a quick glance over my shoulder before chancing my flashlight. The light reflected off the glass, making it hard to read the tiny numbers. I angled the light this way and that as I tried to balance my notebook on my upraised knee. I was trying to make out whether the last digit was a five or a six when I heard the unmistakable scrape of a shoe on pavement. Close by, from the sound of it. I froze as a beam of light bobbed through the hedge. Somebody else with a flashlight.

Wildly, I scanned the yard for a hiding place. The choices were limited—under the car or the shadows on the far side of the house. I chose the shadows. I wedged myself as far into the bushes as I could and held my breath. Silence except for the incessant droning of the insects. Then, faintly, a crunch of gravel. Whoever it was was coming nearer.

I pressed myself harder against the bricks. Then came the twang of the screen door spring. A series of clicks and scrapes, a muffled curse. Someone was trying to get into the house. A squeak of hinges told me they'd made it in. I eased out of the bushes and peered around the corner. Nothing. I gazed up at the windows above my head. The blinds on one of the bedroom windows were only half-closed. As I watched, a faint light played through the slats and disappeared. The window went dark again. They'd moved to the front of the house. Hours crept by as I stood frozen to my spot, but when I checked my watch, less than three minutes had passed when I heard the screen door protest again. They were leaving. I peered around the corner, but whoever it was had moved fast. I darted around to the front of the house where the corner streetlight cast its light. Nothing. Perplexed, I strained my ears for footsteps or a car engine. Nothing. If they didn't go up the street and they didn't go down the street, where the hell did they go? Maybe nowhere, whispered something down the back of my neck. Maybe they're hiding in the shadows waiting for you.

It wasn't easy, but I forced myself to make a complete circuit of the house. I kept well away from the bushes but with each step, I expected to feel the clutch of a hand. There was no one.

I returned to the backyard and flashed my light on the door. It was pulled to, but the intruder had used a jimmy or some tool to force it open. The latch no longer caught. I took my bloody handkerchief from my pocket, drew a deep breath, and pushed. The door swung open. I stepped inside and waited for my eyes to adjust to the darkness.

I was in the kitchen. The refrigerator hummed companionably in the corner. Slowly, I toured the house. Daylight would no doubt have revealed a layer of dust after so many weeks, but everything looked tidy. The living room opened directly off the kitchen. A sofa and an antique rocker, a few tables that looked like family heirlooms. A record player sat atop one of them, a stack of albums and 45s on the shelf below. The TV on its metal stand occupied the corner. If the intruder had been a burglar, he hadn't gotten much. Maybe he was just casing the place. And maybe he'd be back soon with helpers. Time to wrap up this inspection tour.

A tiny hallway separated the living room from the bedrooms. A dripping faucet to my left proclaimed the bathroom. I flashed my light to the right. Twin beds and photos of ball players ripped from magazines on the walls. That left only the doorway immediately in front of me. Delores's room. And, unless I was mistaken, the room where I'd seen the intruder's light.

I stood in the center of the room trying to absorb something about the woman who had lived here. The bed drew my eyes. Someone had pulled up the green chenille spread and propped the pillows against the headboard. The dresser top, covered by a white cotton runner, held only hairbrushes and perfume bottles. My own ghostly reflection stared back at me from the mirror above it.

The closet door hung ajar. I nudged it open with my foot. A flowered housecoat hung from a peg. Even after all these weeks, a faint odor of talcum powder hung in the air. I stepped around the bed to examine the nightstand. My foot hit something and sent it skittering across the floor. I squatted and slowly panned the flashlight until it caught a reflection of something under the nightstand. I stuck the flashlight between my teeth, fished a pen from my pocket and poked around blindly until I succeeded in dislodging the object from behind one of the legs. Slowly, I crouched down and examined my find.

An empty pill bottle.

CHAPTER 16

Miz Turner finally had to call and pose as a neighbor to report the break-in. None of Delores's neighbors noticed all of us parading through the house Saturday night or the back door I'd left carefully ajar, and Warren was anxious for the bottle to be found. I sweated bullets until Hilda called to report the police had found the bottle where I'd left it for them. By then, Warren's high-priced pathologist was already on a plane.

I was at the library before the doors opened the next morning, despite Susie's flatly stated opinion that I wasn't fit to be let out alone. I'd told her a long and complicated story about having to scale a tree to hide from the intruder to explain my injuries and torn clothes. If she'd found out about the shooting, I wouldn't have been let out alone. Much more excitement like last night's and I'd be seeing a lot more of Gary—in his professional capacity.

A pretty, young librarian indoctrinated me in the mysteries of the map section and left me to it. I'd driven the circuit from Delores's house to the Square, her office, the drive-in, and, just in case, Lattimore's cabin, and calculated there was roughly two hundred miles on her odometer unaccounted for. There was no way to know if she'd gone to the office at all. She could have driven around aimlessly for hours or gone from store to store looking for the right tennis racquet. She could have gone out Monday afternoon, but from what we knew of her condition, I doubted it. There was no way to know if anything she'd told

Lattimore was the truth, but it was all I had.

I double checked the scale and drew a circle roughly a hundred miles from Delores's house. Then I moved the compass point slightly and drew an overlapping circle from Lattimore's cabin. I sat back to look at my handiwork.

Delores could have been anywhere or nowhere within those circles, but one name leaped out at me.

Bob flattered Kershaw when he called it a little bitty wide place in the road. The huge textile plant that loomed over the highway, however, made up for it. It was a typical mill village, with rows of nearly identical frame houses on cinder blocks and surrounded by acres of cultivated land bordered by rows of peach trees. The houses got closer together as I neared the center of town.

I cruised the main drag, with its brick-fronted stores, slowly, which took all of five minutes, then circled the outer perimeter, which took another five. The burned-out hulk of a filling station served as the demarcation between "town" and the endless pine barrens that stretched beyond. The streets were deserted. I made a three-point road turn and headed back to "town."

I pulled up in front of the diner, which caused no end of excitement among the dogs on the sidewalk. One even raised up long enough to scratch.

It wouldn't be fair to say the natives were unfriendly, but every question brought the same response—a swivel of the head and a blank look. Within a half hour, I'd covered the feed store, the hardware store, the five-and-dime, the bank, and the drugstore, and was back where I started at the diner. At least the dogs were happy to see me. One even thumped his tail as I stepped over him to enter the diner.

Every head in the place turned in my direction and all conversation ceased. I settled myself on a stool and nodded to the sunburned farmer on the next stool. He stared back at me. Four or five other men in bib overalls occupied the remaining booths and tables, but they might have been store window dummies. No one moved. No one spoke. They just stared. There was nothing hostile or challenging in their stares. They just stared. It was the damned creepiest thing I'd ever felt.

"Afternoon. Getcha something?" The waitress appeared, tea pitcher at the ready.

"Is it too late to get some lunch?"

"Bert!" she hollered over her shoulder. "Any stew beef left?" Bert answered in the affirmative. "How 'bout the green beans?" Bert allowed as how he thought he could eke out another serving. She poured a glass of iced tea without asking and started to move away.

"I was wondering if you might know a family around these parts by the name of Cotter."

"Cotter?" Her eyes wanted to slide toward the men. She kept her gaze on mine with an effort. "Can't say I do."

"I could have the name wrong. The man I'm looking for would be in his early forties, about five seven or five eight, a hundred seventy pounds, with curly black hair and real blue eyes. He goes by Jack Cotter. Does that ring a bell?"

"Nope, sorry. Can't say it does."

Without warning, I swiveled around on my stool to confront the men. "How 'bout any of you?" They shuffled their feet and shook their heads at their plates. "How about a black late-model Chevy? Anybody notice a strange one in town the last few weeks?" They shook their heads. I shrugged and smiled at the waitress, which seemed to frighten her more than my questions. "Oh, well. Can't win 'em all."

We sat in silence for several minutes until she emerged from the kitchen with my plate. She set it front of me and disappeared. It was the best stew beef I'd ever sunk my teeth into.

The green beans were fresh, with a tiny square of fatback swimming in the juice. I was seriously thinking about trying to lure Bert to the big city and a job at the Diamond when the front door opened with a tinkle.

"Afternoon, Margie." I turned on my stool. Damned if it wasn't Gary Cooper—tall and lean, shoulders broad enough to block out the sun, and a big, shiny badge.

"Hey, Hal," she greeted him with obvious relief. "Lunch?"

"Just a piece of pie and some coffee," he said. "Got any peach left?" He greeted most of the men by name and settled himself on the stool to my left. We nodded, but he didn't speak until he had his pie and coffee in front of him.

"That your Falcon out front?" he asked.

"Yup."

"How you like it?"

"Okay. It didn't cost much and it gets pretty good mileage."

"Run all right on the highway?" He stirred some sugar into his coffee.

"Pretty fair."

He nodded. "My brother-in-law's been thinking about one." He glanced over his shoulder. With a great shuffling of feet and scraping of chairs, the men, who'd been sitting motionless during this exchange, rose in a body and trooped silently out the door.

"Passing through?" He took a bite of pie and gazed at me innocently.

"I'm looking for someone, man by the name of Cotter. I was told he's from around these parts."

He chewed ruminatively. "Don't recognize the name. 'Course, I'm a newcomer. Only been here about ten years. I'm Hal Hooks, by the way." He stuck out a hand. I shook it and showed him my license by way of introduction.

"Private, huh? You looking for this Cotter fella in your professional capacity? If you don't mind my asking," he added.

"Let's just say I'm anxious to talk to him," I replied.

"He have anything to do with that black Chevy you're looking for?" His faded blue eyes were guileless.

"I'm not sure. The car and the woman who owned it went missing the Sunday night before the Fourth and Cotter was supposed to be the first person to see her the next morning."

"You did say, 'owned'?" No flies on Hal.

"That's right. The woman turned up dead about thirty-six hours later."

"S'that so?" Hal took a sip of his coffee and stared thoughtfully into his cup. "Anything in particular make you think she was here Sunday night? If you don't mind my asking."

"Maybe. Maybe not. I got lucky. She took her car in for service Friday morning and again Monday morning at the gas station where Cotter worked. I checked the mileage, drew a circle on the map, and there was Kershaw. It struck me as an interesting coincidence."

Hal nodded. "That is an interesting coincidence. But I got one better than that. That very same Sunday night somebody robbed the gas station out by the highway. Beat the owner, Henry Young, pretty bad and then set fire to the place. When he wasn't home for Ed Sullivan and didn't answer the phone, his wife sent their boy to look for him. He got there in time to drag his daddy out, but the station was gone."

"You think there's a connection? If you don't mind my asking," I added.

"Well, like you said about coincidences." He swiveled around to face me. "The boy passed a car on his way to the station and being a teenage boy, he knows his cars and he thinks it might have been a Chevy—a dark Chevy. And whoever it was knew when to hit the station. Henry's station's also the local Trailways depot. Sunday night's the big night for freight. Henry figures there was close to three thousand in the till that night. Any other night, it woulda been thirty bucks."

"Henry get a look at the driver?"

"His attention was mostly taken up with the gun and the stocking the fella had pulled over his face. 'Bout the only thing he is certain of is the guy was at least six feet and white. Couldn't tell anything about hair or eyes with the stocking."

"Doesn't sound like Cotter."

"Nope." Hal set his coffee cup down. "I'm gonna have a word with Margie." He vanished into the kitchen, returning a few minutes later with the coffee pot.

"Margie recalls a young fella who went to the local high school for about a year who could be the one you're looking for." He poured me a cup of coffee and topped off his own cup. "Nobody knew the family much; they kept to themselves and didn't stay long, but apparently the boy was something of a hell raiser."

"Anybody in town who knew them that I could talk to?"

He shook his head. "Margie didn't think so. But I'll ask around. I might be able to get a little more out of folks than you can."

"That wouldn't be hard. If you find anything at all, I'd appreciate a call. The trial will be starting any day now." I put one of my cards on the counter.

Hal squinted up at me. "Likewise. This one's kinda personal. Henry's my wife's uncle."

"I'm real sorry."

He nodded. "Things are gonna be a mite uncomfortable at the family reunion next month if I don't manage to arrest somebody."

"I was never very good at jigsaw puzzles, but I'm beginning to believe there's a picture in here somewhere," I said. "If any of the pieces fall into place, I'll let you know."

"I 'preciate that." We shook hands and I took my leave. I was halfway out the door when he stopped me.

"By the way," he drawled. "Which side you on?"

I banged the door behind me, but his chuckle followed me out to the car.

I returned to the office to find two cryptic messages. The one from Hilda said simply, *Big pow-wow at the doctor's.* The other was a summons to an audience with Owens.

"He didn't say where?" I asked Mrs. Bruno.

"He said you'd know where." She shrugged and waddled back to her office.

It wasn't until I was settled at my desk, where my calendar reminded me it was Tuesday, that it fell into place. Every Tuesday night for time immemorial, Lieutenant Owens has held court at his usual table in the Hotel Charlotte's empty ballroom. On any given evening, his supplicants could run the gamut from parents of troublesome sons or wayward daughters to patrolmen seeking promotion or city councilmen seeking favors. Not much goes on in this town he doesn't know about.

I left a message with Miz Turner and spent the rest of the afternoon typing my report and catching up on bills and paperwork. I called it a day about five and went home to dinner with Susie and the kids.

Promptly at eight, I pulled up in front of the hotel. I knew better than to arrive early. Owens arranges his audiences carefully to avoid any embarrassing encounters in the lobby. The guy before me could be a bookie or the mayor.

Owens was alone at his table in the back of the room. His face gave nothing away as he watched me approach. I stopped at the table and waited until he nodded at the other chair. He raised a finger without taking his eyes from me. A waiter appeared at his elbow with a coffee cup I knew held premium

Kentucky sipping whiskey. Owens would have two such cups during the evening—no more, no less. At ten o'clock, a patrol car would roll up behind the hotel to drive him home.

The waiter set a glass of iced tea in front of me and vanished. I took a sip and waited.

"I used to work this hotel during the war," Owens said, gazing at the faded grandeur around us. "It was some place in those days, 'specially on the weekends, when the soldiers at Camp Green got leave. We'd be picking up drunks and breaking up fights from sundown to sun-up." He grunted. "Used to make us get blood tests once a week. Afraid we'd pick up something from the whores." His sigh was more regret than remorse.

"Aren't you worried about what King will say if he hears you've been talking to me?" I asked.

He made a noise somewhere between a chuckle and a snort. "I been a cop nearly thirty years now. Lord willing, I'll be one for another ten or twenty years. How long's King been D.A.? Five years? And if he loses this case, he'll be out on his ass next year. I'll talk to whoever I damn well please."

He could easily have made chief during those thirty years if he'd wanted it, but he was more interested in being a cop than a politician. His power far exceeds the Chief's and they both know it.

"They seated a jury today." He took a sip and watched me over the rim of his cup.

"Already?" I was truly shocked. I'd scanned the *Times* before leaving the house, but they have a three o'clock deadline, so there'd been no mention of that bombshell.

"Yup. Never seen anything like it."

"Is that why you sent for me?"

"I just thought since you'd been away, you might appreciate being caught up on all the latest developments." His pale face was inscrutable.

"Like?"

"Like, did you hear somebody broke into that poor woman's house over the weekend?"

"What woman would that be?"

"The dead woman."

"That's too bad. Anything taken?"

A faint shadow that was almost a grin flitted across his face. "Not that anybody can tell. It was more like something was left."

He waited, but I had as much practice as he had. "Damnedest thing. I had a whole squad of detectives search that house top to bottom, but when they went in yesterday, there was this empty pill bottle lying in the middle of the floor like it just magically appeared."

"That is something. But I'm a little surprised you're telling me."

"Oh, I 'spect you would have heard about it sooner or later." He gave me a level gaze. The Chief might be baffled about departmental leaks, but Owens wasn't. I met his eyes squarely. We remained like that for a long time, measuring each other.

"The D.A. released the results of blood tests today, too," he offered.

"I didn't know they were back yet."

"FBI sent 'em down yesterday."

"S'that so? Cut it kinda fine, didn't they?"

"Maybe." Owens looked into his cup. "They found a blood-alcohol level of 0.42 percent."

"That's pretty high."

"Uh-huh. Doc says he's known cases where 0.25 was enough to kill somebody."

"That's interesting."

"Isn't it? 'Bout like that pill bottle turning up from outta nowhere like that."

"Mmm."

We sipped in silence for a few minutes.

"I hear you were out of town," Owens said finally. "Business or pleasure?"

"Little bit of both. Found a place serves green beans almost as good as my mama's and stew beef you can cut with a fork."

"Nothing like good green beans," he agreed, "specially with fresh tomatoes and onions cut up in'em."

I was being dismissed. I rose from the table. "Nice seeing you again, Lieutenant."

He looked up at me without raising his head. "As far as I know, I ain't sent an innocent man to jail yet, Mr. Harlan. And I don't aim to start now. You find anything, you bring it to me, you hear? Don't go playing Wyatt Earp." I knew now why I'd been summoned. Somehow he'd found out about the shooting. He pointed a fat finger. "You bring it to me and only to me, hear?"

"And you'll do the same for me, no doubt." My footsteps echoed loudly in the empty room as I made my way across the dance floor. As I went out, I glanced back to see Owens watching me.

CHAPTER 17

I met Warren and the pathologist, Dr. Claiborne, at Warren's office early the next morning. The clerks were gone; even Warren's office had been tidied and dusted. The decks were cleared for battle.

Even Miz Turner was too preoccupied to snub me. Warren and Claiborne checked their files and notes one last time, packed them in their briefcases, then we left for the courthouse. Warren and Claiborne rode in Warren's big, black Buick; I followed in the Falcon.

No problem, this time, finding a parking place. A waiting deputy shifted sawhorses and waved us into reserved spots behind the courthouse. We slipped in through the back door, where we were met by another deputy who whisked us into the freight elevator, up to the fourth floor, and straight into the anteroom of Judge Cecil's chambers.

Lattimore turned from the window as we came in. Warren introduced Claiborne. The two men exchanged a perfunctory handshake; I got a nod. Lattimore and Warren moved to the corner and began to talk quietly. Claiborne took the empty secretary's chair, spread out his notes on the desk, and set to studying them. I settled myself on the hard, wooden visitor's chair and studied Lattimore.

There was a subtle change in him, an air of authority and command that suited him as perfectly as his banker's uniform of blue suit, white shirt, and striped tie. He actually appeared more relaxed than I'd ever seen him. This was the role in which he felt comfortable—the man of action, ready to take charge. Now that there was something to *do,* even if it was defending himself against a murder charge, he was in his element.

The minutes ticked past slowly. The sun streaming in through the windows gained strength, burning off the early chill of the morning, but it had little strength against the chill of apprehension in that room.

Another twenty minutes dragged on. Warren sat calmly while Lattimore paced, his incessant footsteps periodically punctuated by a rustle of pages from Claiborne. Otherwise, the silence remained unbroken.

Without warning, Judge Cecil emerged from his inner sanctum, pulling on his black robe. The tension in the room tightened and became a living thing. Lattimore froze in mid-step, his cigarette halfway to his lips. Warren crossed the room to shake Cecil's hand. They exchanged low-voiced pleasantries, and then Cecil left without ever looking at Lattimore.

"We'll get under way in about ten minutes." Warren directed his words to me and Claiborne, but his eyes were on his client.

Lattimore gave a curt nod and turned his back to stare, stone-faced, out the window. I tried to imagine what must be going through his mind but I failed.

I rose and crossed to the other window to see what held his attention. Below me, people swarmed across the grass and up the courthouse steps like ants at a picnic. A good many of them actually carried picnic baskets, red-checked dish towels protecting their fried chicken, deviled eggs, and tomato sandwiches. It lacked only a tumbrel to make the scene complete. Lattimore's eyes were on the scene below, but I don't think he saw any of it. He was in some other place where none of us could follow him.

A knock at the door brought us both around with a jerk. The deputy poked his head around the door and caught Warren's eye. "They're 'bout ready for you, Mr. Warren."

"Thank you, Ernie. We'll be right along." I moved away as Warren came across to speak to Lattimore. Claiborne carefully collected his papers and returned them to his briefcase. Warren put a reassuring hand on Lattimore's arm before they joined us by the door. We stood in a semicircle, awkward and uncomfortable.

To this day, I don't know what prompted me, but before I knew I was going to do it, I stuck out my hand. "Good luck, Mr. Lattimore."

He accepted my hand and his eyes met mine for the briefest moment. "Thank you."

The atmosphere in the packed courtroom was one of barely controlled frenzy, but the huge, echoing chamber was strangely hushed. Every square inch was filled. White faces were even dotted in among the Negroes in the balcony.

The defense table had been shoved forward to make room for an extra row of chairs in front of the railing. Bailiffs were sliding the last ones in place as we entered. Warren directed me to one of them, behind and slightly to Claiborne's right. Lattimore sat in front of me at the table, Warren on his left, nearest the aisle. I'd barely taken my seat when the clerk called us to order.

The curtain was going up.

Judge Cecil and his clerk disposed of a few procedural preliminaries, and then Cecil nodded to King. "Mr. Prosecutor, call your first witness."

King, in a new suit an unhappy shade of olive, red carnation in the lapel, rose to take his rightful place at center stage. "The prosecution calls Calvin Miller to the stand."

A ripple of speculation ran around the edges of the crowd at the unfamiliar name. I slid down in my seat. Mr. Miller and I had become well acquainted enough he'd felt perfectly comfortable threatening to rearrange my face if I showed it one more time at Jergen's Funeral Home. But how was I to know he was Doc's protegé, hand-picked and personally trained by the Great Man himself?

I was surprised, however, when he took the stand wearing an Army uniform. Great. He probably knew hand-to-hand combat.

"On July 4 of this year you were employed as an embalmer at the Jergen's Funeral Home on Monroe Road, is that right, Private Miller?" King asked.

"Yes sir, that is correct."

"When did you first view the body of the deceased, Mrs. Delores Green?"

"Between approximately six-thirty and seven a.m.," Miller replied.

"Could you describe what you first observed about the body at that time?"

"The body was on an ambulance stretcher. It was clothed in pink cotton pajamas and covered by a sheet and a blanket."

"Did you notice anything else about the body?" King addressed his questions to Miller, but kept his eyes on the jury box.

"Yes, sir. The . . . deceased's face was covered in bruises. She was lying on her back."

"What did you do next, Mr. . . . excuse me, Private Miller?"

"I called Dr. Winston, the coroner, at his home."

"Yes?"

"At his instructions, I drew a vial of blood from the deceased, then proceeded with the embalming of the body."

I shot a glance at Warren, but he showed no surprise. The silence was thick as fog.

"At what time did Dr. Winston arrive to perform the autopsy?" King asked.

"Well, actually, the police arrived first, while I was still embalming the body, to take photographs, so it took a little longer than usual. Dr. Winston arrived about nine a.m., as I was finishing up. I was just closing the incision when he came in."

I shifted in my chair and caught a glimpse of Greg, his face white and strained, surrounded by women in flowered hats. I assumed one of them was his aunt. I also spotted Mrs. Hemingway in the row behind him. She too, looked different somehow, in a way I couldn't quite put my finger on. As I watched, she reached up to rest a hand on Greg's shoulder. He ignored her.

"How long did that take?"

"The autopsy?"

"That's right."

"About two hours, I'd say."

"Then what did you do?"

"Well, after Dr. Winston completed the autopsy, we began the cosmetic work on the body. Then, at Dr. Winston's instruction, I counted the bruises on the body."

King turned to look full at the jury. "And how many bruises did you count on Mrs. Green's body, Private Miller?"

"Two hundred fifty-one." A gasp went up from the spectators.

"Can you describe them?"

"Well, sir, they completely covered the body from head to toe with the exception of the back."

"There were no bruises on her back?"

"That is correct."

"Were these bruises examined?"

"Yes sir. To my recollection, Dr. Winston opened three of the bruises, the largest, which were on the knee, by her . . . left eye, and just under the left breast. The bruises were all different shapes and sizes, but those were the largest."

"Did you examine the dead woman's scalp as well?"

"Yes, sir, we did. It was also bruised and those bruises were counted as part of the two hundred fifty-one bruises."

"Your Honor, at this time, I'd like to introduce the photographs of the body taken by police at the funeral home and ask Private Miller to explain them to the jury."

"Let me see them," Judge Cecil ordered.

King handed them up. Cecil studied them for a moment before handing them to the clerk, who returned them to King. "I'll allow them," Cecil said. He turned to face the jury box. "Members of the jury, these photographs do not constitute evidence of a crime. They are being introduced merely to illustrate the testimony of this witness."

At a gesture from King, Miller left the witness stand and stood before the jury box. One by one, King held up the photos. The men all looked stolid, but the women didn't attempt to hide their distress. A younger woman turned pale and pressed her fingertips to her lips.

"Would you please point out to the jury which of the bruises were opened?" King instructed. Miller did so, pointing from the bruises in the photo to the corresponding position on his own body. When King decided the jury had had enough, he allowed Miller to return to the stand.

"Can you describe for the court, Mr. Miller, just how you settled on the number of bruises?" King asked when Miller was seated again.

"Yes, sir. As I explained, some of the bruises were sizable, others were very small . . ."

"How small?"

"Uh, I'd say, maybe the size of a match head."

"Go on."

"Well, as long as the bruises did not actually touch or run into another, they were counted as separate bruises."

"Thank you, Private Miller." Turning to the bench, he added,

"I have no further questions."

"Mr. Warren?" Cecil invited.

"Thank you, sir." Warren rose and moved to a spot halfway between his table and the witness stand. "Private Miller, how long have you been an embalmer?"

"I trained in funeral work for four years; I have been licensed for two."

"So most of your early training was received on the job?"

"Yes, sir, most of it. But I did have to study and take several written exams to get my license."

"Thank you. From whom did you receive most of your on-the-job training?"

"Well, several of the people I worked with, but I guess I'd have to say mainly from Mr. Huntington who owns the funeral home."

"Anyone else?"

"Well, I worked real closely with Dr. Winston over the years, too. He taught me quite a bit."

"That's Dr. Winston, the county coroner?"

"Yes, sir." Miller shifted in his chair.

"Mr. Miller, can you recall how much blood was drawn from Mrs. Green's body for testing?"

"Well, the test tube holds two ounces and it wasn't quite full, so I'd estimate it was somewhere between an ounce and a half and two ounces."

"And what did you do with the test tube once you had drawn the blood?"

"Well, I labeled it and put it on a rack we have for them in the embalming room."

"The blood sample was not refrigerated?"

"No, sir."

"And the tube remained in this rack on an open shelf in the embalming room until when?"

"Uh, I guess it would have been there until after Dr. Winston finished up with the autopsy."

"And did you personally place the test tube in Dr. Winston's hand?"

"Yes, sir."

"I see. Thank you." Warren turned back to the table and picked up his notes. "Mr. Miller, were you present during the entire autopsy?"

"I was. Dr. Winston usually insists on it."

"Did you watch Dr. Winston open the body and remove the internal organs?"

"I did." Was it my imagination or was there a hint of defensiveness creeping into Miller's tone?

"Can you remember which organs were examined?"

Miller stared straight ahead in concentration. "He opened the cranial cavity and the abdominal and thoracic cavity."

I caught a movement out of the corner of my eye and turned to see Mrs. Hemingway with her face in her gloved hands.

"That would be the head, the chest, and the stomach?"

"Yes."

"Which of these organs did he examine?"

"He examined all the organs and took tissue samples from some of them."

"From which organs did you see Dr. Winston take tissue samples?"

"I couldn't say for sure. I saw him examine the organs but I don't know which ones he took samples from."

"I see. Mr. Miller, how would you describe the 'bruises' you saw on Mrs. Green's body?"

"I'm not sure what you mean."

"Well, their color for instance. Were they black? Blue? Yellowish-green?"

"Most of them were purplish in color."

"Most of them? Are you saying that some of the bruises were a different color?"

"Not really. I'd have to say it was more that they were different shades of purple. None of them were black or blue and none were green or yellow."

"Mr. Miller, are you familiar with a condition in which the walls of the blood vessels become weakened and allow blood to leak from the vessels under the skin?"

"Yes, sir, I am familiar with that condition, but I didn't see anything to indicate that in this case."

"You say there were no bruises on the back?"

"I saw no bruising on the back."

"Were there bruises on the buttocks?"

"Yes, sir."

"So there were bruises on the back of the body, but not on the back itself?"

"That's right."

"Did you notice anything else unusual about the skin other than the bruises?" Warren removed his glasses and pinched his nose as he waited for the answer.

"Yes. There was a rash on the buttocks and down the legs on the backs of the thighs and the inner thighs."

"Are you familiar with the term 'psoriasis,' Mr. Miller?"

"No, I don't believe I am."

"Mr. Miller, when you examined the body, did you notice any scrapes or abrasions?"

"No, sir. That is," he corrected himself, "there were two small scrapes on her knees."

"Did you notice any grass stains, any gravel or small stones anywhere on the body?"

"No, sir."

"Was there a noticeable smell of alcohol either when you examined the body or when the body cavities were opened during the autopsy?"

"I didn't notice any odor of alcohol, but I probably wouldn't have been able to notice it because of the smell of the embalming fluid."

"Mr. Miller, am I correct that the photographs which have been shown to the jury were taken after the body was embalmed?"

"Partially embalmed."

"Had the blood been removed from the body when the pictures were taken?"

"Yes."

"What effect would that have on the appearance of the skin?"

"Removing the blood?"

"That is correct."

"Well . . ." Miller hesitated, unsure what Warren wanted.

"What I mean is, how does the body, the skin, look differently after the blood is removed than before?" Warren clarified the question.

"Oh. Well, it's whiter. There's no color. Unless the body is a Negro."

"So the skin becomes pallid, very white, after the blood is removed."

"Yes, sir."

"So that if there were any discoloration of the skin, it would become much more noticeable, more dramatic, is that accurate?" Warren asked.

"Yes, that's true."

"Mr. Miller, I believe these photographs to which we refer are black and white?"

"Yes."

"And do you recall whether the police used a flash bulb to take those photographs?"

"Yes, sir, they did. They commented that the light in the

embalming room was not very suitable for photographs and they would have to use the flash bulb to get the right contrast so the bruises would stand out."

"Is that the term they used, 'stand out'?" Warren asked quickly.

"Well, I couldn't say for sure after all this time. They might have just said 'show up,' " Miller corrected himself.

"Thank you, Mr. Miller. I have no further questions," Warren said, resuming his seat.

King rose from his seat and made a production of buttoning his jacket. "The prosecution would like to call Jeff Smith."

Smith, a slight, sandy-haired man with the sharp features and thin lips of a weasel, made his way to the stand and was sworn in.

"Mr. Smith, you were previously employed by the Charlotte Ambulance Service, is that correct?"

"Yes."

"And you were employed in that capacity on July 4, 1961?"

"That's right."

King nodded emphatically at nothing at all.

"Did you receive a call to pick up a body at 943 Ashmore Avenue on that date?"

"I did."

"And did you remove the body?"

"We did. We took the body to Memorial Hospital and waited while one of the doctors come out and pronounced her dead. Then we drove on over to the Jergen's Funeral Home."

"Was Mrs. Green's body removed from the stretcher at the hospital?"

"No, sir. The doctor come out to the ambulance and did his tests and pronounced her right there on the spot."

"Could you describe the state of the body as you observed it?"

"Well, she had on pajamas, so I could only see her arms from about the elbows down and her face and neck."

"And what did you notice about those areas you were able to see?"

"Well, she had kind of a bluish look about the lips." Smith glanced apologetically toward Greg and his aunt. "There were some bruises on her face and her arms, specially the inside of one elbow and there was a big bruise over one of her eyes that looked like it weren't very old."

"How so?"

"Well, the bruise was open, like whatever caused it had broke the skin."

"Did you have any difficulty in removing the body from the house?" King asked.

"No. We lifted her real gentle like on the stretcher and wheeled it out easy as you please."

"Was the body bumped or dropped at any time while it was being transported?"

"Oh, no sir. The stretcher has side rails, but she wadn't a real big woman and since, well, she wadn't gonna object, we strapped her in real snug so she wouldn't shift none during the ride. We don't treat the dead folks any different just cause they're dead."

"Thank you, Mr. Smith." King turned toward the defense table. "Mr. Warren?"

"I have no questions for this witness," Warren replied easily.

"Who is your next witness, Mr. King?"

"I plan to call Dr. Winston as the next witness," King replied.

"Do you anticipate that will be a lengthy examination?"

"I do."

"In that case, and if no one objects, I suggest we call an early recess for lunch and begin Dr. Winston's testimony this afternoon."

King looked disappointed, but agreed. "I have no objection."

"Nor I," Warren rose.

"In that case, we are adjourned until one o'clock." Judge Cecil banged the gavel and disappeared in a swirl of black robes.

CHAPTER 18

I grabbed a quick bite at Hilda's favorite diner and was back at the courthouse by ten of one. I felt, more than heard, the murmurs that followed me as I navigated my way through the picnickers on the courthouse lawn.

Inside, I found I had company for the afternoon session. Deborah Lattimore and two other women, one gray-haired, the other in her early twenties, occupied the seats next to mine.

Deborah greeted me warmly. "This is John's sister, Mrs. Brown, and my daughter, Barbara." We murmured politely and shook hands all around. I stepped over their feet to take my seat at the end of the row.

Word must have spread that Doc was going to testify today. I spotted several prominent attorneys who had no other reason for being there than to enjoy the afternoon's entertainment. Kent came in, with Jeff Phillips from the *Courier* at his heels, and took up a post behind a column. I spotted a few television people in the crowd. With their cameramen and bulky equipment marooned outside, they seemed a little at a loss. Kent spotted me and sketched a wave.

Bennett waddled in, carrying bulging file folders held together by thick rubber bands. He took a seat at the end of the witnesses' bench behind King's table. As the woman seated on the far end shifted to make room for him, I recognized Elvira Hemingway. If she recognized Bennett as her rescuer of a few weeks ago, she gave no sign of it.

A sudden burst of laughter drew my attention to the corner behind the jury box. Doc, surrounded by a crowd of admiring deputies, bailiffs, and the stray lawyer or two, had just delivered a punch line. Beside me, I felt Lattimore's sister stiffen. Deputy Ernie glanced in our direction and had the grace to look sheepish.

Precisely at one o'clock, Warren and Lattimore entered the courtroom, trailed by Claiborne. If Lattimore was pleased to see his family, he covered it well. He spoke briefly to Deborah and took his seat, ignoring his sister and daughter.

Claiborne took the chair by Warren's elbow, no doubt so they could confer during Doc's testimony. People began to scurry to their seats.

Judge Cecil's clerk poked his head around the door and a minute later, the jury filed in followed shortly by the judge.

"The prosecution calls Dr. Winston to the stand."

Everyone craned their necks as Doc took the stand, resplendent in a three-piece suit and an honest-to-God cravat, though he'd left his gold-topped cane at home. King led him through ten minutes of preliminaries before zeroing in.

"On July fourth, you performed an autopsy on Mrs. Delores Green, is that correct, Dr. Winston?"

"That is correct." Doc leaned back in his seat and tugged down his vest, which looked suspiciously like watered silk.

"And, as a result of the autopsy, did you determine a cause of death?" King asked.

"I did."

"And what was your finding, Dr. Winston?"

"Based on my preliminary findings, I listed the cause of death as injuries, multiple and extreme."

"And have you had cause to revise that opinion since that time?"

"I have," Doc replied.

"On what basis did you revise your opinion, Dr. Winston?"

"Based on the results of blood tests conducted by the FBI laboratory in Washington, DC, which showed the deceased had a blood-alcohol level of 0.42 percent, I have revised the cause of death to shock from injuries multiple and extreme, combined with alcohol." Doc glanced at the court stenographer to make sure she'd been able to keep up. She thanked him with a quick nod and a smile.

"Is a blood-alcohol level of 0.42 percent sufficient to cause death?" King asked.

"It could be," Doc admitted easily.

"But you do not believe alcohol poisoning was the cause of death?"

"I do not. Although the alcohol was undoubtedly a contributing factor."

"Could you explain the reasoning behind your decision, Doctor?"

"It is generally accepted that a blood-alcohol level of 0.42 percent can cause death. However, it is my professional opinion, based on many years of experience, that that amount is borderline. It could be lethal to some people. But it is my considered opinion, that in order to be solely responsible for death, the blood-alcohol content would have to be much higher . . . somewhere in the 0.60 range."

"We have heard a great deal of testimony concerning the bruises on Mrs. Green's body. Are you satisfied they were in fact bruises, and not, as the defense has suggested, indications of some skin disorder or other condition?"

"There is no doubt whatsoever in my mind that the discolorations—" Doc cut his eyes at Warren, "were bruises."

"Did you observe any other indications of physical injuries during the autopsy?"

"As I testified during the preliminary hearing, there was some evidence to suggest the deceased might have sustained some type of minor whiplash injury. That's in addition to the heavy bruising to which I have already alluded."

King took that as his cue to lead Doc through the autopsy procedure, step by tedious step in an attempt, I assumed, to refute Warren's implication of sloppy procedures. Warren and Claiborne listened intently and frequently conferred in whispers.

Doc was in his element, the urbane professional, carefully explaining the more arcane points to the jury with no hint of condescension.

But after a half hour of this, the spectators began to squirm and shift in their seats. Sensing this, King picked up the pace and returned to the bruises.

"Private Miller has testified that the two of you counted two hundred and fifty-one bruises on Mrs. Green's body during the autopsy," King said. "Is this an accurate statement?"

"It is. The bruises ranged from the top of her head to the top of her feet. They varied in size from less than a centimeter to the largest, which was approximately three inches."

"And where was that bruise located?"

"Under the left breast. The skin was also broken in that instance, as it was on the bruise over the victim's left eye."

"How large was the break in the skin?" King asked.

"In both cases, the cut was approximately a quarter of an inch. I also noted a number of bruises on her arms and legs. Her left eye, the one with the bruise, was swollen and discolored and there was a cut on her lip."

Lattimore's sister reached up to rest a gloved hand on Lattimore's shoulder. He stiffened and turned his head just the barest fraction. She dropped her hand from his shoulder and returned it to her lap.

". . . the autopsy disclosed approximately fifteen to twenty areas of hemorrhage on the scalp under the skin."

"When you say hemorrhages, you mean bruises?" King prompted.

"I would not call them bruises, but they were due to an injury of some kind."

"Do you have an opinion as to what type of injury could have caused the hemorrhages?"

"It would be impossible to say." Doc shifted in his seat and recrossed his legs. "When I removed the upper portion of the spinal cord, I found a small area of hemorrhages on the left side of the cord."

Higgins leaned forward to whisper in King's ear. "Did the dead woman suffer a brain concussion?" King asked.

"My reply to that would have to be equivocal, but as I stated earlier, there is a definite possibility of brain concussion. There were also hemorrhages beneath the skin on the left side of the neck."

"Dr. Winston, how long did it take to perform the actual autopsy on Mrs. Green?"

"I would estimate roughly two hours."

"And how much time have you spent studying your findings and the other test results in order to arrive at your opinion on the cause of death?"

"Between eight and ten hours."

"One last question, Dr. Winston. Would a high blood-alcohol level make a person more susceptible to shock?"

"It would," Doc replied firmly. "However, let me be very clear. In this case, it is my opinion that the injuries Mrs. Green suffered were sufficient to cause death in themselves."

"Thank you, Dr. Winston."

Warren rose to his feet, but remained behind the table. "Dr. Winston, how much alcohol would someone need to consume to have a blood-alcohol content level of 0.42?"

Doc stroked his mustache and smiled for no apparent reason. "It would be roughly equivalent to sixteen ounces of whiskey."

"And you do not consider that amount to be potentially lethal?"

"As I stated earlier, consuming that much alcohol could be sufficient to cause death in some persons."

"Particularly if it were consumed within a short period of time?"

"That is so."

"So it is possible that alcohol alone could have caused Mrs. Green's death?"

"It is possible," Doc replied, laying a slight, but unmistakable emphasis on the last word.

"And is it not true that alcohol poisoning can, itself, induce shock?"

"It can."

"And is it not true there have been documented cases in which persons have died of alcohol poisoning with less alcohol in their bloodstreams than was found in Mrs. Green's?"

"I believe you are correct, Dr. Warren," Doc replied.

A shocked silence. Warren raised his eyes from his legal pad. "I beg your pardon. Did you call me Dr. Warren?"

"Did I?" Doc's surprise appeared genuine, but it was impossible to tell. "I beg your pardon. Force of habit, I suppose."

I would have given a lot for a glimpse of King's face at that moment, but my line of sight was blocked so I had to be content to imagine it.

Warren gazed at Doc for a moment. "Dr. Winston, did you examine the internal organs you removed from Mrs. Green's body? That is to say, did you take tissue samples from them?"

"I did."

"Did you find evidence of fatty tissue in Mrs. Green's liver?"

"I did."

"And is that condition consistent with alcoholism?"

"It can be. It can also be an indication of certain vitamin deficiencies."

"And is it not a fact that persons who suffer from alcoholism bruise more easily than others?"

"No."

"No?" Warren looked surprised.

"No. That is not a medical fact." Doc leaned forward in his chair as if to give emphasis to his words.

Warren shifted tack. "Are you familiar with the term 'reverse tolerance' as it applies to alcoholism, Dr. Winston?"

Doc hesitated. "Only in the most general sense."

"Am I correct in my understanding that reverse tolerance is a syndrome which occurs during the latter stages of alcoholism?"

"I really could not venture an opinion on that point."

"Am I correct that a person, an alcoholic, suffering from reverse tolerance syndrome loses the ability, or rather, the liver loses the ability, to process alcohol?" Warren asked.

"Allowing for some simplification, that's more or less correct, as I understand it," Doc replied.

"And what would be the effect if a person suffering from this condition drinks alcohol?"

"Well, it varies from person to person, of course," Doc replied. "But allowing for variables such as individual metabolic rate, the contents of the stomach, body weight, and a host of others, the effect would be that the person suffering from reverse tolerance would become more inebriated in a shorter period of time than the average person who consumed the same amount of alcohol."

"Dr. Winston, are you familiar with . . ."—Warren reeled off a litany of medical terms—". . . all of which can cause skin discoloration through spontaneous leakage of blood from the circulatory system?"

Doc inclined his head slightly as if in homage to Warren's diligence. "I am familiar with those conditions. However, I saw nothing to indicate their presence in this case."

"Could heavy drinking immediately prior to death cause a body to bruise more easily?"

"No."

Warren shifted tack again. "Is there any reliable way to determine how recent bruises are on a dead body?"

"There is no certain test to establish that." Warren opened his mouth to ask another question, but Doc overrode him. "However, I examined all the bruises on Mrs. Green's body, even to the extent of opening some of them for closer examination, and they all appeared to be recent."

"How recent?"

"I could not pinpoint the hour they were put there," Doc replied.

"Dr. Winston, is it not true that a body can bruise after death?"

"That is true."

"You have heard the testimony concerning the treatment of Mrs. Green's body—that is, how she was transported from the defendant's cabin to her home, the changing of her clothes, and so on. Is it not possible that the bruises you observed occurred after Mrs. Green was already dead?"

"It is possible."

"Is there any way to determine that?"

"Not with any certainty, no."

"So it is entirely possible that Mrs. Green received those bruises, or at least some of the bruises, after her death."

"As I stated before, it is possible."

"Have you prepared the final autopsy report on Mrs. Green?" Warren fired suddenly.

"I have not."

"Why not?"

"My office handles a great many such reports," Doc replied shortly. "It is not uncommon for a year or more to pass before the final reports are prepared."

"Dr. Winston, how large was the sample of blood taken from Mrs. Green's body?"

"Eight cc's"

"Could you convert that to standard measurement for us, please?"

"Roughly one quarter of an ounce."

"I'm sorry, did you say one *quarter* of an ounce?"

"Yes."

"How much blood does the average human body hold, Dr. Winston?"

"About six quarts."

Warren let the silence draw out for several seconds. "Dr. Winston, did the FBI laboratory also test Mrs. Green's blood for barbiturates?"

"The FBI declined to do so because their guidelines only allow them to conduct tests to determine the amount of barbiturate present," Doc replied. "Their procedures do not include testing merely to detect the presence of barbiturates in the blood."

"Is it not a fact that the other reason the FBI did not test the blood was that it did not receive enough blood to test for both alcohol and barbiturates?" Warren demanded.

"The FBI could have conducted the test on a fraction of the amount of blood they received," Doc retorted.

"But is it not a fact that the FBI specifically stated it did not receive enough blood to conduct both tests?"

"That is only partially correct. The FBI did make that statement, but the reason they declined to conduct the test was because of their rules against doing so."

"The prosecution has made much of your many years of experience as coroner for this county, Dr. Winston. Given those long years of experience, did it never occur to you that in preserving such a minute amount of blood, you were effectively depriving the defendant of his right to have sufficient, independent tests made?"

"There was nothing to indicate at the time I conducted the autopsy that anything of that sort would be required."

"Are you aware, Dr. Winston, that Mrs. Green regularly used tranquilizers prescribed for her by her doctor?"

"I have received no official information to that effect."

"But you are aware that the police recovered an empty bottle of tranquilizers from Mrs. Green's bedroom, a prescription which had been filled only seventy-two hours earlier?"

"My understanding is that there is some question—some suspicion about the circumstances under which the bottle came to be in the deceased's room."

"But as a result of that bottle turning up, you are aware that the deceased was issued a full prescription of barbiturate only seventy-two hours before her death?"

"Only indirectly."

"And if you were to learn—directly—that the deceased consumed even one of those barbiturate tablets in conjunction with the alcohol found in her bloodstream, would you then, Dr. Winston, revise your opinion regarding cause of death?"

Doc shifted in his seat. "The presence of barbiturates could certainly have exacerbated the effects of alcohol on Mrs. Green," he said carefully.

"Have you signed the death certificate for Delores Green, Dr. Winston?"

"I signed the death certificate last week after receiving the blood test results from the FBI."

"And despite the fact that the weight of medical opinion is

against you, despite the fact there is now evidence to suggest the deceased might have accidentally or deliberately combined barbiturates with a large quantity of alcohol, despite the fact that as a result of careless procedures by your office, the blood test results were inconclusive—"

Doc opened his mouth to protest, but King was already on his feet. "Objection! That is a slanderous accusation. There has been no indication that Dr. Winston's autopsy procedures were anything but exemplary."

"Sustained."

Warren turned his head a fraction. He studied King, then turned his gaze back to Doc. "Despite all this, Dr. Winston, you remain unwilling to consider any other cause of death?"

Doc looked directly at Lattimore as he replied. "I have never changed my opinion that injuries, multiple and extreme, played the major role in Delores Green's death."

Warren spread his hands in a gesture of futility. "Then I have no further questions for you, Dr. Winston."

"Mr. King?"

King checked his watch and exchanged a nod with Higgins. "The State calls Mrs. Elvira Hemingway, Your Honor."

I watched as she made her way to the stand. Her permanent had held up nicely and, unless I missed my guess, she'd had a fresh coat of blonde applied too. In a pale-blue shirtwaist dress with a strand of pearls at the neck, she looked downright respectable, almost—prosperous, came to mind. Things must be looking up in the Hemingway household.

She repeated the oath in a fluting, affected voice and took her time getting settled, fidgeting with her skirt, her purse, and her hair. King waited.

"Mrs. Hemingway, you were a neighbor of Mrs. Green's, is that correct?" King asked.

"That's right. I live"—she cleared her throat twice—"lived

two streets over from her house."

"You no longer live on Lennox Avenue?"

"No, I mean, yes, I do. I just meant—well, *she* doesn't live there anymore." One hand stole to the pearls at her throat for reassurance.

"And you also worked together for a period of time, is that right?"

"Yes. I worked as a temporary clerk in her office for several weeks."

"That would be at the Southern Life Insurance Company on Tryon Street?"

"That's right."

"And you often rode to work with Mrs. Green?"

"Yes. My—"

"And as a result, you became good friends?"

"Well, friend*ly*. I wouldn't say we were—"

"You spent time at her house? Socially, I mean."

"Yes." She plucked at an invisible spot on her skirt, smoothed the material.

"Did you ever see the defendant, Mr. Lattimore, at Mrs. Green's house on those occasions?"

"Oh, yes. He was there nearly every afternoon."

"And were you at Mrs. Green's house on Monday evening, July 3, the night, or rather the night before, she died?"

"Yes."

"Was Mr. Lattimore there that evening?"

"Yes. Well, he came to the house . . . he arrived shortly after we did."

"When you say 'we,' you are referring to whom?"

"My husband was also there."

"At approximately what time did you arrive at Mrs. Green's house?"

"Well, it wasn't dark yet . . . I'd guess it was about dinner-time."

"Six o'clock? Seven?" King prompted her.

"Probably closer to seven," she replied.

"What time did Mr. Lattimore arrive?"

"About twenty minutes later."

"Was he carrying anything with him?"

"Yes. He had a bottle of vodka."

"A full bottle?"

"No. It had been opened."

"Where was Mrs. Green when the defendant arrived?"

"We were all standing in the kitchen."

"Did Mrs. Green say anything when Mr. Lattimore arrived?"

"I don't—" Again, she groped for her pearls. "I can't remember."

"Did the defendant say anything to Mrs. Green when he arrived?"

"I don't—if he did, it was just hello or something. I don't remember that he said anything particular."

King looked up suddenly from the notes in front of him. "Did Mr. Lattimore knock before he entered the house?"

"I don't think so. The back door was open. He may have seen us or heard us talking. I think he just opened the screen and came in."

"I see. Mrs. Hemingway, could you describe Mrs. Green's appearance on that Monday evening?"

Mrs. Hemingway cast her eyes about the crowd as though one of the spectators had the answer. "She looked . . . she looked like . . . her hair wasn't combed and her face was scraped and bruised."

"Can you describe those bruises?"

Mrs. Hemingway closed her eyes. "Her . . . left eye was swollen and bruised and there was a scrape on that side of her face.

Her nose was red, but it wasn't black and blue. But she did ask me to feel it and see if it was broken."

"Did you ask her how she had come by those injuries?"

She fiddled with an earring and didn't answer right away.

"Mrs. Hemingway?" King prompted. "Did you ask Mrs. Green how or where she received her injuries?"

"I'm trying to remember . . . I'm not sure." She glanced around the courtroom again. "I don't think I ever asked her directly."

"Can you remember what happened after Mr. Lattimore came in?" King asked.

"Well, we all stood around in the kitchen for a few minutes, I think, then she—Delores said she didn't feel very well and she was going to lie down."

"Did Mrs. Green seem inebriated or drugged?"

"Well . . ." She deliberated over her answer again. "She seemed a little out of it, but since she said she didn't feel well, I thought maybe she had a headache from the accident or something."

"Did Mrs. Green say she had been in an accident?" King pounced.

"No. But I thought maybe that's how she had gotten the bruises, from falling down or something. Then."

"By 'then,' do you mean you later changed your opinion of how she came by her bruises?"

"You're confusing me," Mrs. Hemingway protested. "I just meant that's what I thought she meant then. Before we knew."

"Objection," Warren called. "We don't 'know' anything about how Mrs. Green received her injuries."

"Sustained," Cecil agreed.

"Let's go back to the sequence of events after Mr. Lattimore's arrival," King suggested. "What happened after Mrs. Green said she wanted to lie down?"

"Well, I went with her back to her room. I helped her undress—"

"What was Mrs. Green wearing?" King asked.

"A dress."

"Could you describe the dress?"

"Um, it was red-and-white striped—a sundress, you know, with"—she gestured at her shoulder—"straps."

"Did you notice anything unusual about the dress?"

"There was a spot of blood on the front of it, near the"—she made a vague gesture—"the bust."

"How large a spot?"

"About the size of a silver dollar, I'd guess."

"Thank you. Please go on."

"Well, I helped her change into a housecoat and she laid down on the bed. She said her nose hurt, so I went into the bathroom and wet a washcloth to put on it."

"Let me interrupt you just a moment, Mrs. Hemingway. Where was the defendant at this time?"

"He stayed in the kitchen with my husband, talking."

"Thank you. Did you notice anything out of the ordinary while you were in the bathroom?"

"No."

"No? Didn't you tell police in your statement that you saw a spot of blood on the bathroom floor?"

"No, it was the kitchen."

"The kitchen?"

"The kitchen floor. I saw the blood on the kitchen floor."

"Oh, I beg your pardon. And after you returned to Mrs. Green's bedroom with the washcloth?"

"Well, we just sat and talked for a little while about nothing much. After a while, she complained she was hot, so I went back into the bathroom and found a bottle of alcohol and I began to rub her back with it."

"Did she . . . did Mrs. Green disrobe in order for you to rub her back with the alcohol?"

"Well, not all the way. We just kind of pulled down the top of her housecoat to about her waist."

"And did you observe any bruises on that portion of Mrs. Green's body?"

"Oh, yes." Lattimore leaned forward and tried to catch Warren's eye. Warren responded with a brief nod.

"Then what happened?"

"Well, while I was rubbing her back, the—Mr. Lattimore came into the room."

"Was the door to the bedroom open?"

"No. I closed it, well, almost closed it, when she . . . when she took down her housecoat."

"Did Mr. Lattimore knock before he entered Mrs. Green's bedroom?"

"I don't think so."

"What did Mr. Lattimore say when he came in?"

"I spoke to him first, I think. I said, 'Have you seen these bruises?' "

"And what did he reply?"

"He sort of snapped back, 'Well, I didn't put them there.' "

"And then?"

"Well, I said something, I think I expressed some concern about her condition to him."

"And what did he reply?"

"He said, 'Well, don't worry about it. It's none of your business.' " She sniffed. "After a minute, he left the room and went back to the kitchen."

"Was Mr. Lattimore carrying anything in his hand when he came into the bedroom?"

"He had a glass of vodka in his hand."

"How much longer did you remain with Mrs. Green in her bedroom?"

"About an hour."

"At what time did you leave Mrs. Green's house that night?"

"She and the defendant"—he was the defendant now—"decided to go get something to eat about ten-thirty or eleven o'clock, so my husband and I left and went home."

"Thank you, Mrs. Hemingway."

"I just have a few questions, Mrs. Hemingway," Warren said genially. "You mentioned a spot of blood on Mrs. Green's dress and another on the kitchen floor."

She waited, but nothing more was forthcoming. "Yes."

"How do you know the spots were blood, Mrs. Hemingway?" Warren's tone couldn't have been more pleasant.

"Because they looked like blood. And because she was all banged up."

"All banged up? I believe you testified to bruising and swelling around Mrs. Green's left eye, a scrape, and a reddened and swollen nose. No open wounds or cuts that would account for bleeding. Is that correct?"

"I—"

"When Mrs. Green removed the top portion of her housecoat, did you see any injuries, any open wounds or cuts, that could account for blood on her clothing or on the kitchen floor?"

"No."

"So you assumed the spot on Mrs. Green's dress to be blood just as you assumed the spot on the kitchen floor was blood, is that correct?"

"Well, it looked like blood to me."

"But you don't know that to be so."

"No, I suppose it could have been ketchup." Her voice dripped with heavy sarcasm. "But since she was all banged up, I assumed—"

"Exactly," Warren said. "You assumed it was blood. Did Mrs. Green ever tell you it was blood on her clothing?"

"No." Her genteel accent had disappeared, replaced by the whining tone I remembered.

"So it could well have been ketchup or barbecue sauce or rust or anything of a similar color?"

"I suppose it could have been."

"And you likewise assumed that the spot on Mrs. Green's dress and the spot on the kitchen floor were recent?"

"Yes."

"Thank you for clearing that up for us. Now, another point I'd like to clarify, Mrs. Hemingway. I believe you testified that when Mrs. Green removed or lowered the top of her housecoat so that you could rub her back with alcohol, you saw additional bruises, is that correct?"

"It is." This time, her hand stole to the back of her neck to fiddle with her hair. When she became aware of it, she lowered her hand and clasped it tightly around the catch of the purse in her lap.

"However, we have testimony from both the coroner and the mortician that there were no bruises whatsoever on Mrs. Green's back."

"I didn't mean the bruises I saw were on her back. They were all up and down the insides and backs of her arms."

"I see. So that was an inaccuracy?"

"Yes! I'm not a lawyer. I'm not used to getting every little word right."

"I appreciate your patience. We lawyers can be extremely tedious over details. Particularly when something as important as a man's life is at stake. Now, Mrs. Hemingway, I believe there was an additional exchange between you and Mr. Lattimore other than the one you recounted that took place in Mrs. Green's bedroom."

"I don't know what you mean."

"In your statement to the police, you also mentioned that you went out to the kitchen twice from Mrs. Green's bedroom while you were there."

"Oh, yes. I forgot about that. I think I went in and out twice just for a minute."

"On both of those occasions, however, you remained long enough to have two drinks from the bottle of vodka that Mr. Lattimore brought?"

"I might have. It was very hot."

"Perhaps that might account for your memory lapse."

"What memory lapse?" she asked warily.

"The lapse which allowed you to forget an exchange between Mr. Lattimore and Mrs. Green after you expressed concern over Mrs. Green's condition to Mr. Lattimore and he denied having anything to do with her injuries."

"I . . . I don't remember . . ."

"The one in which Mr. Lattimore said to Mrs. Green, 'You're going to die soon from all your drinking. And they won't call the ambulance, they'll have to call the morgue.' "

"I—he—" Mrs. Hemingway's hand stole to her throat again. "He might have said that. I don't remember."

"It's in the official statement you gave to the police, Mrs. Hemingway."

"I forgot. I was so upset when I gave them that. It was right after she died. And it was months ago. I just forgot."

"Precisely. It is so very difficult to remember, isn't it, Mrs. Hemingway?" Warren smiled benignly. "Thank you. I have no further questions."

CHAPTER 19

That wrapped it up for the day. Since it was after four, Judge Cecil dismissed court. Warren shepherded the Lattimore clan out a side door, but Kent caught me before I could make my own escape.

"Pretty juicy stuff," he said.

"Yeah. This one ought to write itself."

"How do you think it went?"

"Off the record?"

"Yeah, yeah, off the record." He tucked his pen behind his ear to prove it.

"Hard to say. On balance, a tie, I think. Maybe a few points on our side."

"Which reminds me. What's this about a suspicious pill bottle?"

"Not for attribution, but it's on the level." I filled him in but didn't mention the search at Lattimore's. "When they went in, there was the bottle."

"Where was the bottle?"

"Don't know exactly."

Kent gave me a level look. "Yeah, I'd call that suspicious. Damned convenient, too."

"Don't look at me. I had to hear about it second hand. Get Owens to confirm it."

"Oh, I will. What's on tap for tomorrow?"

"Dunno. But I'll bet King is itching to get Greg on the stand."

"That's my guess, too." Kent stuck his pen behind his ear. "I'd better see if I can catch him. He's always good for a quote. Or a hundred." He took off through the crowd.

I stood for a moment, uncertain what to do, and finally decided to ask. I found Warren in the back hallway, deep in conversation with Claiborne. There was no sign of the Lattimore women.

"I'll leave it to you, then," Warren was saying as I approached. "Oh, Steve. There you are."

"Anything you need me for?" I asked.

"John's waiting for me to run him home," he replied. "He wants to get together at his house tonight. He has some 'suggestions' for me." His tone was wry. "I hate to ask, but if you could join us, I'd appreciate it."

"No problem. What time?"

"There's no point in your having to give up your whole evening. Give him a chance to run down a little. Say eight-thirty?"

"I'll see you there."

"Could you pick up Dr. Claiborne on your way?"

We made the arrangements, then I said my goodbyes and went home.

Susie was unusually quiet as she put dinner on the table. Overwhelmed, no doubt, by all there is to do at the start of a new school year. I asked about her day and she seemed to brighten up some at my interest. We chatted through most of dinner about which students showed promise and which just promised to be pills. The kids were disappointed I had to go back out, but I had time to exclaim over Christine's spelling test and sit through an interminable reading session with Adam.

The evenings were beginning to cool down, tantalizing us with thoughts of fall. I even imagined I detected a faint tang in the breeze reminiscent of burning leaves and pumpkin pie. More likely just fumes from the paper plant. It had been a long summer, but despite the calendar's insisting it was nearly September, it wasn't quite over yet.

Claiborne was waiting out front when I pulled up in front of the motel. We made small talk about the weather and the pennant race on our way across town. He was pleasant enough, but volunteered nothing. I consider myself a pretty good interviewer, but by the time we pulled up in front of Lattimore's house, I had a sneaking feeling he knew more about me than I'd learned about him.

Warren answered the bell and ushered us into the dining room, where Lattimore waited. The chandelier above his head threw his features into sharp relief. The omnipresent bottle of Planter's Club was by his elbow, an empty shot glass half-buried under pages of yellow foolscap.

The shadows also accentuated the weariness etched on Warren's face. A glass of whiskey sat, untouched, by his elbow. It looked as though it had been a long session.

Claiborne and I both declined the whiskey and helped ourselves to icy bottles of Coke from the refrigerator. Lattimore favored us with curt nods and returned to his harangue. "We should have hit harder on that while we had that character on the stand." There was no need to ask which character.

"I agree it's an important point, but we would have gained nothing by going head-to-head with Doc," Warren replied with admirable patience. "He's not going to budge. Arguing would only have given him the opportunity to repeat his points for the jury."

Lattimore grunted disparagingly but didn't argue. Instead, he poured himself a healthy slug and downed half of it at a gulp. Despite the coolness of the evening, there were damp patches under the arms of his shirt and a sheen on his forehead.

Warren turned to me. "Steve, you've talked with just about everybody Delores came in contact with. We need someone who can testify to her drinking on a regular basis. Somebody who saw her often, but not a friend." Mimi Brown and Peggy Summerfield were already scheduled to testify, although not in that order. Warren was afraid that Peggy, after hearing what Mimi had to say about Delores's drinking, would feel obliged to whitewash her testimony. "How about trades people? The grocery clerk, her hairdresser?"

I stared down at the table in concentration. My reflection frowned back at me from the highly polished surface. It hadn't occurred to me to ask the people on the periphery of Delores's life about her drinking habits. "Do you have a copy of the list?" I asked Warren.

After only a moment's search, he produced it from the bulging briefcase at his feet. I scanned it, looking for a likely prospect.

"Nobody jumps out at me, but I can go back to some of them again." I stabbed a finger at the paper. "This one, the cab driver, is a maybe. Her boss at the insurance company dropped some hints, but you'll never get him on the stand without a subpoena. And it'd be all hearsay anyway. Some of her coworkers might be a better bet, but they're going to be reluctant to testify and I think the company will do everything it can to discourage them. But I can try. You want me to go back and see what I can get?"

"I think so," Warren replied. "Take a day and see what you can come up with."

"Sure."

"One more thing. Get back to your 'source' and get me the exact wording of that letter from the FBI." At the last possible minute, King had released the test results, but not the cover letter. Hilda had tipped me off to that.

"I'll do my best."

"John," Warren turned to Lattimore. "I want to bring in an expert on alcoholism to testify. Dr. Claiborne knows a good one, man who runs a clinic in California."

"What kind of clinic?"

"Rest cure," Claiborne offered. "You know, where the family sends somebody who's bad to drink, to dry out."

"What do we need him for?"

"To supplement Dr. Claiborne's testimony."

"How much will it cost?"

Warren looked to Claiborne. "Roughly a hundred dollars a day plus travel," Claiborne said.

"From California? Do you have any idea how much that will cost? Why do we need two medical experts anyway?" Lattimore demanded.

"To make a point," Warren said. "Dr. Claiborne is a pathologist. He can refute Doc's findings and establish that the results are open to interpretation. His credentials and experience will make Doc look like the small-town demagogue he is. But there are some areas he can't touch on. We want to reinforce the extent of Delores's drinking problem. Bringing in somebody like Dr. . . ."

"Beckman," Claiborne supplied.

". . . establishes it as a foregone conclusion that Delores was an alcoholic. We can use him to explore areas of behavior and psychology that Dr. Claiborne can't address."

"I still don't see why I have to pay to fly another goddamn expert in here at a hundred dollars a day to tell them what me and Peggy and Mimi can tell them," Lattimore protested.

Warren's face became a careful blank. He studied his client. "Gentlemen, would you excuse us for a few minutes?" he asked without turning his head.

"Of course," Claiborne replied.

We rose and went outside. I led Claiborne to the garden wall where Warren and I had waited while the police ransacked Lattimore's house. Through the trees, I glimpsed lights in Deborah Lattimore's windows. As I watched, the downstairs lights went out, one by one, leaving only a small golden square in an upstairs window.

"Cigarette?" Claiborne offered.

"No, thanks. I don't smoke."

"I shouldn't. Ever seen what a smoker's lungs look like?"

I shook my head.

"Oh, well. We're all gonna die of something sooner or later." He inhaled cheerfully.

The sound of raised voices reached us from inside. Or, more accurately, Lattimore's raised voice. Despite the unremitting pressure of the last few weeks, I'd yet to see Warren flustered or angry. This was one time John Lattimore wasn't going to get his way by bullying.

But I was wrong. When Warren joined us thirty minutes later, his tie was askew and his hair rumpled as though he'd plowed his hands through it. To my further amazement, he was puffing on a cigar.

"Everything okay?" I asked.

"Well, I guess it's all in how you look at it," Warren replied. "It appears our client is dead set on taking the stand on his own behalf."

"Oh, my God."

Warren exhaled a cloud of fragrant smoke. "Yes, that says it rather well."

"Harlan!" We turned as Lattimore rounded the corner of the house at a brisk trot. "The police just called." He paused to catch his breath. "There's trouble at your house. They said they need you to come home."

My heart ceased beating and constricted into a dead weight in my chest. Warren put a steadying hand on my arm. "What kind of trouble, John?"

"I don't know," he panted. "Something about a call from your wife about being in danger."

Adrenaline surged through me, pouring into my arms and legs and racing to my brain so quickly it was all I could do to control the shudders that threatened to take over. There was no time to fall apart.

I blundered blindly past Warren and Lattimore, stumbling and falling up the slight rise as I ran for the car. I was vaguely aware of voices calling out behind me, but I didn't stop until I reached the street. I don't remember wrenching open the car door. The next I knew, I was behind the wheel but my hands were shaking so hard, I couldn't fit the key into the ignition.

Warren's face loomed in the window, a lank of silver hair dangling over his forehead. "Slide over," he ordered breathlessly. "I'll drive." I opened my mouth to protest, but I was unable to form words.

Claiborne piled into the back seat. I looked at him. "I'm still a doctor," he said with a weak attempt at a smile. I closed my eyes.

"Do you want me to come?" Lattimore squinted in the window.

"Better not," Warren replied. "I'll call you." With that, he dropped it into second and peeled rubber away from the curb.

CHAPTER 20

Warren drove very fast and with surprising skill through the dark streets. No one spoke. I stared blindly out the window, fists clenched, and concentrated on keeping my mind blank. By the time we hit Queens Road, Warren was doing sixty, weaving in and out of the traffic as though he'd been doing it all his life. He ran the light at Queens and Selwyn without batting an eye. A few seconds later, a flashing blue light appeared behind us.

"Not now," Warren muttered. But he pulled over. The police car rolled to a stop alongside.

"You Harlan?" a disembodied voice asked from the darkness of the police car.

I leaned around Warren. "I am."

"Lieutenant sent me. Follow me." Warren dropped it into gear and complied with relish.

We made it across town in less than ten minutes. At the top of my street, the officer waved us into the cul-de-sac, then angled his car across the entrance, blocking access in or out.

Three prowl cars, lights flashing, were parked in the circle but no ambulance, I was relieved to see. I flung open the door before the car stopped rolling and ran for the house, heart pounding.

"Grab him," someone called. An iron hand caught me by the elbow and spun me around. I drew back my fist.

"Easy there, bud," the uniformed officer rumbled. Lieutenant Owens loomed out of the darkness. His round face gleamed pale in the moonlight, a cigar firmly wedged in the corner of his mouth.

"Calm down, Harlan." But his voice was gentle.

"What's happened?"

"We don't know that anything's happened. Dispatcher got a call about half an hour ago from your wife saying she'd been threatened. We sent a car out, but when the uniforms got here, the house was locked up and they can't get anybody to the door. We need to take a look around."

I had the kitchen door unlocked in a blink but Owens laid a restraining hand on my arm. "Better let us."

My knees turned to jelly as his implication hit me between the eyes. Warren steadied me with a hand on my elbow. Claiborne materialized on my other side. "It's going to be all right, Steve." I couldn't answer. They coaxed me away from the door. We watched as two uniformed officers drew their guns and entered the house, followed by Owens.

The minutes crawled by like years. I became aware of voices and bobbing lights in the trees surrounding the houses. They were searching the woods. I had a momentary image of Susie cowering under a tree, and my vision went red. If anyone had touched me, spoken to me in that moment, I think I would have coldcocked them without conscious thought.

After an eternity, Owens reappeared. "Nobody home." He held open the screen door. "See if anything strikes you. Don't touch anything." He didn't need to explain, but I couldn't let myself think about it now.

I stepped into the kitchen and stood stock still, scanning the room. A few dishes dripped in the drain, but there were more in the soapy water in the sink. The damp dishtowel lay crumpled on the counter. The table had been cleared, but the milk carton and a bottle of salad dressing were still on the counter. In the other room, Big Bill Ward was signing off, exhorting wrestling fans to "Be good sports wherever you go." It was like the *Marie Celeste*.

I made my way through the house carefully, studying everything as though seeing it for the first time. Warren, Owens, and Claiborne followed silently in my wake; the uniformed officers waited in the kitchen.

On the floor in front of the television, Christine's school papers were spread out on the rug. At the sight of the wide-ruled sheets covered in her careful printing, tears stung my eyes. Adam's Superman coloring book lay open on the coffee table, crayons scattered around it. Superman's face had been colored green.

Together, we moved through the empty rooms, but they told us nothing. We returned, finally, to the living room. Owens turned off the television set. "Well? Anything strike you?" he grunted around his cigar.

"No. Everything looks normal." My voice, however, was pinched and unnatural.

"How 'bout a purse?"

I returned to the bedroom. Susie's purse was missing from its usual spot on the corner of the dresser.

"Not there," I reported as I returned to the living room.

Owens and Warren exchanged a glance.

"What?" I looked from one to the other.

"That's a good sign. Means she probably planned to leave," Owens said. "She have a car?"

"I had it."

"Any friends or relatives nearby she might have gone to or called to come get her?" he asked.

"Donna!" I brushed past him and made for the phone in the kitchen. I listened to Ron and Donna's number ring five, ten times, before I hung up. I thought about calling Susie's mother, Helen. But if Susie wasn't there, I didn't want to alarm her. As

I debated, the phone rang under my hand, scaring me out of a year's growth.

"Steve?"

"Susie! Are you all right? Where are you?" Owens, Warren, and Claiborne crowded in the doorway.

"We're at Howard Johnson's having ice cream." Her tone was calm and matter of fact.

"Howard—? What the hell are you doing at Howard Johnson's?" Owens made a noise in the back of his throat. "Did you call the police?"

"Why, yes I did. Did they come by?"

Now that my pulse had stopped pounding it began to sink in that she was pretending for someone else's benefit. "Are the kids with you?"

"Adam had lime sherbet and Christine and I had butter pecan."

"You can't talk."

"That's right."

"Is everybody okay?"

"Perfect," she chirped.

"Who's with you?"

"Ron and Donna."

"I think you better come on home."

"We're on the way," she promised.

"She's okay. They're on their way," I stated to the room at large without meeting anyone's eye. Now that the crisis was over, I felt an overwhelming urge to break into hysterical laughter, but didn't dare because I wasn't sure I could stop. "Sorry, Lieutenant. Looks like we've dragged you out on a wild goose chase."

He grunted. "You don't mind, I think I'll just hang around and have a word with your missus about that phone call."

I indicated the uniformed officers. "Before she gets here with the kids, could . . . you know?"

"Sure." He jerked his head at the two officers. "Get everybody outta here before the young'uns get back."

The kitchen was very quiet. We stood and looked at one another with a sense of anticlimax. "Would you . . . like to sit down?" I asked.

Warren shook his head. "We'll be clearing out of your way." He clasped my hand. "I'm glad everything turned out all right."

"Thank you for your help." I squeezed his hand gratefully. "Some day I must remember to ask you where you learned to drive like that."

"An entertaining but misspent youth," he replied with a twinkle in his eye. I'd heard that expression all my life, but never actually seen one until that moment. Warren turned to Claiborne. "Shall we, Walter?"

"Sure." It was Claiborne's turn to shake my hand. "Glad you didn't need me after all," he said with a smile.

"Me too."

They made for the door but Owens stopped them. "Uh, Mr. Warren?"

"Yes, Lieutenant?" Warren turned.

"How were you planning to get home?"

"How . . . ?" Warren looked at Claiborne. "Why, that's right. My car's at John's."

Owens stumped over to the window and looked out. "Prowl cars are already gone. Whyn't you two have a seat and I'll drive you over to Lattimore's soon as I get through here."

"That's most kind of you, Lieutenant." Warren and Claiborne removed their hats and settled themselves at the kitchen table like old friends.

For lack of anything else to do and to keep my hands busy, I started a pot of coffee.

"Good thing your neighbors were home," Owens offered after

a moment's silence. I nodded without turning around. I didn't need him to remind me I was a pretty sorry excuse for a husband, father, and protector. If I'd been home, Ron wouldn't have had to rescue my family. If I'd paid more attention to what was going on in my own house, I'd have known the calls had started again. I'd told myself I took the case for their sake, but the gods always extract a price.

"You planning to do anything with that coffee or we just s'posed to stand around and smell it?" Owens interrupted my self-flagellation.

"Sorry." I got out cups and saucers and was rummaging in the cabinet for the sugar when the twang of the screen door announced Susie's return. She hesitated in the doorway, surprised to find the kitchen full of strange men. She turned her head to look for me.

In that instant, I saw her as if for the first time. Her beauty owes as much to the vibrant energy that crackles in the air around her, and the disconcerting intelligence behind her beautiful green eyes, as any arrangement of features. I stood frozen, eyes wet, mouth dry, as the full impact of what I'd almost lost hit me like a blow.

"Mrs. Harlan, I'm delighted to meet you," Warren crossed the room to take her hand. "I'm sorry it had to be under such distressing circumstances. Are you and the children all right?"

Susie turned the full wattage of her smile on him. A lesser man would have crumbled. "We're all fine, thank you. They're with friends for the moment."

Claiborne stepped forward and offered his hand. "Walter Claiborne, Mrs. Harlan."

"I've heard so much about you, Dr. Claiborne. It's very kind of you all to . . ." She turned toward Owens, who had remained silent.

He removed his cap and nodded. "Miz Harlan. If you feel up

to it, I'd like to ask you a few questions."

"Of course." She retrieved the milk carton from the counter and dealt briskly with cups and saucers. We squeezed in around the kitchen table and sipped our coffee. Under the table, Susie's hand found mine. I clung to it for dear life.

"You recognize the caller's voice?" Owens asked.

Susie hesitated. "Maybe. There were quite a few calls when the story first broke, then they more or less dropped off until the trial started. I have the feeling the man who called tonight was one of the earlier callers, but I can't go so far as to say I recognized him."

"Why didn't you leave a note?" The minute the words were out of my mouth, I wished them back.

"And tell him where we'd gone so he could follow us?"

"Why didn't you go to your mother's?"

"Because for all I knew, he was lurking outside waiting for us to come out," she replied, evenly. "I didn't want to lead him to Mother's. I called Donna and waited until they pulled up in the driveway, then we went to the Howard Johnson's where there are lights and people."

"That showed great presence of mind, Mrs. Harlan." Warren poured oil on the waters.

"You had many calls?" Owens pursued.

"A fair number, but there was something different about this one, something creepy."

"What exactly did he say?"

Susie closed her eyes in thought. Years as a reporter had given her the ability to recite entire conversations verbatim if she had to. "Um . . . I warned you but you didn't listen. I told you to stop that husband of yours. Maybe if your young'uns had to do without *their* mama, your husband wouldn't be so damn quick to work for a murderer. Maybe I need to come over there and explain it in person so's you'll understand."

"Good God." I got up from the table and went to stare out the window. At Owens' request, Susie repeated it while he recorded it in his notebook.

"I don't want to alarm you, but it might be a good idea if you could find somewhere else to stay until this is all over," he suggested.

"You and the children are more than welcome at my home, Mrs. Harlan," Warren offered. "We have more than enough room and a big yard where the children can play. My wife would enjoy . . ."

Owens rumbled something I couldn't quite hear and Warren trailed off. "Well, perhaps not."

"You, too?" Susie asked.

I turned from the window.

"Well . . ." he smiled at Susie. "In my case, it's routine, but I would never forgive myself if anything happened to you or the children. I insist that the three of you go away somewhere until this is over. At my expense, of course." He held up a hand to forestall our objections. "I feel responsible."

"That's very kind of you, Mr. Warren, but I couldn't possibly accept." Susie's smile was sincere, but I heard the steel in her voice. "I have a job, obligations, and responsibilities. We have a life and I'm not going to uproot the children just because some creep doesn't like what my husband does. And what about the next case? Or the one after that? Steve's very good at what he does, and after this case, there'll be others. We can't run away every time. I knew when he decided to become an investigator, this kind of thing could happen."

I made an inarticulate noise. She turned to regard me. "I know. But I did." She turned her attention back to the three men. "I'm not running away. We'll just have to be careful, take some precautions. I expect your officers and I may become much better acquainted, Lieutenant. Which reminds me, I appreciate the way you all responded tonight. Thank them for me, will you?"

"I can try to convince the Chief to assign an officer to you full-time," Owens offered, with a slight frown of doubt.

My "yes" was drowned out by Susie's "no."

"I appreciate the offer, but the children would be scared to death," she said. "And what about after the trial?" She looked around the table at the three of them. "I'd rather the children didn't know anything about this. I can look after myself and the children." If she had stabbed me with the coffee spoon in her hand, I wouldn't have felt it any more keenly. The three men paid me the courtesy of looking everywhere but at me.

Owens sighed and, bracing his hands on the table, forced his bulk up from the table. Warren and Claiborne followed his example. "Well, I can make sure the patrol car keeps a close eye on you," he said. "If you see anything, anything makes you uncomfortable, you call the station and a car will be here in five minutes," he promised.

Warren covered Susie's hand on the table. "My dear, if there is anything you need, please let me know. And my offer of sanctuary is open at any time if you decide to take it."

Claiborne added his goodnights and Susie began to clear away the coffee things.

I walked out to the car with them. With his hand on the car door, Warren turned to me. "Don't blame yourself, Steve. There was nothing you could have done to prevent this."

"I didn't *think*." I pounded my fist against the door frame. "I was so . . . selfish, got so caught up, I forgot to pay attention, be vigilant. Susie never said a word to me about the calls starting up again."

"Being married to a strong-minded, independent woman may not be easy, but it has its rewards." Warren laid a placatory hand over my fist. "I've been married to one for thirty years.

Just remember why you married her, thank your lucky stars, and don't try to change her."

"Thank you," I said. "For everything."

He patted my shoulder. "I'll talk to you tomorrow."

I watched them drive away, then turned and went back into the house. I stood in the center of the room, not speaking, and looked at Susie, just drinking in the sight of her. She regarded me warily. I held out my arms and she walked into them. I folded them tightly around her. We stood that way for a long time listening to our hearts beat.

Chapter 21

Later, after it was all over, it occurred to me that Warren might have sent me out looking for a new witness to save me from sitting through Greg's testimony. But by then it was too late to ask.

It took two days to find what we were looking for. In contrast to the days before the trial, when everybody was more or less willing to talk to me, hoping for some inside tidbits they could share with their friends, a lot of people I'd talked to no longer wanted to know me. Or maybe the tawdry particulars revealed in the exhaustive accounts of the testimony in the papers every day repelled them.

But my radar must have been on automatic pilot the day I'd first talked with the cab driver, Merriman. Of course, if I'd been on my toes, I'd have pushed a little harder or in a different direction then, but questioning witnesses is like fishing. Things are so murky on the surface, you never know what's swimming around unless you get lucky enough to snag it. Still, it made me feel better that my hunch had been right.

I finally ran Merriman down at home, where he was taking advantage of the cooler weather to catch up on some yard work. It was how he spent most of his time, from the look of it. A small pocket-handkerchief of perfect green lawn was bordered on all sides by flowers and manicured shrubs. Some of them, like the tall gladiolus lining the fence, I recognized, but the rest of them were just a riot of colors and delicate fragrances perfuming the warm afternoon.

Merriman straightened up at the creak of the gate. "Afternoon." Almost as wide as he was tall, he gave an impression of sturdy strength like the trunk of a tree. Glossy black hair undulated from his forehead in waves. His face was naturally ruddy, his shiny black eyes embedded in pouches of flesh like raisins in dough.

"Sorry to bother you at home, but I kept missing you down at the cab depot," I said.

"Oh, that's okay. There's always something waiting to be done." He waved an arm at the lush greenery.

"We talked a few weeks ago about Delores Green," I reminded him.

"Sure, I remember."

"I wonder if I could ask you a few more questions."

He cocked his head slightly and regarded me out of the corner of his eye like an inquisitive robin. "How about we sit out back where it's cooler?" He led the way around the house to a shady oasis of sweet gum, maples, and dogwoods, in the back.

"Take off your coat, loosen your tie," he suggested. "I've got some lemonade in the icebox."

"Sounds real good."

I took his advice, removed my jacket and settled in a wrought iron chair. He returned with a pitcher and glasses.

"Thought I might see you again," he said as he poured.

I took a thirsty sip and raised my glass in silent thanks. "Why's that?"

He shrugged. "Been following the trial in the papers. Kinda funny reading all that medical stuff about somebody you've met. Even though I didn't know her all that well."

"That's kind of what I wanted to talk to you about. You told me before that you used to drive Miz Green fairly often."

He shrugged again. "Pretty regular. Sometimes once or twice a week, then maybe not for a month. I'd recognize the address and pick up the call if I could. Fares like having a regular driver. 'Specially women. They feel more comfortable, they tip better."

"How 'bout Miz Green? Was she a pretty good tipper?"

"Fair."

"Why did she use a cab so often when she had a car of her own?"

He smiled suddenly. "I wondered when you were gonna get around to that. I didn't like to bring it up, but since you ask . . ."

"I seem to remember that I did, but consider yourself asked again."

"Well, most of the time it was because she was in no shape to drive."

"What exactly do you mean when you say, 'no shape to drive'?" I asked, my pen poised.

"I mean she'd had a little too much of the bubbly." He flipped his wrist.

"She appeared to have been drinking?"

"She appeared to be pie-eyed."

"How often did that happen?"

"Most of the time. Sometimes she'd be lit when I picked her up. Other times she'd have me carry her over to the liquor store and she'd be half-lit by the time we got home. Once in a while, she'd call me to carry her to the A&P or the Colonial for groceries, and once or twice, I picked her up from the beauty shop. But nine times out of ten, she'd either be drinking or on her way to do some."

My pen slid across the page as I struggled to keep up. "How did you know she'd been drinking?" I asked. "Was she stumbling? Was her speech slurred?"

"Oh yeah, all of that. Sometimes she'd be weaving so bad, I'd have to help her up the front steps. Couple times she staggered in to get change and forgot to come back out. I had to go bang on the door for my money. Once or twice, there was a young boy come to the door, a couple of times it was that fella Lattimore."

"Did you know him by sight?"

"Not then. But I recognized his pictures in the paper."

"Why didn't you mention any of this when we talked before?"

"I knew you were gonna ask me that." He sighed. "It just didn't seem right. There she was, dead and that poor kid all messed up in it. Just seemed like tittle-tattle. I didn't know all that drinking stuff was gonna be important."

"I'm afraid it is. Very important. Especially to Mr. Lattimore."

"Yeah, that's what my wife said. If you hadn't come looking for me, I probably woulda called somebody."

"Would you be willing to testify to what you've just told me?"

He rubbed his face with a pudgy hand. "It's not that I don't want to, it's just . . ."

"Just what?"

"Well, I mean, all those bruises. What if I got up on that stand and told what I know and they let him off 'cause of it? What if he killed her and I help get him off?"

"But what if he didn't?" I asked. "They could send him to the gas chamber."

He thought about it for a minute. His shoulders sagged. "I guess you're right. And it doesn't seem to me, reading the papers, he's getting a fair trial. I'm just real glad I'm not on that jury."

Him and me both.

I beat Warren back to his office by no more than fifteen minutes. As soon as he and Claiborne came in, I could tell something momentous had happened, but Warren greeted me and inquired after my welfare with his customary courtesy. Claiborne spared me a nod as he hurried back to Warren's office to make a call.

"Well?" Miz Turner saved me the trouble of asking.

"They rested," Warren said simply. His shoulders sagged in exhaustion.

"Rested!" we chorused.

"But they only put on, what, four witnesses?" Clearly, Miz Turner considered this shoddy work. I thought of Bennett and his bulging folders of notes.

Warren shrugged. "Maybe King felt he couldn't top Greg's testimony."

"Was it bad?" I asked.

"We didn't expect it to be good," Warren replied. He sank down onto the visitor's sofa. Miz Turner lifted his briefcase from the floor and began, with quiet efficiency, to unpack it.

"Thank you, Miz Turner. We did the best we could," he continued, "but we knew Greg's testimony would be damaging. King tried to make something of the whippings again, but I think we got our own back. Greg helped some in that area, but I'll tell you, it gave me no pleasure. He's changed."

"How so?" I asked.

Claiborne emerged from Warren's office and perched a hip on Miz Turner's desk. If I'd done that, I'd have found myself four floors down on the sidewalk without benefit of an elevator. Warren looked at him with raised eyebrows. Claiborne gave him an affirmative nod. "He's on his way."

"He's bitter and it came across on the stand," Warren said, answering my earlier question. "He was brittle and defensive, had an antagonistic attitude. His pain is genuine, but now that the shock has worn off, he's angry. I suppose it was inevitable."

"Guess he is entitled," I said.

"Oh, yes. It's just sad." Warren sighed and stretched his legs out in front of him. "I hope that aunt of his has some intelligence or he may never get past this."

"Was Greg the only witness all day?"

"The only one. It was good tactics. King let him go through his story and all the emotion, then used up the rest of the morning going back over details. So when I had to put the poor boy back on the stand and make him go through it all again in the afternoon, I looked like a heartless monster. Which, of course, is exactly what I felt like and, no doubt, exactly the way I'll appear in the press. But," he straightened in his chair and placed his hand squarely his knees, flexing his neck this way and that, "it goes with the territory, I suppose, and a week after the trial, most folks won't even remember my name.

"But what about you?" he asked suddenly, fixing his piercing blue eyes on me. "How did you make out?"

I told him.

"Excellent. Really good work." He patted me on the shoulder, but I could tell his mind was elsewhere, already focused on what needed to be done. King resting his case so abruptly had caught even him off guard.

Miz Turner surprised me by offering the use of her typewriter so I could type up the notes of my interview with Merriman. When I'd finished, I offered to stay and make myself useful, but Miz Turner made it clear she and Warren would be much better off on their own, so I gave Claiborne a lift back to his motel and went home to read about what I'd missed.

CHAPTER 22

Warren called Peggy Summerfield as his first witness the next morning. There were murmurs from the more experienced in the crowd, who had expected Warren to put Claiborne up first.

Mrs. Summerfield took the stand in a short-sleeve flowered dress and a pillbox hat.

Warren had her describe her friendship with Delores, then led her to what we had taken to referring to as "the night of the pills."

"What time was it when Greg called?" Warren asked.

"About seven o'clock, I think." Mrs. Summerfield's glance roamed about the courtroom as if searching for confirmation.

"To your knowledge, had she worked that day?"

"Oh, yes, I'm sure of it."

"So she could not have been home more than what? An hour and a half? Two hours?"

"She usually got home about five-thirty," she agreed.

"What did Greg say when he called?"

"He said, 'My mother has taken too many pills. She's acting funny.' No," she corrected herself. "He said, 'Mother forgot how many pills she took and I think she took too many. She's acting funny.' And he asked me if I would come over."

"Object to hearsay," King called.

"Your Honor, we already have the boy's testimony that he called Mrs. Summerfield because he believed his mother had taken a possible overdose of barbiturates," Warren protested.

"I'll allow the question," Judge Cecil said.

Warren returned his attention to the witness. "So you agreed to go to the house?"

"Well, of course."

"And what did you find when you arrived?"

"Well, I was surprised to find her up and walking around. I guess I thought she'd be unconscious. I know I worried all the way over if I should have told him to call an ambulance."

"Could you describe her condition when you arrived?" Warren steered her back on track.

"Well, as I said, she was up and walking around, but she was wearing her pajamas and it was way before dark."

"Did she show signs of being drugged?"

"Oh, yes. She acted very sleepy and her words were slurred."

Warren next took her through the phone call to the doctor and the black coffee routine. "What did you talk about as you sat with her in the bedroom?"

"Well, I said something about maybe she should take a vacation and get away from things for a while."

"And what did she reply to that?"

"Again, object to hearsay, Your Honor," King called.

"I'm attempting to show the deceased's state of mind, Your Honor," Warren said. "As Mrs. Summerfield and Mrs. Green were the only two parties to the conversation, we can hardly expect confirmation."

"Overruled," Cecil said.

"She said, 'The only place I want to be is with my mother.' Or 'All I want to do is be with my mother' or something like that." Mrs. Summerfield frowned with the effort to get it exactly right.

Warren waited exactly two heartbeats. "And where is Mrs. Green's mother, Mrs. Summerfield?"

"Oh, she's been dead for years." There was a hubbub in the

courtroom. Cecil lifted his gavel, but Warren raised his hand in a request for quiet, and the room hushed instantly.

"Do you know how she died, Mrs. Summerfield?"

"She committed suicide." It did require Cecil's gavel to quiet them then.

"No further questions," Warren said.

King did his best, but quickly reduced Peggy Summerfield to confusion and non sequiturs. He eventually threw up his hands in defeat and sat down.

Warren called Mimi Brown. She repeated the oath in a loud voice that brooked no nonsense and sat down, back straight, formidable front forward.

"You were also friends with Mrs. Green, I believe?" Warren asked.

"That's right."

"You worked together for several years and remained close after that time?"

"That's right."

"Mrs. Brown—"

"It's Miss."

"I beg your pardon," Warren said. "As a close friend of Mrs. Green's, did you have the opportunity to observe her and her habits?"

"Yes."

"You were familiar with her household?"

"That's right."

"Miss Brown, did Delores Green have a drinking problem?"

"Objection." King was on his feet. "Miss Brown is not qualified to offer an opinion on that point."

"Sustained," Cecil agreed.

"I'll redraw the question," Warren said. He turned back to Mimi. "Miss Brown, did you, over the years you were close with

Mrs. Green, observe signs that would lead you to believe she drank heavily?"

"Yes," she answered emphatically. She tightened her lips and shot a steely-eyed glance at Peggy Summerfield. Mrs. Summerfield lowered her head.

"Were you aware of an automobile accident Mrs. Green was involved in last summer?" Warren asked.

"Yes."

"Did Mrs. Green say or do anything to indicate alcohol was involved or related to her accident?" Warren asked.

"She admitted to me she was hung over and as a result, she probably wasn't paying as close attention as she should have been."

"Hearsay," King objected without raising his head from his notes.

"Sustained," Cecil ruled. "The jury will disregard the question and the response."

"Miss Brown, do you recall whether Mrs. Green received a citation or a fine as a result of the accident?"

"She would have, but she said John . . . the defendant, Mr. Lattimore . . . talked to the officer and he let her go with a warning."

"Your Honor, again, this is all hearsay." King was on his feet this time.

"Sustained," Cecil said. "This is becoming somewhat tedious, Mr. Warren." He glanced at Warren over his reading glasses. "I suggest you move on to questions of fact."

"Yes, Your Honor." Warren turned back to Miss Brown. "When was the last time you saw Delores Green before her death?"

"On Wednesday evening before she died."

"That would be, let's see, June 28th?"

"That's correct."

"Would you describe the events of that evening, please?"

As she did so, I watched Greg. When she came to the part about the food falling out of Delores's mouth, he lowered his head.

"Did you ever discuss her drinking with Mrs. Green?" Warren asked.

Miss Brown shrugged. "It wasn't any of my business."

"Thank you, Miss Brown. I have no further questions."

King rose and bared his teeth at her in a humorless, horsy grin. All the better to eat you with, my dear. "Miss Brown," he began with a faint emphasis on the "Miss." "Do you drink alcohol?"

"On occasion," she replied.

"What occasions might that be?" he persisted.

"Social occasions."

"Parties, dances, things like that?" King asked. "An evening out with the girls?"

She gave him a look that should have wilted the carnation in his lapel. "I work for a living. I seldom have evenings out with any 'girls.'"

"But you do drink—on occasion?"

"That's right."

"Is there any alcoholism in your family, Miss Brown?"

"Certainly not."

"Do you, yourself, ever drink to excess, Miss Brown?"

"No."

"Exactly what do you consider excessive drinking, Miss Brown?"

"Drinking enough to become drunk or inebriated—and doing it often," she replied crisply.

"And what do you consider often, Miss Brown? Birthdays and New Year's? Every weekend? Every night?"

"I'd say when it becomes a habit, interferes with your ability to hold down a job, or when you drink because you have to."

"Is that a medical definition?"

"No, it's my definition," she retorted.

"Your subjective opinion?"

"That's right."

He gave her another sickly smile. "Miss Brown, you stated that on the evening of June 28th, you saw Miss Green take only one drink before collapsing, is that correct?"

"That's right."

"But I believe you also stated she showed no signs of having been drinking when you arrived only a few minutes earlier."

"Yes, I said that."

"Yet you're asking us to believe that Mrs. Green, who showed no previous signs of having been drinking, collapsed almost into unconsciousness after consuming only an ounce or two of whiskey?"

Mimi shrugged. "That was certainly my impression."

"Do you recall what the temperature was that evening, Miss Brown?"

"No."

"Was it raining?"

"No."

"Well, given the time of year and the weather conditions, would it be safe to say the temperature was in, perhaps, the nineties?"

"That would probably be close." Mimi stared at him.

"And Mrs. Green was frying something in an open pan on the stove?"

"That's right."

"So would it be safe to say that the temperature in the kitchen, particularly for someone standing directly over the stove, would be at least ninety degrees or above?"

"Probably."

"If that was the case, Miss Brown, and given that you saw her consume only one small drink, isn't it just possible that Mrs. Green did, in fact, collapse from the heat and not from drinking?"

"If that was true, I would have expected her to feel better after resting, but she was still confused and incoherent when I put her to bed an hour later."

"Did you call a doctor?"

"No."

"Thank you, Miss Brown. No further questions. Oh!" He spun suddenly on his heel. "I beg your pardon. I do have one question. Miss Brown, to your *personal* knowledge, did Mrs. Green ever take sedatives or barbiturates?"

She hesitated for a long moment. "No," she admitted finally. "Not to my knowledge."

King smiled. "Thank you, Miss Brown."

Beckman, the alcoholism expert, was up next. There was something familiar about him, and when he ran a hand over his hair as he took his seat, I realized why. He was the spitting image of Van Johnson. Same broad shoulders, same wavy blonde hair and bright Hollywood smile. I could think of a dozen women who'd happily drink themselves into a stupor to spend a few weeks under the good doctor's care.

Warren confirmed Beckman's credentials and let him talk about his clinic until King had enough.

"The prosecution will stipulate Dr. Beckman is an expert witness," he said.

"Proceed, Mr. Warren," Cecil directed.

"Thank you. You're the medical director at the clinic, Dr. Beckman?"

"That's correct."

"How many cases of alcoholism do you treat in a year?"

"Well, that's hard to say. It might be more indicative to say I probably see or treat between forty and sixty cases a week."

"Is alcohol a poison, Dr. Beckman?"

"Ethyl alcohol, the type used in beverages, could be a poison if taken in sufficient quantity, yes. I presume that's what you're asking?"

"It is. Thank you. In your opinion, could a blood-alcohol content of 0.42 percent cause death?"

"It could."

"Do experts in your field, that is to say, the treatment of alcoholism, agree about the lethal amount of blood-alcohol content?" Warren asked.

Beckman hesitated. "I couldn't speak to the agreement, but I personally have seen death due to alcoholism below 0.42 percent."

"Are alcoholics, people who drink heavily, more susceptible to bruises?"

"They are."

"And yet we have had testimony to the contrary." Warren walked back to the table. "Perhaps you would be good enough to explain."

"Certainly. Alcoholics tend to eat poorly and their blood vessels are more fragile. In addition, coagulants from the liver are inhibited by fatty infiltration of that organ. Because alcoholics' blood vessels are so fragile, they're easily ruptured. Our patients often bruise when they are lifted, even with the utmost care, by their arms."

"Isn't alcoholism rather rare among women compared to men?" Warren asked.

"Unfortunately, that's becoming less the case. The number of women who have problems with alcohol is rising alarmingly. Nowadays, more women can drive, many of them are out working. They're not so tied to the house anymore. But by and large, women hide their drinking. And they can be amazingly clever about it."

Warren started to ask a question, but Beckman rolled over him. "You see, drinking isn't as shameful for men as it is for women. Men don't hide how much they drink—until their families or their boss starts to complain, that is, because it's considered masculine to be able to drink a lot and hold your liquor, as the saying goes. Women, on the other hand, hide the fact they drink at all for fear they'll be thought 'low' or a 'loose woman.' "

"Do you treat many women patients in your clinic?" Warren asked.

"Oh, I'm afraid so, yes. Right now, we have several women undergoing treatment."

"What are the characteristics of an alcoholic, Dr. Beckman?"

Beckman shifted in his seat and flashed a blinding smile at Mimi on the second row. "Well, actually, the lady before me put it rather well if a bit simply. A person can be considered an alcoholic if he or she has trouble holding down a job or performing ordinary tasks like driving or keeping up a house. By that point, their drinking is pretty well out of control. They're drinking because they have to, not because they want to. Although it's rather a moot point, because they're physically addicted to alcohol. They crave it."

"Are alcoholics suicidal?"

"It would be a sweeping generalization to say that all alcoholics are suicidal," Beckman corrected him. "However, it is sad but true, that many alcoholics do attempt suicide, sometimes several times, and occasionally they succeed. But most of them don't mean to do away with themselves. It's a cry for help or attention, or to punish their family. Unfortunately, many of them stage their attempts while they're drinking and, as a result, well . . . ." He spread his hands helplessly. "They unwittingly, or accidentally, succeed."

He leaned forward, his expression earnest, hands clasped passionately in front of him. It probably went over big with the families of his patients, but looked like an attack of gas to me. "Alcoholics are sad people, Mr. Warren. They're to be pitied more than scorned. That's why so many of them come to us. They need to be protected from themselves while they put their lives back together."

"Quite so," Warren said, before Beckman could launch another soliloquy. "Are there any theories, Dr. Beckman, on what causes alcoholism?"

"Objection, Your Honor," King protested. "We've been very patient, but I don't see the relevance of this testimony. Aren't we rather straying from the issue here?"

"On the contrary," retorted Warren. "Mrs. Green's drinking is the issue here."

"I think we can allow a certain latitude," Judge Cecil declared. "Perhaps, Mr. Warren, Dr. Beckman"—he nodded to the witness—"you could narrow the focus of your inquiry."

"Certainly, Your Honor," Warren said. "Dr. Beckman, is there a connection, a correlation, if you will, between family history and alcoholism?"

"Do you mean is someone more likely to become an alcoholic if there's drinking in the family?"

"Precisely."

"Well, that point is a subject of much argument among experts in the field," Beckman replied. "On the one hand, there are figures to suggest that might be the case. On the other hand, there are many alcoholics who have no history of drinking in the family. Some doctors believe that alcoholism is not so much inherited as learned."

"The figures you mentioned which suggest a connection between family history and alcoholism," Warren said. "Could you elaborate on those?"

"Well, the studies are fairly recent and deal in raw numbers," Beckman replied. "That is, they don't necessarily take into account other factors which may have a bearing, you understand. But they suggest that someone whose mother or father had a drinking problem is twice as likely to develop a drinking problem."

"You've heard the testimony given here today concerning Mrs. Green's condition in the days immediately preceding her death and you have read the report from the coroner's office detailing the amount of alcohol in her bloodstream when she died. Based on what you have heard and read and your many years experience in the field, would you characterize Mrs. Green as an alcoholic, Dr. Beckman?"

Beckman took the time to frame his answer carefully. "I would say it certainly seems very likely, yes. She was a woman getting on in years, no husband, and the responsibility of raising a son by herself. The loneliness, the despair, all that responsibility, well, for many women, it's just too much."

"And if I were to tell you, Dr. Beckman," Warren rested an elbow on the corner of the witness stand and half turned to face the audience, "that Mrs. Green's mother was an alcoholic and that she committed suicide under the influence of alcohol, would that influence your opinion?"

"Objection!" King was on his feet. "There has been no testimony to support this slander of a woman who cannot defend herself and, in any event, Mrs. Green's mother's drinking habits have no bearing on this case."

"Given Dr. Beckman's testimony, they may have a great deal of bearing on this case," Warren replied. "And no doubt the death certificate could confirm the facts, but in the interests of the court's time, I won't press the issue. I withdraw the question and turn it over to Mr. King."

King was caught flat-footed. He blinked, nonplussed, straightened his lapels, and announced with a sneer, "I have just one question, Dr. Beckman. How much are you being paid to appear here in this courtroom today?"

"One hundred dollars plus travel expenses," Beckman replied. The crowd murmured. Most of them probably didn't make much more than that in a month.

"A total of one hundred dollars?"

"One hundred dollars per day."

"I have no further questions for this witness." King sat down, triumphant.

It was Cecil's turn to be caught by surprise. He looked at his watch. "Very well, unless there's an objection?" He glanced over his reading glasses at Warren, who shook his head. "We're adjourned until two. Dr. Beckman, you are excused."

CHAPTER 23

Cecil banged the gavel precisely as the courthouse clock finished tolling the hour.

"The defense calls Mr. Herbert Merriman to the stand," Warren announced. The spectators around me craned their necks and murmured to each other as Merriman waddled up to the stand. "Mr. Merriman, you are employed as a driver for the Red Checker Cab Company?"

"Yes sir."

"Did you ever have Mrs. Delores Green as a passenger in your cab?"

"Yes sir, she was a regular customer. She would usually ask special for me when she called."

"And how often was that?" Warren asked.

"Well, like I told that fella there," Merriman nodded in my direction, "sometimes she'd call for a cab once or twice in the same week and sometimes months might go by. 'Course," he added, "she might've called in those times when I was off and got another driver."

"And over how long a period of time did you drive Mrs. Green?"

"Well, it's been a while. I'd have to say, eighteen months, maybe going on two years now."

"That would have been shortly after she was involved in a car accident."

"I don't know about that. She didn't mention an accident to me."

"Objection," King called. "Mr. Warren is fishing."

"Sustained."

"When was the most recent occasion you drove Mrs. Green?"

"Well, I checked my logs and it looks like it was three or four weeks before she died."

"And on how many of those occasions, if any, did you take Mrs. Green to the liquor store in your cab, Mr. Merriman?"

"Most of the time, I'd say. Maybe three times out of four."

"Did she, during those occasions, consume whiskey in your cab? In your presence?"

"Most of them. She didn't usually wait till she was home."

"What did you observe about her on those occasions?"

"She would be so drunk she couldn't hardly get out of the cab by herself." Merriman glanced, shamefaced, at Greg. "Sometimes she wouldn't have any money in her purse and she'd go in the house to get some and forget to come back out. I had to go to the door and bang on it till somebody came to pay me."

"Who paid you on those occasions, Mr. Merriman?"

"Usually, it was her boy. But once or twice, it was the defendant there." He nodded toward the defense table. "Mr. John Lattimore."

"Thank you, Mr. Merriman. That's all." Warren sat down.

Higgins rose to take over for the prosecution. "How long have you known the defendant, John Lattimore?"

"I didn't know him. I never even knew his name until he was arrested," Merriman replied.

"To whom did you take this information, Mr. Merriman?"

"I didn't take it to nobody. That there private investigator," he nodded toward me again, "talked to me before the trial, but I didn't say nothing about her drinking then cause it didn't seem right and I didn't know then that it might be important. But he come back to see me a few days ago and asked me some more questions and I told him then about her drinking 'cause—"

"Never mind your motives, Mr. Merriman," Higgins interrupted. "How much are you being paid to provide this testimony here today?"

"I'm not being paid a red penny," Merriman replied heatedly. "In fact, I'm losing money just being here. I'm losing a day's work to sit here and tell this"—Higgins tried to head him off, but Merriman was too indignant to care—"because it didn't seem like to me, reading the papers, that John Lattimore was getting a fair shake and—"

"Objection!" King shouted.

"Sustained." Cecil turned to Merriman. "Mr. Merriman, please confine yourself to answering the questions you are asked."

"I have no more questions," Higgins said.

"Mr. Warren?"

"The defense would like to call Dr. Walter Claiborne to the stand."

A transformation came over Claiborne when he entered the witness box. It was nothing I could put my finger on, but the minute he sat down, he changed from a colorless nonentity to a figure of authority.

"You are a forensic pathologist, Dr. Claiborne?" Warren asked.

"That is correct. I have been a forensic pathologist for twenty years. I served as medical examiner for the state of Maryland for ten of those years."

"You are now a consulting forensic pathologist for several hospitals and universities."

"That is correct." He reeled them off.

"And, I believe you have published several books on the subject?"

"Three textbooks, yes."

Warren paused, but King remained silent. Warren turned toward the prosecution table and raised an interrogatory eyebrow. "Is the prosecution willing to stipulate Dr. Claiborne as an expert witness or shall I go on?"

"Prosecution so stipulates," King muttered.

Over the next two hours, Warren led Claiborne, step by step, through his findings from the autopsy, painstakingly demolishing Doc Winston's conclusions and his infallibility along with them.

Finally, he wrapped it up. "Dr. Claiborne, should the jury find the deceased was a heavy drinker, that her body had two hundred fifty-one discolorations of various sizes, but superficial in nature, there were no hematomas, only minor internal injuries, the blood-alcohol content was 0.42 percent, and the liver of the deceased was fatty, and based on your personal examination of tissues taken from Delores Green's body, do you have an opinion of the cause of death?"

The jury looked slightly dazed, but Claiborne, who had been listening intently, replied smoothly and confidently, "With a reasonable degree of medical certainty, I would say the cause of death could have been acute alcoholism."

A rustle ran through the crowd. I glanced at the prosecution table. King's head was down as he scrawled notes on his yellow legal pad.

"Could you describe for the court, please, Dr. Claiborne, how heavy drinking could predispose someone to death?"

"Certainly. In sufficient quantity, alcohol in the blood paralyzes the vital centers of the brain that control the heartbeat and breathing. Also, the disease of alcoholism—and I should point out that the American Medical Association classified alcoholism as a disease a few years ago—can cause serious nutritional or vitamin deficiencies as well as damage to the liver.

And, finally, heavy drinkers are predisposed to accidents."

Warren consulted the pad in his hand. "Is a fatty liver conclusive evidence of alcoholism or heavy drinking?"

"Heavy drinking and a fatty liver are a fatal combination. I have personally investigated several deaths of heavy drinkers in which a fatty liver was the only pathological change in the body."

"Is alcohol a poison?"

"Ethyl alcohol, taken in sufficient quantities, can be a poison."

"In your opinion, Dr. Claiborne, is a blood-alcohol level of 0.42 percent sufficient to cause death?"

Claiborne addressed his response directly to the jury. "In my opinion, a blood-alcohol level of 0.42 percent can cause death."

"Do you have an opinion as to the result of the deceased drinking heavily and taking sleeping pills or tranquilizers?"

King leapt to his feet. "Objection, Your Honor. The defense has consistently endeavored to introduce tranquilizers and barbiturates into this trial despite the fact there has been nothing but the flimsiest of hearsay evidence to support that the deceased ever took anything of the kind."

"Overruled," Cecil decreed.

"Dr. Claiborne?"

Claiborne hesitated and decided to play it safe. "I have no opinion."

Warren rose, but remained behind the defense table. "If the jury should find that the defendant, John Lattimore, brought the body of Mrs. Green home in his car, that he removed her body from the car, placed it in a sitting position, and then picked it up from behind with his arms around the chest area and the body emitted a sound, a groaning noise, do you have an opinion as to how that sound was caused?"

"It could be the result of air being expelled from the chest or drawn into the chest as a result of squeezing the chest cavity as it was being lifted. That would force air through the larynx or voice box. It is a very common occurrence."

"Thank you, Dr. Claiborne." Warren sat down abruptly. Claiborne blinked. Lattimore leaned over to whisper urgently in his ear, but Warren ignored him.

So, of course, King felt compelled to demonstrate his equal grasp of the medical evidence by going over the same ground, virtually point for point, but instead of impressing the jury, it only served to bore them to the point of mutiny. Eventually, their restlessness penetrated his rapture with the sound of his own voice and he hurried to wrap it up.

"You have testified that you examined slides of tissue taken from Mrs. Green's internal organs. You did not actually examine the organs themselves, is that correct?"

"That is correct."

"Did you at any time see Mrs. Green's body?"

"No."

"Forgive me, Doctor, your credentials and experience are certainly impressive, but wouldn't you agree that a person who physically performs an autopsy is in a better position to determine cause of death than a doctor who did not actually see the body?"

"No."

"If the jury should find that Mrs. Green died from beatings administered by a man the size of the defendant, John Lattimore, on Sunday and Monday night, and that there were two hundred and fifty-one bruises on her body, did she die of injuries multiple and extreme, compounded by shock, Dr. Claiborne?" he asked.

Claiborne smiled faintly as he replied, "Under those conditions, it is unlikely, in the absence of lesions, that this individual died from those beatings."

"Were you present when the moan or groan Greg Green described, emanated from Mrs. Green's chest?"

"No."

"Then you don't know what was coming out of that woman, do you?"

"That is correct."

"Her body could have had life, couldn't it?"

"I don't know."

"Dr. Claiborne, how many autopsies did you perform last year?"

"I don't perform that many autopsies myself these days. Most of my time now is spent teaching or consulting."

"Or testifying in court as you are doing today?"

"That is correct."

"Are you retired, Dr. Claiborne?"

"No. As I said—"

"Are you semi-retired, then?"

"No."

King walked back to the prosecution table and turned to regard Claiborne. "How much are you being paid for your testimony here today, Dr. Claiborne?"

"I am being paid nothing for my testimony. I am being paid for my time."

"And how much are you being paid for your time?"

"Thirty dollars an hour."

"And how many hours would you estimate you have worked on this case?"

"About forty or fifty." There was a stir in the courtroom.

King smiled. "Thank you, Dr. Claiborne."

The judge caught a signal from Warren. "You have a redirect, Mr. Warren?"

"Just a few questions," Warren replied. "What would be your opinion, Dr. Claiborne, of a person who, only days before her death, took one drink and became unsteady on her feet and was unable to feed herself?"

"I would have to say that person was either drunk or ill."

"Do you have an opinion as to whether Mrs. Green's death was preceded or associated with shock?"

"I have no opinion."

"Have you, of your own personal experience, known of cases where persons have died of acute alcoholism with less than 0.42 percent alcohol in their blood?"

"I certainly have."

"And the tendency to bruise easily is associated with alcoholism?"

Claiborne nodded. "Yes. It is commonly associated with death due to excessive alcoholism."

"Thank you, Dr. Claiborne. I have no further questions."

"Your Honor!" King called. "I have a few more questions."

I couldn't be sure, but I thought Judge Cecil stifled a sigh. "Go ahead, Mr. King."

"Dr. Claiborne, can shock be brought on by fright?"

"It can."

"A person receiving a severe beating could go into shock and die couldn't they, Doctor?"

"There is that possibility, I think."

King couldn't resist a triumphant glance in Warren's direction. "I have no further questions, Your Honor."

And that was it. I tuned out as Cecil droned through his daily caution to the jurors. Unless Warren had a surprise witness up his sleeve I knew nothing about, John Lattimore would get up on that stand tomorrow morning and attempt to defend himself against a charge of murder.

I came to with a start as Cecil banged the gavel. "We are adjourned until nine-thirty tomorrow morning."

CHAPTER 24

Lattimore strode to the stand with confidence and repeated the oath in a strong voice. He'd gained back most of the weight he'd lost during the summer and looked fit and healthy. He loomed over the bailiff from the witness stand, a Kodiak in a charcoal gray suit and white shirt.

As soon as he was seated, Warren rose and took up a position halfway between the table and the witness stand, empty hands clasped loosely in front of him.

"Mr. Lattimore, would you state your name, address, and occupation for the court?"

Lattimore complied.

"Your father was both a founder and president of First Mutual Bank before you?"

"That is correct."

"And you worked for the bank under your father's supervision for how long?"

"Nearly twenty-five years, until his death three years ago."

"Did you inherit the position of president on your father's death?"

"I did not. I was elected to the position by the bank's board of directors."

Warren half turned toward the audience. "Do you see any of those board members present here today?"

Lattimore scanned the crowd. "Yes, I see two."

"Thank you." Warren folded his arms and looked at his shoes

for a moment as if considering his next question. "Mr. Latti-more, how long did you know Mrs. Green?"

"About ten years."

"How did you meet?"

"A mutual acquaintance introduced us."

"How would you characterize your relationship with Mrs. Green?"

I could feel the crowd holding its collective breath, but Latti-more replied easily, "We were good friends." He was so extraordinarily calm, I wondered if Warren had slipped something into his coffee.

"Did you become friends with the deceased while you were married?"

"Yes."

"Was your wife aware of your friendship?"

"I don't know."

"Are you married now, Mr. Lattimore?"

"My wife and I are legally separated and have been for some years."

"Is your wife in the courtroom today?"

"Yes." Around me, women nudged each other and pointed out Deborah Lattimore's flattering rust-colored suit on the second row.

Warren plunged his hands into his pants pocket and tossed the question out casually. "Was Delores Green your mistress?"

The question hung in the air for a heartbeat.

"She was not." Lattimore's reply was firm and clear and he looked straight at Deborah as he answered. I thought I saw a fleeting expression of sadness, but it may have been my imagina-tion. Deborah Lattimore raised her chin a fraction of an inch as Lattimore continued, "Despite what you might have read in the press, Delores Green and I were never anything more than friends."

"You did not have a romantic relationship with Mrs. Green?"

"No. I felt sorry for her." A buzz from the crowd. "That is to say, I felt sympathy for her." Lattimore hastened to repair the damage. "She didn't have much money and she was raising a son all alone."

"Were you also acquainted with Mrs. Green's son, Greg?"

"I was. I am." Lattimore shifted slightly in his seat.

"How would you describe your relationship with him?"

"It was good, on the whole. We had disagreements from time to time, just as a father and son might." Skepticism hung in the air, so tangible it was almost visible, but the crowd kept quiet.

"Did you ever discipline Greg?"

"On a few occasions."

"Physically?"

"Yes."

"Why did you do so?"

"Because his mother asked me to."

"Do you recall those occasions?"

"Fairly well. Most of them have been within the last few years."

"Would you describe for the court, please, the circumstances under which you physically disciplined Greg?"

"Well, there was one time where Greg dumped his newspapers in a ditch instead of delivering them and Delores had to pay for them. But she was most upset because when she asked Greg about it, he lied. She asked me to whip him."

"And you did so?"

"I whipped his legs with a switch. Just as I did to my own boys when they misbehaved," he added.

"Not your hand?"

"No. I used the switch to remind him he was still a child and had to mind."

"And the other occasion?"

"It was about . . . well, I guess it's been a year now because it was last summer. A couple of Greg's older friends have cars, jalopies, and I suspect one of them has secretly taught him to drive. One night, when . . ." he flicked his eyes at Warren ". . . his mother was asleep, he took her car keys from her purse and went joy riding. When she found out, she asked me again to whip him."

"With what did you whip him?"

Lattimore drew a visible breath. "The rubber belt off a sewing machine."

"Did it leave marks?"

"Yes."

"Mr. Lattimore, you said earlier that you felt sorry for Mrs. Green. Why was that?" From his tone, Warren might have been asking why Lattimore chose a particular brand of fertilizer.

"Well, money, for one. Her husband died not long after they divorced, but he had remarried, so there was no insurance and Delores was raising Greg on a secretary's salary."

"Did you ever loan her money?"

"Not directly. I would sometimes take her or the both of them out to eat, and I'd bring groceries to the house on occasion."

"Did you pay the rent on her house?"

"I did not."

"You said money was one reason you felt sorry for her." Warren rubbed the back of his neck. "Were there others?"

"Greg was starting to give her trouble. She said to me several times that she worried whether she would be able to control him as he got older."

"And?"

Lattimore looked directly at the jury box, and then lowered his head before he answered. "She had a drinking problem."

"Objection!" King leaped to his feet. "Despite Mr. Warren's

continued attempts to blacken the victim's reputation with this slander, we have no hard evidence that Mrs. Green had a drinking problem."

Warren gave him a disbelieving stare. "May we approach, Your Honor?"

After a few minutes of argument, Cecil announced, "The question and the response will stand."

Warren resumed his position in front of Lattimore. "Did you discuss Mrs. Green's drinking with her?"

"Many times. Toward the . . . just before she died, we had several . . . discussions about it. It was getting out of hand."

"Did Mrs. Green have an automobile accident as a result of her drinking?"

"That's right."

"And did you persuade the police officer who responded not to charge Mrs. Green with driving under the influence?"

"Yes, I did."

"And did you pay to have her car repaired?"

"I did. She didn't want to file it on her insurance, so I loaned her the money, but she paid me back a little at a time."

"Was Greg Green aware of his mother's drinking?"

"I believe he was."

"You believe he was?"

"We never discussed it directly, but he was old enough—I believe he understood what was going on."

"Did Greg Green ever see his mother inebriated in your presence?"

"A number of times. Quite a few in the months before she died."

"And he never commented on it to you or asked any questions?"

"Not directly, no. If we talked about her condition at all, we both said she was sick."

"Did you see Delores Green on Sunday, July 2?"

"I did not."

"Did you attempt to see her?"

"Yes."

"Would you describe the events of that evening, please?"

Lattimore described his attempts to track Delores down that night, the calls to friends and, finally, the hospitals.

"And you suggested that Greg stay with neighbors?"

"I didn't think he should be alone in the house."

"You didn't offer to stay at the house with him?"

"No."

"Have you ever spent a night under Mrs. Green's roof?"

"No."

"When did you next see Mrs. Green?"

"It was about mid-morning the following day, Monday."

"At her home?"

"Yes."

"How did you come to be at her home that morning?"

"Greg had called and asked me to come over."

"Did he say why?"

"He said his mother had returned in bad shape."

"Physically?"

"That was my impression."

"Would you describe her condition when you arrived?"

Lattimore did so.

"And it was your clear impression that Mrs. Green had been drinking heavily?"

"She gave every sign of it and she smelled strongly of alcohol."

"And she was unable to account for her movements the night before or where she had passed the night?"

"That is correct."

"Was Greg Green present during this conversation?"

"No. I sent him outside. I didn't think he should hear any of it."

Warren then steered him through the events of the rest of that day, his return to the cabin, the discovery of Delores's body, and his reaction.

Lattimore was perfect. He didn't sugarcoat or apologize, didn't whine. As I listened, I recalled our session in the squalid interview room where he'd recounted the same events to me some months ago. It was hard to believe this dignified, self-possessed man was the same one I'd confronted in that room.

The spectators hung on every syllable. Warren let him finish describing the scene at Delores's house before asking the question that trembled on the lips of everyone in the courtroom. "Did you consider taking Mrs. Green to a hospital or seeking medical attention for her?"

"I did not." Lattimore compressed his lips and lowered his head, the picture of regret, if not remorse.

"Why not?"

"Because it was painfully obvious to me she was dead." Lattimore raised his eyes to regard the jurors. "There was nothing more that could be done for her medically. She had killed herself with her drinking . . ." He paused at a murmur from the crowd. "Not intentionally. But Delores never really got over her mother's suicide and I didn't want that for her son. I hoped he could grow up thinking it was an accident. Maybe it would keep him from drinking—" He wiped his face, the first sign of emotion he'd shown.

He was good, all right. Very good.

Warren spent the next hour taking him painstakingly over the physical and medical evidence, from Delores's appearance when she'd resurfaced Monday morning to the groan Greg had described so vividly as the two of them heaved his mother's body from the damp grass. He managed to make some good

319

points, but it was stuff we'd heard before. The crowd wasn't interested in Lattimore's version.

"Mr. Lattimore." Warren paused, gathering everyone's attention. He raised his eyes and looked directly at John Lattimore. "Did you kill Delores Green?"

"I did not," Lattimore replied steadily.

"No more questions."

Cecil banged the gavel, the crowd heaved a collective sigh of relief and went off to lunch to fortify itself for the real fireworks to come.

King didn't disappoint us. We were hardly settled in our seats before he launched his attack.

"You have testified that you were 'friends' with Delores Green for ten years." King took up a combative stance, legs spraddled, one fist resting on his hip like a gunfighter. "Did you take her out during that time?"

"I don't recall," Lattimore replied.

"You don't recall whether you took her to public places while you were living with your wife?"

"I may have. I don't recall. It was a long time ago."

"What you mean is, that you don't recall anything that reflects badly on you, isn't that right, Mr. Lattimore?"

"Argumentative, Your Honor," Warren called.

"Sustained."

"The original question stands, Mr. Lattimore." King crossed his arms over his chest. "Did you take Delores Green out to public places while you were still living with your wife?"

"I recall taking Delores to the Pecan Grove Supper Club with a party of her friends on one occasion, but I don't recall whether I was living with my wife at the time. And, as I've said, I took both Delores and Greg out to eat on many occasions if you consider that taking her out in public." Lattimore's tone was cooperative, his demeanor respectful. I wondered again what miracle drug Warren had given him to keep him so calm under King's needling.

"Did you tell Delores Green when you met her that you were a married man with three children?"

"I'm sure I did. I certainly never made any attempt to hide that fact." Lattimore looked out over the crowd, calmly meeting their eyes.

"When did you separate from your wife?"

"It was approximately three years ago. I don't recall the specific date."

"Did you file for separation or did your wife?"

"I . . . my wife did so."

"On what grounds?"

"Objection!" Warren called. "That is completely irrelevant to the issue at hand."

"On the contrary," King protested. Cecil forestalled him by motioning both attorneys to the bench for another conference. After two minutes' vehement argument, Cecil agreed to sustain Warren's objection.

"Was Delores Green your mistress?" King asked sulkily as he took up his position again.

"No."

"You did not have a physical relationship with her?" King persisted.

"Your Honor," Warren pleaded.

"Overruled."

"I did not," Lattimore replied firmly. "As I have already stated, Delores Green and I were only friends. She dated a number of men, but I was not one of them."

"And that's why you killed her, isn't it?" King demanded. Warren was on his feet, protesting, but King overrode him, shouting to make his point. "You were jealous of those other men and when she stayed out all night that Sunday, you assumed she was with one of those other men. You were jealous and that's why you beat on her, isn't it, Mr. Lattimore?"

Cecil banged his gavel. "Make your objection, Mr. Warren."

"Object to argumentative, Your Honor, and Mr. King's remarks are beyond badgering the witness."

"Sustained, Mr. King." Cecil glared at the district attorney.

"I beg the court's pardon," King said smoothly, but he flashed Warren a triumphant smile before turning back to Lattimore. "You are asking us to believe that the night you brought Delores Green's body—strike that," King barked at the court reporter. She glanced to Cecil for guidance. He nodded and she resumed her pecking. "You are asking us to believe that the night you brought Delores Green home and forced her son to help you undress—"

"Objection," Warren called. "There is no evidence or testimony that Greg Green was forced to do anything."

"Sustained."

King tried again. "You are asking us to believe that the night you brought Delores Green home and"—he glared at Warren—"with her son's help, undressed her, was the first time you had seen her unclothed in the ten years you were 'friends'?"

"That is so," replied Lattimore, who had waited calmly throughout the exchange.

"And yet we have Greg Green's testimony that you came to that woman's house at all hours of the day and night, coming and going as you pleased."

"That is not true." Lattimore's tone was calm. "While I was there many times in the evening, most of my visits were during the afternoon."

"Did you love Delores Green?" King barked.

"I did not love her. I was fond of her." The crowd murmured, but Lattimore ignored it and kept his eyes on King.

"Much has been made of your efforts to locate Mrs. Green on the evening of Sunday, July 2." King gestured toward the jury in an effort to force Lattimore to look at them, but Lattimore kept his eyes on the district attorney. "You and Mr. Warren would have us believe that you were motivated by concern for Mrs. Green, but the truth is, you were motivated by jealousy, isn't that right, Mr. Lattimore?"

"No. I was concerned about her. Her drink—"

"You were afraid she was out with another man, weren't you, Mr. Lattimore?" King raised his voice, drowning him out.

"No."

King turned and began to walk toward his table, then whirled, finger outstretched, to demand, "What kind of car do you drive, Mr. Lattimore?"

"A Cadillac."

"A Cadillac. And where do you live, Mr. Lattimore?"

"In Myers Park."

"And do you pay your wife, excuse me, your estranged wife, maintenance?"

"I do."

"As well as the mortgage on the home she occupies?"

"That is correct."

"And where does your estranged wife live, Mr. Lattimore?"

"Her home is also in Myers Park."

"So you drive a Cadillac and maintain two homes in Myers Park, is that correct?"

"Yes."

"And yet you offered Mrs. Green and her son no financial assistance? You did not offer to pay for the groceries you ate or pay the electricity bill from time to time?"

"The Cadillac belongs to the bank," Lattimore replied. "And as I've explained, Mrs. Green and I did not have that kind of relationship. It would not have been appropriate."

Terry Hoover

"But it was perfectly appropriate for you to haul her body around in the back seat of your car like a bag of dog food and undress her to keep your good name clean, wasn't it, Mr. Lattimore?"

"Your Honor," Warren protested. "Mr. King's attack is nothing less than verbal abuse."

"Sustained," Cecil agreed. "Mr. King, I will not warn you again."

King snatched up a bundle of papers from his table. He strode to the box and slapped it on the railing in front of Lattimore. "Look at these pictures, Mr. Lattimore."

Lattimore paled as he complied.

"These are pictures of Delores Green's body. Do you see the bruises on her body, Mr. Lattimore?"

"Yes."

"Were you not responsible for those bruises, Mr. Lattimore?" King looked again at the jury, but Lattimore kept his eyes on the photographs in front of him.

"No. I wish I knew who was."

"You have no idea how she came by those bruises?"

"No."

"I remind you, Mr. Lattimore, that you are under oath."

"I am aware of that."

"And you still maintain that you are not responsible for any of the bruises on Delores Green's body?"

"I do."

"Your Honor." King spun back to face the bench. "I'd like the defendant to stand before the jury box for a brief demonstration."

"Approach the bench, Your Honor?" Warren called.

Cecil agreed. We watched as King argued and Warren responded quietly but vigorously. Lattimore sat quietly, his eyes fixed on a point above the spectators' heads. Finally Cecil handed down his decision. Warren shrugged, shook his head, and returned to his seat.

King produced an easel and cork bulletin board and set it up in front of the witness stand, facing the jury box. "Would you step down here, Mr. Lattimore?" It was not a request. King stood, facing the jury box but carefully angled the easel away from the spectators. Lattimore descended the stand heavily and stood at King's side, dwarfing the smaller man. As courtroom theatrics go, it wasn't shabby.

"I'd like you to demonstrate, for the jury, the location of the bruises depicted in these photographs," King ordered. One by one, he pinned the photographs on the board and had Lattimore point with a massive finger, to the corresponding position on his own body. The spectators were giving themselves whiplash to get a glimpse of the macabre photos.

Finally, King allowed Lattimore to return to his seat, but he continued to pound away at him, firing questions left and right, barely giving Lattimore time to answer. He bored in particularly hard on the time elements and Delores's appearance on Monday morning, trying to trip him up on details.

Many times Lattimore was forced to answer, "I don't recall," to which King retorted, "You have a particularly bad memory for anything to do with this case that's not favorable to you, don't you?"

It went on, by my watch, for four hours. Parry and thrust, point and counterpoint. King strode about in front of the bench, waving his arms and gesturing, over and over at the jury in an attempt to force Lattimore to look at the jurors. As the afternoon wore on, he loosened his tie and mopped his face frequently with a handkerchief. Many times, I expected Warren to object, but he remained silent and in his seat. Through it all, Lattimore remained calm, even when King accused him of dominating the Green household and terrorizing Delores and

Greg with threats.

Finally, a little before five o'clock, King paused for breath. Cecil spoke up. "Mr. King, the hour is growing late. I assume you have further questions for the defendant?"

"Oh, I most surely do, Your Honor."

"Then, if you have no objection . . ." Cecil paused. King shook his head wearily. "Mr. Warren?"

"No objection, Your Honor."

"Then we are adjourned until nine-thirty tomorrow morning."

I caught Warren's eye and received a slight shake of the head in response, so I joined the throng slowly making its way out of the courthouse. Outside, I paused to put on my jacket against the cooling afternoon air. As I stood, slightly removed from the crowd, a bright flash of chrome reflecting the afternoon sun caught my eye. I was just in time to see Mrs. Hemingway's bright curls as she ducked into the front seat of a Bel Air, a '59 by the look of it.

As I watched the car glide smoothly away from the curb, I could almost hear the gears in my head start to turn with a rusty squeak. I stood, transfixed, ignoring the dirty looks and muttered imprecations of the crowd as they jostled around me. Cars. Everywhere I turned in this case, there were cars. Lattimore's Cadillac, Delores's car that refused to start on Monday, the mysterious dark car speeding away from a burning gas station, the tan car that had spirited Cotter away.

The pictures turned and shifted as I stared blindly after Mrs. Hemingway, until, finally, they rearranged themselves into a very sharp, clear picture.

"I'll be damned."

CHAPTER 25

The next morning's headline was "I Did Not Love Her" in sixty-point type. I winced when I saw it, but in Ben's shoes, I'd have used it, too. As soon as the words had come out of Lattimore's mouth yesterday, I'd pictured them on the front page.

He was in for another brutal session with King, but I wasn't destined to see it. I made it to the courthouse in plenty of time, but the person I needed wasn't in court and it took me the better part of the day to track him down. I left a message with Miz Turner that I was following up on some new information. She was suspicious, but, safely at the other end of a telephone, I stood my ground and refused to divulge any details.

The sun had begun its slow, autumnal slide to earth by the time I turned onto the dusty washboard road. My eyes were gritty with fatigue and my hands felt as though they were glued to the wheel. Fences guarding empty pastures hemmed me in on both sides for half a mile before the road curved to reveal a small white farmhouse at the top of a gentle rise. A wide apron of sawdust under a stand of pecan trees served as the driveway. I knew enough to go to the back door.

My knock summoned a tall, spare woman. I almost didn't recognize her without her flowered hat, but she knew me.

"Miz Pickens? I'm—"

"I know who you are," she replied through the screen. "What do you want here?"

I removed my hat. "I'd like to talk to Greg."

"He's got nothing to say to you."

"I beg your pardon, ma'am, but I believe he may have."

"Why can't you people leave him alone?" Her words were sharp, but her tone was curiously without heat, the voice of a woman who had never won and didn't expect to this time. But she persisted. "He's seen enough and heard enough. Leave him alone. He's hurting."

"I know. I lost my father when I was younger than Greg. I know what it feels like. I'm not here to try to get him to change his story. But there is something I need to know and I think he can tell me."

"You expect him to help you get that man off? The man who killed his mama?"

I hoped I could project enough sincerity to penetrate the screen that obscured her. It was like talking to a gray, colorless ghost. "No ma'am, I don't. I leave that to his lawyer. My job is to find facts—the truth, if possible. I think Greg has a piece of the truth." I pressed on. "Miz Pickens, what if? What if John Lattimore is telling the truth? What if somebody else killed her? And what if it comes out years from now? How will Greg feel then? He's hurt and angry and he has every right to be. But whatever problems your sister had, I believe she loved her son. What if his testimony helps convict an innocent man? Is that the legacy Delores would want to leave him?"

"It's all right, Aunt Cathy."

At some point in our conversation Greg had entered the kitchen unnoticed by either of us. He laid a gentle hand on his aunt's shoulder and opened the screen. She started to speak, but compressed her lips and turned away.

Greg descended the steps and, with a gesture, indicated the shady oasis where my car waited.

We leaned against the front bumper like two old pals. Greg

picked up a green pecan hull and began to dismember it. In the fading light, his face was soft, but the last few months had left their stamp of the man he would soon become.

"You weren't in court today," I observed, looking away from him across the fields.

"I'd heard enough," he replied, his own eyes on some distant point.

"Will you be staying on here with your aunt after the trial?"

"I guess." He shrugged. "I don't really have anywhere else to go."

"You like it here?"

Another shrug. "Not really. Never thought I'd end up a farmer. My mother used to threaten to send me down here to go to school. Guess she got her way."

"Have you thought about what you'll do after school?"

"Not really."

"I hear you like cars. You ever think about doing something with them?"

For the first time, he showed a faint spark of interest. "Like what?"

I leaned back on my elbows against the hood and studied the upper branches of the pecan tree. "Oh, I don't know. Build'em, maybe, or design'em. Or work on 'em or even sell'em."

"Yeah, maybe."

"Some of the best mechanics I know tell me they got their start tinkering with farm machinery. Tractors and so on."

He made no reply.

I snuck a glance at him out of the corner of my eye. He had reduced the pecan hull to shreds and was rolling the nut back and forth between his palms.

"I was pretty car crazy when I was your age, too," I lied. "I think I learned to drive when I was about twelve, from my older cousin. He lived out in the country like this." I gestured toward the still pastures surrounding us. "We used to sneak out at night and practice on his daddy's old pickup truck. But it was so quiet out in the country, we had to push that old rattletrap a mile from the house before we could start it. We finally got caught and boy, my uncle, he whaled the tar out of us." I watched him from the corner of my eye as I spoke. His face was closed, but his fingers worked the pecan feverishly.

"You like to get out alone at night, too, don't you Greg? Just you and the sound of the engine and the darkness. Nobody bothering you, nobody talking to you."

"Things aren't as ugly at night," he said, looking away from me.

"No," I answered gently. "It's easy to hide in the dark. But it's time to stop hiding, Greg. It's time to tell the truth. The whole truth."

His profile was a heartbreaking portrait of youth in the gathering darkness.

"You drove your mama's car that night, didn't you, Greg? You went out to the cabin but you weren't alone. Who did you drive out to the cabin that night, Greg?"

He gazed out across the fields for a moment, then he turned to me and, in a strong, clear voice, a man's voice, he told me.

CHAPTER 26

I shifted in my seat for the thousandth time, struggling to find a new position that didn't press my knees into the steering column, but not so comfortable I'd fall asleep. It was no use. Over the last hour, I'd exhausted them all.

I needed to get out and water a tree, too, but with the coming of darkness, the woods had become so quiet I was afraid to make the slightest noise. What happened to all those little woodland creatures that are supposed to populate the forest at night? Crickets and owls and possums and raccoons and the other things that hunt at night? I reached over my shoulder and checked that the back doors were locked.

The trap was set. I was almost certain I had the answer, but no proof, and a lot could go wrong.

I folded my arms across my chest for warmth and settled down again to wait, but straightened up again almost immediately. There. Was that a footstep? I rolled down the window to listen. Silence. Then a faint, unmistakable crack as a twig snapped underfoot. Or paw. I strained my ears to hear. There it was again, a faint rustling, growing unmistakably louder. I slid down in the seat. Finally, after an eternity, a small, bright cone of light, like that from a flashlight, danced through the tops of the trees. I was glad I'd thought to cover the hood and bumpers with branches. The light disappeared. I counted to twenty, and then, just to be safe, to forty, before I raised up to peer out.

The light was inside the cabin now, dancing over walls and

ceiling. It was replaced after a minute by a softer but steady glow, like that of an oil lamp or a candle. This wasn't supposed to happen.

I reached for the door handle, but the silence made me think better of it. It had seemed so simple in the bright light of afternoon, surrounded by people and lights and noise. But here in the silent darkness, the smallest sound seemed to carry for miles. Slowly, painfully, I wedged my shoulders through the open window and wiggled my hips through after them. The window frame bit into my backside and thighs as I struggled to swivel around.

Finally I was out and moving toward the cabin. My heart thudded in my chest. I was in a fever of impatience, but to my heightened senses, every step sounded like a herd of buffalo crashing through the forest.

Slowly, I made my way to the steps leading up to the porch. I lifted my leg high, avoiding the concrete steps for the softer, wooden ones. The first one held my weight without creaking. The second sagged under my weight, but held steady. Finally, I was on the porch. I tiptoed to the door and listened. I could hear faint voices from inside.

I took a deep breath, trying to control my heart, which was galloping like a metronome out of control. Big mistake. If I stopped to think, I'd lose my nerve. Summoning every ounce of courage, I took a deep breath and shoved against the door with my shoulder.

"Good evening, Mrs. Hemingway."

She straightened from her position on the floor in front of the sofa with a startled squeak, banging her shoulder on the heavy pine table.

"Mr. Hemingway."

He stood, frozen, in the act of running a cloth along the mantle.

Elvira Hemingway rubbed her shoulder and stared at me with huge, round eyes. There was cunning and speculation behind them. "Why, Mr. Harlan. Whatever are you doing here?"

"Same as you two, I expect. Looking for evidence."

"Wha—?" Her hand stole to her throat and she couldn't stop herself from stealing a look at George.

He held himself very still and didn't look at her. "What are you talking about?" he demanded.

"I had a long talk with Greg yesterday. He admitted he drove the two of you out here the night Delores died. Died with the bruises you put on her—on Sunday night."

Elvira turned her head sharply to look at him. Could this really be news to her?

"But you didn't tell Greg that, did you? You let him believe Lattimore had beaten her and that you wanted to follow them because you were worried for her safety. You must have been scared spitless when you saw the police cars at her house that morning. Selfless, caring neighbors that you are, you rushed right over to offer comfort to the poor, motherless boy. That's when you discovered John Lattimore had already delivered himself up like a gift from heaven."

I moved closer, keeping the sofa between us. "What happened Sunday night? Did you want to play and she didn't? Did she put up a fight and you had to 'convince' her?"

He split his glance between me and his wife, trying to decide which of us posed the greatest danger, and licked his lips. "I don't know what you're talking about. I never laid a hand on her. She was drunk. Falling down drunk. She hung on me crying and carrying on. I just kinda pushed her away and she went rolling down the hill, through the gravel. She rolled down to the bottom and didn't get up."

It could have happened that way. Or he could have smacked her around a few times and sent her down that hill.

Terry Hoover

"What gravel and what hill, George? You told the police—and me—that she gave you a ride as far as the Square uptown to catch the bus. There's no gravel or hills uptown."

Was that a sound outside? I spoke quickly just in case.

"And then what? You figured as long as she was unconscious, she wouldn't be needing the car for a while and you'd just borrow it to knock over a filling station?"

"I don't know nothing about knocking over no filling station." He began to sidle to his left. I sidestepped, putting my body between him and the door. He stopped.

"The filling station that just happened to be in Cotter's hometown? That just happens to be the local bus depot? The reason you're here now, dusting that mantle."

By the end of my conversation with Greg, he'd been happy to call Hemingway at the garage to tell him I'd come all the way out to the farm to ask whether he'd spent time at the cabin. But Hemingway hadn't become concerned until Greg added that I'd also asked whether he or his wife had ever been there. Under the circumstances, the police hadn't bothered to dust the cabin for prints, but the Hemingways had no way to know that. There hadn't been time to discover whether the police had been able to salvage any useable prints from the burned-out filling station, but I was gambling that Hemingway couldn't be sure, either, and might not be willing to take the chance. It appeared my gamble had paid off.

"How else would you have known the till would be full after the nine-thirty bus?" I continued to keep their attention on me. "Did Cotter go with you or did he just give you the idea and split the take? Enough to buy a new car and leave town before his ex-wife found him."

"You said—" Elvira stopped, just in time.

"Said what, Mrs. Hemingway? That there wasn't as much money in the till as he'd thought? He lied. There were thousands. Cotter left town wearing new clothes and driving a new car.

"Why did you decide to follow Delores and Lattimore that night?" I asked her, changing tack. "Did Delores let something slip that night in her bedroom? Was her memory of Sunday night starting to come back to her? You were careful to see she was never alone with Lattimore that night, but you couldn't stop them from leaving together. If she remembered what happened and told him, you'd had it."

They'd tried to talk Greg into loaning them Delores's car, but seeing an opportunity to drive, he'd insisted on going along.

"She was alive when we got here and alive when we left," Elvira retorted.

"Shut up," George snarled.

"Too late for that," I said.

He calculated for a split second. "All right, then, it's true. We brought the boy out here after he begged us, but neither of us ever laid a hand on her." He took a step in my direction, gesturing with the cloth in his hand. "If the boy told you otherwise, he's lying. That's the thanks we get for trying to protect him. It was him flung her down."

Greg had admitted it, though not quite in those terms, describing a painful scene in which his mother had alternated between screeching justification and maudlin tears. When she flung her arms around his neck in a boozy caricature of maternal affection, he'd recoiled, and she'd landed in a sobbing heap on the floor. But *he* said the Hemingways had ordered him to wait in the car, demonstrating their ignorance of teenage boys.

"Not quite," I replied. "You *had* to know whether Delores had regained any of her memory of Sunday night and told Lattimore. So you convinced Greg that Lattimore had beaten her, and got him to drive you out here because you were worried for her safety," I said. "When Delores turned up dead, you were there, Johnny-on-the-spot, to whisper in his ear, reassure him you knew he didn't *mean* to kill his mother. Man, you got all the breaks on this one, didn't you? Delores was dead and you'd convinced the boy *he* was responsible for her death, and then along comes John Lattimore, doing his damnedest to make it look like a natural death, and oh, so conveniently putting his head in the noose. I almost wish you *had* killed her. They could fry you for that. But there'll be a special place in hell for you for what you did to that boy."

I didn't dare look at my watch, but it seemed to me way too much time had passed since I'd entered the cabin.

Elvira, who'd been silent throughout my diatribe, suddenly rounded on her husband. "This is all your fault. You could have explained your prints in her car. She gave you a ride to the Square. And she was a drunk. It would have been her word against yours. But you couldn't let it alone, could you? You had to try to get in her pants. You had to beat her up and ruin everything." She took a step toward him, her hands clenched into fists.

"I didn't hit nobody," he growled. "She fell."

"The police will call you an accessory, Elvira. They'll say you helped him plan the holdup and kill Delores to keep her quiet."

"I didn't know anything about it. And Delores was alive when we left, snoring like a lumberjack. When Cotter came by the house Monday morning looking for George, was the first I knew about the holdup. Jack was waiting for George at the garage for his share, and when he didn't show up, Jack came looking for him."

She spoke to me, but her eyes were on George. She must have read his intent, because she ducked just as he flung the chunk of firewood at my head. I threw up an arm to protect myself. George took his chance and launched himself over the sofa at me. He caught me around the knees and we both tumbled to the floor. There was a crash of glass. We rolled over and over, struggling. I was younger and stronger, but he was bigger and had more to lose. He crouched above me, his face red and contorted, and raised his right arm to crash the log down on my skull. I heaved my body to the side with all the strength I could summon from my legs, taking him with me. The weight of the log helped overbalance him, but he kept his legs locked around mine and we rolled together toward the sofa.

A cloud of black, oily smoke rolled over us. The crash must have been the kerosene lamp going over when he'd leaped at me. Flames had raced up the cheap nylon curtains and were now licking at the dry wooden roof. The wood around the windows was already blazing. Without warning, the windows shattered, sending lethal shards of glass flying about the room. I let go of George and flung a protective arm over my face. George fastened his hands around my throat. I scrabbled futilely at his wrists, but he had the advantage of weight and leverage. He was coughing and his eyes were streaming, but they were cold and flat, empty, the eyes of a killer with nothing to lose. I clawed for them, but he only tightened his grip. I could barely see for the smoke. I was losing consciousness. Elvira's face appeared over George's shoulder. In her hand was a chunk of firewood. It was the last thing I saw.

CHAPTER 27

I was cold and I hurt. Everywhere. I knew those things without knowing how I knew them. I tried to slip back into the soft, black velvet of unconsciousness, but a voice calling my name dragged me back.

"Harlan. Can you hear me? Wake up."

Reluctantly, I fought my way up through the darkness and opened my eyes. Owens's pale moon face swam into focus.

"Can you breathe?"

I gave it a cautious try. A boulder had landed on my chest and my throat felt like I'd been gargling razor blades.

"No," I croaked.

"You hurt?"

"Yes."

"Where?"

"Everywhere."

"He'll live." Owens straightened up.

"You're late," I croaked feebly.

"Yeah, well, I told you not to be a cowboy. The cavalry only shows up on cue in the movies. Here, sit up. It'll be easier to breathe."

He and a uniformed officer propped me into a sitting position, triggering a coughing fit. I hacked until my eyes streamed, but once it had passed, breathing became marginally easier. I looked around. I was propped against Owens's police cruiser. The forest, so dark and silent before, was now ablaze with the headlights of fire trucks and police cars. Five hundred yards away, smoke rolled up to the sky from the smoldering cabin, but no flames. The woods rang with voices as men moved to and fro in the darkness, spraying the trees and brush to prevent a stray spark from catching again.

Owens handed me his handkerchief. I wiped my face with it.

"You get'em?" I asked.

"Not yet," he grunted without looking at me.

"You lost them?" I looked around me at the officers scurrying to and fro like ants, and the smoking ruin of the cabin. "And the evidence? How the hell—"

"Well, when the place went up like a Roman rocket, I guess we *coulda* let your sorry ass be cremated," he replied, as though seriously considering it. "What the hell did you mean going in there, anyway?" He rounded on me suddenly. "You're what gummed up the works. We didn't know what was going on in there. He coulda had a gun. If we'd come in with ours blazing, he could have shot you or used you as a hostage. Hell, for all we knew, you were already dead."

"But they were never supposed to make it into the cabin," I insisted, setting off another coughing fit.

"Well, now, there mighta been a slight miscommunication there." He ground out the words slowly, as though it pained him to do so. "And we'll be having a Come To Jesus meeting about surveillance techniques in the morning. The boys were watching the road, but them two had come in two cars and musta got here way before us. We spotted the first one hidden up in some trees about a mile away. Then they musta doubled back in the other car to the other side of the lake that comes in from another road that just dead ends. It's a narrow cove, only about a couple hundreds yards wide, but to get from one side of it t'other by road, you'd have to double back five, eight miles." He shook his head. "They parked the second car in somebody's driveway and walked around by the shoreline."

"It's a lake. You didn't think about that?"

"We didn't know about the second car and there ain't no open shoreline on this side of the cove. We couldn't be sure how far they were ahead of us and it's near impossible to follow somebody through these woods without making an unholy racket. So we hung back and sent a man around by the road on foot with a radio. But by the time he got here, the Hemingways were already in the cabin and he found your car empty, so we had to assume you'd gone in after'em."

To be fair, we had all assumed the Hemingways would wait for full cover of darkness to make their move, so I could almost understand how they had slipped by us, but how had they escaped a forest full of policemen?

"We still didn't know about the second car, remember," Owens retorted when I posed the question to him. "I left a handful of men between here and the car, just in case. When the cabin went up like merry hell with you in it, we rushed the place, but the smoke was blacker'n Satan's soul. The only doors and windows is"—he turned and surveyed the rubble—"*was* on the front, but hell, half the walls was gone in minutes. They musta kicked their way out at one of the ends and made for the lake. We found a rope attached to nothing on a tree by the shore a couple lots over, so we figure they 'borrowed' a neighbor's canoe or fishing boat and rowed across the cove. They didn't make it back to either car, though, and they won't get far on foot, so we'll pick 'em up soon enough."

"Unless they rowed down to the marina and hitched a ride," I pointed out. "Or called a cab." The marina and the adjoining dive were popular hangouts because of the lax enforcement of the liquor laws on the South Carolina side of the lake.

Owens scowled. "We'll get 'em."

"My guess is you'll find both cars registered to innocent, law-

abiding patrons of the filling station where Hemingway works,"
I added.

At that moment, a uniformed officer sidled up with the
expression of a Christian who can smell the lion's breath, to
whisper in Owens's ear.

"Sonuvabitch," Owens swore. He turned to us. "If it wadn't
for bad luck, Harlan, you'd have no luck a'tall."

"What?"

"The jury's out. I told King plain as day, to stall. I swear if
the voters don't throw that sonuvabitch out this fall, I may do it
myself." He put a meaty hand under my elbow and hauled me
to my feet. "Can you walk?"

"Do I have a choice?"

"Can you drive? Never mind." He turned on the beleaguered
uniform. "You. Follow us in his car."

I turned over the keys. "Can't you stop it?"

"Nothing stops jury deliberations unless somebody drops
dead," Owens growled, moving with more speed that I would
have suspected him capable of. "And even then, it has to be the
defendant or the judge. I'll get on the radio and let the lawyers
know, but I doubt it'll make any difference."

The uniformed officer made short work of clearing the
branches off my car. There was no need for quiet now. Men appeared from nowhere and piled into the police cars, calling out
directions to one another. We arranged ourselves into a ragged
sort of caravan and set out for town at full speed with the sirens
blaring.

CHAPTER 28

Warren and Lattimore were waiting for us in an empty conference room at the courthouse. The overhead lights were off. Two lamps on tables in opposite corners of the room cast pools of light, highlighting the silver of Warren's hair as he sat with his head bowed, hands clasped before him on the table. Lattimore, pacing as usual, hands in his pockets, took one look at my bedraggled state and stopped in his tracks.

"Steve." Warren lifted his head. "Are you all right?"

"Nothing seriously damaged but my pride." I limped to the table, pulled out a chair, and sank gratefully into it.

"I got the gist from Lieutenant Owens, but perhaps you'd give us the details," Warren said.

It took a while to tell it all. Warren leaned back in his chair with his eyes closed, but I knew he was listening carefully to every word. There was silence when I finished.

"Well," Warren roused himself finally. "This is good news. I must let Judge Cecil know—"

"No!" Lattimore spoke sharply from the corner.

"I beg your pardon?" Warren, halfway out of his chair, stopped. "I have to let him know there's new evidence. We have to stop the deliberations," he said.

"No." Lattimore stepped into the light. His voice was quieter, but no less determined. "We say nothing."

"John, I don't think you understand—" Warren began.

"No, *you* need to understand," Lattimore replied. "We are

not saying a word about this. To the judge or anybody else."

"John, we only have this one opportunity to enter this new evidence. If we don't, we can never use it."

"I understand that," Lattimore said flatly.

From his seat behind Lattimore, Owens cocked his head and regarded the man thoughtfully.

"Well, I'm afraid I don't," Warren replied with his customary courtesy, a small miracle under the circumstances. "This evidence could exonerate you."

"Exonerate me?" Lattimore placed his palms on the table and rested his weight on them. "That's rich. That jury is not going to convict me." He swept the three of us with his gaze. "But it won't make one damned bit of difference. My life is over. The life I knew is gone."

"John, people will forget in time—" Warren tried again.

Lattimore straightened up from the table. "Do you think I don't know what you people think of me?" He turned his head to include Owens and me. "I see it in your eyes every time you look at me. You don't say it. But I see it. Same thing they," he made a sweeping gesture with his arm to indicate the street below us, "think about me. I still don't see that I did anything so terrible. I didn't kill Delores Green." He looked hard at Owens, who gazed back, impassive as a rock. "If anything, I helped keep her alive. But I accept that involving Greg was . . ."—he struggled to get the word out—"wrong. My life is over, but he still has his ahead of him. We are not going to ruin it by dragging him into this."

"I agree," Owens spoke.

"What?" Warren and Lattimore said together.

"I agree the boy ought not be dragged into this," Owens repeated. "Why the hell do you think I agreed with this cocka-mamie scheme of Harlan's?"

Taking my new information to Owens had been the biggest

gamble of the whole thing, but years as a reporter had taught me something about human nature and how to read it. I'd had a feeling that Owens would be as determined to protect Greg Green as I was. And Lattimore, as it turned out.

"When we catch up to the Hemingways," Owens continued, putting stress on the first word, "we may or may not have enough to charge them with murder or even accessories after the fact. But I'm sure we can convince them to see that it's in their best interests not to mention the boy's involvement."

Lattimore turned back to Warren. "That's it. It's settled." He picked up his jacket from the back of the chair beside him.

Warren stopped him with a hand on his arm. "John, your intentions are noble and do you credit, but as your attorney, I urge you to think very hard. You're gambling with your life."

Lattimore looked down at him. "I told you. My life is over." He shook off Warren's arm and strode out without looking back.

Silence reigned for several minutes. Warren broke it finally. "To a certain extent, John was right. Whatever the verdict, people will never forget his callousness towards the boy. But those two—" he shook his head. "To kill her and let Greg think he was responsible. That is truly monstrous."

Owens and I traded looks. "I'm not sure we'll ever know for sure," I said. "They told Greg to stay in the car and keep watch in case Lattimore came back. They obviously don't know much about teenaged boys. And she was *his* mother. It could be that when they found her alone at the cabin, George saw his chance. By following them, Greg may have saved his mother's life."

"Only a temporary reprieve, unfortunately," Warren said.

"True. After he pushed his mother away, he rushed out of the cabin and back to the car. According to him, if Elvira hadn't arrived right on his heels, he probably would have roared away, leaving them there. He was so upset, it was difficult for him to judge time, but he estimates it was at least another five minutes before George joined them. When Greg took off, taking the car keys with him, Hemingway would have had to think fast. In his shoes, I'd have hit her in the back of the head and arranged it to look like an accident—like she'd tripped or fallen, and hit her head on the logs. But there were no splinters in the wounds or Doc would have found them. Maybe he only had time to slam her head against the floor and hope for the best."

"Monstrous," Warren repeated. He looked at Owens. "When you find them, I want to know. We *have* to find a way to make them pay for what they've done without involving the boy. For his sake and his mother's."

"Well, I'd say you've set yourself quite a problem, then." Owens rose ponderously to his feet, his leather belt and holster providing a creaking crescendo. "Since you and some very high-falutin' experts just spent the past week doing a bang-up job of convincing the jury that woman drank herself to death." He dipped his head a fraction of an inch and walked out, leaving silence once again in his wake.

CHAPTER 29

Fred, the porter, was waiting for us at Warren's office. "Us three, we've spent many a evening like this together," he said, as he fumbled for the elevator key. Our voices echoed loudly in the empty building. "Us three, we've spent many a evening like this together."

"That we have," Warren agreed.

Fred punched the button for the third floor.

Miz Turner was waiting at her desk. She ushered us into Warren's dimly lit office, then disappeared, to return a moment later with a whiskey bottle and some glasses on a tray. The banker's lamp on Warren's desk cast a cone of light on its surface, leaving the rest of the room in shadow.

"Don't mind if I do," Fred said. With neat, careful motions, he removed his uniform jacket and hung it over the back of a straight-backed chair. Miz Turner served us, then, to my surprise, poured herself a generous tot and settled on Warren's sofa, where the shadows obscured her except for an occasional gleam off her glasses.

Warren lay back in his chair with his fingers laced together over his stomach. He inspected me from under half-closed lids. "Are you sure you're all right?"

"I'm fine," I replied, gingerly touching my tender face. I took a sip from the glass to soothe my parched throat, but I was too tired to risk more. Or to remain seated. I moved over to the window and gazed out toward the courthouse.

"Pretty different being on this side of the street for a change." Against the lighted windows of the courthouse, I could see figures moving about in the tiny basement room reserved for the press.

"Why'd you quit?" Miz Turner asked from the shadows. The customary acid was missing from her tone, washed away, perhaps, by the whiskey. I turned to regard her, but it was too dark to see her expression. I turned back to the window. Which truth to tell?

"I had a birth defect," I spoke to my own reflection in the dark window.

"A birth defect. You look all right to me. What's the matter with you?"

I glanced at Fred, dignified and upright in his chair. "They decided I was color blind."

"Color blind?"

The quiet room and the darkness encouraged intimacy. In these long hours of waiting, all secrets could be revealed, only to be forgotten in the bright light of day.

"There was another dead mother. She left three little children. But she was colored. Didn't rate the front pages or a big investigation."

"But if you loved it so much, why didn't you stick it out?" Miz Turner persisted. "Discovered you couldn't change the world singlehanded?"

"It wasn't so much I thought I could change it," I replied. "But I was naive enough to think if I could just hold it up for people to see, things would change."

"But they didn't."

"It wasn't that they couldn't see. They didn't want to see."

A long silence followed my words. I turned, afraid I had offended Fred, and found him smiling at Miz Turner in the shadows.

347

"What's funny?"

Her voice floated from the darkness. "When I was a little girl, we lived in the country. Me, my mother, and my five brothers and sisters. My daddy died when I was two and Mama was left alone with all of us to raise. We were poor, but we lived on a farm, so we could raise most of what we needed."

She leaned forward into the light and stared into her glass, rolling it between her palms. "When I was six, there was a fire. We lost everything. The relatives came, of course, one at a time, and offered to take one or two of us. But Mama refused. She knew if we were ever split up, we'd never be a family together again." She was quiet for a long moment. "There was a colored family that lived near us, on the other side of the railroad tracks, a sharecropper family. When all the relatives had come and gone, the daddy came to Mama with his hat in his hand and told her we were welcome to live with his family as long as we needed. Five children of his own to feed and he was offering to take us all in. The relatives were mortified, but that's exactly what we did. We moved in with them and stayed for six months until my oldest brother got out of school, got a job, and moved us all into a house in town." She tilted the glass and swallowed the last of her whiskey.

"Purty little thing you was, too," Fred said. A gentle smile creased his ageless black face. "Used to go down to the creek and play school with the cows while the other young un's was off at school. Get mad at'em, too, for being so stupid."

"Some of them were still smarter than a lot of people I've come across," she answered tartly. She rose to refill their glasses. She held the bottle up in mute invitation to me, but I shook my head.

"How did you come to be a newspaper man, Mr. Harlan?" Fred asked.

"It was the only thing I ever wanted to be," I replied, looking out the window again.

"Used to lie on the floor with his feet on the radiator and listen to Edward R. Murrow on the radio and say, 'Some day that's gonna be me.' " Warren spoke without opening his eyes. He'd been quiet for so long, I'd almost forgotten he was there.

I stared at him. "How did you know that?"

"Your daddy used to talk about you. In fact, you were his favorite subject. He was mighty proud of you."

"You knew my father?"

"He was my barber for twenty years," he replied, eyes still closed. "And my friend. Damn fine barber, too. But what he really wanted to be was a lawyer. Did you know that?"

I shook my head, too stunned to answer.

"He studied law through correspondence school," he continued. "He'd have made a damn fine lawyer. We had some spirited discussions about the law. Your daddy was much more conservative than I in those days. But then, liberality is a young man's privilege."

Warren opened his eyes to meet the silent accusation in my own. "No, Steve." His voice was gentle. "I hired you because you're good. I kept up with you, where you were and what you were doing, because of your daddy, but anything you've achieved, you did on your own."

"You didn't have anything to do with my license?" No one had been more stunned than I when my application for a private investigator's license had been approved, despite my lack of experience.

"No, sir, I did not. I suspect you'd find our Irish friend across the street had something to do with that."

"Owens?" It was too much to take in. Lieutenant Owens pulling strings to get my license approved.

"Understand, I don't know it of my own certain and personal

knowledge, but if I was a betting man, I'd say the odds were in my favor."

There were a thousand questions whirling in my brain, but before I regained my equilibrium, the phone at Warren's elbow pealed. Miz Turner rose, but he waved her away and answered it himself.

"Thank you very much." He hung up and placing his palms flat on the desk, rose to his feet. "The jury's in." Silently, Miz Turner rose and began to clear away the bottle and glasses. Fred wiped his mouth with a spotless white handkerchief; Warren combed his hair with his palms and shrugged into his jacket.

Still without a word, we made our way through the outer office. As Fred gently pulled the door to behind us, I glanced back to see Miz Turner sitting motionless at her desk in the outer office, her head bowed over her clasped hands as the harsh overhead light reflected off her hennaed hair. When Warren returned, defeated or victorious, he'd find her there, waiting.

It was odd and disorienting to be in the brightly lighted courtroom so late at night. There were fewer than a dozen people in the cavernous room, most of them reporters, huddled in the corner. Kent looked at me curiously as I came in. I must have looked like I'd been in a war, but he gave me a high sign as I took a seat on the front row. The rest of them ignored me.

King and Higgins were already seated behind the prosecution table. Warren and Lattimore took their places at the defense table. With a jerk of his head, Warren invited me to join them, but I shook my head.

Judge Cecil appeared, his robes askew, and took his seat. A moment later, the jurors filed in and self-consciously took their seats, carefully avoiding anyone's eye. Judge Cecil and his clerk whispered together for a few minutes, then Cecil banged the gavel.

"Court will come to order. Mr. King, are you ready?"

"We are, Your Honor."

"Mr. Warren."

"The defense is ready, Your Honor."

Cecil regarded the jury over his glasses. "Mr. Foreman, has the jury reached a verdict?"

The tall, skinny one—an accountant, Warren had told me— rose and cleared his throat. "We have, Your Honor."

"The defendant will please rise." Lattimore and Warren rose. King and Higgins also came to their feet.

The judge regarded the jury again. "In the case of the State versus John Lattimore on a charge of first-degree murder, how find you?"

The accountant kept his eyes on Cecil as he replied, "We find the defendant, John Lattimore, not guilty of the charge of murder."

A commotion broke out in the back of the room as the reporters trampled each other on their way to the door. As the doors swung shut behind them, a silence fell over the courtroom. Warren put a hand on Lattimore's arm, but Lattimore ignored it and kept his gaze on the judge.

King and Higgins stood silently, also regarding the judge.

"Mr. Lattimore, you have been acquitted of the charges against you. You are free to go." He thanked the jurors for their service, reminded them they didn't have to talk to anyone if they didn't want to, discharged them with a bang of the gavel, and disappeared in a swirl of robes.

I stood, bewildered by the sense of anticlimax, unsure what to do. Higgins came over and shook Warren's hand. They exchanged a few low words. King stared down at the polished table, watching his political dreams crumble to dust. Finally, he squared his shoulders, rose, and offered Warren a perfunctory handshake. No words were spoken.

The courtroom emptied until only the three of us were left. Warren stuffed a few papers in his briefcase. Lattimore waited, motionless, saying nothing and staring into space. Silently, the three of us walked down the aisle, down the echoing corridor and out onto the front steps. We paused in the crisp autumn darkness.

Warren turned to Lattimore and offered his hand. "Well, congratulations, John. You're a free man."

Lattimore returned his handshake only briefly. For the first time since the verdict had been pronounced, he spoke. "Well, it sure as hell cost enough. I told you all those damn experts were a waste of money." He spun on his heel. Warren and I stood and watched him stride away into the darkness.

CHAPTER 30

"So it was Hemingway in Delores's house that night?" Susie raised her voice over the tumult from the back seat.

"Pipe down, guys or I'm pulling over," I warned. They ignored me. "That's right. I don't know whether he found the pills or took them from her purse deliberately. For that matter, we can't be sure they were ever in her purse. He or Elvira could have helped themselves to them when they were at the house that night. They were both in and out of the kitchen. But when we started to argue her death was accidental, from mixing alcohol and pills, he figured he'd help us out and maybe we'd stop worrying about where she spent Saturday night or how she got the bruises. So he left the bottle where we'd be sure to find it. My showing up when I did was just stupid luck. He probably planned to call the cops and report the break-in himself. We just saved him the trouble."

"And he was behind the phone calls?"

"Probably. Maybe he figured if he couldn't get me to back off one way, he'd try another. But if they ever catch them, he'll pay for that," I promised.

"But how did they know Delores was at the cabin?" she asked. "Wait." She interrupted herself to hand the kids a handful of peanut butter crackers. "Nothing else until we get to the beach, understand?" Merciful silence descended.

"Greg overheard enough of Lattimore's interrogation of his mother Monday morning to pick up her reference to watching the water," I replied.

"But once the Hemingways admitted they were at the cabin, they could have explained their fingerprints being there and claimed they didn't speak up because they were protecting the boy," Susie said. "Were they afraid of being charged as accessories?"

"It's unlikely Greg would have been charged—at least not with murder," I replied, dropping my voice. "The real danger was that George's fingerprints might show up in the cabin *and* at the filling station. His fingerprints must not be on file anywhere. So if they showed up at the filling station, they couldn't be identified without a suspect to compare them to. But if they identified his fingerprints at the cabin, there'd be something to compare them to. Although," I broke off as I floored the accelerator to pass a slow-moving delivery truck, "I find it hard to believe this is their first brush with the law—or crime."

"Why didn't they just run?" She adjusted her visor to block the sun from her eyes.

"That appears to be their modus operandi, but if—when, the police found out they'd been at Delores's house a few hours before her death, and they were bound to, they'd want to talk to them and it would look awfully suspicious if they'd disappeared. Once they gave a statement to the police, they were stuck because they'd be called to testify. As long as Greg believed he was responsible for his mother's death, they were reasonably safe. It was safer for them to stick around and keep an eye on developments—and Greg. Once the trial was over, they could disappear and if anyone noticed, well, they'd figure they were hoping to get away from the notoriety."

"What if he had cracked? He's just a boy."

"I don't like to think about it," I replied. "If he'd shown signs . . . maybe an unfortunate accident? Suicide? It's one of the few lucky breaks in this whole thing, that his aunt took him away and that she lives fairly far away and in a small farming community where strangers would be noticed and remembered."

"If they ever find them, do you think Owens will be able to convince King to charge them?"

"We'd have to have Greg's evidence to tie them to the cabin that night, but there's no direct evidence to tie them to her death. Even if we could, you read what the juror said." I indicated the folded newspaper on the seat between us. "They didn't acquit because they were convinced of Lattimore's innocence, but because the State didn't prove its case on cause of death. And this close to election, King's not anxious to repeat his public humiliation."

Personally, I thought Higgins would be our next district attorney, and Owens hadn't corrected me when I made the observation, so I figured it was a pretty sure thing.

"They have issued a warrant for armed robbery and there's my warrant for assault. But they've got to find them and Cotter first. Owens seems pretty confident they will, now that they have a serious charge. The beating they gave the gas station owner, and the fire, are enough to put them both away for a long time. Owens and that long, tall drink of water from Kershaw have been burning up the phone wires. When I left his office yesterday, they were arguing the merits of worms over spoons for bass. I think we've seen the start of a beautiful friendship."

"Well, I'm ready to see a ladies room and quick."

"I anticipated you, my beautiful bride and we should be coming up on one just about . . ."—I slowed as we topped the hill—"there." I pointed to the sign a few hundred yards ahead.

Susie and the kids piled out and headed for the bathrooms. I helped myself to a grape Nehi from the machine and wandered out to the car to wait.

"Nice day," the attendant offered, vigorously swiping at the rear window.

"That it is," I agreed.

He moved around and began to attack the windshield. The folded newspaper lying on the front seat caught his eye. The headline, "Lattimore Acquitted of Murder" was clearly visible.

"Lattimore," he squinted through the glass and turned to look at me. "That's that fella that killed his girlfriend, idn't it?"

"He was acquitted."

"Oh well, yeah, but hell, that don't mean he didn't kill her, does it?"

ABOUT THE AUTHOR

Terry Hoover, winner of the Malice Domestic grant in 2001, has been writing for local, regional, and national publications and corporate clients for 20 years. *Double Dead,* a finalist in the Malice Domestic/St. Martin's Press contest for Best First Traditional Mystery, is the first book in the Steve Harlan series. Hoover, a native of Charlotte, NC, where *Double Dead* is set, now lives just outside the city, with her husband, a public relations consultant. To learn more, visit her website at www.hoover mysteries.com.